A DAGGER IN THE WINDS

Books by Brendan Noble

The Frostmarked Chronicles:
A Dagger in the Winds
The Trials of Ascension
The Daughters of the Earth

Frostmarked Tales:
The Rider in the Night
The Lady of Rolika

The Prism Files:
The Fractured Prism
Crimson Reigns
Pridefall
White Crown

For Grandma and Grandpa.
Niech Bóg błogosławi ich dusze.

Major Gods and Their Marks

Marzanna - Frostmark
Winter, Disease, and Death

Dziewanna - Bowmark
Wilds, Hunt, and Spring

Jaryło - Springmark
Spring, Agriculture, and War

Mokosz - Mothermark
Women and Divination

Perun - Thundermark
Thunder, Justice, and War

Weles - Serpentmark
Underworld and Lowlands

Swaróg - Forgemark
Celestial Fire and Smithing

Dadźbóg - Sunmark
The Sun

Pronunciation Guide

Major characters

Wacław Lubiewicz: Vahtswahv Luubeeayvihch
(Little Name) - Wašek: Vahshehk
Otylia Daryczówna: Ohtihleeah Dahrihchohvnah
(Little Name) - Otylka: Ohtihlkah
Xobas: Kohbahs
Kuba: Koobah
Ara: Ahrah
Narcyz: Nahrsihz
Marek: Mahrehk
Jacek Lechowicz: Yahsehk Lehkohvihch
Juri: Yuuree

Major Gods

Marzanna: Mahrzahnah
Dziewanna: Djehvahnah
Jaryło: Yahrihwoh
Mokosz: Mohkohsh
Perun: Pehruun
Weles: Vehlehs
Swaróg: Svahrohg
Dadźbóg: Dahdzbohg
Strzybóg: Strihbohg

Other Terms

Żityje: Zhihtyeh
Dwie Rzeki: Dvee Zehkee
Krowik(ie): Krohvihk(ee)
Szeptucha: Shehptuuhah
Płanetnik: Pwahnehtnihk
Rusałka: Ruusawkah
Chała: Hahwah
Kwiecień: Kvihehchehn

A DAGGER in the WINDS

BRENDAN NOBLE

Prologue

Wacław

We're going to be in so much trouble...

"WAIT FOR ME!"

I scampered into the moonlit woods, clutching my wool cloak in one hand and my makeshift spear in the other. It was nothing more than a poorly sharpened stick. In my mind, though, it was a mighty weapon, capable of killing the demons and monsters lurking in the shadows.

Otylia glanced back with a smirk. Her bright green eyes pierced the sea of white surrounding us as her breaths fogged the air. "Hurry up! Dziewanna waits for no one."

With a sigh, I hopped through the snow after her.

Otylia was my best friend, but all she'd wanted to talk about recently had been the wild goddess. Like me, she'd turned twelve last summer, and she would soon be initiated as a szeptucha—a channeler of the gods, capable of amazing sorcery. She wanted to be chosen by Dziewanna more than anything. I worried I was going to lose her.

"You're so much faster in your soul-form," she quipped, hopping over a log once I caught up. Her herb bag flapped against her leg as she ran, but even with the hindrance, she was quick. "Why don't you just stay in it?"

"I have to wake up *eventually*," I replied.

Whenever I slept, I emerged from my body in what we called my soul-form. I was invisible when I wanted to be but could interact with the world like normal. Mom and Otylia were the only ones who knew about it, and Mom had forbidden me from exploring at night. Tonight, though, was the eve of the spring equinox.

With Otylia's father, High Priest Dariusz, out late preparing the festival's rituals, Otylia had snuck to our cottage once Mom was asleep. I had slipped out to meet her.

This wasn't our first time wandering the dark woods, but tonight was supposed to be special. The stories said you could *see* the spring gods as they traveled to kill Marzanna, goddess of winter and death. Dziewanna was among them, so Otylia had demanded we go.

I shivered as I leaped over another log. The snow had lingered unusually late this year, but Dziewanna and Jaryło, god of spring and war, would rid the world of it come morning. Part of me would miss its beauty.

"Where are you going?" I asked, stopping as Otylia ducked deeper into the forest. "Mom says there's demons away from the trails."

She stomped back to me with her nose wrinkled. Her long black hair, braided and wrapped in twine, swept behind her as she snatched my hand. "It'll be fine! Mother showed me the way to a grove in autumn. We'll be able to see Dziewanna flying from there."

"Why do you always talk about her and not Jaryło? He matters too."

Furrowing her brow, she pulled me along. "Because *he* gets all the attention from Father and the tribe. Dziewanna's the one that Marzanna can't kill in winter. She keeps the wilds alive during Marzanna's moons, but she's been forgotten by everyone except Mother and me."

We wandered on for a long time. I had no idea how she knew where she was going in the darkness. Though I knew much of the forest around our village of Dwie Rzeki, to me, every tree seemed the same this far from home. And with the clouds obscuring the stars, it was impossible to tell which direction we were headed.

The eight winds whistled through the branches above when we finally reached a small clearing.

Otylia grinned and twirled, swinging the skirt of her deep green dress around her. "Come on, Wašek!" she said, using the affectionate 'little' version of my name—Wacław—that only she and Mom called me. "Drop your spear and dance with me!"

"Of course, Otylka!" I replied with the same form of her name.

We danced hand-in-hand, spinning with the gales as they blew our hair and stung our cheeks until they turned red. Joy filled my heart. Otylia brought me the freedom I was too afraid to fight for by myself. With her, I felt like I could fly.

A growl ripped through the night.

I turned, placing myself between Otylia and the noise. My heart pounded as six pairs of ice-blue eyes glared at us from the trees. *Wolves.* They closed in, their snarling growing louder.

"Wašek, don't," Otylia said with a grip on my tunic's sleeve. "You can't fight all of them."

She was right, of course. But on the wolves' jaunt faces, I could see Marzanna's winter had been hard on them. They were hungry. Both of us would die if I didn't do something.

"Run," I whispered.

Otylia screamed as I dove for my spear.

The wolves charged, but my hands found the spear's shaft. The first wolf's jaws raced toward me as I swung its tip. Wood struck flesh, and with red streaking from its throat, the wolf yelped and fell, dead.

What did I just do?

The strike was just instinct. I had never wielded a real weapon before, let alone hunted something larger than a rabbit. My breaths shortened as my stomach churned. *So much blood...*

"Wašek!"

I spun as the other wolves charged, angered by the first's death. They came from every side. Their sleek white fur flashed through the shadows with the moonlight gleaming against their fangs. *There's too many.*

I stabbed at them as they reached me, but it wasn't enough. Teeth closed on my arms. Claws scraped my face and chest. I collapsed, screaming for Otylia to run.

Time slipped away. I prayed to Weles, god of the underworld of Nawia, to bring me paradise's peace. But death's release did not come.

A blast tore across the grove, flinging me through the snow as a brilliant light shone behind my eyelids. The wolves whimpered. My whole body shook against the frigid snow, the fear too much for me to look. Though the wounds were to my soul-form, when I awoke, the damage would remain on my physical body. So would the pain.

Eventually, the grove went quiet, and I gasped as I opened my eyes.

All six wolves lay dead, their bodies strewn amid a pool of blood that merged with the snow, staining it a deep crimson. Otylia stood at the grove's edge. Her fair skin glowed bright enough to illuminate the carnage, and her sharp green eyes were fixed on me. Horror filled them.

"What… What just happened?" I stammered, struggling to a knee as I clutched my throbbing torso. My head was woozy. Blood trickled down it and dripped to the ground. *Am I imagining this?*

Wide-eyed, Otylia stared down at her hands. "I think I just channeled."

A new fear struck me as I studied her. "How?" My best friend had channeled before being chosen by a god. What did that make her? I tried to stand, but my legs failed. I fell as Otylia rushed to my side.

"I don't know." Her voice trembled as she tore open her herb bag and pulled out a small clay poultice. "Just stay with me. Mother's healing salve should help."

I took her hand as my mind began to drift. "Whatever you just did, Otylka, thank you."

"Stay awake, Wašek." Tears welled in her eyes. "Stay awake!"

My grip slipped. I tried to call her name, to beg for her help, but tiredness washed over me. With my last breaths, I met her glowing eyes one last time before I fell into the black.

Part One

The Drowning of Marzanna

1

Wacław

FOUR YEARS LATER

He's winning... again.

"STOP HESITATING," XOBAS DEMANDED, circling me with sweat beading on his olive-skinned brow and his shield held tight to his chest. When he lunged, his cavalry sword clashed against my shield, knocking me to the dirt. "It's not your day, Wacław, is it?"

My arms ached as I pushed myself to my feet and sighed. *It's never my day when we're sparring.*

At Father's command, Xobas had trained me to fight ever since the wolf attack four years before. I was sixteen now. Still, the swordsman repeated the same instructions. Though Father believed his general's foreign style would teach me to adapt to any opponent, all it had given me was a sore butt.

A wicked grin crossed Xobas's face as he took his stance. "We go again. It's time for you to shake off the winter's chill and become the warrior the high chief expects you to be."

With a deep breath, I readied myself for the next blow, holding my wooden shield in front of me and my short spear alongside it. The cold shaft burned against my fingers. Despite the sun now hovering at the tips of the trees, its warmth had yet to reach our sparring ring.

"Why must we spar at first light?" I asked. "It's the equinox, and... you know..."

He advanced, chuckling as he did. "You Krowikie and your festivals. You believe this one is your time to find a girl?"

"Maybe..." I whispered to myself, unsure whether to hope as I thought of Genowefa dancing with the grace of the winds.

Xobas yelled and swung again, catching me in my thoughts. His sword sliced toward my head, and though I raised my shield to block the blow, the force was enough. I stumbled before he swept my legs and sent me to the ground.

His jagged gaze met me as I picked myself up for the fifth time that morning. "You can't be distracted like that in a battle," he said. "Solgawi swordsmen won't spare you if you let down your guard thinking about a girl's pretty eyes. In solo combat, you must take charge, understanding how your opponent will react."

I had grown up listening to warriors telling stories of Solga's many invasions from west of the Krowik River. Our tribe was named after that great river, and only it and a few miles of swampland separated their latest advance from our territory. Father had spent his life as the high chief working to unite the other Krowikie chiefs against the Solgawi. That unity had been enough to maintain peace for the last six years, but warriors in Father's inner circle were demanding we retake our lost land. I could only hope cooler heads prevailed.

Xobas's words spurred me. Despite my body aching from the beating, I gripped my spear tighter. He smiled as I shuffled forward, bending my knees so the circular shield covered more of my torso.

While he danced back and forth, I waited for my moment. I had seen this game far too often. He wanted to throw me off balance and strike the opposite direction. This time, I promised myself that I wouldn't let him.

For only a second, he hopped to the left. *Don't flinch.* I held my position as he spun back around, using his momentum to swing the curved cavalry sword. His stomach flashed beneath his tunic as his shield lagged.

Now!

I thrust my spear through the gap, striking Xobas just under his ribs and sending him to the ground.

As he wheezed and pushed himself to a knee, guilt swelled within me. The training spear had a blunt end, but he would be sore through the festival regardless. While he had given me more than my share of scrapes and bruises since we'd started sparring, I didn't enjoy hurting him.

"That's more like it!" he said, reaching his hand out to me as the light of Dadźbóg, god of the sun, split through the bare trees.

Grabbing his arm, I pulled him to his feet. He never covered his forearms, and on his right one, a tattoo of a horse traced the lines of a gruesome scar. I had always wondered if it had come from his time with the eastern Simukie clan before he'd joined our tribe. My curiosity had gotten the better of me once, but I had learned my lesson. Little angered Xobas. That question did.

"Have I earned myself a rest?" I asked, failing to hide my anticipation. There was much to do before the start of the two-day spring equinox festival surrounding the Drowning of Marzanna, but Father would be angry if I left before Xobas excused me.

Dirt covered his brown tunic, but he brushed it off without breaking eye contact. "Yes, you may go. It would be a shame if your gods struck me down for keeping you away from your *true love.*" He chuckled. "Run along. Paint your pretty eggs and set your doll on fire."

"We're all part of the egg hunt, but only the girls paint them," I said, strapping my shield to my back and doing the same with the spear. "And it isn't a doll."

He sheathed his sword and crossed his toned arms. "Ah, yes. The burning and drowning of the winter goddess's effigy sounds like the perfect time to woo a beautiful woman."

He has a point. I blushed. "Won't you be coming? Last time I heard the stories, there was no age limit on having fun."

"But there definitely is on the belief in true love."

I shrugged. "Okay, suit yourself, but that just means more food for me."

With that, I took off, racing and sliding through the trees. In our settlement of Dwie Rzeki, there was nothing to do but farm, herd the cattle and horses, and wander the forest. There had to be *something* more.

As much as I didn't want to put my faith in a silly festival to fall in love, I would jump the fire tonight and be declared a man, eligible to wed. Our tribe considered the rituals of the summer festivals to be the peak time for couples, but the courting began now.

My doubts slid away with every second that passed. Just the thought of it made me giddy. *I listen to Mom's stories too much.*

Brown and gray ruled the forests, but today, the spring gods came with the dawn. Jaryło would bring life to the crops and his golden shield to protect us from our enemies, and Dziewanna would make the wilds bloom and rivers flow.

Each of my steps crunched more of the dried and dead leaves that had been preserved beneath the snow. I leaped with each landing, trying to crush as many of them as I could. Mom always said the forest, not the village, was our home. As I listened to the trees creak in the wind and the leaves crinkle under my boots, I had to agree.

I reached the farmland at the edge of the village and jumped over a log, feeling the breeze skim the back of my neck. The cattle watched me run, but they paid me only a moment of attention before returning to their grass. *Just like the girls.*

With the trees sparser here, the daylight illuminated the sloped thatch roofs of the wooden houses, sunken below ground to keep in as much warmth as possible during the long winter moons. Besides the sound of my heavy breaths, the winds, and my boots thudding against the dirt, it was silent. I treasured that as I turned down the trail to our home.

There was something magical about the woods beyond Dwie Rzeki's wooden walls. They brought a peace that the day's work and busy village center lacked. With nobody around but the trees and birds, I was myself.

That magic faded as I passed the place Otylia and I had entered the forest four years before. Our final late-night journey. My heart ached at the thought. So much had changed since then.

A trail of smoke stretched to the sky ahead of me. *Mom's up.* She was always an early riser, which made life difficult for me. While she found her energy from the second her eyes opened, I struggled to find that morning spark. My nightly wanderings in my soul-body stole that from me.

I hopped down the four steps to our house and pushed open the wooden door. It creaked as I slid inside, setting my shield and training spear on the dirt floor in the corner as the warmth of the stone stove washed over me. The house was only eight strides long and half that wide, so the stove never failed to keep us warm, even in the midst of winter's grip.

Mom turned from her kettle and smiled, the blaze illuminating her pale skin and loose golden hair. "I was wondering how long Xobas would keep you. Here, I'm sure you're freezing."

She handed me a steaming bowl of soup, which I accepted eagerly. As she went about making one for herself, I sat at the small table in the middle of the room and wrapped my hands around the clay bowl, letting its heat flow through my body. For just a few seconds, I didn't care that it burned my palms. "It took some effort to convince him to let me go this early."

"Your father will be pleased he's pushing you," she replied, sitting across from me.

All my life, she'd referred to him as *your father*. I assumed it was because Father had agreed to the request of High Chieftess Natasza that he throw us out of the longhouse, ending Mom's time as a concubine—a secondary wife. I had only been a baby when it'd happened. In a village with little in the name of drama, though, it had apparently been talked about for moons.

I didn't mind living apart from Father, Natasza, and my five half-brothers and sisters. Mom and I had a cottage to ourselves. We'd been forced beyond the village walls' protection, but Father's longhouse wasn't far. Just distant enough to typically avoid Father's stern control and close enough to see my siblings—or at least the ones I liked.

11

I stared at my spoon as it drifted through the steaming liquid. "I doubt my fighting will ever satisfy Father."

"Jacek is a difficult man to please." Her gaze dropped to her bowl before she smiled up at me.

Even with nothing but the stove's aura and the flickering candle on the table to provide light, her eyes were a bright blue like mine. *She's faking joy for me.* I let her do it. She wanted me to be happy, but she deserved it too.

"Are you excited for the festival?" she asked.

My heart jumped. I forced myself to sip the soup to give me time to think. All that accomplished, though, was burning my tongue, and I let out a yelp.

"Oh, that nervous?"

I wiped my mouth on my sleeve as I blushed. "Is it that obvious?"

"No, just a mother's intuition. Is there a girl in particular who has your heart fluttering like the birds? Genowefa? Otylia?"

How does she always know? All the boys wanted Genowefa. One glance from her was enough to make my heart stop. "Does it matter who I'm fond of? Father will probably just marry me off to some chief's daughter to keep his loyalty, and he's made sure I haven't had a real conversation with Otylia in years."

An understanding smile crossed her face. "I remember jumping the fire with hope in my heart." Her eyes drifted to the stove. Memories swirled in them. "Jacek was the second-born, like you, and all the girls were fond of him."

"Not like me…" I mumbled.

Chuckling, she reached across the table and squeezed my hand. It was a small thing, but it calmed my heart. "Oh, my Wašek," she began. "I would not wish upon you the trials your father faced. With prestige, it's often difficult to know who truly loves you and whose heart is full of greed. The others may scoff at you because of me, but when you find someone who sees beyond that, you'll know they're the one."

I picked at the calluses on my palm, avoiding her gaze. Being the son of a concubine didn't make me untouchable, but it was enough.

Though I was Father's second-born, my family name was Lubiewicz, son of Lubena, instead of Jackiewicz, son of Jacek. Only bastards took their mother's name, and even now the other boys mocked me for it. To them I was the Half-Chief and nothing more.

"But you loved him?" I asked.

"It was hard not to. Your father could charm any girl, but at the summer solstice that year, he chose me." Her spoon slipped into the bowl. She stared at it for a few moments before letting out a sigh. "Of course, you have heard the rest of the story."

With a reassuring smile, I shrugged. "He got stuck with wicked Natasza, and you got me to help feed the horses and plow the field."

"And I thank Mokosz for that blessing." She tapped the wooden amulet of the Great Mother that hung from her neck, then stood without finishing her soup. As she pulled her dress from around the stool, she glanced at the stove and clicked her tongue.

During our meal, the fire had dwindled, and sorrow filled her eyes when she turned back to me. "I'm sure you would like to prepare for the festival, but can you grab more firewood first? They needed so much for the bonfire, and I—"

"Happy to," I said as I followed her to the stove. "There's still time before everything begins, and I'll never turn down an excuse to wander the woods."

"Don't travel too far, and don't—"

"Follow the leszy's whispers," I interrupted again, grabbing the iron ax leaning against my bed, where she'd probably placed it as a hint—one I had missed. Mom had constantly warned me of the forest spirit's call for years. Not that either of us had ever heard it.

She swept across the room, placing the bowls next to the bucket of water by her bed that she must have already pulled from the well. "I sometimes forget how old you've gotten."

I kissed her on the cheek and headed to the door with the ax swung over my shoulder. "Never too old to love your stories. Be back soon."

"When you return, I'll likely be feeding the animals. I love you."

I flashed a smile in response and climbed back into the daylight.

Overhead, the eight winds carried the gray clouds, and I prayed to Perun, god of sky and thunder, that he'd stay his storms.

Please let me have this one day.

As I wandered through the woods, though, the air battered my back. I tried to ignore it as I searched for suitable downed trees to chop, but after a few minutes of enduring the torrent, I stopped and let the head of my ax rest against an exposed tree root. A chill ran up my arms.

"What are you telling me?" I asked Perun as I stared into the sky.

The bushes rustled nearby.

My breaths caught, and I whipped around, ready to fight as I studied the forest. Demons didn't often attack during the day, but other spirits lurked, and rogue wolves or bears could strike a lone wanderer. I shuddered. *Otylia can't protect me this time.*

A buck watched me from less than ten paces away, its eyes full of the fear I had felt moments ago. I loosened my grip on the ax. "Hey there."

It huffed and swung its head like a restless horse.

"What's wrong?" Deer weren't a rare sight, but they normally ran if you got too close. This one just stared at me and repeated the motion. *Is it trying to point?* I looked to the clouds. "You want me to follow it?"

The buck took off before skidding to a stop and looking back at me. It let out another sharp breath.

I glanced toward our cottage. *This isn't a voice, right?* A thrill rose within me as the winds returned, forcing me to stumble after the deer. Soon, I gave in and ran myself. What harm could a deer be?

Dashing through the trees, my arms and legs ached. I cursed Xobas for my soreness as the ax weighed me down. I struggled to keep up with the buck, but whenever it reached the edge of my vision, it stopped and waited, its eyes judging my slowness. "I'm coming!" I called after it.

Am I actually talking to a deer? Is that worse than talking to the sky?

Without answers, I kept running. The air seemed to chill the longer I went, and the ground grew hard against my boots as frost replaced the muck of spring. I knew the forest well, but by now, I had no clue where we were. Wherever the mysterious deer was leading me, I was trapped in its wake.

My patience soon wore thin and my legs tired. I stopped as we reached a rock outcropping, dropping the ax and placing my hands on my knees as I caught my breath. When I looked up, I lost it again.

The deer transformed, morphing into a spiraling tower of bark and leaves, roots and dirt. The creaking deafened me, and I froze to my spot as it grew to over twice my height. It twisted out, forming legs, arms, antlers, a mask of bone, and... *No*...

From the top of the tower, two green eyes stared down at me. A mouth formed among the vines, and the leszy's voice rumbled the whole woods when he spoke, "Hello, Wacław. I've been waiting for you."

2

Otylia

I hate festivals.

THE BLACK HELLEBORE FLOWER on my bedroom nightstand seemed to suck away the candlelight as my toes met the chilled dirt floor. Most hellebore would never bloom so early in the spring, but I'd channeled the power of Dziewanna, goddess of the wilds and spring, to keep this one alive year-round. Unlike most girls and their pretty red and blue flowers, it wasn't a decoration.

It was a reminder of Mother's death.

Mother had loved the festival around the Drowning of Marzanna. Every year, after the arrival of the spring gods, she'd led me deep through the woods at dawn to welcome spring's warmth against our bare feet.

Her dark brown hair like that of a sprawling willow would cascade down her back as she'd freed it from her headscarf. Married women in our tribe were supposed to cover their hair at all times, but Mother had claimed it was best to experience spring's birth free, if only for a moment.

As we'd wandered, she told stories of beautiful girls finding their love in the moons following the equinox. I'd lamented I would ever be a wife.

"Oh, my little Otylka," she'd said with her hand at my cheek. "Even the wild goddess was forced by her father to be wed. But when your time comes, the man you marry will be of your choosing. Dziewanna's spirit is yours, and no man will tame you."

When Mother had died just weeks after the spring equinox four years ago, the festival lost its meaning of new life. She'd suffered from the illness we called Marzanna's Curse since the end of winter, and her potions hadn't been enough to keep the curse at bay.

The day after she passed, I'd found that black hellebore next to me in the woods as I wept. I still didn't know whether it was a fluke or a gift from her wandering spirit as she traveled to the underworld of Nawia. It didn't matter which. I'd never stopped missing her.

This morning, I'd heard the commotion outside before the sun had even risen.

Every spring the tribe's chiefs came to Dwie Rzeki with their eligible daughters and strongest sons. Every spring they thanked Jaryło for protecting the crops and ending the thaw. And every spring they forgot Dziewanna—the one who actually killed Marzanna and ensured there was anything left to restore.

With a deep breath, I gripped Dziewanna's amulet of an hunter's bow on my necklace and said a prayer, asking the goddess to give me the strength to make it through the day. I'd need it.

The hellebore held my gaze as I tied my long black hair into our tribe's traditional braid. The weave signaled that I was unmarried—and as of tonight, eligible to be wed—but the bone talismans I wore within it usually kept boys away.

Once I finished, I changed into my simple gray dress, blew out the candle, and grabbed my herb bag.

Our house's main room was quiet besides the meowing of our sleek black cat, Maryn, and the crackling of the fire in the stone stove as I pushed aside the cloth separating it from my small bedroom. I crouched for a second to scratch the cat's head. He was a stupid little thing that knew only how to knock the ingredients for my potions off the table. Father said cats protected their homes from evil spirits,

17

but as I looked down at Maryn, his purring filling the space, I doubted he would be any use against a mouse, let alone a spirit.

Over a dozen wood-carved statues of many of the gods lined the room, their eyes watching me as I moved to the door. Father's staff was missing from the corner. He must've been away, helping prepare for the festival's rituals already. He would come home soon, and I didn't want to be there when he did.

Our cottage was bigger than most in the village. As high priest of our tribe, Father received land, the house, and all the food we needed. I had continued potion-making after Mother's death, but the bartering barely earned enough to trade hunters for their spare animal bones. They always raised a brow at me but accepted.

I stepped into the early morning daylight and scowled at the villagers hobbling by. While they drank and danced, I had work to do.

I served as one of the szeptuchy, whispering sorceresses able to channel the power of the god who had chosen us. It was our responsibility protect the gods' altars and do what they asked. Every channeler trained from a young age to prepare for initiation when we turned twelve, but the gods never chose many of those who went through with the rituals. No szeptucha had ever channeled more than a single god.

I channeled two.

A group of stumbling boys, likely no older than me, eyed me as I ducked through the village's eastern gate and into the woods. Their taunting whistles followed, and my fingers twitched. *I could strangle them.*

Dziewanna was my primary deity. Mokosz, her mother and the goddess of women and divination, had also chosen me, but my connection to Dziewanna was the strongest. With the wild goddess's power, I could whisper to the trees, waters, and animals, calling them to my aid. There would've been a thrill in shutting up the boys. But I had better things to do.

I headed toward the deeper parts of the forest, away from the drunkards in search of herbs. The festival guests would need relief from their sickness when they drank themselves into a stupor.

Even before I could channel Dziewanna, I'd had a keen sense of where to find the right flowers, herbs, and fungi to use in potions. Mother had always sent me to collect them for her before...

Tears threatened my eyes as I knelt to pick an edible mushroom. *Gods, I miss her.*

When Father had scolded me as a child for running into the forest with my hand clasping Dziewanna's amulet at my collar, Mother had smiled and encouraged me to get so lost that only the goddess could guide me home. Father was a follower of the eldest god, Swaróg, and didn't approve of me serving Dziewanna. To him, she was nothing but the headstrong, rogue goddess. I didn't care what he thought.

I ripped the mushroom from the earth and threw it into my bag. Then, with my dress's skirt sweeping behind me, I stomped through the woods, crushing the leaves underfoot as I went.

The festival had me agitated. It happened every annually when the tribe ignored Dziewanna, but this year was worse.

On top of the drunk boys eager to put their hands on anything with breasts, I had plenty of motivation to avoid the crowds. I was sixteen now. Despite Mother's claims I would choose my husband, Father wished to marry me off to another influential priest or chief to increase his own standing in the tribe. That just encouraged me to stay away even more.

Even now, when I knew them well, the woods were a rare haven. They were Dziewanna's realm, untouched by the corrupting hand of man. As far as I knew, she had never chosen a szeptucha before me. That made serving her lonely. But I liked it that way.

With each stride I took deeper into the wilds, my array of bone-carved amulets rattled against my hips. Besides helping me connect to the gods, they did a fine job keeping people away. Still, I'd heard the villagers' whispers through the years.

"There goes the witch of the woods."

"Maybe those bones are human."

"I bet she poisons us all with her potions."

I would only smirk and shoot them a glare in response. They

blindly believed me to be a witch. While witches used spells like szeptuchy, they channeled dark spirits for their selfish magic. A szeptucha's power, instead, was useless if she acted against her god's wishes.

Many of the unclaimed initiates pursued witchcraft after their rejection. That power didn't make them like us, but that didn't matter to the simple-minded villagers. To them, I was a sorceress. Whether I channeled the gods or black spirits didn't matter. I was strong—a girl with power they couldn't have—and that scared them.

Maybe that was why they excluded Dziewanna too. She'd dared to challenge Perun's rule over the Three Realms: Prawia, Jawia, and Nawia—the lands of the gods, living, and dead. When she'd failed, Perun had forced her to marry his rival, Weles, who was the god of the lowlands and underworld. Father said that was how to tame a wild girl. But no one could tame Dziewanna, not even Weles. I would be no different.

I shivered and pulled my sleeves over my forearms. The breeze was cool this morning. *Odd.* Dziewanna and Jaryło should've started to warm the earth by now.

My hand drifted to the dirt alongside a willow as I whispered to Dziewanna, calling for her connection to nature. Through the goddess, I sensed everything within the tree, its vast system of roots underground, and the wilds that stretched around it. The forest was part of me—joined with my soul. I craved that. I was whole with Dziewanna's power flowing through me and nature's senses mixing with mine.

Frost stung the ends of my fingers and raced up my arm. I staggered back, breaking the connection. "What are you doing, Marzanna?" I whispered into the winds.

Marzanna's death was the only thing I looked forward to during the spring equinox. Her illness had taken Mother from me. Burning her effigy and watching it drown in Dziewanna's river was my annual bit of revenge.

Marzanna was Dziewanna's sister and Jaryło's twin. No one knew why she was bitter rivals with her spring siblings. Some claimed she hadn't always brought despair, but Father and the other priests dismissed them.

Tribal customs banned the channeling of Marzanna's power, and the priests had exiled her worshippers to the cursed Mangled Woods in the far east of our lands. Many of her szeptuchy hid after their initiation. Like all channelers, though, they bore their goddess's mark on their neck. Anyone with a Frostmark who refused to leave was executed.

It was stupid. There were rumors that those Frostmarked had established a cult in the Mangled Woods. Pushing channelers into their arms was asking for trouble. But I was just the weird witch girl. Why would my opinion matter?

After an hour of collecting herbs, I'd filled my bag, but I wasn't ready to return. Dadźbóg was still early in his journey across the sky. I had time before Father would expect me.

I pulled the skull of a muskrat from my bag and placed it at the base of an oak. The hunter I'd traded with had demanded I cure an infection on his foot in exchange for the skull. After I'd narrowed my eyes and started chanting to the trees, he'd settled for a potion that would help him sleep. The last thing I'd wanted to see was his disgusting foot.

Bones were powerful when used correctly. Since they still held elements of the animal's life force, or *żityje*, they helped channel a god's power—or strengthen a witch's own. They were especially helpful with Mokosz's divination rituals.

On the day I would jump the fire, I needed to know what Father had planned. Tension balled in my stomach at the thought of what type of man he would arrange for me, but curiosity was stronger than my fear.

Mokosz's Mothermark—four diamonds divided by a X—stared back at me from my wrist. I traced each of them, anticipating the rush that came with her rituals. All channeling brought power coursing through me, but divination was seeing what would be—or at least what could be—and nothing was like it.

Mokosz's diviners, like all szeptuchy, were women. The men had their doubts. That never stopped them from visiting me in search of the future when it suited their purposes.

"Great Mother, bring me your sight," I whispered in the old tongue of the gods, clutching Mokosz's amulet with one hand and hovering the other over the skull. "Show me what is to come and what is done."

The world faded as darkness swallowed me. The ritual understood my will, my desire without words. Mokosz led me into the river of time, guiding me toward what she wanted me to see. I surrendered to her.

When the vision formed around me, I stood deeper in the woods than I'd ever gone. A thin layer of frost covered the hard ground, and the surrounding oaks lacked their leaves as their dark, dead ones meshed with the frozen earth.

I sighed. *This isn't Father's plan. Why are you showing me this?*

Something cracked in the grove ahead. My hand snatched Dziewanna's amulet, and I hesitated before creeping forward, not sure what I was about to find. Within Dziewanna's power, I sensed a spirit—one I had only felt once before.

The leszy stood amid a snow-covered clearing. Before him trembled a scrawny blond boy, dressed in a dirtied brown tunic.

"Half-Chief?" I asked, using Wacław's nickname, though I knew he couldn't hear me. What was High Chief Jacek's second-born son doing so far from the village with a forest guardian?

I studied the frost covering the leszy's typically lush body. The towering spirits were supposed to be friendly to Dziewanna and Weles—as the masters of the forests—but another deity's mark stained this one. A shiver ran down my spine as I recognized it.

Marzanna…

The leszy spoke, but when his words pierced the air, the ground split. I cried out as the darkness pulled me away.

"I needed to see that!" I shouted to Mokosz with my fists clenched. "Marzanna is planning something."

"Oh, little one," she said in my head, *"you will see all of it in time."*

When I opened my mouth to reply, everything spun. My stomach turned as the void faded and more visions flashed before me.

In the first, a whirlwind caught Wacław in the forest, lifting him off the ground. Air rushed from his lungs as I fought my way to him. Each step felt like an eternity. The gale's power tore at my arms, forcing me to collect. Then, I let loose a scream with a strength that came from neither of my goddesses. The gusts ceased, and when Wacław dropped to the ground, the vision slipped to another.

I stood at the edge of a moonlit pasture in an elaborate dress. Rain poured. Wacław knelt in the muck and stared through the storm at a zmora, one of Marzanna's undead minions and the most frightening type of demon I'd ever faced. Blood dripped from his arms and chest. His breaths were shallow, weak, and when he struggled to his feet, the monster snarled and lunged.

They never clashed.

Instead, light swarmed over me, and I found myself back-to-back with Wacław in a forest I didn't recognize. Snow blanketed the ground and shouting filled the air as warriors charged at us with blood in their eyes. I swung my dagger and reached for Dziewanna. But her power was distant, fleeting. I was defenseless as the warrior's blade streaked toward me.

A moment before the blade struck, Wacław slid his shield into my grasp. Now vulnerable himself, he spun through a group of trees as he sparred with a warrior of his own. When my voice called after him, Mokosz pulled me away once again.

Why are you doing this?

I begged for it to stop as the tide of time drowned me, yet the goddess's grip would not relent. She forced me deeper, and my mind followed.

I floated in an endless pit of darkness, but this wasn't time trying to drag me away. It was cold, deathly still. Neither Dziewanna nor Mokosz answered my call as a sharp crackling encircled me.

Then came the pain.

A being of pure light clutched my throat, choking me as sparks surged from its fingers and seared at my skin. I kicked at the creature, but no matter how hard I fought, it wouldn't relent. Wacław knelt nearby—his eyes glowing as lightning arced through his veins. I sensed his power in my soul, unlike anything I'd ever felt.

When he stood, time swept away the light once again and left me drifting in its wake. Every part of me shuddered at what I'd seen.

What is he?

Many in the tribe had nicknamed Wacław the Half-Chief—the concubine's son that nobody bothered to respect. I had wondered if that was why we'd been so close growing up. Despite our fathers' disdain for each other, he'd always defended me when people called me a witch, and I couldn't have cared less about who his mother was. He had been kind and understanding when others scoffed at me for hoping to serve Dziewanna. *Had.*

A hundred memories filled my mind of our time as children, running from our fathers' quarrels. We'd been Wašek and Otylka, a warrior and sorceress adventuring through our imaginary worlds and slaying demons—he with his soul-form and I with my channeling. Besides Mother, he'd been all I had as a child.

That night four years ago had changed everything.

Somehow, I'd *channeled* before completing my initiation. The power had been raw, as if I'd unshackled something inside me in my desperation to save Wacław from the wolves. Even now I didn't understand it.

There had been fear in Wacław's eyes that night, and the next day, he'd trembled when he met me at our usual place in the woods. He'd worn a black eye and bruises on his neck that hadn't come from the wolves. When I'd asked about the wounds, he'd shook his head. "They were there when I woke up."

Wacław had always been quieter than the other boys, but the few days after that, he barely spoke. He insisted we meet where no one could see us, refusing to answer why. Then, one overcast morning, he came with tears in his eyes.

"I can't be seen with a witch anymore," he said without meeting my gaze.

Though I tried to take his hands, to ask him why, he gave no answer. After that, he avoided me like the other foolish boys, and when Mother died only a week later, he didn't come to comfort me.

In one moon, I'd lost my best friend and Mother. I knew Jacek had kept Wacław away, but his betrayal still felt like a knife in my gut.

Pushing away those memories, I spoke to Mokosz, "I don't understand. All I wanted was to figure out Father's plan."

"That is not what you wished to see, only what you believed you needed to see."

"What?"

One last vision rushed through my mind.

Wacław stood with me under the crescent moon. Snow drifted through the air, obscuring the rolling plains as I shivered and looked from the moon to him.

His hair was longer than usual, oddly unruly for the son of a chief, and patches of red covered his face and the tips of his ears. Passion shone in his light blue eyes as he stared at me. I hated it. And when he stepped forward, wrapping his arms around my waist and leaning in, I screamed and tore myself from the ritual.

My heart hammered my chest as I dug my hands into the cool dirt, clinging to reality. I'd seen war and murder in my visions before. This was worse than all of them. *Anyone but him…*

When I raised my head, the forest no longer felt safe. I saw his gaze everywhere I looked—the gaze of the boy who'd abandoned me when I needed him most.

No, I told myself. Father had despised whenever I went near Wacław, and that was no different now. It didn't matter what he'd been like when we were kids. We'd changed, and Mokosz only ever showed what *could* happen.

Gripping her amulet, I shook my head. "I'll never kiss him."

An animal's panting approached.

I shot to my feet, ready to channel. The blur of orange bolted through the corner of my vision, darting between the trees. It circled around me, and when it stopped a few strides away, I let myself breathe.

It's just a fox.

Most red foxes were friendly with Dziewanna, and I sensed her connection with this one.

"Follow her," Dziewanna said, her voice swirling through the branches.

"Where?"

"Don't ask questions. Go!"

The fox took off, heading deeper into the woods. I groaned. The festival hadn't even started, and I was already sick of the day. But Dziewanna had given me a command, so I forced away my reluctance and ran after the fox.

3

Wacław

I should have listened to Mom.

I SCRAMBLED BACK, my heart racing as the leszy's long legs stepped toward me, roots and vines twisting as they closed in.

Where's my ax?

Its iron head glinted against the snow between us. I lunged forward, but the creature's vines engulfed it, stealing whatever hope I had of putting up a fight.

"No ax," the leszy said, shaking the trees with his deep voice.

My eyes sought an escape, but trees and undergrowth stretched everywhere I looked. *Which way did I come in?* With the wind gusts smothering me and the leszy lumbering closer, I had lost my sense of direction. I ran anyway.

Roots snatched at my feet with each stride. Before I could escape the grove, they dragged me into the frost.

I was trapped.

The spirit lumbered within a few paces, and his stench of rotting wood overwhelmed me as I gritted my teeth. "What do you want from me?" I shouted.

"Lady Marzanna has need of you."

I swallowed and tried to hold my gaze on the leszy's eyes, but everything on him slithered and creaked. "Why would the goddess of winter want my help?" We were to burn and drown her effigy that night, sending her to the underworld of Nawia until autumn. Why would she speak now, at her weakest?

"She has seen your trials, your pain," the leszy continued. "The goddess understands what it is to be rejected by those who should show you affection."

My breaths slowed. I should've been afraid, but the guardian's words touched me and smothered Mom's warnings. "She's watching me?"

He seemed to smile. "Marzanna sees the power in you that others are blind to. Follow her words, and she will grant you what you seek. There is a place for you at her side."

What I seek? Peace? Acceptance? A purpose? Which of my many dreams does she want to grant? I shook my head. "I don't understand."

A shout rang out from behind me. I spun and studied the tree line, trying to identify where the noise came from. A figure appeared, but it ran through the trees too quickly for me to tell who.

"Obey the words…" the leszy carried on, followed by a gust of air that tickled my neck as the figure reached the grove.

"Half-Chief!" a voice yelled. "What are you doing out here?"

"Otylia?"

The szeptucha narrowed her sharp green eyes as she held out her hand and chanted in the old tongue, the language of the channelers and gods. The roots released my leg at her command, and awe filled me as the muck and earth engulfed them in seconds.

Otylia tossed her long, braided black hair over her shoulder and marched toward me. As she walked, the pendants of various gods clattered at her waist, and her ashen dress trailed behind, biting at her heels. From the furrow of her wide brow, I knew I was in trouble.

I glanced at where the leszy used to be. It had transformed into the buck once again, and it touched its nose to the ground before scampering into the woods. Something glimmered where it had stood. I covered it with my boot as I turned to Otylia.

She watched the deer go with curiosity, then returned her gaze to me. "You didn't answer my question."

I puffed up my chest, trying to match her intensity. Secretly, though, I was flustered by her sorcery and the array of bone talismans woven into her hair—everyone was. "I could ask you the same thing."

"Yet you won't," she replied, circling me, "because you're afraid of me, just like the others."

"What makes you think that?"

"You're too scared to tell me you spoke with a leszy." She noticed my surprise and smirked. "I'm a szeptucha, remember?"

I could never forget Otylia was a whispering sorceress—not after that night four years before.

Our fathers had been rivals our entire lives, and Father had seen Otylia as High Priest Dariusz's way of manipulating me. Still, Mom defied his wishes and allowed me to meet with her most days. When I showed up to the equinox festival the morning after the wolf attack covered with scrapes and scars, though, he called Otylia a cursed witch. I pleaded that she'd saved my life. It didn't matter to him. He *forcefully* forbade me from ever seeing her again.

Despite Father's beatings and my shock at what she'd done, I snuck away to meet Otylia the following days. She told me stories of the gods, their powers, and the szeptucha initiation rituals. I was in wonder of it all. Then Father discovered us.

He landed blow after blow to my arms and torso, where no one would see the bruises, and swore he would exile Otylia to the Mangled Woods if I dared to seek her out ever again. So, I put my head down and backed away. Though the decision had cost me our friendship and turned us bitter toward each other, it was better than losing her forever.

"I followed a deer," I finally said, the guilt of leaving her weighing heavy on my shoulders. "Then it transformed into a leszy, yes."

Otylia knelt and ran her fingers through the frost. "That was foolish, but considering it led you *here* and you're alive, it told you something." Her eyes flicked to me, and I could feel her poking at my soul. "What was it?"

"Why would I tell you? You'll just run to Dariusz so he can use it against Father." On a day where all the chiefs and priests would be there, I couldn't let that happen.

"You trust a spirit more than me?" she asked, furrowing her brow as she stood and brushed the snow off her knees. "I would expect a concubine's son to see me as more than a witch by now. There was a time we trusted each other more than anyone."

Her words rang true. She was an outsider too, yet ever since Father had forced me to shun her, I had treated her like everyone treated me. All I could do was stammer as I searched for a reply, but I came up empty.

She sighed and shook her head. My heart sunk. Though I could see the burden she carried, I couldn't bring myself to tell her the truth. It was too late. Nothing I could say now would fix four years' worth of distance.

"You can keep your secret," she said, "but a fox guided me here. Dziewanna sent me to find you for a reason."

I searched for a reply, but she clutched her sack of herbs and stomped back into the forest. My throat burned watching her go, as if Swaróg, god of celestial fire, punished me for my silence.

Alone again, I shivered, suddenly aware of how cold I was. I had wandered deep into the woods, fallen into the trap of Marzanna's messenger, and was now lost with more questions than answers.

My foot's throbbing reminded me of the object the leszy had left behind.

A small dagger lay buried in the snow. Its hilt was black as the night and a leather sheath covered its blade. When I picked it up, the cool metal hummed in my hands, glowing as I drew it and gasped.

The flat of the dark blade crackled as icy-white designs etched themselves into its surface, forming a set of symbols I didn't recognize. Our tongue had no written word, but a whisper in my mind told me their meaning.

"Blood."

The dagger slipped from my fingers as Mom's warnings echoed in my head. I stared down at the blade, its white letters taunting me in the early morning sunlight, before surveying the forest to ensure no one had seen.

But I was alone. Normally, that would've been a comfort, yet as that word haunted me, I wished Otylia hadn't left. Though our relationship had soured, a channeler seemed helpful when a goddess was demanding my blood.

Why does Marzanna want me?

My breaths shallowed. The blade tugged on my soul, as if the etching was a demand, not a request. I had prayed to the gods all my life for something to happen. Marzanna's answer was not what I'd expected, but the leszy had said she needed my help—that she *wanted* my help—and denying a goddess's call never went well in Mom's stories.

I gave in and picked up the dagger from the frost and dirt, feeling its dull chill against my fingers. Mom's voice begged me to stop, but the dagger's pull grew stronger. I held its point to my palm and tore my gaze away.

"Do it."

I froze. My fingers gripped the hilt, turning my knuckles deathly white. The thought had not been mine. Whether it was Marzanna, the dagger, or the leszy, it scared me all the same. My hand trembled as I tried to pull away the blade, but it wouldn't budge.

"You cannot fight destiny, Wacław. Join me, and you will have more than you ever dreamed of."

A vision tore me into the darkness, tumbling me to its depths until the world swirled to life, too real to be a dream.

I stood on the highest peak of Perun's Crown. Genowefa smiled at my side, her soft hand in mine as all the lands of the tribes stretched before us in an endless display of their glory. Each breath of the cool alpine air relaxed my mind and soul. And with the winds blowing Genowefa's golden blonde hair through the warm rays of Dadźbóg's light, she left me breathless.

The ground gave way. I panicked and grasped her hand, but her fingers slipped from mine, stealing the joy in my heart as I watched her disappear. I shut my eyes.

Seconds later, the smells of alcohol and warriors coated in sweat washed over me. I dared to look, and my mouth gaped.

I sat in Father's fur-covered chair at the head of his longhouse. In front of me knelt the chiefs of not only the Krowikie but of tribes both east and west—kings and chiefs, warriors and priests. One by one, each set their swords, spears, and axes at my feet. Pride swelled within me as I reigned over them, tasting power for the first time, but then the scene shifted again.

This time, when the ground vanished, I didn't continue to fall. Instead, I danced through the air over the Krowik River, the wide forests and plains stretching in every direction. At first, I feared plummeting from the sky, but each gust seemed to ask for my command, lifting me as I flew far above the highest of trees. The eight winds were one with me. Each traversed the land as a limb of my body. *Is this what it feels like to be a god?*

A sharp cold tore me back to reality.

My legs wobbled. I dropped to my knees, desire replacing my fear and pulling my hand to the dagger's jagged point.

"This will all be yours," the voice whispered. *"All you must do is gift me your blood."*

The sweet visions swirled through my mind as I stared at the dagger, its tip sharp against my palm. I felt cold, empty. Marzanna had shown me a life with power I could've only dreamed of. Something in my soul craved it more than anything.

I sliced my hand.

Pain shot up my arm. The dagger slipped from my fingers, dropping to the frosted ground. I staggered back, shocked, as blood seeped over its blade and filled the inscription.

"You have done well," Marzanna said. *"Take the dagger. Listen to its commands—my Frostmarked."*

Frostmarked? Trembling, I held my bleeding hand in the light. Agony tore through me as the cut grew. It spread across my skin like an invisible blade, carving until it formed Marzanna's Frostmark—a X, crossed at each end.

What have I done?

Father, like the chiefs before him, had banished all Frostmarked to the Mangled Woods. I had become one of them.

It was common for the gods to demand a sacrifice, but we feared Marzanna for a reason. She was the goddess of death and disease as well as winter. And now, I had gifted her my blood.

As another inscription etched its way across the dagger, I slid it back into the sheath, shoved it into my bag, and took a breath. I hadn't even realized I'd been holding it, but my lungs screamed as I clutched my knees. My stomach flipped. *I need to get out of here.*

Without knowing where I was, I took off in the direction Otylia had gone, hoping I could find a familiar section of the forest.

The chill nipped at my ears as I ran. What scared me most was that I could *feel* something pulling me back to that frozen patch. Dreams, hopes, passions—they all whispered for me to return, but I kept going. It didn't matter where I ended up. Anywhere was better than there.

A musty smell soon hit me, and I let out a sigh of relief as I reached the bank of the wide Wyzra River. *Hello, old friend.* Panting, I knelt by its bank and washed my face with the cool water.

What just happened?

I stared down at my reflection as water dripped from my nose and chin, disturbing the image. Minutes before, I had been searching for wood. Now... It was difficult to know what the leszy had meant. Why would a goddess want my help? Why had I given into her temptations?

I splashed more water over my face, wishing it was all a messed-up dream. But I didn't dream.

Frostmarked.

That symbol stained my mind, its pain throbbing in my hand. *I have to get home.*

Father would be upset if I was late to the festival preparations, but I was a long way from the village. Luckily, though, the bubbling, slow Wyzra would guide me back home, where it joined with the Krowik.

Mud caked my boots as I trudged along, trying not to think about the dagger tucked away in my bag and the Frostmark branding my palm.

In the chaos, I had almost forgotten my anxiety and excitement around the Drowning of Marzanna. Those feelings seemed childish now, and I regretted my wish for change and adventure. All I wanted to do was curl up next to our fire and hear Mom's stories or begin preparing for the spring planting season. Yet, instead of that simple, safe life, I now faced blood magic and the opinions of girls—I didn't know which frightened me more.

Dadźbóg was well on his way through the sky when I finally reached the gate at the eastern edge of Dwie Rzeki covered in bites and a layer of sweat from head to toe. While Marzanna's winters brought death and starvation, I wished Dziewanna's breath of life didn't awaken the bugs. I hoped no one would see me, especially the girls.

Unfortunately, the trails weren't as lonely as usual. Even beyond the walls, people hastily walked toward Perun's Oak at the heart of the village, carrying food, drinks, wood, and materials for Marzanna's effigy.

Since Father was the high chief, all the chiefs and priests visited Dwie Rzeki for major festivals. Our settlement was the largest in the tribe, yet it rarely had more than a hundred and fifty adults. Within my first few minutes back on the trail, though, I saw at least that many—most of them strangers. Considering what most of the girls in the village thought of me, I welcomed that.

When I was about to turn off the main trail, someone called my name. I took a sharp breath and stopped as Mikołaj, my half-brother, grabbed my shoulder.

"Wacław!" he exclaimed. "Father has been asking for you." He looked me up and down before pulling back his hand in disgust. "What happened to you?"

I hung my head. Mikołaj was three years older than me, and Father had been grooming him for years to take his place as high chief when he passed. Despite my isolation, Mikołaj had always seen me as his competition for the position, so he never missed an opportunity to show he was better. If I was late, he would be smitten that I'd disappointed Father—again.

"I went to collect some firewood for my mom but ended up a little lost," I said. "Luckily, I found the Wyzra."

He smirked and ran his hand through his light brown hair—his mother Natasza's hair. "Well, go clean yourself up and find Father before he throws a fit. Would *hate* for the girls to see you like this."

"Please let him know I'll be there soon."

"I'm not your servant. Tell him yourself."

Without waiting for a reply, he turned and jogged back down the path he'd come from. I watched his bulky frame go. We'd both inherited Father's height, but somehow, I had missed out on the wide shoulders and firm jawline.

When Mikołaj had turned sixteen and jumped the bonfire, every village girl had descended upon him, trying to seduce the heir of the high chief. In the end, he'd picked the girl everyone had their eye on: Chief Serwacy's daughter, Kinga. All the other boys had applauded him for snagging the most beautiful of our tribe, but the two of them argued endlessly.

While their union kept Serwacy, the tribe's third most powerful chief, within Father's sphere of influence, I doubted their marriage was a joyful one. I didn't know what I hoped for, but it wasn't that.

Mom was feeding the horses when I made it back home, her long hair draped freely over her shoulders as she worked—the hair of a woman neither married nor seeking a man.

The chestnut stallion I had claimed as mine, Tanek, seemed to be enjoying the attention and followed her around until he noticed me hopping the fence. With a huff, he trotted over and practically threw his head onto my shoulder.

I chuckled and blew into his nose like mothers did to their foals. "Hey there. Did you miss me?" As he nuzzled my side, I smiled and rubbed his neck. "Sorry, my friend. No treats today."

Just a magic dagger coated in blood.

Mom finished dispersing the bucket of grain and wandered over with concern in her eyes. "Your hand is bleeding."

I looked down at my palm and the stream of blood trickling from it. *How did I not realize that sooner?*

She took my face in her hands. "What happened, Wašek? Talk to me."

"I'm all right, I think."

"Then where is the wood and your ax? Did you—"

"Encounter a leszy?" I sighed and stepped back. "Yes."

Gasping, she held my uninjured hand. Hers shook. "Oh, my son. How did you escape? Why did you follow the voices?"

"There weren't voices, just a deer and a wind that seemed to drive me deeper into the woods. I thought that maybe it was Perun or Strzybóg leading me somewhere, but when we reached a frozen patch and the leszy appeared, I knew I was wrong."

She released me and stepped back with fear in her eyes. "Strzybóg's winds may guide us, but if this beast serves Marzanna… We must speak with Dariusz."

As she walked past me, I pleaded with her to stop, "We can't trust him! If you tell Dariusz of this, then he will exploit it to hurt Father." *And he'll send me away as one of the Frostmarked.*

Her thumb dragged across her fingertips as she thought for a moment, staring at the ground. "Your loyalty to your father is admirable, even if he doesn't reciprocate it. Does anyone else know about this?"

I bit my cheek. "Otylia was there."

Something glimmered in her eye. "She spoke with it as well?"

"No, only me, as it fled when she arrived. She claimed Dziewanna's fox guided her to that spot."

"And what did the leszy speak of?"

I hesitated. *Why am I afraid to tell her?* Whatever fueled the doubt, I pushed it away. "It said Marzanna knew my pain and the power within me—that she would gift me what I sought. And…" I tried to reach for my bag, but a force held me back as I considered showing her the dagger. "I have no idea what it meant," I finished.

Compassion filled her face as she wrapped me in her arms. "I am so glad you are safe and alive. Please, though, promise me you will be more careful?" She brushed the strands of my mangled hair back into place with amusement. "You are all I have left, and I don't know what I would do if I lost you to a monster like that."

"I promise. No more wandering that far into the woods."

When she let go, she looked to the midday sun. "Thank you for trusting me with the truth. We will try to solve the goddess's riddle, but for now, it sounds to me like you owe both Otylia and Dziewanna your thanks."

I must have been scowling, because she lifted my chin and smiled. "Do not allow your Father's rivals to dictate who are yours. I remember when you two were inseparable. You used to speak of your Otylka day in and day out. Besides, she is a cute girl herself."

"Mom," I grumbled. My cheeks flushed as I glanced toward the house, eager to change the subject. "I promise I'll trade for a new ax, but Mikołaj said Father has been looking for me. I should clean up before I meet with him. Will you be okay without me?"

"Of course," she said with a smile. Though I knew she didn't want to let the topic of Otylia go so easily, I was grateful that she did. "You'll remember this festival for your entire life. You deserve to enjoy it. Just don't go chasing any deer on your way there."

Bowing my head, I replied, "I promise."

She smiled. "And the girls would probably appreciate it if you covered that cut. Unless your goal is to bleed on their dresses."

I laughed, but my mind drifted to the dagger in my bag. "I'll wrap it in flowers for them. Love you."

"Love you too."

4

Otylia

Visions, a leszy, and now I'm late. Wonderful.

I WASN'T LOOKING FORWARD TO FATHER'S GLARE as I wound through the woods, heading toward the high chief's longhouse. Avoiding the paths would make me even more tardy to the gathering of the diviners, but it was worth it to avoid the crowd for a few more minutes.

Every year at the spring equinox, Mokosz's chosen szeptuchy met to combine our channeling strength and predict the year's harvest, wars, and other events. I was far less skilled than the eldest ones. Father demanded I attend regardless.

But it wasn't the future of the tribe that was on my mind. I couldn't stop thinking about that patch of frost and Mokosz's vision. Marzanna had called a leszy to talk to Wacław, but why?

He's hiding something.

Some men were able to persuade or intimidate their way past anyone. Wacław was not one of them. He'd trembled our entire conversation. As much as I enjoyed instilling some of that fear in him, this was different.

After the ritual, even I was worried. Marzanna should've been focused on survival when the spring gods were coming for her. Instead, she was courting the foolish second-born of the high chief.

Even more frightening was that Wacław might've been dumb
enough to agree to whatever she'd asked of him. Like Jacek, he had
little experience with the gods or their calls, but unlike him, Wacław
wasn't a skeptic.

The noise of the preparations flowed from the village gates to the
woods. I clenched and flexed my fists as I waited at the tree line,
nervously watching the people before checking my braid. *They don't
care anyway.*

When I finally reached the village center, Father stood at the base
of Perun's Oak with another priest. Skulls of game that he'd sacrificed hung from the tree's branches above him. They were said to
amplify the power of the thunder god, like the bones I wore and
those I placed at Dziewanna's altar in the swamps. Above Father,
though, they seemed an omen.

A headband held an amulet of Swaróg's Forgemark at Father's
brow—its hollow iron diamond wrapped by rings. It was hard to
know if my disdain for the god of fire and smithing was because of
Father's loyalty to him or another reason. It didn't matter. My job
was to serve Dziewanna and Mokosz, not Father.

A jolt ran down my spine when his brown eyes snapped to me. I
took a deep breath. The mysteries of Marzanna, Wacław, and my
divinations would have to wait. I wrinkled my nose and joined them.

"You're late," Father began, running his hand through his long
gray hair. It flowed down his ceremonial red robes, trimmed in a
white pattern that mimicked that of a rope.

"The Great Mother sent me a vision," I replied without offering
any more of an excuse.

The other priest's eyes lit up. "Was it of any interest to us?"

"No." I turned to Father. "Have they started?"

He studied a group of giggling girls near the longhouse—too
close to the divination ritual for his comfort. I noticed Ara's laugh
among them and smiled. With her dark skin and hair, it seemed
Weles himself had crafted my only friend from the purest earth he
had.

Ara was one of the Zurgowie refugees from the far east who had fled their nomadic clan's wars in recent years. For some reason, she had quickly decided she didn't care whether I was a channeler or just another girl. It was a rarity I had clung to since the moment we'd met.

"They have not," Father said when he returned his gaze to me. *Unfortunate.*

The second priest nodded. "We should not keep the women waiting. They have their tempers."

I gritted my teeth to avoid snapping at him as Father gestured to the girls. "Would you mind ushering away those who might overhear the ritual? I must speak with my daughter."

"With pleasure."

The priest left, and Father stared into my soul with all the power of Swaróg's fire. Despite not being a diviner, he always believed he knew exactly what I was thinking. He didn't.

"This is an important day for you, but don't get caught indulging temptations, Otylia," he said.

Anger flashed through me. "I told you! I was conducting a ritual with Mokosz. I want nothing to do with the boys and their stupors."

Only part of that was true, but I wouldn't admit that to him. While Father had his own plans, the other girls gossiping about boys ahead of the festival had gotten to me—only a little. It was impossible to not look around and wonder.

I shuddered as the sight of Wacław in the final vision returned to my mind. After everything we'd been through, he was the last boy I wanted to be with, and the thought of divining again so soon was not appealing.

Father let out a deep sigh. "Your unwillingness to explain what that ritual showed you doesn't ease my doubts."

"Then take it up with Mokosz." I pushed past him. "If they're waiting, I need to hurry. The horses get restless."

He grumbled, but I wasn't going to give him another chance to demean me. There was no way I would admit to him I was talking with Wacław. Besides, whether or not I was kissing anyone in the woods should've been the least of his concerns. It was up to him and the other priests to convince Jacek our visions were true. With the high chief's lack of trust in us, success was doubtful at best. But that wasn't my problem.

I passed through the trees at the rear of the longhouse and reached Mokosz's Grove. A wooden statue of her with open hands and a full body stood in the center of the circle. It was supposed to represent the inviting arms of a mother to her children. I found some comfort in that.

"Oh lovely, she's here," Arleta said in her sweet voice from alongside the statue.

As the eldest diviner, it was her responsibility to ensure the success of the ritual. I didn't care about upsetting Father, but Arleta was a different story. She had always claimed to see something special in me and had defended my adventures in the forest after Mother died. That was enough to make me feel guilty for delaying her.

"Sorry I'm late," I replied, glancing at the eight diviners gathered along the rim. "I received a vision from Mokosz that I couldn't understand, so I needed time to think."

Most of Mokosz's szeptuchy were far older than me, but this year, we had a twelve-year-old initiate—Adelajda. *She's so young.* The skin around Mokosz's mark on her neck was still inflamed, and I doubted she'd done much channeling. I remembered my first equinox divination three years before, scared with no clue what I was getting myself into.

Arleta placed her hand over my heart. "May the Great Mother's gift bless you, child. Your arrival is at the perfect moment. We were about to begin."

I took my spot in the circle next to Adelajda. The girl's eyes were wide, and I offered her a small smile. "You'll be okay," I whispered as Arleta signaled for the horses to be brought.

"I've only divined once before," the girl replied.

"Take my hand and breathe. We're all here to help you."

Her hand clenched mine as five mares charged into the circle, snorting and tossing their heads. But as Arleta chanted to Mokosz, the horses halted and stared at her. It was always shocking to see Mokosz's power tame the wild, powerful beasts. She never failed.

With a wide smile, Arleta dipped her fingers in a bowl of blue liquid and approached the mares. It was our responsibility to summon Mokosz's vision and then read the horses' reactions as a signal of war or peace. For now, they bowed their heads as Arleta smeared the paint across their faces. That calm would soon fade.

Arleta whispered to the horses one last time as another bowl was passed around the circle. When it came to me, I shivered, dipping my fingers into the cold paint and drawing the Mothermark of Mokosz on my forehead. *We already bare her mark,* I grumbled to myself. *Why is this even necessary?*

Adelajda tried to follow my lead but instead created a smudge more than the four diamonds of Mokosz. I held in a snicker as she beamed up at me. "Did I do it?"

"Close enough," I said with a grin.

As Arleta moved into the circle, we joined hands and chanted to the Great Mother. Her power flowed through our connection, growing stronger with all of us joining in the call.

Every spring since my initiation, Mokosz had shown the Solgawi slaughtering our warriors, so we'd encouraged Jacek to avoid war. He'd listened—for now. His doubts of our powers and intentions were no secret, though. If I hadn't been a diviner, I could've understood his skepticism, but this was Mokosz's ritual. Defying it meant defying her.

The darkness soon engulfed us all. Time flowed past me like in my own visions, yet with all of us calling to the goddess together, the ritual's power would drown anyone who let go. We clung to each other as the current pulled at my face, hair, and soul.

I quickly lost track of how long we'd been in the void. Seconds? Minutes? Hours?

The ritual was different every year, and in the gap, my mind drifted to the visions she'd shown me earlier. No matter how much I hated to see Wacław's power by my side, I couldn't deny the vision. But what did Mokosz want me to do?

Time's current stopped.

My breaths were shallow, my entire body on edge as the ground met my feet. We stood on an endless sea of rolling hills and short grasses. Brown and a dull orange hue covered the whole terrain as the dry air left me already wishing for water.

The Anshayman Steppe.

I'd never traveled beyond our tribe's borders, but Father had spoken of his journeys with Jacek to negotiate beyond the Mangled Woods. A dozen nomadic warlords constantly clashed for supremacy of the Anshayman Steppe. From here, however, the lands appeared to be barren. Why would anyone want to rule a wasteland? And more importantly, why were we there? Mokosz had never shown us the east before, and an eerie feeling gripped my chest as the ground began to rumble.

Adelajda stared up at me with her mouth ajar. "What's going on?"

"I don't know…"

Then they appeared—hundreds of riders yelling and clanking rounded swords against their thin wooden shields. They wore no armor on their dark-skinned torsos, where tattoos of battles and creatures stretched across their chests. At the rear, archers rode with their short bows in hand and quivers hanging at their sides. The ground rumbled as if Weles's rage had reached the surface, and their shouts blanketed the valley with their calls for blood.

I clenched my jaw and studied the riders. Ara and Father had told me about the clans and their skill with archery on horseback, something few in our tribe possessed, but this was overwhelming. I'd never seen so many horses in my entire life.

A man wearing a bright red cloak bearing the insignia of a steppe vulture rode out front as they stopped at the peak of a hill. His voice thundered throughout the valley. I couldn't understand his words, but his rage was obvious.

Ara could've identified them. The general's tongue wasn't the shared one of the Zurgowie and Simukie. I'd picked up enough bits of the language from Ara's conversation with her family to tell this was another clan.

After the initial surge, we stood forever in the silence, waiting with the riders. Unfortunately, that gave me time to ponder what was to come.

Tribal politics meant little to me, but this vision had me curious. Was this our next war? Was Jacek foolish enough to send our warriors to die on the distant Anshayman Steppe? The other diviners whispered among themselves in confusion, but no one dared to break the circle.

My legs were stiff by the time the second army arrived across the valley. The air grew deathly still as the stampede approached, their advance louder than rolling thunder.

A horde of over a thousand men charged the first clan on the blackest horses I'd ever seen. Their own mounted archers led the way, holding oddly curved bows and bone-tipped arrows. Behind them, riders wielded long bone spears and cavalry swords that they held high as they shouted. None wore armor except for leather helmets with flaps that covered the back and side of their necks.

Fear filled the eyes of the vulture clan as the wave of black split. The horde archers moved to encircle the clan at full gallop, leaving a single horseman ahead of the wedge that the remaining men had formed.

The lead rider wore the simple brown tunic of the rest of his warriors, but he rode a pure white horse that was blinding in Dadźbóg's harsh light. From a thousand strides away, I sensed the power flowing from him—neither demon nor channeler.

The white rider raised his spear and loosed a yell that pierced through the noise.

As I clutched the weeping Adelajda into my chest, the bone archers fired from every side. The arrows filled the sky, casting a shadow over the earth before they even struck. And when they did, I winced at the screams.

"Shut your eyes!" I ordered the little girl as I shook in horror.

Blood carpeted the grasses and sands as the remaining vulture clan riders surged forward in an unruly charge. Horses and men alike cried out with each volley of arrows that fell upon them. Their own archers attempted to return fire, but it was sparse and slow. Before the clan's cavalry had even reached the horde's, they were surrounded.

The horde leader seemed to laugh as he stared down the red-cloaked general. His men swept forward alongside him, engulfing the clansmen in a tide of darkness as he plunged his spear through the general's chest. The clan's warriors cried out, but it was too late. Less than a minute later, none of them remained.

The horde circled the battlefield, cheering and chanting as their leader dismounted. Each of his massive strides brought him toward the clan's fallen general, who lay dead alongside his horse, the spear holding his bleeding torso off the ground like a gruesome trophy.

My blood curled as the horde leader pulled a blade of bone from his side and gripped the general's hair.

I can't watch.

I turned away, and though I couldn't see it, the noise of him slicing at his victim's head over and over cut through my mind. When I looked back moments later, he held the general's scalp high for all his men to witness.

The chants surrounded me as darkness faded into my vision again. It took everything I had not to vomit as the torrent of time pulled me away.

Who was that? When I closed my eyes, I saw the horde leader's black gaze, his hand gripping the bloodied scalp. We'd seen war in our visions. But this was far worse. There was something dark about that horde, beyond even the bone weapons and savage brutality. I couldn't shake the power that had flooded from him. *Is he a god?*

I was ready for the ritual to end. For once, I wished szeptuchy were allowed to drink and forget. We couldn't. And it wasn't over.

The darkness cut away to a burning village in the black of night. The new moon provided no light in the cloudless sky, but everywhere I looked, snow covered the tree-tops, illuminated by the houses and fields ablaze.

Corpses lay scattered around a smoldering bonfire. Smoke burned my eyes and nose, and I cried as rage boiled within me. These bodies weren't warriors. They were women and little children—*our* women and children—clutching amulets of Mokosz, Perun, and Jaryło in their lifeless hands.

This isn't winter.

Despite the snow, this had to be Noc Kupały, the summer fertility celebration of the sixth moon—Czerwiec. The dead boys wore our tribe's white and red-trimmed ceremonial garb. Some donned flower wreaths upon their heads—a sign they'd been favored by a girl during the festival.

Beyond the burning buildings, the crops were little more than kindling, barely peeking above the snow. It was supposed to be the summer solstice. Only Marzanna could be responsible for the frost. *But how?*

Arleta's voice broke through the crackling of the fires, tearing us from the vision as quickly as we'd entered. I welcomed the chill of the grove's air as I dropped to my knees, drained.

Sorcery always came at a price. The more we channeled, the more *žityje* the ritual took from our life force, and this time was the worst yet. Sweat coated my skin. Everything seemed cold and distant as I cradled myself in the dirt.

Next to me, Adelajda wasn't doing any better. I forced myself to reach out to her. The little girl came from Chief Serwacy's village of Klist in the north, far from our past wars with the Solgawi. She'd probably never seen bloodshed—vision or not. I pitied her.

All around the circle, the other diviners were just as shaken as me. Even Arleta quivered, and she'd experienced these visions for at least forty years. The mares bucked and squealed—the sign of an imminent, destructive war—but we'd witnessed enough without studying them. Mokosz's message was obvious.

The horde is coming.

Arleta eventually steadied herself with the help of two other diviners. Her lost eyes fell on me as she shuffled toward the statue of Mokosz.

"Find Dariusz and tell him to bring the chiefs," she said. "They must know what we've seen."

5

Wacław

He won't be pleased with me.

FATHER WAS SPEAKING WITH KAJETAN, our tribe's ambassador, when I approached Perun's Oak at the heart of the village center. Crowds gathered all around, preparing for the festival. None gave me a care as I ran my fingers along the oak's rough bark.

According to Father, the oak represented the Three Realms of Prawia, Jawia, and Nawia—Perun's realm of the gods in its branches, the lands we knew as its trunk, and Weles's underworld as its roots. Dariusz disagreed with Father's view of Perun as the chief deity, instead choosing Swaróg to reign in Prawia. It didn't matter much to me as long as Jaryło granted us a plentiful harvest and Perun protected us from those who would destroy the village. To Father, though, it was yet another symbol of his rival's disobedience.

"Ah, Wacław, I had been looking for you," Father said as he adjusted his wolf-pelt coat and examined me.

Even in my traditional white and red-trimmed tunic, covering me to my knees before giving way to my white pants, I felt inadequate under the gaze of his deep blue eyes. The warriors often spoke of Father's prowess in battle against the Kingdom of Solga and how he'd united the Krowikie chiefs. Though his blond hair was receding, he was still built like a warrior. I would never match his prestige.

I bowed my head and instinctively held my wrapped hand behind my back. He'd assume it to be nothing more than a trivial wound, but guilt weighed heavy on me. "My apologies, High Chief. Mom had me gathering some needed supplies for the house before the festival."

Kajetan furrowed his brow, deepening the already prevalent wrinkles in his forehead. "A boyish excuse for evading one's responsibilities…"

"Kajetan, my friend," Father said forcefully, "go on and continue greeting the chiefs. Ensure they're comfortable and happy."

With a disapproving click of his tongue, the ambassador bowed his head. "Of course, my chief, but you are too easy on the boy."

He left, his chin held high. I didn't miss him. Kajetan never bothered to acknowledge me—except to inform everyone in earshot that my presence irritated him.

Father's eyes drifted to the people setting up the torches throughout the clearing. He shouted over for them to change the arrangement before turning his attention back to me. "While Kajetan could stand to be less direct, his point stands. Lubena should've known you would be needed for the preparations. There is much to do, and my son going missing does not reflect positively on me when the visiting chiefs and priests are watching."

"I doubt they noticed," I muttered, surveying the area.

Yet, sure enough, a group of chiefs across the circle whispered and shot glances in our direction. Chief Serwacy stood in the center, stroking his long graying beard. At his side was Chief Marek—a pimpled, brown-haired chief only four years older than me. His village had no more than fifteen people, but Marek was a giant who always seemed to find himself standing next to the most powerful man around.

Father snatched my shoulders and forced me to look him in the eye. "It is not important to them that you are Lubena's son. All that matters in their eyes is that you are mine, and that means you must

48

be aware of the consequences of your actions. They are watching for weakness in us. So are the Solgawi."

I nodded. "Yes, my chief."

He stepped back and pointed toward the confluence of the Krowik and Wyzra, where other villagers prepared the bonfire. "Tonight, you will jump the fire and become a man. I pray to Łada that I will find you a suitable woman who strengthens our tribe's alliances, but until then, do not make a fool of me."

"Jacek! My high chief!" a voice called. I groaned as Natasza strode from her and Father's longhouse with one of my youngest half-sisters, Nevenka, following closely behind.

Like all married women, the high chieftess wore a headscarf that covered her brown hair. Age had not worn her round face as much as Mom's, but Father had chosen Natasza because of power, not natural beauty.

Natasza's brother was Boz, the king of the Astiwie. Though his southeastern tribe worshipped our gods, they were few and caught between the Mangled Woods and the end of the sweeping mountain range we called Perun's Crown. Still, Father's marriage with Natasza had gained him an ally in Boz—an ally that had given him enough warriors to convince the most stubborn chiefs to kneel.

Natasza grabbed Father's wrist and pulled him toward the longhouse. "The diviners have conducted the rituals. It would be foolish to leave the priests and chiefs waiting while wasting time on unimportant tasks." Her gaze snapped to me as she finished.

Father nodded and followed her away without another word to me. I let out a disappointed sigh. *A couple minutes with him is apparently too much to ask.*

Nevenka had lingered and tugged at the bottom of my tunic. She must have been running around outside, since her little nose and wide cheeks were red from the morning's chill, but she beamed up at me anyway. As identical twins, she and Maryla were difficult to tell apart. The mole gracing Nevenka's temple and her permanent smile always gave her away, though.

"Waci," she said, using the nickname she'd given me. "I found something! Come with me?"

I crouched to her level and brushed the stray dirty blonde hairs from her face—Natasza was never good at braiding her daughters' hairs. "Only if I can show you a secret after," I said, waving for her to come closer and whispering. "But you must promise not to tell anyone."

Her brown eyes lit up, and she twirled, giggling as she did. "Come, Waci!"

She gripped my hand as we raced across the courtyard. Out of the corner of my eye, I caught Serwacy and Marek's stares, but if they judged me for exploring with a child, they needed more heart.

Nevenka pulled me through the eastern gate and down a side trail before darting into the woods, her breaths louder than the snapping of the twigs at our feet. *Someone's excited.*

Soon, we stopped, and she crouched behind a pine tree, pointing into the branches of a tall willow in front of us. "Look," she whispered.

I knelt next to her and peered through the needles, cursing my eyes as I tried to figure out what she was pointing at. Then I spotted the white birds sitting within their large nest. With a smile, I patted her head. "You found a stork nest on your own? They're lucky, you know. Maybe you and I are in for a great day."

She dropped her chin. "Mother didn't look."

Of course she didn't. Natasza was too concerned with playing politics to worry about her children's interests. "I'm sorry, but I think I have something that'll make you feel better."

"The secret?" she asked, her mouth wide.

I lowered my hands and shushed. "Be very quiet. We don't want the leszy or rusałki to hear us. Can you do that for me?"

When she nodded again, I took her hand and led her through the woods, toward the Wyzra. During my trek back from the leszy, I'd made a discovery. Showing it to her seemed like more fun than carrying wood for the festival while Father spoke with the priests.

We reached the riverbank where the Wyzra split around a long, thin island before rejoining with itself. When the river was high, the only way to reach it was by boat. It was low for now, though, and I'd found another route across. The cool blue water broke over a line of rocks, both jagged and smooth, that seemed to connect the shoreline to the island—if you were adventurous enough to cross it and not worried about getting a little wet.

Nevenka gasped when she saw it, her cheek twitching in excitement. "You cross?"

"Not yet," I replied, staring at the channel.

"Together?"

Grinning, I shook my head. "You're only six, but how about this: When you turn ten, the two of us will celebrate by climbing across those rocks together. Then, we'll have our own island and make our own rules."

I hadn't thought her smile could get any wider, but it did as she gripped the skirts of her blue dress and twirled. With all the fun she was having, she forgot to reply.

"Is that a yes?"

She stopped and wobbled for a second, probably dizzy from all the spinning. "Can I bring anyone I want?"

"I don't see why not. It's your island."

As she tapped her finger against her chin, she grinned. "I'll bring you, and Seweryn, and Gośka."

"Hmm." I thought for a moment, intrigued that she'd take along her youngest brother and eldest sister. "What about Maryla?"

She cocked her head. "What if nobody can tell which of us is in charge?"

"Fair enough." I stood and took in the breeze before nodding back toward the village. "We should get you back before Natasza wrings my neck."

She protested while I pulled her along. In truth, I needed to return too if I didn't want to invoke Father's anger for being tardy twice in a row. He was, luckily, still in the longhouse when we returned, and when he emerged, I had already joined with the others, carrying a pile of split wood toward the bonfire. *Just in time.*

51

I helped finish the preparations until the call for lunch came. For a little while at least, my mind could focus on the labor instead of wrestling with Marzanna's Frostmark and the upcoming festival.

Even as I worked, though, I caught the snickers of the other sixteen-year-old girls and boys when they thought me out of earshot. Their mocking stung like a blow of Xobas's sword against my shield, but I wouldn't let them see the pain. I couldn't.

Once I finished hauling the last stack of firewood, I took a deep breath and looked over the powerful Krowik River. Tonight, we would throw Marzanna's flaming effigy into its depths. I should've been excited. But one thing never left my mind.

I had wrapped the cut on my palm, yet the Frostmark still seared. With each passing minute, the pain continued to grow.

6

Wacław

At least Marzanna can't taint the golden egg.

WHEN DADŹBÓG'S LIGHT WAS AT ITS PEAK, High Priest Dariusz stood under Perun's Oak and waved for us to gather around him, a crooked smile on his face as he did.

"The egg hunt shall begin soon," he said, speaking elaborately with his hands as the tree's hanging skulls blew in the breeze above his head. "Each of you children has a crucial responsibility to collect the decorated eggs of Jaryło so that he may come and bless us with a plentiful spring."

My thumb drifted along my wrapped palm. With each mention of Jaryło's name, the Frostmark's pain was enough to make me wince. *Am I going to be stuck with this?*

When I raised my head, Otylia's cold glare was fixed on me through the crowd. I shuddered before staring at my boots. *What does she know?*

The priest continued, "…and whoever finds the golden egg will receive a special reward from our glorious gods. This gift shall remind us of their dominant power from whence our annual prosperity comes."

The other sixteen-year-olds and children chattered in excitement.

I sensed it too. Though I had never been particularly good at the egg hunt, it was a welcomed distraction.

Dariusz cleared his voice. "There is also news sent by the gods. The diviners of our tribe have gathered and completed the horse divination rituals." He swept his arm around, gesturing to the eldest few of Mokosz's szeptuchy, their long, uncut hair mangled and their fingers clutching their bone and iron amulets. "They have seen a great tide of darkness coming from the east, one that will test us all. Deformed horsemen, their black steeds trampling the dead, and the sky raining ash…"

I took a sharp breath as the crowd murmured. Some questioned what he said, others feared it, but I didn't know what to believe. Our chiefs and warriors were focused on the Solgawi, not the east. If the diviners were all saying the same thing, though, then something was coming. *But why?* I looked to Otylia, but her face revealed nothing.

Dariusz raised his arms in an attempt to calm the crowd. "These visions are all the more reason to worship and fear the gods. There must be balance in our world: with prosperity, suffering, with light, darkness. Fire creates fertile soil. Winter is necessary for spring. So, let the children gather the eggs and begin Jaryło's reign. Let us all vigorously prosper and prepare for the times to come."

The contest's usual excitement faded after Dariusz's speech. Girls no longer giggled and danced along the edges of the village center. Boys stopped their games.

Among the crowd, Father leaned over to Xobas and whispered something with his brow furrowed. With him and Dariusz competing for influence among the villagers, Father was always skeptical of those who claimed to know the gods' wills, but surely, even he couldn't ignore a threat that large when the diviners spoke in unison. Could he?

While the older children mulled about, the youngest ones danced to their own music with white willow catkin necklaces swinging around them.

Nevenka grabbed my hand. "Why sad, Waci?"

Besides the forbidden symbol sliced on my palm? It was hard to know if my half-sister read me well or if I was that obvious.

I faked a smile and picked a twig from her braid. "I'm only disappointed that you may not be my partner for the egg hunt."

"But we did bad last year."

I chuckled. "We found all the places the gods chose not to hide them. Adventure for the sake of adventure is just as fun, right?"

"Ad-ven-ture?" she asked, sounding out each part of the word.

"You know, exploring?"

She scrunched her nose. "Mom says the gods like girls who find the eggs."

"Nevenka, come along," Natasza called from near the longhouse, glaring at me.

Speaking of the high chieftess. I gave Nevenka a little smile and nodded.

As she ran off with her mother, the priests met at the base of Perun's Oak, praying to the gods for guidance on selecting teams. Without a real knowledge of their art, I didn't know how much of a role the gods had in creating the groups and how much was the priests' infamous match-making.

I hadn't cared most years who was on my team. Today, though, I just wanted to forget about Marzanna's Frostmark and dagger for a few minutes. If only my palm would let me.

When the priests finished and summoned us, I caught a glimpse of Genowefa and her long blonde hair arching down her back. Her eyes met mine, and my heart stopped. I cleared my throat and looked away, my cheeks burning as Marzanna's vision of us on the mountain flashed in my mind. *This will all be yours.*

Someone smacked into me. I stumbled and crashed to the ground, catching the ire of the elders nearby.

"Didn't see you there, Half-Chief," Narcyz said sarcastically.

Dusting the dirt off my tunic, I glared up at him. The brown-haired ironsmith's son was one of the other boys who would jump the fire tonight. I'd never known who'd created the Half-Chief nickname, but my gut told me it had been him.

His calloused hand grabbed my forearm as he gave me a wry smile. "Let me help you up."

I allowed him to pull me to my feet, even though I knew what he was doing. Father wouldn't want me to make more of a scene than Narcyz already had. He'd made it clear many times my first responsibility was to not ruin his reputation. "Excited for the search?" I asked with a challenge in my voice.

Narcyz yanked me closer and whispered in my ear, "You'll end up in worse places than the dirt if you keep looking at her."

Before I could reply, Father emerged from the crowd. "Wacław, come. You can wrestle with your friends later."

I bit my cheek but let my anger out in a sharp breath. "Yes, Chief." I stared at my feet as I shuffled behind him, avoiding the gaze of both Narcyz and Genowefa. *Maybe the storks weren't so lucky after all...*

I stood at Father's side, away from the others, as Dariusz announced the teams in the shade of Perun's Oak. It was entertaining to watch each group's reactions, ranging from ecstasy to embarrassment or pure annoyance. The groups weren't supposed to be a potential romantic pairing. The eligible boys and girls thought otherwise.

Narcyz was among the first names called. With his chin held high he strode forward, shooting me another glare, and I held my breath as he awaited his partner. Part of me knew the answer before Dariusz opened his mouth. *Genowefa.* The priest confirmed, and my heart sunk as she joined with Narcyz.

I felt like a fool clutching to hope from Marzanna's visions. Even with my Frostmark covered, I was ashamed to have believed them, to have surrendered to the goddess of winter and death. They had just been so *real*, and that pull in my soul had commanded me to accept. *You were too weak to fight the temptation. Accept it.*

"Wacław!"

I jumped. Everyone was staring at me.

"Go," Father said, pushing me forward.

Dariusz waved for me to join him. "Come on, boy! We don't have all day."

With a glance at Mom in the crowd, I swallowed and stepped forward, anxiously rubbing my thumb against my palm. *It'll be okay. Relax.*

The smell of charred wood smothered me as I stood before Dariusz. There was judgement in his glare as he raised his arms and summoned the next name. When he spoke, it came out as more of a squeak than anything, "Otylia?"

Definitely not lucky.

Straight-faced, Otylia joined me under the oak tree. I folded my arms and stepped away under her father's ominous gaze. Whispers spread through the crowd, followed by laughter from the boys. Though part of me was excited to have the chance to talk to her again, Father would see this as his rival trying to humiliate his son.

"There must be a mistake," Father said, stepping into the circle, his forehead wrinkled. "I will not allow my son to be forced onto a team with the likes of *her.*"

Dariusz sighed and ran his hands through his long ashen hair. "This would not be my decision either, my high chief, but the gods have spoken through us. Unless you wish to defy their will—"

Father scowled. "Or is it you are hoping to manipulate my family with all of the chiefs here to see?"

I glanced at Otylia. She hadn't moved, and her gaze remained fixed on her clasped hands in front of her. As much as I knew our pairing would displease Father, this was not a confrontation he would win.

"It's all right," I said, turning to him and spurring gasps from the crowd. "If the gods want this, then I will do as they wish. It's only a fun egg hunt."

Father's brow furrowed. *I'll pay for this.*

"Very well," he said with a shake of his head. "May Perun's wisdom guide you."

I opened my mouth to reply, but I was left with the sound of his boots marching away. The murmuring continued through the crowd as my eyes met Mom's. She gave me a nod as Dariusz cleared his throat, and I returned my attention to him, unsure how much I had harmed Father's reputation.

"This pair," the priest continued, "will lead two young children: Wincenty and Zenobia."

Otylia bowed. "Thank you, Father."

Dariusz's gaze fell on me, and I bowed as well before joining with the children and moving to the side with the other teams. Otylia had yet to even glance at me since her name had been called. After our encounter earlier, that made me suspicious, but with a little boy and girl to wrangle for the rest of the ceremony, I was too distracted to dwell on it.

Soon, Dariusz signaled for the search to begin, and we set off with woven baskets in hand. Wincenty seemed content to wander aimlessly, bumbling to himself as the slightly older Zenobia sped away, her braids flapping in the wind behind her.

"You're going to be a handful, aren't you?" I asked Wincenty as he spun around me, not at all interested in where Zenobia was headed.

His only reply was to plop his butt on the ground. I sighed and looked to Otylia, who watched the little girl like an eagle as she skipped through the woods. *Guess it's up to me.*

Scooping the boy into my arms, I walked after Zenobia with Otylia trailing close behind. We followed one of the side trails until Zenobia decided she wanted to dart another direction. I chuckled and followed her. "Stay close. I can't run and carry a child."

Wincenty giggled. "That's me!"

A smirk flashed across Otylia's face before disappearing as quickly as it had come. I nodded toward Zenobia. "I remember you being like that at her age. What happened?"

"I grew up," Otylia snapped, still staring forward. "Losing your mother and best friend does that to you."

My shoulders slumped. "I was just trying to make conversation, sorry."

"Found one!" Zenobia shouted from ahead, hopping and holding up a bright blue egg.

I offered her a smile as she slid it into the basket. "Well done! I'm sure Jaryło will be excited for you to bring it back. Do you think you can find more?"

She nodded and took off again without hesitation, forcing me to jog to keep her in sight. The pattern continued for nearly half-an-hour, and Zenobia slowly found a small collection of eggs while Wincenty fell asleep with his head on my shoulder. Drool coated my tunic, but I figured that was better than having him waddling off and getting lost.

When Zenobia slid her fifth egg into the basket, green this time, she huffed. "Am I doing good?" she asked, hopeful as she stared up at me.

Despite there being no chance we'd win, I smiled down at her. "You're doing really well, especially since one of our partners is asleep and the other..." I looked around for Otylia, but she wasn't anywhere among the trees. "Huh. Not sure where she went."

I had been so focused on keeping track of Zenobia's energy that Otylia had slipped away somehow. With her gone, the conversation level was the same, so I couldn't blame myself too much for losing her. Though, I was curious where she'd went.

"Come on," I said, "Let's go see if we can find our missing witch."

Can a diviner ever be lost? I didn't know, but returning with my partner seemed like the best option, even if Father might have wished for me to leave her stranded.

We wandered, crunching twigs and running along logs with no luck. Then, as we came up to another side trail, my Frostmark's burn intensified. I winced.

Zenobia grabbed my unbandaged hand. "What's wrong?"

I took a shallow breath and shut my eyes for a moment. Desire swept my mind as I remembered Marzanna's visions, but I pushed them away and focused on the task ahead. The pain was leading me somewhere. When I turned down the trail, it faded, yet when I stepped toward the woods on the other side, it arced across my entire palm.

"This way," I said, trying to cover my discomfort.

Zenobia hopped on the dead leaves as we slipped through the underbrush. Each little *crunch* helped distract me from my worry as I followed the mark's signals. In a way, I was glad Otylia wasn't around for this part. I felt ridiculous. Luckily, the children weren't attentive enough to see it.

As we reached an oak grove, an agonizing pain shot up my forearm and tore through my muscles. I staggered ahead, my breaths weakening. *What do you want from me?*

Then I saw it.

Nestled among the trees at the edge of the clearing was the true prize—the golden egg. My palm seared as I rushed forward and scooped it into my uninjured hand, smiling down at the treasure.

I had never touched the golden egg before. It was at least three times larger than all the others we'd collected, and it hummed with power in my grasp. Even if Marzanna had somehow led me to it, my heart soared as I imagined the possibilities of what reward the gods would have for me.

"Whoa!" Zenobia hopped toward me and reached for the egg.

I held it away from her. "Do you promise to be careful with it?"

She nodded, and I reluctantly let her take it. As I watched the awe in her eyes, I smiled at her innocence. Neither Marzanna's Frostmark nor threats of a distant army were enough to ruin that. I missed those days.

Footsteps in the soft ground came from behind me. *Now she decides to show up.* I stood and smirked back at Otylia. "You are an excellent teamma..." My voice trailed off as I noticed her basket full of eggs. "Oh."

Grinning, she paced around me to Zenobia and reached down for the golden egg. "Trade?"

The little girl surrendered it and took the full basket. With all the eggs, though, it was too heavy for her, and she ended up on the ground with it on top of her.

Otylia was too fascinated with the golden egg to notice, running her fingertips along its smooth surface before she returned her triumphant gaze to me. "You were saying, Half-Chief?"

I opened my mouth to reply, but Wincenty gasped. *Oh, now he's awake.* I set him down, letting him waddle over to Zenobia and practically rip the basket out of her hands. Otylia stepped between them and handed him one red egg, which he held in his palm, his mouth wide open.

"Apparently he's more impressed by quantity than quality," I said, jealously rubbing my boot into the dirt. My hand hurt more than I was willing to admit, and I twitched in desperation to have the egg back.

Otylia rose and closed the distance between us. "You expect me to believe you found the golden egg without assistance?"

"What are you implying?"

Sliding the egg into my cut hand, she whispered, "What did Marzanna want from you?"

My Frostmark seared against the egg. I staggered back, lightheaded. Its hum became a roar—voices deafening me as they swirled.

What's happening to me?

Energy rushed from the egg and through my body. It grew with each passing second as a gale danced at my fingertips. I gasped for air, but none came.

A wall of wind had encircled me, lifting me into the air. Otylia fought through it, her eyes ablaze and her chants caught in the gales. Though the winds pulled at her amulets and whipped her hair across her face, she pushed on.

The power burst through my veins. I felt more alive than ever, yet I teetered on the edge of death, its surge threatening to rip me apart. *Is this the end?* Somewhere ahead, Wincenty whimpered and Zenobia squealed. As tears rushed down my face, I pleaded to the winds, *Spare them...*

Otylia fought closer. The torrent whipped through her hair and dress, threatening to tear her away, but she chanted in the old tongue.

Roots emerged and tied her feet to the ground. Then, she threw out her arms with a mighty shout.

The winds ceased.

I dropped to my knees. Every inch of me shook as my hands gripped the earth, clinging to reality while the chilled air sent a shiver down my spine. Around me, the gales left behind nothing but the noise of a distant woodpecker.

Otylia took a cautious step toward me as I gulped each breath of air into my screaming lungs. Fear covered her face, yet she was staring down at her own hands, not me. As the children gawked, I wished I could claw my way into the depths.

"Please, don't say it," I said, my voice hoarse.

Her dress swept behind her as she shook off her shock and examined the circle, running her fingers through the soil. "What don't you want me to say?"

I groaned and lifted my gaze to Dadźbóg's sun. *Why couldn't you have chosen me? Why did it have to be Marzanna?* My heart wrestled with dread. Though I wanted more than anything to will it away, Marzanna's icy grip wouldn't relent. All I had hoped for was one day of fun and adventure before jumping the fire. Instead, it had become a nightmare. "I don't know…"

A twig snapped behind me. I snatched the egg and spun, ready for the worst.

Narcyz emerged from the woods with Genowefa and their two little partners in tow. *Anyone but them…*

He raised his brow, noticing my discomfort. "What's going on here?" He looked from the golden egg to the full basket that Zenobia clutched in her arms. "You found it?" he asked, the cockiness wiped from his voice.

Still rattled from the whirlwind, I struggled to find a response as Genowefa studied me. Father would've wanted me to stand tall and take pride in my victory, but all I could do was stagger back, woozy. *How much did they see?* I looked to Otylia to bail me out. Unfortunately, she stayed kneeling, silent with her hand in the earth.

Narcyz stormed forward, ripping the egg from my grasp. "Of course they found it," he spat. "She's a witch!"

Otylia stood and wiped the dirt from her hands without a word, a twinge of pain on her face. I knew that feeling too well, and something stirred within me.

"No." I stepped toe-to-toe with the ironsmith's son and matched his glare. "She's a szeptucha, and we both know the gods don't look fondly on those who insult their rituals."

His hazel eyes darkened. I had surprised myself with that defense, but as far as I could tell, Otylia had saved my life. It didn't matter if Father believed her to be a witch too—Narcyz's mocking was undeserved.

Genowefa stomped her foot. "This isn't fair! It would be impossible for us to find that many eggs."

Narcyz wrapped an arm around her, flashing a grin at me as he did. "I know it is. C'mon. Let's get back before they cheat again and steal our eggs."

They started toward the woods, but Zenobia swept past me and snagged Narcyz's white tunic. As her feet dragged in the dirt, he tried to keep walking, and I could only chuckle and watch him struggle in a tug-of-war with the little kid.

When he finally tore his tunic from her grasp, Otylia took the girl's hand and fixed her fierce gaze on Genowefa. "You're going to let him steal from a child?"

Genowefa looked to Narcyz with a shake of her head. "She's right. It's just a silly game. Let her have the golden egg and let's get out of here."

Trapped between Otylia's intensity and Genowefa's plea for him to hand it over, Narcyz rolled his eyes and gave Zenobia the egg. The little girl beamed and hopped to Otylia as Narcyz made a show out of holding his arm around Genowefa. The pair shuffled back to the trail, their silent partners at their heels.

My shoulders slumped as I looked away, trying to focus on what had happened only a few minutes before. The egg's energy still buzzed on my fingertips. I had no idea what it had done to me, but whatever it was, it had to be more important than my feelings toward a cute blonde girl. That didn't fill the void in my chest, though.

Something pulled on my pant leg, and I looked down to see Zenobia's wide eyes. She held the golden egg gingerly in her hands. "Did we win?"

I glanced at Otylia, who gave a close-lipped smile. "I guess we did," I said as I looked up at the sun. Dadźbóg had begun his slow descent toward the horizon. "We should probably head back."

Wincenty waddled past, apparently now full of energy, and led the way toward the village center. Naturally, Zenobia was right behind, and I chuckled before following with Otylia.

The two of us had a lot we needed to discuss. With the children so close, however, our conversation would have to wait. Until then, I sighed and let my fingers dance through the breeze at my side, trying to forget the dread creeping within me.

7

Otylia

What have I gotten myself into?

SONGS FILLED THE AIR upon our return to the village. Around Perun's Oak, the musicians plucked their strings, played their flutes, and sang of Jaryło's blooms replacing the frost.

No songs were sung for Dziewanna.

Dinner had yet to be served, but men both young and old already staggered around with mugs and horns full of oskoła—fermented birch sap—dangling from their fingers. When they saw us approaching from down the trail with the golden egg in hand, a loud cheer erupted. But I wasn't excited.

Wacław had almost died in that whirlwind. The flash of power in him had been raw, like the golden egg had ignited something. Two of Mokosz's visions had come true already, and if Marzanna had led him to the egg…

I shuddered. Could Marzanna have been using him, increasing his power so he could wield lightning like I'd seen in the visions? Whatever power I'd channeled to save him from the whirlwind hadn't been that of Dziewanna or Mokosz. Was she manipulating me too? It felt as if it'd come from my soul—just like it had four years ago with the wolves—and that scared me nearly as much as Marzanna herself.

Wacław feigned a smile at the crowd, looking toward Jacek, but his worry was written all over his face. Instead of returning his son's smile, Jacek glared at me and shook his head.

I had badly wanted to pin Wacław to a tree and force him to tell me the truth. With the kids running everywhere, however, it had been impossible to talk in the woods. Narcyz, that idiot, had interfered before I had been able to get a good read on the egg or even the ground around us. There had been an obvious residual power. He'd cost me precious minutes, and it was too late by the time he'd left.

Just like his father, Narcyz despised me—even more than the others. They were ironsmiths and only believed in the gods as immaterial guides. That made us szeptuchy nothing more than witches, channeling spirits we claimed were the gods.

Fools. If the gods were distant, how could they direct the world without us to channel their power and carry out their wills?

We approached Perun's Oak, and Zenobia scampered up to the gathered priests, beaming at Father and holding up the golden egg for him to see. I followed close behind but let her have the moment. Between my visions, Wacław's secrets, and now the whirlwind, the day had been awful so far. We all needed something to smile about, even the aloof Wincenty, who had hopped over to his mother and was now cradled in her arms. Part of me envied his obliviousness.

Wacław was still staring into the crowd, this time at his mother. Lubena stood alone with a grin as she held her slender fingers to her lips. *A mother's pride.* My heart twitched knowing I'd never see my own mother's smile again.

"The golden egg has been found," Father declared as he held his arms to the sky. "May the gods be praised! And it appears that this team has found quite the large number of Jaryło's eggs as well. He will be pleased."

Will he?

If Marzanna had granted Wacław the golden egg, then I doubted any of the gods would look fondly upon us. Sure, I had used Dziewanna's power to find so many of the colored eggs myself, but the golden egg had real power. There was a reason Marzanna wanted Wacław to have it. A pit opened up in my stomach knowing that.

Father looked from Zenobia to me and smiled with pride. "Which among you was the one to find the golden egg? For all of you shall be blessed by the gods, but only the one who made the discovery shall keep the egg and receive their gift."

Wacław's mouth hung open, and he stammered before giving up.

Rolling my eyes, I spoke for him, "Wacław, Father."

A frown replaced Father's smile, and his gaze shot to Jacek in the crowd. While their glares clashed, Wacław stood there, silent. His cheeks had turned bright red. When he looked up, he stared right at Genowefa, that airhead from the woods whose only goal seemed to be finding an equally stupid warrior to bring her jewels from war. The boys couldn't keep their eyes off her. But it appeared she'd already found her prey in Narcyz.

"Is this true?" Father asked, stepping toward Wacław and smothering us in the smell of ash and soot.

Wacław nodded without a word, and I groaned in disappointment. *He'll never be a chief.*

"Then the victor has been chosen," Father said. He held up the golden egg for the crowd to see before cupping it in Wacław's hands.

As it graced his palm, Wacław winced, like he expected a storm to rip the village to shreds. But there was calm.

"May the gods bless you and spare you from suffering," Father finished. His voice sounded forced, and I doubted he meant any of it.

How much does it pain him to give the egg to Wacław instead of me? It was a high honor, and Father's twitching lip had shown his greed when we'd approached. He should've known the competition meant nothing to me. I'd found the eggs I did because I couldn't stand walking with Wacław for another second.

Mokosz's vision of his arms around me hadn't left my mind. The more accurate her predictions became, the more my heart panicked. I wished I could've been anywhere but by his side, but to figure out Marzanna's plan, I needed him.

With the hunt over, Father dismissed everyone to prepare for supper and the drowning of Marzanna's effigy. I swept across the village center, eager to get away from both Wacław and Father. But someone caught my arm. I growled and ripped it from their grasp before looking back to see Ara's raised eyebrow. "Oh…" I mumbled, my cheeks burning.

"What's wrong with you?" the Zurgowie girl asked with a smile. "You won!"

"Half-Chief won," I corrected.

"Jealous?"

"No."

"Then what's got you so flustered?"

I bit my cheek, but she meant the best. "It's been a long day," I said. "Walk with me?"

"Sure!" Her arm locked with mine, and we walked down the trail toward both of our houses. "I was going to ask if you wanted to get ready together."

"Get ready? I… Oh…"

"There's no way you forgot."

I wrinkled my nose. *Forgot* wasn't the right word. Every girl knew about the flower crowns and dresses we'd wear for the rest of the festival to honor the gods and, just as importantly, catch a boy's eye. What I'd done was ignore it in hopes of it never having to happen. Father had sternly forbidden me to even look at a boy the wrong way before, but I would jump the fire tonight. Even if he had the final say, I couldn't help but be anxious.

"You spend an hour with Wacław and now your cheeks are stained red," Ara said, giggling through my silence.

"Seeing a demon will do that to you," I replied flatly.

There was only one possible explanation for Wacław's power. He was a płanetnik—a storm demon. I had known about his soul-form for years but had never considered it to be anything more. Between his lightning in the visions and that whirlwind in the woods, however, the answer seemed obvious now that I was away from the crowds.

But how?

Some priests told stories of days long ago when demons were more than just those who died in unjust ways or whose corpses were not burned. Father called the stories fabrications. If Wacław was a living demon, though, could there be others?

"Oh please," Ara said. "If any boy is a demon, it's not Wacław. We both know how you used to be fond of him. Mother says those feelings don't ever go away."

She's wrong. I gripped my Bowmark necklace. "You can get ready with me if you don't mention Half-Chief again."

Her hand seized mine. "Deal! I can't wait to see you wearing those white anemones."

Before I could give a snarky reply, she pulled me along and talked about all the rumors from the egg hunt. I tried to listen, but my mind spun with Mokosz's visions of the eastern horde, Marzanna's schemes, and Wacław's eyes gazing into mine. Until I had answers, nothing else mattered.

We soon reached Ara's family cottage near the southern edge of the village. Both Ara and her father were hunters, and her mother was a masterful seamstress. Still, they had little after only settling in Dwie Rzeki two years ago. Their house was dirt-floored and only one room. Most of it was usually covered in her mother's projects, and this time, it was both of our dresses.

Ara kicked off her boots and grabbed her sky blue, pink, and white dress from on her bed as I tentatively shuffled toward mine. "You like it?" she asked, twirling with hers. It swept out before her, the spiraling patterns of a hundred flowers dancing across its torso and sleeves.

Despite my mood, her joy was contagious, and I let myself smile. "It's beautiful enough to make even Łada jealous." Łada was Swaróg's wife and the goddess of love. Between today and Noc Kupały, every eligible girl in the tribe would pray to her in hopes of finding a boy to jump the fire with during the summer festival.

"Mother never disappoints." Beaming, she grabbed the purple flower wreath next and placed it on her head, dancing to the silence with her bare feet drifting through the dirt. "If only more of your people saw beyond our accent and dark skin."

I scoffed. "They can't even see beyond the sorcery of those of us who channel their own gods. You're better off without them."

She continued her dance over to the table, where my white and black-embroidered dress lay. "You don't mean that."

Hesitating, I approached the dress and ran my fingers across the sewn black plants winding their way from the skirt to the chest. I had no skill in dressmaking, but from the look of the work, her mother had spent a long time on it. And I loved it.

"I... I don't know what to say," I stammered. "How can I repay her?"

"Consider it repayment for all the potions you've provided Father ahead of his hunts. We couldn't pay you then, but Mother still has her skill."

"That she does."

It was foolish to be so focused on this after everything I'd seen, but I didn't have an army to stop the horsemen, and even if Marzanna had plans, the ritual this evening would send her to Nawia. I took a deep breath. *Relax.* Dziewanna hadn't warned me of anything. For now, at least, I could enjoy myself.

Ara handed me the anemone wreath with anticipation in her eyes. Streaks of black rushed across the white flowers as leaves wove their way through the crown. Her mother had made a headscarf to match the dress too, and I tucked my braid into it before placing the wreath on my head. "What do you think?" I asked her, wishing I didn't care about her response.

A dangerous smirk crossed her face as she held the dress up to me. "You'll have them regretting they ever called you a witch."

8

Wacław

Why do they tolerate us?

WITH THE WOMEN AWAY, men drank and boys wrestled around the village center. It was a rare time without feminine oversight—the most chaotic hours of the year.

Soon, the girls would return, wearing their elaborate head wreaths made of flowers and carrying the effigy of Marzanna. Most of the boys didn't give care about the work they put into the wreaths. I thought they brought a certain elegance and beauty. Every year when the girls emerged wearing them, they became women. We were just boys rolling in the mud.

I lingered by a patch of trees away from the commotion. These were my nicest clothes, and I didn't want to tarnish them before the ceremony, especially now that I had won the egg hunt and would have to light the effigy with Otylia.

As I looked down at myself, though, I saw the dirt and foliage that speckled my lower half. Marzanna obviously didn't intend to let me forget what had happened.

"You win the egg hunt and then run away?" a voice said.

I smiled as my clumsy friend, Kuba, ran toward me. He was the son of an iron miner, but you wouldn't know it by the way he held his chiseled chin and unblemished face high like the strongest of warriors. "I've had my share of fights today," I replied. "Xobas put me on my back more times than I would have liked."

He snickered and jabbed me in the ribs. "Didn't realize he liked your spear that much."

"Oh, come on!" I exclaimed, my cheeks flushed. I should've expected a vulgar joke from Kuba, though, I had set him up for that one. "If only this egg would protect me from your humor."

"Then your life would be far less interesting."

I shrugged and slid the golden egg into my bag, alongside Marzanna's dagger. "True."

The trees creaked in the wind as Kuba jumped and grabbed a hold of a young oak's lowest branch, hauling his lean, muscular frame up over it before sitting down.

"You know the girls haven't come back yet, right?" I asked.

He rocked his head back and forth, as if he was considering the question. I knew he wasn't, but he needed the time to come up with his next quip. "Doesn't matter. I've got mine all lined up."

"Still have your eye on Maja?"

"And after tomorrow, I'll have more than my eyes on her."

Leaning against the trunk of another tree, I raised an eyebrow at him. While we technically would become adults at tonight's fire jump, tomorrow was when the courting games would begin the journey to Noc Kupały's fertility festival in summer. "If you talk like that around a girl as pretty as her, you'll end up with a swollen cheek too."

His eyes widened as he covered his face, faking a gasp. "Not my extraordinary face. What will I do without it?"

"Considering your hopeless personality, I'm not sure what you'll do *with* it."

In one swift motion, he swung from the branch and pounced on me. We fell to the ground in a heap, and before I could defend myself, he had me in a headlock. The golden egg slid from my bag as I wheezed.

"Take it back," he said.

72

"All right, oh great Kuba! All the girls fawn over you, and the strongest metals of the earth rise at your word."

He released me. "See," he said, the dirt meshing with his brown hair as he grinned like a maniac. "That's all you had to say."

As I bent over, holding my knees and gasping for air, Father approached. "My son, I had expected you to treat a festival tunic with more care."

Kuba's eyes widened, and he bowed his head. "High Chief! Sorry, it was—"

"Me," I said. "It was my fault." The other boys could wrestle and ruin their tunics all they wanted, but they weren't the son of the high chief.

Father stepped forward and brushed the dirt from my chest. "I hope that when the young women return, you will put on a better face. They are away, ensuring that they look their best for the festival. The least you can do is attempt to do the same, especially with the chiefs watching."

My eyes dropped to my feet. "Yes, my chief."

"Kuba," he said with a tight grip on my arm, "run along and help with the final preparations. I wish to talk with Wacław in private."

As Kuba stumbled off, I wished to flee with him. I assumed Father intended to discuss the golden egg, but after coming so close to death, it was the last thing I wanted to think about.

Father paced, running his strong hands through his thin blond hair. He was as fit as a workhorse for his age. Knowing he could still physically punish me only heightened my anxiety.

Eventually, he sighed as he looked up into the afternoon sky. "Dariusz questions whether you were truly the one to discover the egg. Why do you hang your head when you should stand tall with pride? You are the second-born son of the high chief. You are to receive the gods' blessings, yet you cower when asked if you are the victor."

I struggled to find a response. With all the chiefs and priests here for the festival, he was too distracted to handle the truth of what had happened. Even beyond that, though, he was cynical of anything related to sorcery and the gods, and it was by his order that the Frost-marked had been banished. No, telling him would only make the problem worse. "I... I'm not sure."

"The people expect us to lead with confidence, especially in times of potential war. Each of them doubts you because of your mother. If you're going to prove them wrong, then you must rise to the challenge and become a man."

My shoulders slumped. He'd called me his son, yet I never felt like one. "I won't fail you, my chief. I give you my word."

With a nod, he picked up the golden egg from the dirt and placed it in my palm. His stern grip closed my fingers around it. "Soon, you must fulfill your duty to the tribe. I pray to Perun that you do so."

He marched away, leaving behind a sour taste in my mouth. *What duty?*

For years, I had watched him conduct diplomacy with other tribes and clans, but I'd never sought that responsibility. If the choice were mine, I wanted to travel the world and see what lay beyond the forests and fields of Dwie Rzeki. I could take Mom, find love, and be free of Father's expectations. In my gut, though, I had a sinking feeling that I would never be able to make that decision.

I wiped the rest of the dirt off of my tunic as the first girls returned to the village center. My heart fluttered in my chest, but I swallowed my anxiousness and returned to Perun's Oak. As I passed through the crowd, the girls from the other villages whispered among themselves and glanced at me. I just stared at my boots and kept walking until I tripped.

I fell forward face first, but at the last second, someone caught me. "Watch it there, Wacław."

I staggered back to my feet and studied Mikołaj, unsure whether my brother wanted to make a fool of me or was honestly helping. I decided to give him the benefit of the doubt. "Sorry, was a little lost in my thoughts."

Chuckling, he crossed his arms and surveyed the gossiping girls and their flower wreaths. "I understand. There is plenty to think about."

"I didn't mean it like that…"

"Your cheeks say otherwise, brother, but worry not," he whispered before raising his voice to a shout. "Genowefa didn't see, or are you concerned about Otylia?"

The egg's energy seared through my veins as I turned away, regretting my decision to trust him. "Can you back off, Miko?" I snapped. "I have enough to worry about without your mockery!"

He stepped back, his brows raised and the ends of his mouth curled. Around me, the giggling continued, and I realized I had yelled. I couldn't help it. He and so many others had always talked down to me. With the stress of Marzanna's call on top of the pressure of the festival, I had finally had enough for a day.

My gaze dropped as I tried to steady my breaths, each a battle against the air. The winds danced, taunting me with whispers. *Please, whatever this is. Not now. Please, not now.*

I stumbled away without direction as Mikołaj called after me. I ignored him. All I knew was that I needed to be alone for a moment to clear my head.

When I reached an empty side trail, I leaned against a tree and slid down its trunk, out of breath and disoriented. Voices circled me. Their whispers carried on the breeze and drowned out the world.

"Who are you?" I asked as they grew in number and volume. Though my ears were numb, the whispers pierced my mind, no, my soul, as if their very essence was linked with mine.

"Wacław? Come back to me, Wacław. I'm here…"

A force snapped me to reality. I blinked away my blurry vision, and Mom's face appeared above me. "What's happening?" I asked.

"I was wondering the same thing," she said, her eyes concerned. "What caused you to be in a daze against a tree? Was it too much oskoła?"

My mind cleared, but the whispers lingered in my soul. "I wish it was."

Her calloused hands slid into mine, and she pulled me to my feet before wrapping me in a hug. A calm flowed through me as she cradled the back of my head. "Whatever you are facing, know you can always tell me."

I quivered in her embrace, not knowing what to do. The constant throbbing of my palm scared me more than I was willing to admit to myself, and when I stepped back, all I could say was: "I messed up, Mom."

A gust whipped through the trees, sending goosebumps running up my arms as she folded her hands in front of her. "What do you mean?"

"There was a… a dagger. The leszy left it behind, and when I held it, it asked for blood."

A chill ran down my spine as she uncovered my palm and traced the Frostmark with her fingers. I looked away in shame.

"There is power in blood," she said. "You obeyed Marzanna's call, and I have a guess that she gave you the egg in return."

"Probably. But what does she want with me? Winter is to end tonight, and she'll be sent to Nawia."

"A goddess's power cannot be underestimated, whether in Jawia or Nawia. Who else knows of the dagger and this mark?"

"No one, not even Otylia. I was too scared to show her, especially with what happened when I touched the egg…"

As group of girls skipped by, I averted my gaze. Father would expect me to be at the center of the festival, drawing attention like Mikołaj, but I wasn't like my brother. Nor would I ever be.

When they passed, Mom held her palm to the trunk of a tree, her eyes distant. "Narcyz quite loudly spoke of a disturbance in the forest."

I nodded, remembering how the power had suffocated and drawn me in at the same time. Fear paralyzed me at the thought, but some part of me wanted more. "When the egg touched the cut on my palm, a whirlwind spun around me and sucked the air from my lungs. I would've died if it Otylia hadn't stopped it. Now, I'm stumbling into the woods, light-headed and hearing whispers in my stupor. I don't know what Marzanna wants from me, but I just want it to end."

Worry returned to her eyes, and she cupped my face in her hands. "I've always believed you have a gift. I do not know the gods' wills, but perhaps Otylia—"

"No." I pushed her away and circled the tree. "What if she told the priests and the chiefs about the dagger and me being Frost-marked? What would they say about the Half-Chief then? All of them have looked down on me my entire life, and this would finally give them what they need to cast me out forever."

"Has she told her father or anyone else what she has seen?"

"Not yet, but she's probably just waiting to use it against me. She's hated me ever since Father forced me away from her. Why would that stop now?"

A close-mouthed smile crept across her face as she glanced at the light of the sun. "Your father was wrong, and that girl possibly saved your life twice today. Have you thanked her?"

Wincing, I dug my heel into the dirt. I hadn't, and she knew it. *Why must she always know the truth?*

Desires and fears swarmed in my head. I couldn't trust my own thoughts. They had convinced me it was smart to cut my hand with a goddess's blade. How would they tempt me next?

A horn blew from near Perun's Oak, and my heart sunk. I wasn't ready to face the crowds. They had seen me shout at Mikołaj. They knew I would never have his strength, his prestige, or his looks. On the day I'd dreamt of love, all I had instead was dread and an infinite number of questions. My hopes seemed petty when I was choking to death, yet they were all that warmed my heart as I pondered my return.

Mom took my hands one last time. "You must go, but be careful. If Marzanna is scheming on the eve of her banishment, I fear something may be coming."

I offered a weak smile. "Yes, Mom. I will."

She kissed me on the cheek, and we started back down the trail, listening to the chirping of the birds and the crunch of the soil underfoot. A buzz of energy still danced through my veins, jarring me, yet I tried to focus on what lay ahead.

I would have the honor of lighting Marzanna's effigy. With her help or not, I had found the golden egg. I didn't know what the gods had in store for me, but I prayed to Jaryło that his spring growth would bless our crops and his golden shield would protect me from the dangers I faced.

As I prayed, the burning returned to my palm, strong enough to make me wince. We had reached the village, though, so I swallowed the pain and joined the boys. Music flowed through the air as they eyed the girls who sang and swayed to the tunes. Unlike our more neutral tunics, the girls' wreaths and dresses were an array of beautiful colors. I couldn't blame the other boys for gawking and found myself doing the same.

Among the crowd, a girl with hair nearly as white as the snow stared at me without the sarcastic giggle of the others. Pink orchids spread like a crown on her head, accenting her lips and the painted lines along her cheekbones. The skirt of her high-neck dress twirled around her as she danced. Each time she spun, her blue eyes returned to me and stole my breath. The ends of my mouth twitched upwards, the closest thing I could offer to a smile as nerves took over.

A hand clasped my shoulder. "Stare any longer and you'll drool," Kuba said with a smirk.

"Who is she?"

"No idea, but you'll never find out standing here with me." He slid something into my hand—a horn full of oskoła. "Drink up. Knowing you, you'll need it."

My mind felt numb as I drank without thinking about anything but her. *Gods, I'm pathetic.* I had never seen the girl before then, but somehow, she'd already stolen my heart. Genowefa and the sight of Narcyz's arm around her waist faded away. "What do I even say?" I asked.

"You're the son of the high chief. I'll tell ya now. If you can't woo a girl like that, you can't woo kings and chiefs to your side."

I scoffed and handed him the horn. "Luckily, I don't hope to bed kings and chiefs."

He slapped me on the back, forcing me to catch my balance. "That's more like it!"

I shook my head and brushed off my tunic—as if it would do any good after the golden egg's storm.

The crowd around the white-haired girl raised their eyebrows, snickering but allowing me to pass. My heart raced as I approached her.

What am I doing?

When I bowed, a smile crossed over her face. "I don't believe I've had the pleasure of meeting you," I said. "Wacław Lubiewicz, son of High Chief Jacek of Dwie Rzeki."

"It would be impossible for me to not know who you are," she replied, her voice sweet like a blooming spring flower. "My name is Yuliya Arkadczykówna, daughter of Arkady of Koberec."

I bowed my head. "I'm grateful your father brought you all this way for the festival."

She glanced away, her blue eyes studying a group of nearby girls for a moment before she returned her gaze to me. "I do hope you wish to discuss something other than our fathers."

I gripped the end of my sleeves, realizing my mistake. *You're doing fine. Remember the music.* "You seemed to be enjoying the songs."

"I was," she said with another smile. "It has been too long since I have had the chance to dance."

"Would you like to… with me?" I rubbed the back of my neck and looked at my feet, my confidence waning as quickly as it had come.

She grabbed my hand and began skipping to the beat. Without another thought, I followed along, much less graceful than her. *That actually worked?* Apparently it had, because Yuliya laughed and smiled as we danced, never releasing my hand. Joy swelled in my heart, and for a few minutes, my fears and anxieties faded. All I saw was her face. All I felt was the passion in her eyes.

When a lull in the music came, I met Otylia's gaze as she lingered with her friend Ara near the torchlit edge of the clearing. How long had she been watching me?

My heart skipped a beat. I tried to look away, but something was... different... about her. Like the girl I'd once known. White anemone flowers with streaks of black adorned her wreath, matching her headscarf and dress, and a necklace of stones had joined the Bowmark of Dziewanna around her neck. Flour concealed the blemishes on her face while lines of green marked her cheeks and chin.

How could this elegant girl be the same as the wild sorceress who'd intimidated me in the woods just hours before? And why couldn't I take my eyes off her?

Before I could wrestle those questions, though, Yuliya swept me away again.

It wasn't long before the songs died and food was laid out within Father's longhouse. Flickering torches and candlelight illuminated the main hall as we grabbed our share and sat at an empty table.

The longhouse was by far the largest building in the village. There were hundreds of guests, yet the hall, decorated with the wolf and bear pelts of Father's greatest kills and a massive ax along the front wall to honor Perun, could hold nearly all of them.

"What's it like in Koberec?" I asked Yuliya.

Her eyes glowed as she surveyed the hall and the drunk men flirting with the unmarried women. With her head turned, the edge of a birthmark became visible on the side of her neck for only a second before she looked back to me. "A long journey from here, though far less eventful than this. Honestly, it's rather dull. Have you ever seen it?"

"No, Father never let me travel with him." I sighed and pushed away the sorrow I felt for all of those missed adventures. "But perhaps it's best that I've stayed here and helped Mom till the fields. I'm not sure I would want the weight of the tribe on my shoulders anyway."

"You speak of your Mother, Lubena. I had wondered why you called yourself *Lubiewicz*. Is that why the other girls giggle about you?"

My heart sunk. "Yes."

She touched my arm, but I couldn't bring myself to look at her. I'd hoped that her not being from my village had kept her from hearing gossip about me. A foolish wish. "Why don't you laugh at me like the others?" I asked.

"Why should I? Power comes from the gods, not the opinions of fools."

Besides the blood magic I've gotten myself into and the fact even my father didn't want me? Without a reply, I deflected, "You asked if I had visited your village, but I know you've never been to Dwie Rzeki."

"What makes you think that?"

I took her hand and felt her smooth skin against the calluses of my palm. "I'm pretty quick with names and faces. I would have remembered yours."

When she blushed, I puffed up my chest with pride. I had no idea what I was doing, but I figured if she was laughing and smiling, I was doing something right. Before she could reply, though, Kuba slid onto the stool across from me, beaming and jabbing his spoon at me like a spear. "Want to introduce me to your new *friend?*"

I shot him a glare. He knew exactly what he was doing, but my revenge would have to wait. "Kuba, this is Yuliya Arkadczykówna, daughter of Arkady. Yuliya, this is Kuba Piotryk, son of Piotr and the clumsiest iron miner known to the tribe."

Kuba bowed his head as Maja joined him. "I would contest that," he said, "but he's right."

"Well, it's a pleasure to meet you, sure-footed or not," Yuliya replied with a smirk. She looked to the newest arrival. "And you are?"

Adjusting the purple flowers that covered her light brown hair, Maja replied shyly, "Maja, daughter of no one important."

Yuliya reached for her hand. "Whether your parents bring prestige or not, you are stunning." Her eyes drifted to Kuba. "I hope you let her know that."

His jaw dropped as he stammered, "Oh... We're not... She's not... Are we?" He grabbed his mug and drank, sending us all into a fit of laughter.

"Were you asking her a question or just vomiting words?" I asked.

"Probably both." He held Maja's arm, whose round cheeks were flushed, before glancing at me. "Uh, can you excuse us for a moment?"

Likely trying to avoid embarrassing Kuba further, Yuliya nodded, and the pair escaped. I grinned watching them go. *Good luck with that conversation.*

Yuliya glanced at my bag with curiosity in her eyes. "Now that we're alone, I'm curious. Can I see it, the golden egg?"

"I…" I cleared my throat. "Of course." The egg hummed in my hand, tingling my fingers when I slid it into hers. *Please don't notice.*

She examined it in the torchlight. "Do you believe the stories—that its holder receives a gift from the gods?"

"I don't know." My thumb drifted across my palm. Would the spring gods reward or curse me for being guided by Marzanna?

The ground shook as the warriors around the room stomped their feet. Conversation stopped, and all eyes turned to the front.

Father stood with Natasza beneath Perun's Ax, holding up a horn with a fierce look on his face. Already he wobbled, and the horn spilled over as he spoke, "Perun and his son, Jaryło, have granted me the glorious honor of hosting all of you today. While the plague of winter fades, we must unite once again. The Solgawi lurk beyond the great river. If they smell that we are divided, they will surely overtake us, so I ask you all: Do you stand with your tribe?"

The chiefs scattered throughout the room nodded and shouted in approval, trying to assert themselves as always. Chief Mieczysław—the most powerful of Father's chiefs—and his allies remained silent.

In the wars of the past, the chiefs near Mieczysław's northwestern village of Talis had lost more of their land than most. Father had become famous for his previous victories over the Solgawi, yet reputation could fade quickly when warriors watched their homes burn.

As Father droned on, the diviners' visions of the eastern riders rang in my mind. Many chiefs doubted Mokosz's szeptuchy, but I hoped they heeded the warning. If the diviners were right and we marched west, Dwie Rzeki and all our lands east of the river would be defenseless. Only our use of the woods and rivers to surprise the Solgawi had kept us alive in the past. There were a dozen nomadic clans east of us and our Astiwie allies. Any of them could raid our villages while we were occupied in the west.

"I believe in the egg's power," Yuliya said, pulling me from my thoughts once Father had retaken his seat. "And I believe you have been chosen."

I huffed and flexed my Frostmarked palm—covered once again. Its throbbing had intensified during our dance, and throughout the meal, it had only gotten worse. "I'm not sure if being chosen is such a blessing…"

Her hand fell on my arm. As she drew close, what I'd thought to be a birthmark shone on her neck. "Queen Marzanna's chosen are the most blessed of all."

My heart stopped as I pulled away, my cheeks flushed. Her high-necked dress had hidden her Frostmark before, but now, it pulsed along with my own. *Of course…* Flirting with her had been too easy.

"To be Frostmarked is an honor, Wacław," she continued, "and our queen does not appreciate those who ignore her gifts."

"What does she want from me?" I muttered. My instincts told me to flee, but I *needed* to know what was happening.

With an intense gaze, she wrapped my hands around the golden egg. "Keep the egg close, listen to the dagger's commands, and do not trust the witch. Queen Marzanna grows impatient with you already. It would be a shame if you felt her wrath."

Then, she smirked and slipped into the crowd.

I stood. If I could follow her, maybe she would lead to some hint of Marzanna's plans. But the longhouse was packed full.

By the time I caught sight of Yuliya again, she had reached the shadowed wall. She glanced at me over her shoulder and held up a glowing hand. A second later, she disappeared, leaving behind only a patch of white where she'd stood.

Around me, no one stirred. It was as if I had been the only one to see her simply dissolve. The golden egg still hummed, and I swallowed, quivering with it in my grasp. *I need air…*

The door let out a creak as I stumbled into the cool evening and took a deep breath. My hand throbbed while I paced and thought about the dagger and egg, now tucked away in my bag. Yuliya had told me to listen to the dagger, but I couldn't bring myself to unsheathe it. It had been an error to pierce my skin with it in the first place. I wouldn't listen to Marzanna's temptations any more. At least, that's what I told myself.

A hunger grew within me. It desired the golden egg and the power the goddess had promised. Had Marzanna sensed my doubts and sent Yuliya to ensure I obeyed?

I groaned, holding my head in my hands.

What a terrible day. Yuliya had made it so much worse, granting me hope and then tearing it way in a matter of minutes. All I had wanted was someone to care about me the same way I did for them. *Is that too much to ask?*

The dirt crunched behind me. "I was wondering how long you'd last with her."

9

Otylia

This'll be fun...

"WHO'S THERE?" WACŁAW STAMMERED as he spun to face me.

I smirked, stepping into the light of the torches. "I would've expected you to recognize the voice of the girl you've played with since you were a child."

He closed his eyes and clenched his fists. "Go away."

"Still afraid of me after everything that's happened?" There was something enticing about his agitation, so I pushed further. "Are you and that lovely ashen-haired girl to be wedded already, or did you jump straight to having children?"

Wacław had stumbled out of the longhouse after flirting with some girl who'd done nothing but gawk at him. Even from a distance, I could tell she was soft—the type all the boys were fond of—but Dziewanna's Bowmark had burned my neck watching her. Usually, it only did that when I was near dark spirits. I doubted that frail girl could hurt a flower if she tried, but Dziewanna's warning could not be ignored.

As she and Wacław had danced around Perun's Oak, giggling and smiling, I'd gritted my teeth. It shouldn't have annoyed me to see him having fun with another girl. He was just a foolish boy, and Mo-kosz's vision had only shown what *could* happen between us. I would make sure it didn't.

He studied me for a second but hung his head when he spoke, "No. Marzanna sent her."

Sent her for what? I scowled. "I knew she had dark intentions."

"What good is a szeptucha if you don't tell me that before I dance with her?"

"Did I not save your life today?"

"That's a fair point." He paused and brushed his thumb against his nose. "I didn't get the chance to thank you for that."

A band of drunk men spilled from the longhouse and stumbled toward us, bantering loudly and whistling in my direction. *If they knew who I was, they'd never touch a drop of alcohol ever again.*

Scowling, I grabbed Wacław and pulled him down a side trail where the fading sunlight barely crept through the trees. Their shadows covered his face as I replied, "Tell me what's going on or I'll let you suffocate next time a whirlwind strikes. First the leszy and now this girl. You're hiding something."

He stared down at his hands, yet again testing my patience. *Why does he have to think so much about everything?* I tried to remember that interacting with the gods was new to him and that he'd almost died just hours before. If I was right about Mokosz's visions and the whirlwind he'd caused in the forest, though, he was a płanetnik. It was hard to pity him when I'd seen him control lightning.

"Marzanna sent both of them as messengers," Wacław finally said, his voice hushed, "and the leszy gave me this dagger."

He pulled a black blade from his bag and unsheathed it. In the fading light, three white words in the old tongue were etched into its surface. *Let war come.* His eyes widened like he hadn't seen them before.

"Let war come," I repeated aloud. "What war?"

"I don't know… I just heard it in my head when I drew the blade. Before, it asked for my blood."

That piqued my curiosity. I stepped forward, studying the dagger.

Thunderstone. The metal was made whenever Perun's lightning struck the ground and was said to have power beyond that of any other. The sight of it made me shudder, but my curiosity was stronger. "This explains the cut on your hand. What? You think I didn't know what a cloth wrap like that meant?"

His jaw hung open. I pinched the bridge of my nose, fighting the pounding headache that had arrived unwelcome in my mind. Around us, Dadźbóg's last light swept across the trees and disappeared completely, leaving us alone in the black.

"Before," I began, "I just said it because it was fun, but you truly are an idiot."

"Today seems to be a lot of that."

I muttered under my breath, clutching Dziewanna's amulet as I begged the goddess for an answer. This was not how I'd wanted the festival to go, and my expectations had been low. "Typically, when an enchanted object asks you for blood, you shouldn't give it. Let me see your hand."

He trembled as I gripped his wrist, unwrapping his palm to reveal a scar of Marzanna's mark. I cursed at the sight. *He's Frostmarked.*

Gods could exert influence over demons and people through their symbols—just as they did to szeptuchy. Though we wore amulets to amplify our channeling, I bore Dziewanna's Bowmark and Mokosz's Mothermark on either side of my neck, forever devoting me to them. The Frostmarked had been exiled for years. If he was one of them...

What do I do now? I asked Dziewanna.

Silence.

Why aren't you speaking to me?

The wild goddess had never been so quiet before, but I needed her now more than ever. It was undeniable that her sister was scheming on the eve of her death. But what was Marzanna's plan?

Lost at what to do, I took a deep breath and snapped my glare to Wacław. How could he have done something so stupid? Well, of course *he* could've, but it was unnerving that Marzanna had managed to convince him to take her mark. Even if he hadn't known what he was doing, I needed to stop it.

"Tell me what the szeptucha's message was," I demanded.

"She… She said to keep the egg close and to listen to the dagger's commands. Apparently, Marzanna is already upset with me."

"She's not the only one." I stepped closer. Wacław was half-a-head taller than me, but he wavered. "Is that all she said?"

He sighed and dropped his gaze. "She also told me to not trust you. Then she just walked into the shadows of the longhouse and disappeared."

"She's a Frostmarked szeptucha…" I raised my brow. "Do you trust me?"

He nodded slightly. It wasn't much, but with everything that'd happened, I took it. "Fine, then hold out your hand. I'll see if I can get rid of her mark—or at least dull its effects."

Whispering in the old tongue, I held my palm to his. Dziewanna's power rushed into me. The trees and roots around us rustled as I called for her blessing. There was no way to know if it would work, but without the goddess's guidance, my options were limited.

Wacław's palm glowed as his Frostmark and my Bowmark cast a sheer light over the trail. Seconds later, he cried out, and I lunged forward, covering his mouth.

"Be quiet," I sneered. The last thing I needed was to be discovered in the woods with him, especially considering he was Frost-marked.

A stupid smirk crossed his face. I grabbed his tunic and glared at him as fear replaced amusement in his annoyingly blue eyes. It took everything I had not to slap him. "Stop laughing," I snapped, glancing down the trail. "Nobody can know about this."

He stepped back, his smirk replaced by a softer smile. "Sorry. It's just, this is the first time since your initiation that you look like a girl instead of a witch."

"I'm not a witch." I pushed him back and pacing around the trail. "This isn't a joke! Marzanna has your blood."

"What does she want from me?" he asked, looking down at his glowing palm.

I sighed. Mother would've known what to do. She had always had a keen understanding of the gods, even when I failed to understand their riddles and symbols. *I miss her.*

"Only Marzanna can answer that," I finally said, "but if she is calling to you now and sending a spirit and a szeptucha as messengers, something's wrong. I just wish I knew *what*. For now, stand still so I can finish."

Without waiting for a reply, I snatched his wrist and began chanting again. Dziewanna's *żityje* merged with me and danced at the ends of my fingers. I traced the mark of shattered ice, remembering what Marzanna had done to Mother. My breaths shortened. My heart raced. Emotions were a potent force in channeling, and as my resentment, my hatred, burned in my chest, Dziewanna's power intensified with it.

A chill fought back the harder I pushed. It crawled up my fingers and numbed my palms, forcing me to close my eyes and find the center of Dziewanna's presence in me. I latched onto the goddess's unbridled desire to free her wilds of Marzanna's curse and allowed her rage to become mine. Her power surged through me. When I opened my eyes, the Frostmark was blinding.

Then it went dark.

Everything rushed out of me at once. I released Wacław and stumbled back, disoriented as I fell into a tree across the trail. My legs felt alien beneath me, like I'd forced them to carry me for miles. They gave way as I struggled to remain conscious.

When the world stopped spinning, I touched my hand to my head. *What just happened?*

Channeling came at the cost of *żityje*, but now, every breath I took was desperate. I'd never experienced so much power rushing through me at once. With it gone, my soul felt cold and drained along with my body. I cursed my weakness—I couldn't even bring myself to stand.

Across the trail, Wacław knelt with his fists dug into the dirt. His breaths were as weak as mine, and neither of us spoke for a few long minutes. Even if I had the energy to, I didn't know what I'd say. I was a szeptucha. I served the gods every day. But this wasn't praying at the altars and protecting them from a stray demon.

Somehow, behind his hesitance and thin frame, the foolish boy in front of me was a powerful demon that had surrendered to Marzanna. If I failed to stop her... I shook my head. Failing wasn't an option.

"What... What did you do?" Wacław said, his voice shaky.

Testing my legs, I clawed my way up the tree and clutched my side, already out of breath. "Dziewanna's blessing *should* prevent Marzanna from having influence over your thoughts. But she will try to contact you with the dagger or another creature. I'm sure of it."

"You're hurt."

"Channeling the gods' powers comes at a price. I'll be fine, but that dagger's Frostmark is more than a symbol."

"Why would Marzanna do this? What was the whirlwind when I touched the egg?"

With a groan, I pushed myself off the tree and limped toward him. I couldn't get Mokosz's ritual out of my head—Wacław's battle with the zmora, his shield sliding into my hand, and the lightning arcing from his skin. Based on the moon and the dress I'd worn in the first of those visions, he'd face the zmora tonight. I would see then if I was right about him being a demon.

"I don't know for sure," I said. "The power of the golden egg combined with Marzanna's mark and something inside of you."

He shook his head, and for only a second, I pitied him. "Inside me? You're telling me there's a power in me?"

"I don't know," I snapped, "but the egg's power is very real. That's why Marzanna led you to it."

"How do you know she showed me where it was?"

"Besides her szeptucha telling you to keep it close? You're too much of a fool to find the egg while carrying a sleepy boy and corralling a girl without direction. I knew you were lying to me."

And I felt her influence...

A horn blew from the center of the village, signaling that it was time to head to where the rivers merged for the fire jump and effigy burning. Wacław looked toward the noise before glancing at me with a hint of sorrow in his eyes.

My skin crawled as I clutched Mokosz's amulet. *Why'd you have to show me that stupid vision?*

"Will you be okay?" he asked. "They'll expect us to light the effigy."

I couldn't muster the energy to answer, so I just scowled and hobbled back toward the village center. In truth, I didn't know whether I'd be fine. But I did know I was ready for the day to end already.

10

Wacław

Let war come.

THE DAGGER'S WORDS HADN'T LEFT MY MIND since Marzanna's whisper had chilled my ears. It seemed an ill omen after the diviners' visions of the eastern horde, but what role did I have to play?

When I emerged from the woods, everyone else had already gathered around Perun's Oak. Others would notice that I was sneaking in late; though, I hoped no one saw Otylia come from the same direction as me. People talked too much. In a village our size, if someone had seen us alone in the forest, Father would've heard in minutes. I felt my neck. *I would rather not be choked to death before jumping the fire.*

Around me, boys and girls whispered about who had danced with who and which relationships would work. I didn't have the spirit to join them. Between the endless burning of Marzanna's mark on my palm and the omens the diviners had spoken of, the thought of finding true love seemed childish.

Father reluctantly stood alongside Dariusz and the other priests at the base of the oak. A hush came over the crowd as the priest raised his arms, but their energy lingered in the air. "Let Swaróg's light guide us as we end Marzanna's frigid grip!" Dariusz called out. "Men, bring the sheep to sacrifice."

Drunk men and boys cheered around me as one of Weles's shamans grabbed the sheep.

Though the shamans weren't szeptuchy, they claimed that the god of the underworld and cattle spoke to them through their drug-induced dances and visions. Father believed them even less than the diviners. All I knew was that I didn't want to be in their way when they called for Weles to speak.

With the priests, diviners, shamans, and chiefs all leading us, we began the march down the trail. I tried to keep my head down, but someone grabbed my shoulder. "There's the lost son," Narcyz said.

Why do the gods hate me?

I faked a smile and turned to face him. In the moonlight, it was hard to see his expression, but was safe to assume he smirked as Genowefa clutched his hand, her gaze judging me more than was comforting. "I'm shocked you missed me," I said, raising my brow.

"We didn't." His hazel eyes snapped to her before returning to me. "Doubt that blonde broad does either."

An anger rose within me without warning, but before I said something I would regret, I turned away and jogged ahead. His glare burned the back of my head as I did. Though he had gotten under my skin again, I wouldn't let him have the satisfaction of provoking me further. Father wanted me to avoid public conflict on today of all days. After my argument with Mikołaj earlier, a fight with a brute like Narcyz would not help my case.

We soon reached the confluence of the Krowik and Wyzra. The smell of the water bubbling over the rocks and mud filled my lungs as the cool wind skidded across the surface of the rivers, sending shivers up my arms.

I let the tension in my back release with a deep breath. When so many looked down upon me in the village, I knew the twin rivers would never betray me.

Where the rivers met, the shamans wore wooden masks and fox pelts draped over their heads. They drummed and danced alongside the wood-carved idols for the various gods—Perun with his wise beard and thunderous ax, Swaróg with his smithing hammer, Mokosz with her woven threads of life, Jaryło with his golden shield and eight swords at his back, and many others.

The bonfire's flames stretched to the sky before the carvings. Against the black night, it seemed to tower over the shamans as sparks floated through the air and drifted to our feet as little more than ash.

I wanted to fight the racing of my heart, but my anxieties were stronger.

Once I jumped the fire, the rest of my life would begin. I wasn't entirely sure what that meant—especially now that I'd found myself caught between Marzanna and the spring gods.

An energy buzzed through the crowd as Gośka, the eldest of my half-sisters, appeared next to me. I tensed as her gaze flicked from me to the fire. Besides her blue eyes, she looked exactly like her mother, and while I knew it was unfair to dislike her for that, I saw too much of Natasza in her.

"Don't singe your feet," she said with more than a touch of sarcasm in her voice.

"I'll try my best not to, but if I do, at least I can say I walked on fire."

"And I can say I saw my brother eaten alive by Swaróg's rage."

I glanced at Gośka and the vicious little smirk on her face. *Just like Natasza.*

"Only two more years until you make the jump too," I said. "Remember that boys tend to run from girls on fire."

Lines creased her forehead, and she glared at the gathered boys. "Now I'm considering it."

I chuckled as Dariusz took a long knife from a shaman and knelt next to the sheep, which had been placed before Jaryło's idol. His gray hair draped down his crimson robes as he muttered a prayer to the gods and the shamans' drums echoed over the river. Then, in one swift motion, he slit open the sheep from front to back. I looked away as it let out a last blood curdling bleat and died.

The crowd cheered—the ritual had begun with the sacrifice.

Dariusz rose and held his arms to the idol with the other priests. "May our gift please you and bless the coming days of warmth!" As the shamans moved the sheep, Dariusz grabbed two unlit torches and called for Otylia and me to come forward.

Taking a deep breath, I weaved through the crowd until I stood next to the priest and his daughter.

With the torch in hand and everyone's eyes on me, I felt naked, exposed. My insides twisted within me, and when I raised my head, my palm ached. I'd squeezed the torch so hard that my knuckles had turned even whiter than before, ghostly.

Dariusz cleared his throat, tearing me from my thoughts. "With the dark nights of winter, Marzanna brings an essential element of our world's cycle, a balance among the gods. With Jaryło's bloom, there must be death. With warmth, a freeze. We worship and fear Marzanna as we do Swaróg, Perun, Weles, and others, but we must continue the cycle. Wielding Swaróg's fire, we shall light Marzanna's effigy and allow the great river to carry her to Nawia, where Weles shall contain her fury until the time comes for her to rise again."

His hand closed around my arm, and, with more force than necessary, he yanked me to the fire as Otylia followed. I gritted my teeth but didn't fight it. The priest may have been the gods' messenger to us, but that only meant I had to listen and comply in rituals. I didn't need to like him.

I swallowed my fear and stuck the torch into the fire, its heat drawing sweat from my brow. Then, with the torch lit, I stepped aside and nodded to Otylia. Instead of furrowing her dark brows like usual, she returned the gesture.

That took me aback at first, but there was a sense of understanding between us now. Though it couldn't fix the divide Father had made, I owed her—she was my only hope to figure out what was happening to me.

The flames crackled and danced at the end of my torch, trapped in their stream of unending motion while Dariusz guided us to the effigy. Shamans spun around it, and their loud chants hammered my ears as they drummed in the herb-induced stupor.

How will you punish me for this? I silently asked Marzanna as I stared up at the crude figure's black eyes. Its mangled hair and tattered clothes barely covered its body, made of tuffs of wheat and straw.

Goddess of winter, of pestilence, of death.

No matter what Marzanna offered, I promised myself I would never serve her. I feared Marzanna's wrath, but I could never follow someone who left so much destruction in her wake.

Time slowed as we approached the effigy. The crowd, shamans, and priests all seemed distant, as if a barrier had formed between us and them. I looked to Otylia, but she marched on, staring up at the effigy with vengeance on her face. We all feared the goddess, yet this was personal for her. The illness we called Marzanna's Curse had taken her mother. Nothing had been the same for her since.

A chill ran up my arms when we stopped. Each of my breaths turned to fog, and the ground was unusually hard beneath my boots. I remembered the lone patch of tundra around the leszy and shivered at the thought of the visions. *I won't surrender to you again.*

"Wacław, what are you doing?" Otylia muttered.

The barrier dropped. Everyone was staring at me as I stood there like a fool, and heat rushed to my cheeks. "Sorry…"

We held our torches to the effigy. The flames raced through it, deforming it even worse than before. When we stepped back, the chanting continued, and the pain from Marzanna's Frostmark arced up my arm.

"No," I whispered as I met the effigy's burning glare.

Soon, the yells of the other boys and girls replaced the shamans' chants. They rushed to the effigy, ripping it from the ground with the fire reflecting the passion in their eyes as they threw it into the Krowik. In the darkness, it was impossible to see the effigy float along, but it didn't matter. Spring could finally begin.

"Marzanna will despise you for this," Otylia said, still watching the river.

"Why just me?"

"You gave her a blood offering and then betrayed her on the same day, Half-Chief. I cast a blessing on your Frostmark, but there's a reason szeptuchy don't take our gods' marks lightly. I can't save you if Marzanna decides to collect what is hers."

A cold breeze blew through my hair as the others ran toward the fire. It was time to make the jump, but her omen hung in the air, freezing me to that spot. If she spoke the truth, it didn't matter if I found a girl or earned the village's favor. Marzanna would come for me.

"What about the egg?" I asked as our fathers took their position before the flames. "It grants a gift from the gods."

Otylia glanced toward the others. "The gods don't care what you want as your gift. You'll get it when they decide, but since Marzanna seems to be scheming, by then it will probably be too late."

As she walked away, I looked to the sky. *Why me?*

The boys shouted for me to get in line. I forced myself to take a breath, collecting what little confidence remained in my soul as I ran to them. I had almost reached the back of the line when Kuba snagged me. "Your dad is gonna want you up front."

"Not my biggest concern right now," I said.

"What happened with Yuliya?" he asked. "You were gone when I came back. Sorry I wasn't there."

I sighed. "It was stupid to think a girl like her would be fond of me. What about you and Maja?"

With a shrug, he glanced at the girls ahead. "We talked for a while, but I got too nervous to ask her anything serious. Whatever. But no more changing the subject." He gripped my tunic. "Listen, we've known each other forever, and all you've talked about for the last year is hoping some girl notices you when you jump the fire. I can't blame you for at least *trying* for once! Heck, I would've with her if you didn't."

Maja stepped up, her eyes narrow. Horror replaced Kuba's cockiness as she tapped her foot. "I was about to ask if you wanted to jump together," she said, "but it seems you would rather talk about other girls, so if you'll excuse me…"

She hurried off toward the front of the line with her chin held high. Kuba winced and ran after her.

Alone again, there was nothing to distract me from my longing as I felt the golden egg in my bag. My palm throbbed against it—the same pull that had tempted me to pierce my skin with the dagger. I shook my head to myself. *Why did I listen? Am I really that desperate?*

"Wacław!" Father yelled to me. "Make haste!"

No one remained between me and the fire. I looked from Father's judging eyes to Mikołaj, who laughed at my hesitance with his older friends. Mom was nowhere to be seen. Instead, all the chiefs and villagers watched me, eager. Father stood among them with his bulging arms crossed.

I sprinted toward the fire.

Wave after wave of heat washed over me as I ran with the shamans' chants in my ear. Marzanna's call echoed in my mind and her mark stung my palm, beckoning some power within me. I wasn't ready. In a few steps, I would become a man, yet I felt more like a boy than ever—more alone than ever.

Alone.

Across the fire, Otylia studied me. I'd abandoned her when she'd needed me most. How alone had she felt losing her best friend and mother? How could I blame her for the years of scorn that had followed when I was the one who'd turned away? Whatever power the golden egg held had merged with me, and I needed her to figure out why.

I needed *her.*

Time froze as I leaped with the flames snapping at my boots and legs. Though I wasn't far off the ground, I seemed to fly as the cool winds wove through my tunic and nipped at my ears. For a moment, I forgot what troubles faced me and embraced the freedom of the air beneath my feet.

When I returned to the earth, a thrill raced through my veins. *I did it.*

A beaming Kuba ran up to me, and I shared a hug with the only real brother I'd ever had. "You finally made it," he said as music began around us.

"And Maja didn't kill you," I replied.

"If I can survive a fight with her, I'm going to be the best skirmisher in the army. Those Solgawi bastards better be ready."

I chuckled as he ran off to join Maja, who danced by the fire now that everyone had jumped. As I watched the crowd follow the shamans' drums, though, nausea replaced my joy. *Let war come...* Had it meant the Solgawi?

The melodies flowed around me as I slid through the crowd in a trance of thought, the emotions of the day drowning my soul in a dense fog. Perun's clouds rolled overhead. This time, I prayed for his rain to end the festival. So many hopes had filled my heart when I'd finished my training with Xobas. Now, as Marzanna's call and Yuliya's omens weighed on my shoulders, all I wanted was to return home, curl up in my bed, and forget this day had ever happened.

But I couldn't forget. My throbbing Frostmark wouldn't let me, and when Otylia approached me where the woods met the clearing, I grimaced. "Go ahead, make a joke."

The ends of her mouth curled as she slid into the shadows next to me. In the fire's flicker, the green of her eyes matched her necklace and face-paint. I hated that there was something both threatening and alluring about that. Between the flower wreath, flowing black and white dress, and headscarf, she looked like an entirely different girl to the jagged channeler she'd become since her mother's death. I missed her.

"What is there to joke about?" she asked.

"I don't know whether you're being sarcastic or kind."

She chuckled. "You should know the answer to that."

"Then why did you save my life and cast Dziewanna's blessing on my hand?"

"Because if you died in the woods with me, people would blame the witch, and it's my job to stop Marzanna's influence from spreading in Dziewanna's realm."

"And why are you here with me instead of talking with Ara or some boy?" I nodded toward the fire. "Seems like everyone over there is having a lot more fun."

With her brow raised, her hand drifted to Mokosz's amulet. "Ara *is* dancing with some boy."

"Jealous?"

"Hardly."

"Good, because otherwise, I would still be suspicious why you've come to me and not your father or anyone else after jumping the fire."

"Father is busy."

I let myself smirk, half-expecting her to smack it off my face when I did. "As are all the other boys, right?"

Her nose wrinkled as she spun and glared up at me, enough to make my heart twitch in fear. "I came over here to check you were okay after I placed Dziewanna's blessing on the Frostmark. Obviously, that was a mistake."

Frustration gripped me as she turned to leave, but before she got far, the pounding of a horse's hooves approached from the trails. A rider burst into the firelight at full gallop, his shield and spear clanging with each stride. Screams rang out from the crowd as they scrambled out of the way. The rider's light blue cloak flapped behind him as he dismounted before the fire. *Astiwie.*

I would've recognized the kalina symbol of our southeastern allies anywhere: white flowers and red berries. Purity and bloodlines. *What is he doing here?*

"Where is High Chief Jacek Lechowicz?" the rider asked, his voice carrying through the night.

There was nothing but the crackle of the fire for a few moments until Father stepped forward, his gaze fixed on the visitor. "I am here."

The rider dropped to a knee. "My name is Andrij Myroslavovych Yakymchuk, and I bring a message from your great ally Boz Vladyslavovych Kramarenko, king of the Astiwie. An army has amassed itself east of our lands. We are all in danger."

11

Wacław

If this messenger speaks the truth, then war is coming. Is it the one Marzanna wants?

THE ENTIRE TRIBE HAD PILED INTO THE LONGHOUSE. I stood near the ring of chiefs and priests that had formed around Father, who sat beneath the ax of Perun.

Age seemed to wear on Father's face in the torchlight as he looked from his warriors to the kneeling messenger, Andrij. "What threat does Boz believe this army poses?"

"The Zurgowie have always been one of the most aggressive nomadic clans roaming the Anshayman Steppe," Andrij replied. "But something's changed. They have united with the Simukie and taken up camp north of the Narrow Pass. Together, the clans sent an envoy with an ultimatum."

The clans have united? Around me, the crowd shifted at the notion of raiders from the east after the diviners' warnings.

Chiefs and warriors alike had told stories of the many clans beyond the Mangled Woods and mountains of Perun's Crown. Xobas had taught me much of the clans' shared tongue. Beyond that, however, he had spoken little more about the Simukie beliefs and culture he'd left behind.

"The allied clans claimed that a substantial force has driven them from their lands," Andrij continued, ignoring the noise. "We've been given until the new Kwiecień moon to allow them safe passage through the Narrow Pass. If we don't, they will attack with an army considerably larger than our own."

My heart sunk. I found Otylia among the crowd, and her gaze met mine. *Let war come.* If Marzanna wanted war, though, what could *I* do to stop it? I didn't know, but Otylia nodded. *Do something.*

Father had never spoken highly of Boz, despite his brother-in-law's help in our last war with the Solgawi. If Boz believed that this nomadic coalition was truly that powerful, though, our hold on the dense eastern forests and southern hills were at risk. Only the Astiwie and their control of the Narrow Pass through the mountains of Perun's Crown stood in the clans' way.

Dariusz stepped into the circle as Father considered the messenger's words. "This confirms the visions of the diviners, my high chief. A great eastern horde and an attack on our villages during the celebration of Noc Kupały."

Xobas crossed his arms at Father's right hand. "I fought the Zurgowie many times with my people. Even in the face of a horde, I find it difficult to believe the two clans would ally."

Andrij shook his head. "I am merely delivering King Boz's message."

"What proof does Boz have that this army is any threat to our lands?" Chief Mieczysław said, approaching the messenger with a battle-ax hung at his side and a cloak of bear furs trailing behind. Just the sight of the war-seeking chief made me nervous.

Andrij staggered back as Mieczysław towered over him. "None, Chieftain, but King Boz honored our alliance during your wars against the Solgawi. He asks that High Chief Jacek does the same for us now."

It wasn't a surprise to see Mieczysław's resistance. His allies had the most to gain from a war with the Solgawi. Defending the Astiwie would bring his warriors no spoils and him no land. It said something, though, that he valued raiding more than honoring an alliance with a tribe that shared our blood.

But how do I ensure peace?

Mieczysław began to reply, but Father held up his hand to silence him. "I do not wish for a war in the east either," Father said, "but it is in our duty as a tribe to defend our brothers. Regardless of the threat, however, we cannot leave our lands unprotected when the Solgawi continue their raids west of the Krowik."

Nodding, Chief Serwacy replied, "I must concur. The Solgawi will look eagerly at us if we march east, and the last thing we need is a war on two fronts. I suggest no more than a quarter of our men be sent to aid our allies."

"If we were to sow for a more permanent peace with the Solgawi, my chieftain," Kajetan said from his left hand, "then we could send up to half of our army."

Why do you have to be the one making sense?

"We cannot make peace with the savages that raid our western lands," Mieczysław snapped, turning to Father. "I pledged my clan to you nearly twenty years ago because you swore you would never let them steal what is ours. I have never asked for anything in return, yet now you ask me to drag my men far to the east when the Solgawi hold territory within two days' march of Talis. My patience wears thin…"

Father scowled and stood, pacing around the circle. "My promise to you still stands, but we must uphold our side of the agreement. The Astiwie shed their blood defending our land. What would you have me do? Go to war with the Solgawi and leave our brothers' homes and women defenseless?"

"He dares to doubt what we have accomplished," Natasza sneered. "The tribe will never be unified as long as he is allowed to be a chief."

"This is not your place, High Chieftess," Serwacy replied.

Mieczysław glared at Natasza before pointing at Father. "I'd have you grow a set of balls and secure the Krowik! Every day our enemies piss in the tributaries of the great river is another disgrace to our ancestors. You act as if you've forgotten that we choose to follow. All I've heard since I swore my ax to you has been lies and excuses. And now, you want to send my warriors to die far from their homes because you married a king's sister!"

He turned and held out his arms to the other chiefs. "Before all of you tonight," Mieczysław declared, "I shall invoke my right of *Dar* and demand that the high chief honor his word."

The crowd gasped, and my breaths quickened as I shook my head.

Any chief could request a *Dar*, a gift, after ten years of willful allegiance to the high chief. It was usually a piece of land, a village, or even a woman, but a chief as powerful as Mieczysław could use it also for war. He'd served Father for twenty years with no *Dar* until now. It would be hard for Father to resist his demand—there would be war.

Father stepped back and sat in his fur-covered chair. Exhaustion replaced anger on his face. "I have not forgotten our traditions or our ancestral western lands. Our time will come to retake what we have lost, but we are nothing if our word cannot be trusted when our allies need us most. I cannot honor your request."

"You're a liar and a coward!" Mieczysław shouted.

I have to stop this.

"What if there's another way?" I said, pushing my way into the circle.

The weight of the chiefs' scowls fell upon me. I had spoken out of turn and Father would make me regret it. With Marzanna's desire for war, though, peace was more important than Father's wrath.

"There is no alternative," Mieczysław spat.

"Let him speak," Xobas said, looking to Father.

With a deep breath, Father nodded for me to continue.

Gathering my confidence, I stepped to the circle's center. "What if instead of fighting the Simukie and Zurgowie, we brought them into our lands, settling them and gaining powerful allies for when the

Solgawi attack in the future? If the clans are fleeing the horde Mokosz's diviners saw, then they're desperate for help. Let's give them land to fight for."

Murmurs spread through the crowd, but I gritted my teeth. "Father, you've heard Xobas speak time and time again of the Simukie clan's skilled cavalry, of their hunting prowess. Imagine if we could bring them into our tribe."

"The boy shows a rare spark of wisdom, my chieftain," Kajetan whispered, leaning over to Father.

Mieczysław's fur cloak swung behind him as he plowed across the room and gripped my tunic. "You are a child who has no place in these talks! We cannot continue to hand out our land to whoever threatens our borders."

Father stormed toward us. "Unhand him!"

When he grabbed hold of Mieczysław's arm, his rival turned and drew a dagger. The iron blade shimmered in the light of the torches as he held it to Father's throat, pushing him into a wooden pillar.

The crowd stirred around us. Xobas pulled his sword as the chiefs unsheathed their weapons, each chieftain's allies staring down the other's as the room seemed ready to explode.

"Everyone out!" Serwacy shouted before stroking his graying beard and shooting me a glare.

What have I done?

All I wanted was peace, unity. Yet my words had done the opposite, and now the call of our allies threatened to tear apart the tribe.

Dariusz stormed forward, hissing and pulling at Mieczysław's cloak as the crowd filed out. "End this! There are far greater powers at play than two quarreling chieftains. May the spirits of the Krowik drown you both if you drag our tribe apart."

"We can reach an agreement, Mieczysław," Father said with an arm raised to signal the others to lower their weapons. "Drop the blade, and let's talk like men."

Mieczysław scowled as he looked from him to Dariusz, but after a few seconds, he released Father and marched back to his allies' sides. "Talk, or you'll find your head on the end of my spear instead of a Solgawi one."

Father's gaze fell on me as he returned to his chair. Without the crowd in the room, my stomach fluttered as we waited for him to speak. "Wacław's proposition has merit. A peace with these clans could allow us to focus our efforts on the west and honor your *Dar*. The diviners have not seen defeat at the hands of the Solgawi, only the clans' attack. Xobas, you know your people. Do you believe an agreement to be possible?"

Xobas studied me, then faced Father with one hand on the hilt of his cavalry sword. "My clan has never allied with the Zurgowie or run westward. The situation must be dire. I agree with Wacław, but the Zurgowie are not known for their want of peace."

"Where would we settle them?" Serwacy asked. "I doubt nomads would accept life in the eastern forests, and I have no wish to grant them free reign over my northern coast."

Father nodded. "That is why they will be settled in my lands: the southern foothills. Their open plains should provide a suitable environment for the nomads. Do you not agree, Xobas?"

"I do," the general said.

"And Boz would not object to us removing the threat without war?" Father asked the messenger.

Still kneeling in the center of the circle, right next to me, Andrij looked stunned by the exchange. He took a moment before stumbling over his words, "I... I believe he would accept such an agreement."

"Then it is decided. Kajetan will lead Xobas and a team of boys to the east to earn the loyalty of the nomads. The rest of our men shall march against the Solgawi once the chiefs have had time to rally their warriors. Upon Kajetan's return, we will have a fresh army to help in the effort."

Mieczysław bowed his head ever-so-slightly but kept his eyes fixed on Father. "Glad to see you finally see sense, Jacek. My warriors will be ready."

I winced. In my attempt to find peace, Father had given into

Mieczysław and started the war we'd fought for years to avoid. *Is it the one Marzanna wants?* I stuttered, "But—"

"You've said enough," Father interjected as he stood. "The chiefs will discuss the plan and bring it before all the tribe present for a vote tomorrow. For now, though, I must have a word with Wacław. I will send Xobas to fetch all of you when we are finished."

As the chiefs and priests bowed and left, Mikołaj grabbed my shoulder. "Really enjoyable show, little brother."

I didn't have the energy to reply, so I just pushed away his arm as questions strangled my mind. Would we have any chance against the Solgawi? Would the clans accept our offer to join our tribe in the southern hills? And would Marzanna be pleased with my failure?

Andrij stood in the midst of the confusion, obviously unsure what to do, before he shuffled out with the chiefs. Father was right about our alliance with the Astiwie, and I could only hope my suggestion would not strain our relations. Though it was our duty to protect our allies as they had us, peace in the east had to be a better option.

With the room empty except for us and Xobas, Father staggered toward me. I hung my head. "I'm sorry, my chief."

Anger filled his eyes. I didn't flinch until his backhand struck my cheek, knocking me to my knees. "You make me a fool! You may have jumped the fire, but you have shown tonight that you are still a boy. What made you believe you should intervene in a negotiation among the chiefs?"

"It all happened so fast…" My face throbbed from the blow, and I fought against the tears that stung my eyes. "He attacked you, and I thought he would sway the other chiefs if I didn't step in."

"You need not protect me from my chiefs," he said, pacing. "Mieczysław and I have fought for longer than you've been alive, but interrupting him only ignites his already powerful rage." He stroked his beard and let out a deep sigh. "While your idea was a good one, you must know your place. There is a way things are done."

"I just wanted to prove I had a purpose, that I can be more than a boy you can marry off for political gain. I wanted to make you proud." There was more, but I couldn't tell him the truth. Father would never believe my claims.

He shook his head and took a swig of oskoła from a mug on the table. "Have I not given you enough of a purpose? When I pass, Mikołaj will be the next high chief if all goes well, and he will need warriors like you to support him." He leaned forward on his knees, looking up at me as if I were a puzzle he was trying to solve. "It is not your role to interfere in my discussions with the chiefs."

My hopes burned away as I stared at the floor. *Then my role is to be irrelevant.* "And if I wish to be more than a warrior?"

"You must be a warrior to earn the respect of the tribe and defend our lands in times of war!" Father growled. "Though you are not Natasza's son, you have a role to play in ensuring your brother continues my work."

"He's not my brother."

"He is!" he exclaimed, pulling me to my feet by my arm. "My blood runs through both of your veins, and you will serve Mikołaj and the tribe. It matters not who your mother is. You are *my* son."

Memories of every time that hadn't been true filled my head— when he'd beaten me and turned away when I'd needed him most. On my twelfth birthday, he'd ignored the traditional cutting of my hair, making Mom do it instead. That rejection declared that I was not his son in name or in succession. I would inherit none of his lands, not even the tiniest of villages. His words said I was his son, but his actions declared I was nothing.

Swallowing my emotions, I raised my gaze to him. "What do I do now that we march to war?"

He threw me back. When I recovered, his look sent a shiver down my spine. "Now, you must execute the plan *you* created. You will travel with Kajetan to the clans, find an agreement, and bring me an army."

I'm leaving? I had always dreamed of seeing the lands beyond our village, but that meant leaving behind Mom and everything I knew. Suddenly, the thought of adventure seemed daunting.

I held my arm across my body and forced myself to breathe. "When do we go?"

With a sigh, Father slumped back into his chair. "Time is short. I did not believe the diviners' omens before, but Boz's messenger confirmed the threat. The clans will march at the beginning of the Kwiecień moon. With only three weeks until then, you don't have time to cross Astiwie lands and the Narrow Pass. You will need to travel through the Mangled Woods if you are to succeed. And you *must* succeed. If you don't, our warriors will be caught in the west, and we will be defenseless."

The Mangled Woods. Everyone knew the stories of the unsettled eastern forests. Hundreds of years ago, a powerful witch had tamed demons and warped the trees, creating the twisted trunks and branches that gave the woods their name. Perun had led our ancestors into the forest and killed the witch before cutting off her head and burying it separate from her body. Even now, though, people claimed many of the witch's demons remained. It was also rumored to be where Marzanna's exiled cultists and szeptuchy hid. The thought of walking into her grasp made me shiver.

"Are you listening to me, Wacław?" Father continued. "You asked for a chance to prove yourself, so I'm giving you an opportunity."

A hundred emotions swirled in my heart as I dropped to my knee and stared at the floor. "Yes, my chief."

Father signaled to Xobas at the door, and seconds later, a stampede of footsteps followed. *The chiefs are here. Father wants them to see this.*

I thought of Marzanna's visions and the power of the golden egg rushing through me: distant memories after all that had happened. Ever since I had picked up that dagger, my life had been turned on its head, and as I felt the stares of the tribe's most powerful chiefs and warriors on my back, I wished I had never followed that stupid deer.

"Are you ready for us?" Serwacy asked with his narrow eyes trained on me.

Father nodded. "Stand, Wacław, and be off. We will speak more when Dadźbóg rises."

When I stood, I became light-headed and stumbled. Mikołaj cackled from behind me, but Father raised his fist, silencing him instantly. I bowed my head one last time and shuffled for the door, avoiding the gaze of the chiefs and wiping the tears from my eyes.

Before I could leave, though, Xobas caught my arm. "Do not regret speaking for peace, you hear me?"

I nodded.

"Good. Now get out of here and stop believing in true love."

That felt like a stab in my heart, but I knew he was trying to be kind. "Thanks, Xobas," I said, stepping into the cool night, where the festival continued despite the disturbance.

More eyes turned to me, and I walked as quickly as I could toward the path home. Though my ears were numb, I heard their snickers and gossip in my soul. It was all I'd heard my entire life. Now, it had finally become too much.

This journey should've been my chance to prove myself to Father and the tribe, but with their mockery and Marzanna's mystery circling me, one thought ruled my mind. *Why did I wish for change?*

12

Otylia

The boy who wants peace more than anything started a war... ironic.

THE MOONLIGHT SHONE SOFTLY ACROSS ARA'S FACE. We'd gathered at the end of the village center with the other girls, waiting for Wacław to emerge. Storm clouds had rolled in from the west while we'd been in the longhouse, but that sliver of light was enough to show the warriors' smirks.

The Drowning of Marzanna had been nothing but a complete disaster. While I hadn't really known what I expected, it wasn't this. Dziewanna still wasn't talking to me, my childhood friend turned rival was apparently a demon, no boy had dared to approach me the entire night, and now, the tribe was about to march against the Solgawi.

Let war come.

We hadn't gone to war since I'd become a szeptucha, but the other channelers talked often about the chiefs' use of our sorcery in battle. That was the last thing I wanted. My job was to serve the gods, not help the generals prove who was the most arrogant.

Even the fire jump had gone wrong. It was supposed to have represented my crossing into adulthood. Instead, all I'd done was worry about the mark on Wacław's hand.

It was stupid to care. Wacław had turned his back on me, scorned me like everyone else. I wanted to do the same to him. I wanted to forget our childhood and focus on fulfilling my role. But I couldn't. I hated that.

We anxiously awaited the decision of the chiefs after Mieczysław's outburst. While I didn't understand all the chiefs' intricate diplomacy, the strain on Jacek's face had been obvious. Mieczysław had backed him into a corner—abandon his allies or lose his most powerful chief.

Wacław had given his father a way out, but as I'd looked at the warriors gathered, licking their lips like they could already taste blood, I'd known war would come anyway. Whether it was against the Solgawi or the eastern clans didn't matter. They were blind to the real threat. We'd seen the army chasing those clans, and whether Jacek believed it or not, if we failed to prepare, we were doomed.

When the chiefs emerged, the oaf, Chief Marek, quickly revealed the agreement they'd reached. I doubted Jacek appreciated him loudly preaching his war plans, but Marek's mouth was even bigger than his muscled arms.

"The Solgawi will die!" he so eloquently proclaimed, his ax held high as the warriors joined him in a chorus of cheers.

I rolled my eyes. *Idiots.*

"Why do they blame Wacław?" Ara asked me. "He came up with the idea."

The warriors around us did exactly that. In one group, Narcyz sneered and insulted him for choosing to settle the clans in the southern hills. Marek seemed more content with the fight but imitated Wacław's surprise when Jacek had declared his intention to march west.

Ignoring the men's arguments, I shrugged and fixed my wreath. The thing was beautiful but itching worse by the minute. "Because he disobeyed his father," I said to Ara. "The chiefs don't appreciate others having opinions." *And often, neither do the gods.*

Marek lumbered toward me, each of his steps more awry than the one before it. "Little witch," he slurred.

One flick of the wrist.

"You look *different*," he said with another swig of oskoła.

"Shouldn't you be sober for a war council?"

"My mind is better when…" He stumbled and caught himself. "Your father would like you with a chief."

I scoffed. "I'm sure Father would be very impressed by the five valiant warriors from your village. Go throw yourself at someone else."

I snatched Ara's arm and pulled her to the trails. Waiting for Wacław's embarrassed face wasn't worth it with thugs like Marek around. I just wanted the night to end, but if Mokosz's next visions was true, Wacław would face the zmora tonight. I cursed myself for starting that ritual.

Why did I have to get curious? Maybe, if I hadn't reached out to Mokosz, I wouldn't have been wrapped up in Wacław's stupid submission to Marzanna. But I knew that thought was a lie.

"He really is a brute," Ara huffed as we passed by Perun's Oak. "I swear Marek popped a vein when you called out his village, though."

"Good," I muttered, glancing at the longhouse one last time.

What are you hoping for?

I didn't know, but something pulled me back there—a tether wrapped around my soul that forced me to stop at the trailhead. No matter how much I wanted to keep walking, I knew I couldn't. Wacław was the key to figuring out Marzanna's plan, whether she was dead or alive. Dziewanna would be disappointed if I walked away.

Ara looked back at me. "Otylia? What's wrong?"

I gritted my teeth. "Go find your boy. The gods still need me here."

"You sure? I can—"

"Just go!"

The shock in her eyes twisted my stomach. Undeterred by my pleading, she stormed toward the boys who had gathered near the trails to the river. *Why can't I just keep my mouth shut?*

Snickering erupted from the crowd as Wacław shuffled from the longhouse, his head hung with the warriors hurling insults at him. He'd stood up to Narcyz and Genowefa during the egg hunt. Despite Wacław's obvious fondness for her, he'd fought for me, and I pitied him as he disappeared into the woods without a glance in my direction.

With a sigh, I clutched Dziewanna's Bowmark amulet and whispered into the winds of the gathering storm, "What do I do now?"

No reply came. I'd known the answer before I'd asked, but something in me craved her affirmation. After following her directions for so long, her absence made the world feel cold and isolating. It was almost like when Mother had...

Goddesses don't die. They're not the same.

I shook my head and forced away my doubt. There was no time to dwell on Mother's death when Marzanna's presence still stained the earth.

A downpour began as I charged after Wacław, winding my way through the shadows and toward his house. My wreath grew heavy, and I tossed it away. Ara's mother had worked hard on it. None of the boys bothered to care, and with both it and the headscarf gone, my hair flowed freely behind me.

I treasured the cool rain against my scalp, a rare moment when my hair wasn't pulled tightly back in the traditional braid. No one's rules could control me here in the dark woods. I was free.

The yelps of couples scrambling for cover filled the forest. I grinned at their foolishness. The storm had been gathering for hours, but they'd been too busy drunkenly kissing and groping each other in the shadows to notice. Now they paid the price.

When I reached the tree line near Wacław and Lubena's farm, I only caught a glimpse of him slipping into the house, their stove's light casting a dull glow over his white tunic before he disappeared.

I knelt next to an oak and rested my hand on its trunk. The bottom of my dress was coated in mud, but I could clean it with the goddesses' powers. All that mattered was watching for Wacław.

There was no way to know when he would emerge in his soul-form, but I would be there when he did. I needed to see his power. I needed to understand why Marzanna wanted him. But most of all, I needed to know if yet another of Mokosz's visions were true. *Please let it be a quiet night.*

For almost an hour, I waited there on my knees. My hands braided my hair again. Then, I pulled twine and the bone talismans from my bag and wove them into the braid. It would've felt wrong without them.

When I finished, I whispered to the gods and hoped for a reply. I sensed Mokosz and her flow of time, yet Dziewanna was distant. Her power was there, but the usual warmth of her presence was gone, replaced by a void that left me chilled.

I rubbed my arms as I shivered and let out a sigh. *He's not coming.*

If Wacław was going to sneak out in his soul-form—as I'd seen him do many times when we were younger—surely he would've done it already. My energy was fading along with my patience, but as I stood and stretched, the door crept open.

A shadowy figure appeared in the cottage doorway. When it moved into the moonlight, an ashen glow illuminated Wacław's body. At once he seemed both there and not—neither in this world nor the afterlife. My heartbeat quickened. *It's been so long since I've seen his soul-form.* There had been a time when he'd needed to make himself visible to me in it, but I was a szeptucha now, capable of seeing hidden spirits and wandering souls.

With a glance over his shoulder, Wacław ran toward the forest across the trail. My legs ached watching him go, but I took a sharp breath and followed. *When will this stupid day end?*

13

Wacław

I wish I could dream.

SLEEP WOULD BE NO WELCOME ESCAPE for me that night. It never was.

When I returned home, soaking wet and frozen to the bone, Mom forced me into a hug. Although my mind was distant, I told her everything. I vented about Otylia, about Yuliya and Marzanna, and about every hope that Father had stolen from me.

Through it all, she held me in her arms. Then she sat on the edge of her bed, her face heavy. "Your father lost the meaning of love many years ago, and now he wishes to send you away like a mistake. If Marzanna truly commanded you to let the chiefs march our men to war, then speaking for peace was brave—far braver than anything your father has ever done."

I sat next to her, rubbing my thumb along Marzanna's Frostmark, now uncovered. "It didn't work. Father is attacking the Solgawi anyway, but what if the diviners are right? What if these riders from the east are the real threat? What if Marzanna wants the destruction to happen?"

"Then we pray that the gods protect us."

That's not enough. I stared up at the ceiling. "Marzanna called *me* for a reason. She awakened that power in *me* for a reason. Praying to the gods and hoping they answer isn't enough. Our journey will bring us allies in case this horde does come. I just… My heart says by surrendering to Marzanna's call, I've wound myself into something bigger than I can see. That scares me."

"This power that Marzanna has awoken in you is yours alone," she said, wrapping her hands around my Frostmarked palm. "I believe you will use it for what is right. If you refuse to speak with Dariusz, however, you should at least trust Otylia. That girl will never betray you."

I winced. "All this day, Marzanna has haunted me, but it's Otylia I keep thinking about. Why does it hurt so much to be around her? Why does it hurt so much to leave when I know it's the right thing?"

She gave a motherly smile—an uncomfortably knowing one. "Because, despite Marzanna and your father's interruptions, you've always dreamed of love and your own adventure. Our hearts rarely follow our minds. You deserve the world, and I'm sorry the world is too fickle to feel the same."

I laid my head on her shoulder and forced myself to breathe. "You'll be okay without me?"

She stroked my hair, soothing me as she sighed. "I will miss you every moment, my Wašek, but I've always known you're meant for more than a life with me on this farm."

"What if I don't care what I'm meant to be?"

With a chuckle, she kissed my head. "The gods hardly give us a choice."

When I fell asleep and rose in my soul-form, Mom's sobs from across the room had ceased. She'd said many times that she wished I couldn't hear her cry to the gods for my sake. My heart always ached at the sound.

Something pulled my mind as I stood and felt the warmth flowing from the stove. The air seemed to hum in the small room, and my breaths caught as I reached into my bag and rolled the golden egg in my hands, wondering of its secrets.

Otylia and Yuliya had said the stories of the egg's gift were true. Still, I doubted whether the gods would truly grant me such a blessing. Whatever lay within me had combined with the egg to cause the storm. While a part of me craved the thrill of the power coursing through my veins, it was frightening how close I had come to death.

It wasn't the egg that called me, though. Nothing changed with it in my hand, and dread filled me as I drew Marzanna's dagger from its sheath.

The room's warmth faded into a sharp chill. My Frostmark stung. Around me, the hum morphed into a voice as I rubbed my thumb along two new symbols etched in the blade, *"Find me."* There was power in the words, coaxing me to follow their command—Marzanna's command.

With a shudder, I drove the dagger back into its sheath. Otylia had protected me with Dziewanna's blessing, so I wasn't under Marzanna's influence any longer. At least I hoped.

The whispers continued, though, and I groaned as I snuck toward the door, hoping Mom wouldn't hear. No sound came from her bed.

It's all in my head.

Outside, a storm raged as the trees bent beneath the weight of Strzybóg's winds and Perun's lightning strikes. I stood in awe of the gods' powers, and though the rains soaked my soul-form, I let out a laugh as the voices disappeared from my mind. There were times in which I wished my night journeys would leave forever. This was not one of them.

I sprinted into the woods, free from Marzanna's calls and the judgmental glares of Father and his chiefs, Mikołaj and his friends. For a few precious moments, I was truly alone.

Then the whispers returned.

"Find me…"

I spun around, examining the dark forest as my heart raced. The voices were no longer in my head. Someone, or something, was out there, baiting me to follow Marzanna's call. "Who's there?" I asked.

Silence.

Stepping back, I froze as my foot squished against something that definitely wasn't mud. When I regained my footing, I stared down at my boot in the dim light. Red covered it.

A deer carcass lay among the trees, but this was no hunter's kill. The entire side of it had been torn out. Deep claw marks ran from the deer's shoulders down its back, where traces of a black substance coated its hind legs.

As I knelt to examine the deer closer, a shrill squeal came from the pasture. *Tanek.*

I took off toward the horse without a second thought. The rain obscured my vision as I darted through the tree line and hopped the wooden fence. He was nowhere in sight, but he never screamed like that. Revealing my soul-form to Tanek, I whistled and trudged through rain-soaked pasture.

Another cry came from the other end of the pasture, opposite of our house.

"Tanek!" I yelled, rushing toward him as the wind and rain whipped my face, tearing at my skin. I wished it wouldn't leave marks behind, but any damage that my soul-form took, my physical one suffered as well.

Tanek's outline came into view. He bucked and spun, whinnying as I closed in with my hands up. Pain arced across my Frostmark palm. "Whoa boy... Whoa..."

Lightning flashed. A second of light—just enough to illuminate the creature upon his back.

I shivered as the bony, white-haired beast laid its cold eyes on me. Shaped like an unfed woman, decaying skin hung loose on its body and dark pus oozed from where the skin no longer covered.

Demon.

As it screeched and scampered off Tanek on all fours, I cursed myself for not bringing a spear. Each of its movements cracked and creaked, like bones snapping against each other. An eerie mist streamed behind it as I scrambled back, but the mud closed around my ankle, sending me into the muck. I writhed, desperate, as the creature approached.

The dagger! I fumbled with the sheath, my hands shaking. The demon was mere strides away now, and the smell of decay choked me as I pulled the blade.

The demon snarled and lunged. I stumbled. Its bloodied claws streaked toward me, each a knife of their own, but I spun just in time.

Sliding past, the demon struggled for footing in the mud. My breaths were weak as I looked from it to Tanek. In the moonlight, deep streaks bled on his side as he let out another squeal and charged the beast.

"No!" I shouted. But it was too late.

Tanek reared and struck at the creature, crunching what few solid bones seemed to remain. For a moment, the demon wailed and curled into itself. Then it lashed out at him.

The sound of claws slicing flesh hit me. Tanek's cry tore a hole in my heart. He kicked free, but blood coated his leg. As he limped away, the creature screeched again and turned to me, a savage thirst in its eyes.

My hesitation was gone. Rage replaced fear. Tanek may have been only a horse, but he was one of my best friends. I couldn't let this creature kill him.

With a shout, I gripped the dagger and charged as it did the same.

We clashed in a battle of claws, blades, and gnashing teeth. I stabbed at where I thought its brain to be, but it was too quick. Each time I lunged, it dashed around me and raked its claws across my arms and torso, tearing my tunic to shreds as blood dripped to the muck at our feet.

"What do you want?" I growled as I clutched my chest.

It circled me without an answer. Black poured from its eyes, oozed from its broken body. I sensed its craving to kill, but as it charged, Xobas's lessons flashed in my mind. I waited until I could smell its rancid breath. Then, I dove to the side, letting the creature pass and driving the dagger into its back.

A blood curdling cry escaped its gruesome mouth. Its glare bore into me as it spun, ripping the blade from my hand.

I staggered. The winds whirled around us, but the deathless monster ignored their force. It scampered forward, its body slithering like a hunting dog excited to make its kill. Then the dagger began to glow upon its back.

"The winds serve you," a voice whispered. *"Call and they will answer."*

A power raced through my veins—the same as when I'd first held the egg—swelling within my chest and arcing between my fingers. The creature creaked closer, but I focused on that energy and the eight winds that carried the storm on their gales. I shut my eyes and took a deep breath.

The air surrounded me, consumed me, became me. Memories of my flight in Marzanna's vision filled my mind. I clung to them and sensed each shift of the winds, expecting them, knowing them, and then controlling them.

When the demon bounded forward with a screech, I shouted with all my rage, commanding the winds to sweep it away.

Nothing happened.

The demon's claws flew toward me. I panicked and covered my face, waiting for the end.

A blast knocked me from my feet. The creature screamed as the sound of crunching bones filled the air. I dared to open my eyes as the winds intensified. The beast fought the torrent and crawled toward me, pus and black blood covering where its arms used to be. Mangled flesh mixed with the mud, and only fear stopped me from vomiting as it struggled closer.

The power pulsed within me now as the winds traversed the land. Everywhere they touched, I sensed like the tips of my fingers, and I let my anger merge with them as I clenched my fists.

The winds went mad. They smacked the creature to the ground. As it screeched and fought to stand again, another gust sent it flying into the fence.

Tanek neighed from across the pasture, but the winds and my rage deafened me to his calls. I felt all the resentment that I'd forgotten I had at Father, at Narcyz, at Mikołaj, at everyone who had ever laughed at my struggle. The eight winds fueled the storm within me. I plunged my anger into them, demanding they destroy the creature.

They obeyed.

The demon cried out as the winds collided like two great armies, crushing it between them. Its bones cracked and its muscles tore as I pushed the gales harder, as if I was driving my spear through its heart. All of its screams, its pain, they felt good. I wanted it to pay for what it had done to Tanek, how it had injured my friend.

After a minute of the screeching, whatever life filled that decrepit creature gave way. Its body went limp, and I released the winds. The power faded, replaced by a void of exhaustion.

The air stood still. The storm ceased. In the distance, a crow cawed and took flight. It soared through the trickling rain as I dropped to my knees, allowing the muck to cover me.

What was that? Blood and muck coated my hands. The power had faded as quickly as it had come, along with my fury—both scared me as much as the demon. I had commanded the gales and destroyed a monster, yet with regret filling my heart, I wondered if I had become one in the process.

Tanek whinnied and shuffled over to me, apparently in better condition that I'd thought. The rain had washed much of the blood away, but the gruesome cuts remained. Exhausted, I forced myself to stand and wrap my arms around his neck.

"I knew it!" a voice called from across the trail.

I whipped my head around as Otylia hopped the fence, no longer in her white and black head-wreath. The flashes of lightning in the distance illuminated her green eyes as she stared directly at me, smirking. *Can she see me?*

"I know you're there, Wacław, cradling your horse."

Tanek exhaled as she drew nearer. "How can you see me?" I asked. "It's been four years since I willed my soul-form to be visible to you."

"Despite you shutting me out, I am a szeptucha and see some of what lies beyond the physical world—including wandering souls like you." She studied the wounds across Tanek's side, care replacing the usual fierceness of her gaze. "His wounds should heal on their own, but if you'll let me call Dziewanna to mend her animal, I can speed up the process."

I nodded reluctantly. Otylia had a nasty knack of appearing when I least expected her, leaving me with more questions than answers. Though she had helped me more times in the last day than I wanted to admit to myself, it didn't make me forget our bitterness from the past few years. Something inside me hoped that could change.

"Thank you," she said. "Hold him still. That'll make this easier."

I did as she said, resting my head against Tanek's muscular neck. His heart raced. "It'll be okay, buddy. The crazy witch will make it better."

"Call me a witch one more time and you'll wish I hadn't saved you from that whirlwind." She pulled a tuft of herbs from her bag and chanted as she held her hand over the wounds, calling a blessing on them one at a time. Though she winced at the sight of the deep cuts, her hands were calm, unshaken.

When she finished, the plants in her hand withered, and she dropped them into the mud. Confused, I asked, "What was—?"

"I told you. All sorcery requires some life force to draw from, even though my powers come from Dziewanna and Mokosz." She looked to the dead creature before returning her gaze to me. "When I healed Marzanna's mark earlier, I drew from my own strength. It takes time for the goddesses to restore my *żityje*, and it wasn't worth me wasting more of it on your horse."

"Tanek."

She raised her brows.

"His name is Tanek."

A grin crossed her face as she rested her hand on his back. "You would name your horse *Immortal*."

"Jealous?"

Her eyes narrowed. "No. Horses are Dziewanna's creatures, so

as a follower of her, I connect with them too. He says you smell."
She turned away and approached the demon, the bottom edge of her
dress dragging through the mud behind her.

I sighed and followed. "What is that thing? What did you mean
when you said you 'knew it'?"

When we reached the broken fence, she examined the demon's
long claws and jagged teeth. Dark blood coated its entire body. The
smell of decaying flesh had only gotten worse, and it took everything
I had not to gag.

Disgust covered Otylia's face as she gingerly moved the strands
of white hair from the demon's face. "You killed a zmora. If you
hadn't caught it drawing the life from Tanek, it would have come for
you next. As for what I knew... Let's finish here first."

I tried to remember the stories I'd heard of zmory as a child.
There wasn't much besides that they, like most demons, were the
restless souls of the dead who never reached Nawia.

"It was drawing from Tanek's life force?" I asked.

She wrinkled her nose as she touched the dagger in the zmora's
back. "His *żityje*, yes. That's what zmory do—suck away their victim's
life, usually as they sleep. Demons are powerful but don't regenerate
their own *żityje*. They need to draw it from another source to survive.
Animals have less life force than people, and people have less than
szeptuchy. A horse, though, is an easier target."

"Why would it come for me? I doubt it's a coincidence it showed
up after Marzanna summoned me." I pointed to the dagger in the
zmora's back. "There was another message. *Find me.*"

"I told you Marzanna would punish you for your betrayal, but I
didn't expect it to be so soon." She stood and pulled a knife of her
own. "Draw the dagger and replace it with this. When people question the zmora's death, you'll say you killed it. Maybe then they'll
forgive you for trying to settle clansmen in our territory."

Ignoring her last comment, I knelt and pulled the dagger. Black
blood spewed from the wound, and I winced as she handed me her
blade. "Why are you helping me?" I asked. "After everything we've
been through, I thought you hated me."

"Maybe I do. Maybe I don't. But helping you is in my best interest. My divinations were not as clear as the combined efforts of Mokosz's szeptuchy, but I sensed it too. There is something coming. More than just the clans. We need to be united if we're to defend Dziewanna's forests from whatever it is."

I drove the knife into the zmora's skull and quickly stood, trying to get the noise of it squishing through flesh out of my head. "You care about the woods but not the tribe?"

She sighed and stared into the trees just across the trail. Her braided black hair shimmered in the moonlight as it draped down her shoulder and over her chest. I forced myself to look away, hating that I'd looked at her like that again.

"Chieftains and their petty struggles come and go," she said. "Our tribe is not the first. It won't be the last. The powers of these woods sustained our ancestors as they have us. If we were to lose them, we would lose our identity and our connection with the gods, with Dziewanna and maybe even Mokosz."

Her eyes snapped to me, the fierceness I had always known returning to them as she continued, "So, yes, if protecting the tribe saves the wilds, then I will work with foolish boys and cruel warriors to do as Dziewanna wishes."

Before I could reply again, she strode toward the woods and left me alone with the dying winds and a sinking feeling in my chest. "Where are you going?" I asked, jogging to keep up.

She entered the forest and glanced back. "Stop talking and follow me."

My energy from before was gone as I stopped on the path's edge, watching her push on. In a flash, the winds had given me all the strength in the world and taken it away just as quickly. Was this emptiness me lacking the life force, the *żityje*, she'd talked about?

A chill tickled my back, and the trees creaked in the wind overhead. I took a deep breath and felt the breeze's rustling along their bark as if it were my own fingers. The fear of my new power faded only slightly, but with my eyes closed, I let myself enjoy the sensation.

Though my feet never left the dirt, I could've sworn I was dancing with the winds.

"Come on, Half-Chief. Unlike you, I'm not currently sleeping, but I would like to be before dawn."

A laugh escaped my lungs as I smiled and ran after her. I had no idea what power coursed through my veins, but for the first time since I'd picked up that dagger, hope filled me. *Adventure, here I come.*

14

Wacław

What is happening to me?

OTYLIA'S SHADOWED FRAME led me deep into the woods without a word.

Around us, the forest seemed to have forgotten it was night. Birds fluttered, their wings beating against the air as they searched for either food or a place to nest. Each flap was a tingle on a fifth limb, and if I focused, I could follow each one's movements until they disappeared into the distance. When that focus faded, I became aware of everything once again—a sea of sensations drowning me.

The longer we walked, the worse it became. My brain spun at the onslaught of senses the winds sent through me, but I was numb to the touch of my body against anything physical. All I felt was the air and the rain. Then I tripped over a log.

Pain rushed through my shoulder as I hit the ground, coating my arms in another layer of mud. *Mom would kill me if this was my actual tunic.*

When I stumbled back to my feet, Otylia crossed her arms. "I appreciate the help," I quipped.

She rolled her eyes and turned. "We're almost there. Try not to let a mud demon eat you before we arrive."

"You put that log there, didn't you?" I caught up and walked beside her. "Like those pranks you played on me after…" My voice trailed off, but we both knew what I meant—after I had stopped seeking her out.

Her head dropped for a moment. "This isn't a prank, and those… We need to keep moving."

My chest ached as I followed, wondering if I could ever fix what Father had broken. "Why does—"

"Shhh," she whispered as she pulled me down to kneel next to her. "We're here, but something isn't right."

We were at the edge of the swampland near the Wyzra. I pushed aside the line of brush that blocked my view and swallowed when I saw the lurking demon ahead. The strips of moonlight creeping through the barren trees illuminated the slimy skin and gills along its neck. *Why can nothing be easy today?*

"What is that thing?" I asked. My Frostmark throbbed at the sight of it, just as it had done near the zmora.

Otylia's eyes remained fixed on the demon "I don't understand. An utopiec would never defile Dziewanna's altar." She looked at my blank face and groaned. "It's the restless soul of someone that drowned in the swamp. I need to move closer. Stay here."

The cuts on my arm almost tickled as I gripped Marzanna's dagger, reluctant to use it again but too curious not to continue on. "Why don't we, you know, try to settle it instead?"

Her eyes narrowed. "You want to *settle* a monster like that? Go ahead if you want your guts ripped out."

"Then I could come back and do the same to you," I muttered. "If it's only a demon because of how it died, are you certain there's no way for us to calm its soul and send it to Nawia peacefully?"

The rain pattered against the soft ground as she furrowed her brow. Around us, the breeze picked up again. My hesitation faded along with my fear as the power danced at my fingertips, as if the gusts longed for me to command them. Though exhaustion still gripped me, my craving for that strength was stronger.

With a flick of my wrist, the winds brushed against the creature.

Slime, fungus, and soaked, decaying flesh covered it from head to toe. My stomach churned. I released them and stepped back, cringing.

"What?" Otylia sneered.

"It's disgusting," I said as I tried to shake the awful taste out of my mouth.

Her eyes widened. "You used the winds again?"

"How do you know that?" I asked, agitation creeping into my voice. All day she'd been concealing something, and I was sick of her not telling me what was going on.

"Be quiet! I'll tell you once we—"

The utopiec leaped from the shadows. It pulled her into the deep swamp waters ahead as she fought and tried to crawl away. But it was far faster than a beast of its size should've been.

"Do something!" Otylia cried out.

I forced away my daze and charged as the creature spun, gurgling and fixing its yellow eyes on me. With the force of the winds at my back, I drove the dagger at the utopiec's head, but before I struck, it dropped Otylia and dove into the waters.

Where'd you go?

I scanned the bog, dagger ready. There was nothing but the breeze, the distant birds, and Otylia's curses as she struggled to stand. I choked as fear took over. The demon could be anywhere, and we were just sitting ducks in the middle of its hunting grounds.

"What now?" I asked.

Otylia scowled and flexed her hands. The marks of Dziewanna and Mokosz glowed on her neck as the waters stirred around her, feeding on her rage. "It'll return, and I'm going to kill it when it does."

"Apparently someone else already did that."

Something grabbed my ankle. Suddenly, water filled my nose and mouth. I lashed out, kicking at the utopiec as it dragged me through the swamp. But this was its territory.

My lungs burned as I fought to bring my head above the surface, for one gasp of precious air. The utopiec surged on with me in tow.

I felt my mind slip, darkness edging into my vision and regret filling my heart.

Seconds later, the utopiec threw me through the air. Pain arced through my back as I crashed into a tree. Slumping into the muddied waters, I fought for each breath.

The creature slithered closer with hunger in its snake-like eyes. I scrambled for the dagger, but it was gone, lost somewhere in the swamp's endless waters. *Marzanna will definitely hate me now.* At the moment, though, I wasn't worried about the goddess but the reeking horror in front of me. Desperate, I pulled myself up the tree and reached for the distant winds.

There was no answer.

The creature grabbed my arm, its claws tearing into my skin before I kicked out, striking its stomach. As it stumbled back, I called for Otylia and ran deeper into the swamp.

My spine throbbed with each step, a constant reminder of the utopiec's strength. It would catch me if I remained in the depths. I desperately needed drier ground.

Its bloated gurgles drew closer as I sputtered and trudged on, the rain obscuring what lay ahead, but I dared not look back. The hope of dry land was all that kept me moving. One more glimpse of the beast would ensure panic took over. So, I ran on, not knowing if my efforts brought me closer to freedom or deeper into the creature's grasp.

These were not my woods—the ones that greeted me each morning and night. No, this maze of stretching roots and vines, murky waters and still air, was something far more carnal, raw. All I knew was that I wanted to leave and never return.

"Wacław!"

I snapped my head around and hoped, if only for a moment. "Otylia? I'm here!"

Based on the echo of her call, she was too far, and the demon stood between us. I gathered what little confidence was in my heart as I reached into the air. The winds were still but ever-present. *I just need something. Please…*

The creature seemed to smile with the sight of me stopping. I swallowed and pushed harder, grasping for the power I'd felt in the pasture and woods. Finding the winds was a puzzle, though, and I couldn't solve the pattern. I cursed whatever had given me those night wanderings and squared up with the beast. Hopefully, Xobas's lessons could buy me enough time for Otylia to arrive with her sorcery.

The utopiec dove into the deeper waters again. This time, I saw it coming and cut off the move. It snarled and snapped as I wrapped it in a sloppy chokehold. Every muscle in my body complained, but I clung on.

I didn't know if I had the pressure applied right. I didn't even know if the beast could be choked. Before I found out, it grabbed hold of my tunic and tore me off its back.

I sputtered in its grasp and shouted for Otylia. With everything I had, I fought to remain on my feet, but it swirled around and drove my skull into a rock.

My head stung as I dropped into the bog. I tried to cry out in pain, but that only let more water fill my throat as I shut my eyes, willing myself to focus and avoid the fear surging through me. Instinctively, my hands found the muck coating the bed of the swamp. I lowered myself and allowed the creature to hold me against it. Then I pushed.

The force shot me up into the beast. As it stumbled back, I gulped down every breath of air I could as my head broke the surface. I shivered, suddenly aware of how cold I really was, soaked to the bone in the chilled swamp water.

Where are you, Otylia? How long had it been since I'd heard her call? My spinning mind had no clue, and as the utopiec gripped my arm again, I had no time to search for her.

With the little energy I had left, I shouted in frustration and swung at the demon's face with my free hand. The blow landed, but it barely flinched.

"You can have your swamp," I told it, trying to pull away. "I never wanted to come here anyway!"

The utopiec's webbed hand closed around my throat, cutting off my already sore lungs. I pulled against its arm and fingers, but it was too strong. It had failed to kill me twice. From the vengeful look in its eyes, I knew it wouldn't let me escape again.

As my air faded away and my hands dropped into the water, a current brushed against them. It was faint, but with my vision fading, I could see a pair of striking green eyes in the moonlight.

Then the world turned dark. An eerie calm replaced the pain, the struggle. The air and water flowed around me as if I was flying through both land and sea. *Is this death?* When the creature released me, the thought of Mom weeping beside my battered corpse filled my mind as I drifted to the depths of the swamp. *I'll never get to say goodbye.*

15

Otylia

I hate demons.

THE UTOPIEC SLASHED AT THE ROOTS that swallowed its legs, gurgling and groaning as I channeled Dziewanna's power and willed the roots to pull it down. My arms were heavy and my body exhausted, but Wacław had gone under almost a minute before. He wouldn't have much air left. And the demon stood between him and me.

Now or never. Dreading the state of my dress, I dove into the thick water. Each stroke was through more mud than anything, but I made progress. Slowly.

The monster fought against the roots as I swam. Their strain tore at my strength, the pain of Dziewanna's life struggling against the undead. *Almost there...* My herb bag, my only extra source of energy, was somewhere back near the altar, and the little *žityje* I had left drained steadily from my soul.

Seconds later, Wacław's body appeared at the bed of the swamp. My hand closed around his wrist, but just when I started to hope, pain shot across my back. The demon's claws tore into me, ripping through my dress. With my muscles screaming and my lungs begging for air, I ignored the pain and pulled Wacław to the surface. He still wouldn't wake.

"Gods help me!" I yelled as the utopiec attacked.

His claws raced toward me, slicing through the darkness as I gripped Dziewanna's bow amulet. I wished I had the knife I'd given Wacław. I wished I hadn't wasted my energy on his stupid hand. Wishes didn't matter. But Dziewanna's power did.

A shock ran through my body when the demon's claws struck. My skin glowed bright for an instant. Then, all went dark as *życie* rushed from my soul.

Hissing, the utopiec tumbled backwards with steam rising from its hands. I fell into the shallows as a rancid smell pierced the air.

What was that?

My hands shook as the utopiec fought the roots covering its decaying body. The force was the same that had calmed the whirlwind earlier—the one that had saved Wacław four years before. Its source was neither Dziewanna or Mokosz.

It had come from me.

Whatever the force was had passed, though. And the demon's eyes were fixed on me.

I whispered for Dziewanna to finish the utopiec, my calls hanging in the still air. At first, there was no answer. But when the utopiec growled and charged, the willows around us creaked. Their branches reached toward the demon, entangling its arms and legs. I smirked as I wielded the trees like my own body. Their strength was at my fingers, and with every bit of *życie* I had left, I sent a branch through the utopiec's head. It released a final shriek, dropping into the waters.

I collapsed with the creature. Rain poured on me and matted my hair. An exhaustion worse than I'd ever felt gripped me as I knelt in the shallows, my hands in the muck and my dress ragged and torn.

I hate festivals.

The demon shouldn't have been anywhere near Dziewanna's altar. I'd fought a few demons in my life to protect the wilds around Dwie Rzeki. Occasionally, they would wander around altars before being driven off by the god's power, but this one had been strides away from the willow where Dziewanna's altar stood. As it lay in the murky waters ahead of me, I sensed Marzanna's chill on it.

A growl escaped my throat as I struggled to my feet. Between Marzanna's plots and Dziewanna's silence, I had a sinking feeling things weren't going to get any better.

Wacław floated in the shallows. An array of willow catkins had fallen onto his face and chest. If I hadn't been frustrated and exhausted, I would've laughed at the demonic boy covered in flowers. Instead, I trudged my way through the water and grabbed hold of him.

At least he's light. He was thinner than Marek, but the altar was back toward the entrance to the swamp. Every muscle in my body throbbed as I dragged him along.

I hadn't known where the utopiec had taken him after its first attack. The stupid thing had lunged out of nowhere and surprised me. I wished it hadn't been because I was distracted by Wacław, but remembering his betrayal had jarred me for just long enough. I wouldn't let it happen again.

Still, there had been a tether between us. It had led me to him before he'd called out, and without it, he probably would've drowned. That shouldn't have scared me as much as it did.

As I pushed forward, I failed to fight the questions in my mind. Why had Wacław forced me away from him? Was it his father? Mine? My channeling? My jaw throbbed—I'd been gritting my teeth.

Why does he get to me so easily?

All the other boys had ignored me the entire festival. I could shrug that off. But something in me refused to hate Wacław for ignoring me when I'd needed him. In less than a moon, I'd lost my mother and best friend. My heart had never stopped longing to have both of them back. *Grow up.*

Wacław's tunic was torn like my dress. Despite the waters washing away the blood, the deep slashes across his chests and arms didn't look good. I would do what I could at the altar to heal his soul-form, but the scars would linger on his body.

The rain lightened by the time I finally reached half-dry land.

Mud covered the ground near Dziewanna's altar—a wood-carved idol alongside her willow. A dark wooden table stretched before it with roots twisting up its base. I'd prepared hundreds of sacrifices here since Dziewanna had chosen me, and despite not completely understanding how it amplified the goddess's power, I'd done what she asked. Having the answers was the gods' responsibility, not mine.

When I finally pulled Wacław out of the water, I dropped next to him, fighting for each breath. Dziewanna's statue stood over us, a nocked bow in her hand and vines climbing her legs as her long hair flowed down her body. *Why won't you answer?*

My heart stopped as the moon exposed the black spots across the willow's trunk and branches. I scrambled forward and examined the disease. "No, no, no, no, no!"

Tears burned my eyes, and I drove my fist into the trunk as I screamed in rage. Only one thing could've done this. Only one thing could've sent the zmora to attack Wacław and the utopiec to poison Dziewanna's altar.

Marzanna.

I knelt in the mud, shaking from exhaustion as my soaked hair coated my face. "I'll kill you! You hear me, Marzanna? I don't know how, but I'll find where you're hiding and feed you to the wolves. If the gods of spring failed, I promise you, I won't."

First, I needed to find my herb bag and tend to Dziewanna's Willow. It had to be around here somewhere. I peered through the rain to the trail we'd taken in. There, the bag floated in the shallow waters, half the herbs I'd collected surrounding it.

My legs were stiff as I forced them to carry me back into the water and toward the bag. I didn't shiver, despite the cold. Between the rain, my rage, and the eternity it'd taken to drag Wacław to the altar, my body had numbed a long time ago. It was rare for me to wish for home, where Father would surely be ready to scold me for my tardiness, but the relentless grip of the dress's sopping cloth against my skin and emptiness I felt in my soul were enough.

Why am I the one stuck with him?

Any experienced channeler would've known what to do with Wacław. They would have slain the utopiec before it had the chance to attack, and they would know how to stop Marzanna. But Mokosz had whispered to *me*. Dziewanna had sent her fox to guide *me* to Wacław. Why?

I remembered the first time I'd heard Dziewanna's voice.

After the initiation rituals, Dziewanna's spirit had connected with mine the moment I stepped into the woods. I sensed every root, every hair on a fox's back, every bristle on a willow's leaves, and the craving of an army of ants.

Then Dziewanna appeared as a beautiful young woman, a cyclone of leaves around her as she drifted to the forest floor. With a dress the color of willow's bark, a long cape of leaves swirling with the winds, and a crown of antlers adorning her head, nature itself made her its queen. I knelt as her striking green eyes studied me above her amused smile.

"Kneeling is for boys who cower before men they hope to kill," she said. "Stand."

My hands trembled as I did. Knowing that the goddess I'd always adored had revealed herself to me—her only szeptucha—was overwhelming. The initiation had formed me into her vessel, part of her wilds and made to serve her. It was every dream I'd ever had as a child. Yet, all I felt was fear.

Her hand cupped my cheek. It was wet like her swamps, yet it brought warmth to my face. When I struggled to look upon her, she pulled my gaze to hers and forced me to take in her stunning face, undamaged and unblemished. "You are mine above all others, Otylia. You are my only szeptucha, my only daughter."

"Why me?" I stammered. "Why would you choose me as your first?"

She smiled. "Because I see myself in you—young, ambitious, and willing to fight for what you believe in. When all of Perun and Swaróg's priests had forgotten me, you didn't."

"Mother... Mother gave me your amulet and showed me your ways. We prayed to you every night, but she got sick and—" Tears welled in my eyes and stopped me in my tracks.

"Odeta loved you. I have seen her in Nawia, and she is proud of the woman you are becoming. She had to leave you too soon—that changes nothing." Her fingers wiped the tears from my cheek as she cradled my head and untied my braid. "I heard your prayers, little one. I know the pain of your solitude, of your loss, but I will never leave you. Together, you and I are free, even if fathers and warriors seek to control us."

"I don't understand. Why am I chosen by more than one?"

"It's for the best that you don't know everything now, my child, but I promise, when the time is right, I will tell you all the secrets of the Three Realms." She stepped back and joined her hands with mine. Her power flowed through our connection as sorrow seemed to creep into her eyes. "Until then, you will protect my altar and my wilds. You will make sacrifices and worship me. And my power will be yours."

I will never leave you. Now, those words stung my ears as I reached my bag and clutched its mucky cloth against my chest.

I felt like a fool kneeling in the shallows with a half-full bag of herbs, blood trickling down my arms and back. Everything had fallen apart so quickly. I should've been home, but Marzanna had poisoned Dziewanna's altar. My goddess needed me. Wacław needed me. Sleep could wait.

Wacław's breaths were shallow when I returned to the altar. Streaks of red and pale skin crisscrossed his chest where the demons had clawed him. I'd thought him dead when the zmora charged, but then he'd called the winds.

And they'd listened.

I had no doubt that he was a płanetnik now. Father had told me stories about the lost spirits of men who had been hung or drowned. Some served Strzybóg, god of the winds, and his eight grandchildren, but there were ranks of the płanetnikami. The storm demons that collected the clouds, lightning, and rain often chose the most powerful among them to be their leader. They could either help villages or cause chaos and destruction with their power. Only rumors had ever spoken of one being alive.

I threw my bag on the table and grabbed the wooden mortar and pestle from within it.

Mother had taught me how to make hundreds of potions. None of them were for healing whatever Wacław's soul-body was, but one came to mind. She'd said it would mend a broken soul. If he was a living demon, I couldn't think of anything more broken.

It was a long time before Wacław heaved awake. The noise startled me, and I dropped the pestle as he spun toward me with his arms raised.

I rolled my eyes. "Relax. The demon's gone. Here." I shoved the mortar to his mouth and forced him to drink the potion.

As he slurped the first drops, his lips puckered. He pulled back, but I insisted, "All of it." From experience, I knew it smelled and tasted foul, like the contents of a rotten egg, but there were more pressing issues than his taste buds.

He drank with his forehead wrinkled, and I let myself snicker at his struggle. "What did I just drink?" he asked when he finished, shuddering at the aftertaste.

"It's a potion Mother used to make me drink before she..." My throat caught. I stared down at my hands before swallowing my sorrow and meeting his gaze. "It's supposed to be good for the soul and healing. Given that this isn't your real body, I figured it might help."

Wacław gasped as I paced over to the altar to begin the potion for the tree, "Your back..."

"I'm fine!" I snapped.

It was a lie. I didn't want to talk about how alone I felt without Dziewanna's voice guiding me or how each slice on my back was a jagged line that stung with every movement. Instead, I focused on cutting the herbs as agitation surged through my veins. *Why am I so tense?*

Wacław groaned, pushing himself to his feet and standing awkwardly near the water. "Thank you... I guess I owe you for saving my life, again."

For a second, I looked at him and the regret in his eyes. *Is that for me or Mother?* I nodded, not knowing what to say, and returned to my work. Only the breeze and the sound of distant frogs in the swamp broke the silence between us as I continued cutting. But then Wacław approached.

"That's close enough, Half-Chief," I said without looking up from the table.

He stopped and took a deep breath of the musty swamp air. *He'll regret that.* Like the potion, it stunk like rotting eggs. "What is this place?" he asked.

"Dziewanna's altar."

"You're in quite the talkative mood tonight."

My slicing quickened. "It's safe to say I have spent more than my fair share of time with you since I found you in the woods."

I bit my tongue, instantly regretting those words as he stepped away. Whether he was a demon or not, it wasn't his fault Marzanna had sent the utopiec and poisoned Dziewanna's Willow. There was just so much unsaid between us. I didn't know where to start.

"I'm sorry to be a burden," he finally replied, rubbing the back of his neck, "but you were the one that told me to follow you into the creepy monster-infested swamp."

"Fair point." I failed to hold back a tight-lipped smile. "I brought you here because I thought Dziewanna's altar would provide us a safe place to talk, away from Marzanna's ears and demons. I had hoped that maybe my goddess's voice would guide us. Instead, she's silent and her tree is poisoned." I sighed and leaned on the table, closing my eyes and wrinkling my nose. "I don't believe it's a coincidence that all of this has happened to you around the Drowning of Marzanna."

"This *thing* inside of me is connected to the festival?"

"No, your power has been there all along. I think."

He groaned. "You think?"

Without needing to look at him, I sensed his agitation as I scraped the bits of herb into the mortar. I knelt at the base of the tree, whispering a spell to finish the healing potion. The herbs turned to a light green soup, and I rubbed it along the black splotches on the willow's bark.

"All I know is what my father has taught me," I said, "and I've only learned bits about demons like you."

"Demons?" He stepped back as fear blanketed his face. "What are you saying?"

Once I finished with the tree, I placed the mortar back on the table and clutched Mokosz's amulet. The bone was warm to the touch. My chest ached knowing the pain the truth would cause him, but he had to know. "If I'm right, you're a płanetnik. You can control the winds and weather—at least according to the legends. You're not supposed to be alive…"

A small breeze circled us, like Strzybóg was confirming my speculation, as Wacław stared down at his mud-coated hands. How a boy like him could be anything like the zmora or utopiec we'd faced? Despite the bitterness of his betrayal gripping my heart, he was far from those beasts. I pitied him.

"I always knew my night wanderings meant something," he finally said, his voice hushed. "This, though, was not what I expected. What does this mean? I'm dead?"

"You're obviously not dead, but I don't know. The only legends of living demons are from a long time ago. Even then, Father doesn't believe them." I huffed. "Apparently, he was wrong."

Wacław clutched his stomach and leaned against a nearby tree. "That whirlwind that almost killed me… Did Marzanna do that? Is that why she called for me?"

"Like I said, the golden egg's power somehow awakened your own. I don't know why you can only control it now, when you're asleep, but all of this has to do with the ice goddess." I grimaced. "The ritual should have weakened her strength and allowed the spring gods to defeat her, but she sent that zmora and must be behind the fading protections of Dziewanna's altar. She might still be alive."

I shuddered at the thought of Marzanna surviving. The past years had brought bountiful harvests, but no crops could be planted in the hard ground. If spring never came, our food supplies, everything, would be depleted before long. The wilds would die, and so would we.

"Are you certain it's her?" he asked. "Any of the wild spirits could have done this. Even the zmora may have been just a rogue soul searching for prey."

I furrowed my brow. "You speak as if you have studied the spirits and gods yourself. No, it must be her. The tree is sick... No ordinary spirit has the power to poison Dziewanna's Willow. Only the goddess of pestilence and death could do such a thing."

"But why Dziewanna?" he asked, stepping closer as desperation flooded into his voice. "And why would she need *me*?"

"I don't know!" I shouted.

My eyes widened in shock, and I clenched my jaw as I sat against the tree with my head in my hands. *Gods help me.* Each breath was sharp. Marzanna had already taken Mother from me, and I couldn't let her take Dziewanna too. The fear of not knowing how to fix it had my mind scrambling for an answer.

"I'm sorry," he said, barely louder than a whisper.

"For what?"

He stepped closer. "In one day, you've saved my life more than once, helped me heal, and answered the question of my night journeys that I've wrestled with my entire life. All I've done in response is pester you with questions while you try to repair Dziewanna's altar."

I met his gaze. Tears ran down my cheeks, and despite my attempts to fight them, they kept coming. "It doesn't matter. The tree was fine yesterday. If the poison is progressing this fast, there's nothing I can do to stop it..."

"Most of the tribe's priests and szeptuchy are here," he said as he crouched before me. His eyes seemed to glow against the dark swamp. "We can summon them. Surely, they can fix this together."

"No." I stared up at the willow and the black death creeping across it. The potion wasn't working. "This tree must be maintained by a follower of Dziewanna, and I'm the only one. The others consider her a lesser goddess—she doesn't even have an idol at the river—but they fail to understand how crucial she is to protecting nature."

"Apparently Marzanna didn't make the same error."

My hand closed around my Bowmark necklace as Wacław joined me against the tree. "I can't fail her, but I have no answer to what is happening. If Marzanna truly has survived the ritual, then we have far more to be concerned with than the squabbles of chiefs. *Let war come*. She wants us distracted."

He sighed. "Speaking of distractions: Father wants me to travel with Kajetan to the eastern clans. I wish I could help you here, but he says it's my responsibility to fulfill the plan. If this is a chance for peace, I have to go."

An idea sparked in my mind. In that moment, I knew there was no turning back. "Then I'll come with you."

His mouth gaped. "But…"

I breathed through my teeth as anticipation replaced my sadness. If Wacław was going east, then he could help me face Marzanna. Maybe, I wouldn't be alone. "The gods must have a representative at this meeting, and if the rumors are true, Marzanna's cult lies in the Mangled Woods. She killed Mother and poisoned Dziewanna's Willow. I have to find her and end this."

"How do you plan to do that?"

"Marzanna gave you a Thunderstone dagger. Father says its strong enough to kill a god."

"You believe him?"

"I believe Marzanna needs to die if Dziewanna's forests are ever going to be safe."

"There's just one problem," he said, staring down at his Frostmarked hand. "I lost it."

My forehead fell into my palm. "Please tell me that's a stupid joke."

"I wish it were."

"Then we'll find another way. I don't care how. I *will* find her."

He huffed and laid his head back against the tree, staring up at the few stars visible through the clouds. "Ironic. That's exactly what the dagger's last instructions were."

I thumbed Dziewanna's amulet. "Then it's decided."

"You don't want to think about this more? Neither Dariusz nor my father will be keen on allowing you to come. Even then, sure, we'll pass through the Mangled Woods to reach the clans, but I highly doubt Kajetan will be fond of this side-mission. And then we have to figure out how to kill a goddess."

Always hesitant. He was right that it was a risk, but there wasn't another option. I'd seen the destruction caused by the horde and had recognized Marzanna's presence in the demons. Both were threats, and the only way to stop them was to go east. "I can handle my father, but you must then convince the high chief. Tell him what we've discovered. I'd leave out the bit about you being a demon—I doubt Jacek would appreciate that part."

He cringed. "If you get to call me a demon, I most definitely get to call you a witch."

"It may take a demon and a witch to stop her."

"You really want to go into the Mangled Woods—where she probably has an army of demons, cultists, and channelers waiting for us—without any idea how to actually kill her?"

I slid my fingers across my muddied dress. It was a waste of such fine work. Knowing Ara's mother would see it tattered hurt almost as much as my wounds. "You and I fought hundreds of evil spirits together," I replied, the corner of my mouth flicking up for only a moment. "They might've been fake, but a death goddess can't be much worse than a child's imagination."

"Not sure I believe that." He shook his head. "Honestly, it's hard to believe any of this is happening—Marzanna, the war, me... any of it."

With exhaustion creeping into my head, I grabbed my bag and stood. My wet boots sloshed against the mud with each step as I paced toward the water. "It doesn't matter whether we believe it.

You started this when you took Marzanna's Frostmark, but it's up to us both to stop her. Talk to Jacek and convince him to let me come. Tell him to bring Ara too. She's good on the hunt, and those clans used to be her people."

16

Wacław

I'm a demon.

WHEN I AWOKE THE NEXT MORNING to Xobas shaking me, I groaned and rolled over, sick to my stomach. Leaving my soul-form for my physical one was never comfortable, but this was worse than ever.

"Wacław," Xobas's stern voice said. "You're late for training, and I'm sure Lubena doesn't appreciate my intrusion."

I winced as I struggled to sit up. The pain from last night's fights raced through my ribs and arms. I didn't know if the powers I'd wielded or the intensity of the fight had dulled the pain, but now, it flooded my mind. "Can you please tell Father that I'm incapacitated for the day?"

He huffed and dragged me from the bed. "We both know the high chief won't tolerate—" His jaw dropped when he noticed my bloodstained clothes. "Gods! What happened?"

Mom turned from the stove and gasped as I shook myself loose from Xobas's strong grasp. "I'm all right. Don't worry," I said.

"You're covered in blood!" she exclaimed, rushing to me to inspect my wounds. Most of the scrapes had closed overnight, but many still stung on my arms and chest. "Was this that Narcyz boy?"

How could I explain what had happened without revealing I was a płanetnik? The idea that I could command the winds was still so alien to me. All of yesterday seemed a dream—more like a nightmare—but dreams never came to me. I wished I could tell Xobas about my wanderings. If he learned now, though, he would inform Father. That would not end well for me.

"No," I started. "I heard Tanek screaming late last night and went to check on him. When I hopped the fence into the pasture, I saw a demon on his back, and, well, this happened."

"Why didn't you tell me?" Mom asked as she took my hands.

I relented to her care for a moment. After almost dying more times in one day than I bothered to count, she felt safe. I needed that. "By the time I killed it and finished treating Tanek's wounds, I could barely stand. I passed out when I fell into bed." I turned to Xobas and chuckled. "It didn't occur to me that Father would still expect me to train on the second day of the festival."

Arms crossed, he raised his brow. "A warrior's training never stops, but you're in no condition to fight. With your shield work, you would be writhing on the ground in less than a minute."

"If I had learned nothing from your lessons, I wouldn't have killed that demon."

"That is true," he said with a proud smile. "Dress yourself. The high chief will want to hear about this."

I smiled as he followed Mom outside. I knew stroking his ego would work, like it did with all the warriors. Each of them was different, but they all wanted glory, even if their share of it was teaching the Half-Chief how to hold a pointy stick.

Once they left, I pulled off my bloody clothes and examined the deep cuts on my arms and chest. At least a couple would undoubtedly scar—adding to those from the wolves four years before. I traced a particularly jagged slice from where my collarbone met my shoulder to the center of my ribcage. The skin was still reddened and raised, and it burned to the touch. Despite the pain, something in me hoped the other boys would see them and finally realize I wasn't the weakling they thought I was.

I knew the truth, though. They would think of the scars as nothing more than another set of imperfections, more reasons to mock and scorn me. I picked an earthen long-sleeved tunic to hide them. Someday, I would display my scars proudly like Xobas, but today was not it.

Mom returned after a few minutes, her caring eyes meeting me before she gave me one last hug. "I love you. Stay safe, and please don't fight any more demons."

I bowed my head. "I will try my best."

"You always do," she said with a smile and a soft hand on my cheek. "Even when others don't see the light in your actions."

I kissed her cheek and stepped out into the cool morning air, feeling the breeze drift through my hair. As I joined up with Xobas, though, something seemed off. Without the connection I had with the winds in my soul-form, it was as if I had amputated a limb by waking up. Nothing but the phantom sensations remained.

We followed the trail into the woods. The songs of the birds lofted through the trees above us as they conducted their own festival, hoping to find the love I had sought yesterday. What had been less than a day before seemed like an eternity ago. Now, I had to figure out life as a demon and stop whatever Marzanna planned.

What are her true intentions? Was she behind the approaching horde the diviners spoke of? Was she fighting desperately to survive instead of spending another seven moons trapped in Nawia? What did she want from me? I was dizzy just thinking about it all.

Halfway down the path to the village center, Xobas shifted his sheathed sword at his side. "You have never been much of a talker in the morning, but I can tell something's weighing on you. Speak."

My head dropped. I stared down at my boots in the thin layer of mud leftover from last night's showers. "I thought I had a chance to prove my worth and make a life for myself. Instead, it feels like everything important is decided by someone else."

"Sometimes, it is."

"And now Father expects me to travel through the Mangled Woods and negotiate with the clans."

"The high chief trusts Kajetan to keep the peace."

"Then why is he sending me?"

He wriggled his sharp jaw, considering the question for a second. "I don't know his secrets, never been interested in them, but your father will do what it takes to defend his legacy. He knows one of his sons will need to know how to negotiate."

I wrinkled my brow. "I would rather not have the fate of the tribe resting on me."

Isn't it already? Whatever Marzanna had planned would be far worse than the clans' horsemen. Still, my lip curled thinking about the ambassador's smug grin. I didn't know why Kajetan had it out for me, but it was unlikely he would paint a favorable picture of my involvement in the journey.

We reached the village center, where Perun's Oak glowed in Dadźbóg's early light. Father believed Perun to be chief of the gods, but I wondered what the god of thunder would do to stop Marzanna. While he was as distant as ever, his daughter's presence loomed over me.

Xobas caught my arm when we reached the door. "He's in a rough mood after last night. Don't make it worse."

"Is that an order, general?" I asked, trying to distract myself from my impending conversation with Father.

The look on his face told me he wasn't joking. "It's the advice of someone that wants to see you succeed. I've worked too long on you for him to kill you for saying something stupid."

Once I nodded, he released me and led the way into the dim longhouse. Father's glare hit me, and part of me wished he was a demon instead of the high chief. At least I knew what *they* intended to do.

"Wacław," Father began, standing from his chair, an array of brown and gray furs hanging loosely off him as he shuffled toward me. His skin was nearly white, and there was a hesitation in his step.

The sight stopped me cold. *He's sick.*

Father always took every measure to disguise any weakness, pestilence among them, and those heavy furs on a warm day were admitting his suffering. An uneasiness washed over me as I thought of

Marzanna and the diseases she brought upon us annually. His sickness may have been a coincidence, but he'd appeared to be fine yesterday. After what I'd seen last night, too many incidents pointed to the same culprit.

"Come." Father waved for me to join him as he sat at the long table in the center of the room.

Pushing aside my hesitation, I did, and in the eerie silence of the longhouse, the only noise was the shuffling of my leather boots against the dirt floor.

Xobas turned to leave, but Father raised his arm as I took a stool across from him. "Stay, I value your advice in times like these, as a friend and a general."

Xobas nodded and sat next to me. I glanced at his muscular forearms as he set them on the table, that horse tattoo and scar on display. It was in his veins to be a warrior, to follow what the chiefs told him to do—whether that chief was from his Simukie homeland or our tribe. He and I were different, but I envied him. While I searched for a purpose, he had found his a long time ago.

Father's gaze remained fixed on me. Even with the fatigue of the last day evident, there was a strength in him that could never fade, no matter what plagued him. After a few moments of silence, he spoke again, "I see you have chosen to skip your training."

Xobas started, "High Chief, the boy—"

"I hastily rushed a demon last night when I discovered it preying on Tanek," I interjected. "In the end, I managed to defeat it, but it scarred me in the process." I rolled up my sleeves to reveal the crisscrossed marks dancing up my forearms. Xobas had spoken for me enough. It was my turn to take the blame.

"My son…" he stammered. "What has come upon you with the end of the winter? Speaking out of line among the chiefs and now charging monsters that put your home in danger? Those are not the actions of my quiet second-born son."

Whatever energy I had seeped out of me. I studied my sliced and bruised arms, red and purple splotches harsh against my pale skin. "I'm sorry, my chief."

"What you did last night was foolish," Father continued, pausing to cough. "You have those scars because your actions were those of a young man so desperate to prove himself that he fails to think before he acts. Like I once was."

"You weren't mocked as the Half-Chief, though."

"No, I wasn't, but I was also the second-born, forced to watch my older brother receive all the praise and attention. You may not believe me when I say that I understand how it feels. Either way, it matters not. You defended your land and your mother last night. That bravery will inspire others as long as you do not allow your jealousy of Mikołaj to blind your judgement."

I tried to hold his gaze, but my eyes dropped. Compliments were a rarity from him. It should've been reassuring that he had gone through many of the same experiences as I had. I doubted, though, that he'd been told he was a demon at sixteen.

"I will do my best to make you proud, my high chief." I shifted, knowing further questions would upset him. "I wanted to ask if the chiefs discussed the dark horsemen from the diviners' visions."

He dismissively waved a hand. "The gods guide us, but I trust neither the priests nor the diviners that are surely under their influence. We will march against the Solgawi. Until I hear any reports of these riders doing anything more than attacking the nomads, I will not send my warriors to the eastern frontier to waste away."

"And if they do appear, we will face them with the speed of a thousand horses," Xobas replied. "In my homeland, the Simukie survived by always moving and fighting off whoever threatened our territory. If we must be swift, we will be swift."

I shook my head. "This is a mistake. Otylia believes that Marzanna—"

Father slammed his fist against the table, shaking the bowls and mugs scattered across it. "Did I not tell you to stay away from her?" I swallowed in fear. "I am your high chief, and you will obey my decision. You are to listen and learn how to act among chiefs, not to lecture me on military strategy."

"Yes, Chieftain." I lowered my head and wished I could disappear. The last thing I'd hoped to do was anger him further, but he couldn't understand the true threat that lay ahead. Though even I had my suspicions about the diviners, what Otylia and I had discovered last night had instilled enough fear in me to take their warnings seriously. Whether Marzanna's cultists or dark riders, threats lurked in the east that Father refused to see.

Xobas patted my shoulder as he looked to Perun's Ax, hung at the front of the hall. "I do not know your gods as I know my clan's bond with the horse, but in war, it is said gods choose their sides. I hope yours are with us."

"Indeed," Father said, following Xobas's gaze. "Perun's mighty ax shall lead us into battle, and his tribe will once again rule the lands west of the Krowik. I will not allow my legacy to be squandered."

Nothing else ever mattered to you.

Father scratched his scraggly beard, filled with more than a few strands of gray. "These clans will be crucial to defeating the Solgawi. You must leave tomorrow morning to reach them before the start of the Kwiecień moon. Once the warriors have had their drinks and women, we will meet this evening to call upon the villagers and chiefs to voice their approval."

"Or disapproval," Xobas said pointedly. "Given the distrust of my people, many will not support this."

A low growl escaped Father's throat. "Then may Perun's bolts strike them down for their blindness."

"Perhaps it would be best to ensure they understand that we cannot hold the western lands without joining with allies from the east," I said. "People will respect honesty."

He rose with a groan. "You sound like Kajetan."

"Why do you insult me so?" I joked back, hoping to cool his temper. He chuckled, and I let out a sigh of relief. "If I may ask, I have one request for you."

He coughed, the deep, throaty kind. When he spoke, his voice was raspy, lacking its usual power, "Speak."

My anxiousness took over as I stood and shuffled toward him, running the tips of my fingers along the grooves of the tabletop. If this went poorly, Father would rather cut off my tongue than hear me say another word. "I believe it would be beneficial to bring both Ara and Otylia on the journey. Though I know it's unheard of for women to be part of an envoy, Ara has knowledge of the Zurgowie, and we will need a representative of the gods to bless the negotiations."

For a moment, his eyes bore into me, his mouth set in a fine line. The only man in the tribe he disliked more than Mieczysław was Dariusz, and I doubted the idea of sending his rival's daughter on a crucial journey would be favorable in his mind. My only hope was that his pragmatism outweighed the passion of his heart. "If the Zurgowie girl, Ara, wishes to come, you could use her understanding of their culture," he finally said. "But there are other priests."

"No others that are both diviner and sorceress."

Clutching his fur cloak around him like a shield against a charging enemy, he stepped closer. His blue eyes seemed darker than ever, and though I matched his height, he loomed over me. "What poison has that child poured into your ears?" he sneered. "She is a witch!"

Something clicked. I locked eyes with him, pushing away my fear. "She is not! Dziewanna has gifted Otylia with the ability to channel her power against demons and beasts alike. She is a szeptucha, Father. I have seen it."

Xobas sighed and paced, crossing his arms as he stared up at a fox pelt hung on the side wall, its red fur like blood staining the wood. "Among the Simukie, I saw many women far stronger than men on the field of battle. Some claimed to be driven by the spirit of their gods, others by hatred of their enemies, and even more by love of those they protected. In that girl, I see all three."

"I cannot allow Dariusz to influence these discussions," Father roared. "Otylia is just a girl who whispers into the winds like the witches. It matters not if she claims to be driven by the wild goddess or not."

Frustration flooded my voice as I clenched my fists at my side, my nails digging into my palms. "All I want is for her to give us the advice of the gods as we negotiate an agreement that could save or destroy the tribe. Cynicism will not unite us. Only our common trust in our gods and ancestors can do that."

He huffed and shook his head, looking at his feet as he did. "You have much of your mother in you, boy. That steady passion could sway me at any moment. It's why I loved her."

"Don't speak of her!" I spat. "You threw Mom and me aside for a scheming foreigner."

The disrespect he had shown Mom was one of the few things that ignited me at a moment's notice. She had raised me without the support of Father in the house, and I had taken it as my responsibility to protect her. *Why did I ever seek his approval?* Though Jacek had my respect as my high chief, I would never forget what he had done to Mom and to my relationship with Otylia. He had never been a real father.

His hand struck my cheek, sending a sharp pain arcing across my face as I staggered back. "You will understand one day that I made the choice that was best for the tribe," he said.

With my pride wounded enough, I turned toward the door before glancing over my shoulder. "This is a crucial day for you, so I won't keep you any longer. Accept or deny my request and I will leave you."

Xobas stepped to my side first. "There are few priests that we can trust, my chief," the general said. "Why not send the girl? She is not a threat, unlike the others."

"I cannot—" he began in a rough voice before descending into another coughing fit. He gripped the edge of the table as he heaved, his face turning bright red as he waved his arm wildly at me.

Spite held me for a moment before I sprung across the room and handed him his mug, which he downed. I looked from him to Xobas, not knowing what to think. "My chief," I said, "were you ill last night?"

He let out a groan as he forced himself to stand. Concern replaced his usual confidence. "I was not. It seems Marzanna took one last stab before we completed the ritual."

As he struggled, I gripped his arm. I wished in my heart that I could reveal to him what we had learned, but his skepticism of the priests had blinded him from the truth. Though my desire to please him waned with each second, he was my high chief. I needed him, despite his flaws. "You must rest. If the other chiefs were to see you like this—"

"Do not tell me what I must do!" He pushed me away and tightened his furs around him as he lumbered to his chair. "I cannot burrow in my longhouse during one of our most important festivals. The people are on edge after last night, and once rumors of your kill spread, they will panic if demons start appearing. I must be there to display that our strength is not lost."

I bowed my head. "Of course. And what is your decision on Otylia?"

With his brow furrowed, he sat and looked up at the ceiling, asking Perun for guidance. "The little whisperer may join you, but she is your responsibility. Never forget whose blood she is and where her true loyalties lie."

A knot in my chest released as I nodded and left, testing how sore my cheek was as I did. It stung, but for the first time in what felt like years, I was able to breathe. *I don't need to prove anything to him. I'm nothing in his eyes anyway.*

What lay ahead was a frightening unknown. In a way, so was Otylia, yet as I stepped into the brisk spring winds, I couldn't imagine facing it without her. She knew my secret and entrusted me with hers. Though I failed to understand her completely, after the last day, did I even understand myself? I doubted I could find the answer to who I was without her help.

17

Wacław

I'll miss this.

SWEAT RAN DOWN MY FACE as I tilled the field, swinging the hoe over and over. If Tanek hadn't been injured, we could've used the plow, but instead, I worked an endless dance with the tool as we prepared to plant the year's crop.

It had been hours since Dadźbóg had begun his race toward the horizon. The tribe would meet soon to vote on Father's decision, but I just wanted to keep my head down and avoid the crowds. Word traveled quickly around the village. Rumors of my fight with the zmora would have spread by now, and I didn't want to suffer through Narcyz's sarcasm, especially after all I'd been through over the past day.

Mom had gone inside to prepare supper for herself—away from the festival—but she had worked all morning and afternoon beside me. When she appeared again, her face was sunned like mine. "It has been a long time since I've seen you this upset," she said. "You know, no matter what your father thinks, I will always be proud of the young man you've become. Even if you hide the truth from me."

My chest tightened, but I didn't stop as I threw my stress into each swing of the iron head. "How did you know?"

"I'm your mother, and Mokosz has given us all the gift to see through our sons' lies," she said, lifting her face to the warm sunlight. *Why is she always right?* I huffed in annoyance and swung the hoe again. Still, I loved her more than anyone, and I treasured moments like those. "I assume whatever actually happened last night has to do with Otylia?"

My cheeks burned. Otylia had saved my life and suffered for it. I couldn't shake the sight of her tattered dress when she'd turned away after the utopiec attack. The pure white cloth had been stained as brown as the earth, its tears revealing four long, jagged cuts that tore through her pale skin—wounds she'd taken to save me.

It was a shame the dress had been destroyed. As much as it pained my heart to admit it, she'd looked graceful wearing it. Even during the festival, though, her eyes had been sharp enough to kill. I hated seeing her suffer, but that had been the real her in the swamp—covered in muck in the wilds. I missed that.

"I thought so," Mom said when I didn't reply.

"It's not like that..."

She smirked. "Would you like it to be? She was very pretty last evening with that flower crown."

"Mom!" My spine curled at the memory of us sitting against Dziewanna's Willow—Otylia's eyes almost fluorescent in the moonlight and her long, braided hair wrapped in twine and decorated with enough bone talismans to make the strongest warrior shudder. Covered in swamp water and muck, there truly was no else like her. "She's hated me ever since Father forced me away from her. Besides, she's abrasive and secretive and it wouldn't matter anyway. Father made sure of that."

The words had tumbled out quickly. Whether I believed them or not, I wanted to move on.

"Dariusz is quite the powerful priest as well," Mom said. "If your father seeks to prevent the tribe's division, he need only look at those he alienates."

My hands gripped the wooden handle of the hoe, feeling its splinters jabbing into my calluses as I went to work again. There were enough things on my mind already without worrying about Otylia. "If I tell you what happened last night, will you let the topic rest?"

Curiosity flashed in her eyes. "Sure. Though, I have never seen you so flustered about a girl, even Genowefa."

"This is different. Genowefa was a cute girl. Otylia is a frightening sorceress who even makes the warriors uneasy. Of course I'm flustered, especially after our journey through the swamp last night…"

I told her everything from my newfound ability to our battle with the utopiec and revelations about Marzanna. The entire time, her bright blue eyes just watched me work, putting the puzzle together in her mind. The silence would have unnerved me with anyone else, but Mom always said she saw something in me. I figured mothers could get away with staring at their children.

When I finished, she lowered her gaze, sorrow creeping onto her face. "I've wondered if your moonlit travels meant something, but it seems you know now. Jacek would lose what little sense he has left if you told him of this."

"And that's why I can't," I replied as I wiped the sweat from my brow. "He believes the priests and diviners are conspiring against him, and he would think I was allying with them if he knew I was a demon. I'm concerned about this trek, though. How do I know this is what I'm meant to do, who I'm meant to be? What if this is just me falling deeper into Marzanna's trap?"

In the distance, a figure emerged from the trees, but I couldn't tell who. "I never wished for you to leave home," Mom replied, "but I know the gods have a purpose for you, Wacław, whether it is to help Marzanna or oppose her. Is that not what you have always wanted?" She rested her hand on my arm as I stopped working.

The breeze picked up as she spoke. With no real idea of what was true, I took that as a sign.

The figure had approached the fields. I smiled as Kuba clambered through the mud, almost falling on his face more than once. Taking a deep breath, I pushed away my anxieties, but they lingered beneath the surface.

"Is that Jaryło, god of the crop?" I called to him with a chuckle.
"Oh, no, it's just Kuba, the greatest miner boy to ever live!"

"Shut it," he muttered as he stumbled into me. "At least Marzanna doesn't ruin my boots, eh."

"But she does ruin fences," I said, nodding to the destroyed one in the pasture.

A wide smile crossed his face as he snapped his eyes from the puddle of zmora blood to me. "Everyone's already talking about you slaying the beast! Did you really do it?"

I nodded, and pride swelled in my chest as I showed him my scars. "It got both Tanek and me pretty badly, but I finished the job."

He chuckled and rubbed his hands together, practically hopping up and down in his glee. "Narcyz is sulking around with a swig o' oskoła, so you slayed two demons in my mind."

"That boy could use a knock to his pride," Mom said, taking the hoe. "You should run along and enjoy what time is left of the festival. It will be the last you see of home for a good while."

"And girls," Kuba said, his head dropping. "I'll miss her."

Mom smiled and gave a small wave as I threw an arm over Kuba's shoulder and walked with him back toward the trail. "Maybe, you should tell Maja how you feel for once instead of dancing around the subject like an intoxicated shaman," I teased.

"But what if she says she hates me?"

"If she hates you, why does she bat her eyes like that and lurk wherever you go?"

He smiled. "True, but speaking of girls that hate us, you better tell me what's happening between you and the witch."

She's not a witch! I bit my tongue. *Why am I so eager to defend her?*

"Silence is an answer," he said as we entered the shade of the forest.

"Nothing is happening. Father forbade me to even see her, remember?"

"Then why did you convince your dad to let her come on the journey east?"

"We need someone to speak for the gods. Would you rather have her or slimy Dariusz?"

He wrinkled his nose, and I laughed as he replied, "I don't know which is worse."

"Can you trust me, then, when I say there's more to Otylia than what meets the eye?" I asked, stopping him at the crossroads of a few of the trails, my hand gripping his arm. "That zmora wasn't the only demon I fought last night, and I would be dead if she hadn't saved me."

He shook his head. "What's going on with you? You two have avoided each other for years, and now you're going on romantic demon slaying strolls with her? What aren't you telling me?"

A group wandered by and studied us. I stepped back, digging my heel into the dirt until they were out of earshot. "Something is happening that's bigger than any of us. This advancing army the diviners spoke of, the zmora, the festival—it's all related. Marzanna might have survived the ritual."

"You've been spending too much time with witches and monsters," he said as he grabbed my arm and pulled me toward the village center. "Let's get you a drink and a girl that isn't a sorceress."

My breaths became short as he dragged me along. If my best friend didn't believe me, why would anyone else? Until the vote tonight, however, there was nothing I could do but wait, so I let Kuba lead the way. He was right about one thing: I needed a rest.

18

Otylia

Blasphemous idiot.

MEN CHEERED as Chief Marek stood on a table in the longhouse, drunkenly dancing with a horned mask of Weles covering his face. The smell of alcohol and unbathed people filled the room while the warriors sang songs of victories long past. Ara and I huddled in the back and avoided the chaos. The vote couldn't come soon enough.

In the opposite corner, Wacław sat alone, sipping his oskoła from a ram's horn. Convincing Father to let me go to the clans had been easy. He'd snatched at the excuse to get rid of me for a few weeks so he could focus on his work. Jacek had been the real question, yet Wacław had succeeded. Why was that not reassuring?

"You sure nothing else happened last night?" Ara asked, grinning.

"Shut it. I told you he's—"

"An actual demon? Yeah, but I know that look. Go. I won't mind a few minutes to mingle."

I gritted my teeth. After the Drowning of Marzanna, Ara had been the only one I could trust with the truth about Wacław being a płanetnik. Father would've only sought to gain from the knowledge, but Ara was good with secrets. She slid past me with a mug in her hand before I could object.

Szeptuchy were barred from drinking out of fear of what we might do with our power while intoxicated. Others complained. But as I pushed through the stumbling mob, I didn't envy the drunkards.

Each group sent a passing glance my direction as they made room. Now that I was wearing my ashen dress and amulets again, none of them wanted to be near the wild whisperer. It was better that way.

Wacław didn't look up from the horn cupped in his hands when I slid onto the stool across from him. Whether he sulked over Marzanna or the fact he was a demon, it was hard to not smirk at his long face.

"I've been told I'm not much to look at," he said.

"You're not. I'm simply trying to figure out why you thought it was a good idea to drink ahead of the vote. What the people say will determine whether the tribe stands behind the chiefs' decision."

He set the horn aside and groaned as he rubbed his temples. "Even Kuba didn't believe me, so why would any of them listen to my opinion? They want war, and I'm just the Half-Chief."

"Kuba is a fool," I replied, adjusting Mokosz's amulet around my wrist and surveying the room.

"You called me a fool too."

The ends of my mouth curled. "You are, but less so than most of the other boys and glory hounds in this hall. You showed that when you convinced Jacek to allow me to come."

He scoffed and looked to his father, who sat at the front and oversaw the affair with a solemn look. *Odd.* The high chief usually loved these events. It was his responsibility to ensure the festival kept his allied chiefs and warriors happy, and that meant the mead and oskoła had to flow. But today, something was off. His face and lips were as white as Marzanna's frost.

"Do you think we can actually stop Marzanna if she defied death?" Wacław whispered.

I considered that for a moment before shaking my head. "I don't know. The true power of the gods is beyond our knowledge. Even I can't completely understand Dziewanna. All we can do is listen to their whispers on the winds you're *apparently* connected with."

"If they're so powerful, why must we be the ones to stop her? Can the spring gods not?"

"Father says that on the equinox, Strzybóg carries Dziewanna and Jaryło to Marzanna. Though the god of winds doesn't fight, if Marzanna survived, then she may have defeated two gods. Maybe even three…"

I shuddered at the thought of the spring gods' deaths. Everything was a cycle. Marzanna slayed Jaryło annually in the autumn and sent him to Nawia—unlike Dziewanna, who maintained the wilds year-round, protecting what life she could from the frost. Marzanna was supposed to die upon their return in spring. It was impossible to know what chaos the destruction of that balance would bring.

The same shadowed expression crossed Wacław's face. "Then what can we do?"

"We can learn more," I said. "All we have is guesses until then."

A horn sounded, interrupting the music. Jacek stood in the front alongside Mikołaj, Mieczysław, Serwacy, Marek, and the other chiefs. Pelts of various animals covered each of them differently, depending on their village or clan's traditions, and a sword, ax, or spear hung from their backs or sides.

Jacek wore no blade in the sheath at his side. Warriors often displayed their weapons, but at a festival like this, the real influence was with those who need not carry one to be a threat. The high chief knew that. It was his job to convince the crowd of his plan. While the chiefs made most decisions, tradition demanded a high chief have his people's support before marching to war or making any agreement with another tribe.

"Father always hated this," Wacław said, studying Jacek. "Honestly, though, I'm glad there's some check on the chiefs' bloodlust."

"If only people thought more than cattle," I muttered.

Jacek coughed, and my fears grew as he struggled for each word. "After last night's news, the chiefs have spoken. We have created a plan to ensure our lands are protected and Perun's glory honored. I am sure you have heard rumors of our decision already."

His gaze flicked to Marek for no more than a second, but I grinned at the oaf's twitch. "While we march to war in the west," Jacek continued, "a group of twenty-five under Kajetan's leadership will meet the united clans in the east. We will negotiate a peace and settle them in the southern hills, where our crops struggle to grow. Their cavalry will help us strike the final blow to the Solgawi heartland."

People grumbled across the room, and Wacław and I swapped worried glances. Zurgowie and Simukie refugees like Ara and Xobas had fled from the eastern wars since we were children. With each wave, more resentment had grown against them for their disbelief of our gods and, more importantly, the Zurgowie tradition of marrying within their family. I found Ara in the crowd, flirting with a brown-haired boy with more pimples than I could count. *Thank the gods her parents don't follow that practice.*

"I know this will not sound appealing to many of you," Jacek said, "but allowing the Simukie and Zurgowie to settle our unused lands will only strengthen our tribe and gain us valuable allies."

Albin, the tribe's most infamous warrior, stepped forward. Scars covered his exposed arms, and a black swirling tattoo stretched from the side of his neck to under his dark, sleeveless tunic. As he spoke, I couldn't help but wonder what the rest of the design was. "High Chief, I understand your strategy, but it is a disgrace to our ancestors to allow our lands to be settled by those who do not worship our gods."

"They're inbreeds!" another man yelled as the crowd rumbled in agreement.

Ara's head dropped as she slid away from the torchlight.

Jacek furrowed his brow, any glimpse of his earlier weakness fading as he approached Albin. "Would you rather the clans' warriors burn our fields, disgrace your land and your wife? You're a strong man, Albin. Tell me you have a brain as well."

Albin stepped back as Jacek towered over him. "How can we know they'll aid us against the Solgawi?"

"They are desperate," Jacek replied, gripping Albin's shoulders. "And desperate men will do whatever it takes to survive."

Albin clenched his jaw but knelt and planted his fists firmly on the ground. "Then you have my support, my chieftain."

With a crude smile on his face, Jacek continued his path through the crowd, ensuring everyone met his gaze. "Does anyone else wish to object, or shall we vote and prepare to regain our lost lands?"

A chorus of shouts filled the air as men stomped their feet and shook the ground. Wacław stared down at the horn in his hand. "Father commands respect," he said, "yet I hide in the corner, frightened of a crowd of strangers. How can I face Marzanna, face the clans, when I can't even gain the respect of our own people? Maybe it's best Mikołaj handles the warriors when Father is gone."

I shifted uncomfortably. *Stop making me feel bad for you.* His cheek was bruised where it hadn't been last night. *Jacek hit him again because he asked about me.*

I glared at the high chief as he returned to the front. Father and I never had the best relationship, but I thanked Swaróg for controlling his temper. "Mikołaj will never leave Jacek's shadow," I said. "If the people never loved you, why do you seek their approval?"

"I don't know."

He raised his horn, but I ripped it from his hand. "Pull yourself together! We're leaving for the Mangled Woods in the morning, and I swear to Weles, if you're hungover I'll send you to meet him."

"I'm a demon. Aren't I dead already?" He mumbled under his breath.

Before I could snap back, Jacek coughed and called out for votes in favor. Albin spurred on the warriors, who hadn't stopped shouting, but around the outskirts of the room, the women were hushed.

"Do the women not wish to support the plan?" Wacław asked me.

"You wouldn't either if you were to be left alone for many moons while your husband and sons die across the river. It's a lonely life."

Father had often marched with the armies as an advisor for Jacek, even if both of them despised being near each other. Every time, Mother had tried to hide her sorrow. I'd felt it too. He and I fought, but he was still my father. He was trying to do what he thought was best.

Wacław sighed. "I guess I wouldn't know what that's like. Whenever Father left, I was free from his grasp for once."

How many times has he hit you? I glanced from Jacek back to him, studying the dark circles under his eyes as his father asked for the opposing votes. A few men and most of the women grumbled, but they knew they'd lost. Jacek took it as enough. "Then it is decided. Kajetan will lead the team, and they will leave as soon as possible tomorrow."

The chiefs dispersed. Some in the crowd returned to carousing while those from the more distant villages headed for the door. They'd come a long way through forests, fields, and swamps with few to no trails. Jacek had expanded the tribe's territory. That didn't mean he'd connected its villages. Demons and other spirits lived in those unsettled lands, and when we left tomorrow, we'd be heading directly into their grasps.

I studied the demon in front of me. Two days before, I would've never expected to be placing my hopes in a demon and the boy who had abandoned me, but here we were. "Gods save us," I whispered, clutching Dziewanna's amulet.

A scuffle broke out along the side wall. Ara's thin frame emerged from the crowd, scrambling toward us. Three shirtless warriors stumbled after her, their eyes wild.

I shot to my feet. "Back off."

"Oh, I'm sorry," the burly, balding one in front said with a crooked smile that revealed more than a few missing teeth. "Does she only like her brothers?"

I bit my cheek, but Wacław was at my side. "I would listen to the witch," he said, fists clenched. "Rumor has it, she strangled a demon twice your size and only half as disgusting last night. It would be a shame for my father to lose three warriors because they picked the wrong fight."

I smirked. *Drunk Wacław's got guts.*

The brutes mumbled something I couldn't hear before leaving as quickly as their wobbly legs would let them. People murmured around us, but Kuba stepped into the circle and threw his arm over Wacław's shoulder. He raised a mug and shouted, "Drink for Jaryło tonight! And tomorrow, we march for Perun!"

As the crowd roared, I took advantage of the distraction and pulled Ara out of the longhouse. The glow of the moon chased us as we ducked into the shadows, catching our breaths.

"That was insane," Ara said, her brown eyes fixed on the men singing around Perun's Oak. "If this is how they honor their gods, I'd hate to see how they act when they defy them."

I let go of her wrist and took her hand instead. She squeezed it hard as I shook my head. "They use Perun and Jaryło as an excuse to do whatever they please."

"Thanks for stopping them. Having a channeler friend has its advantages—and apparently a demon one too."

"Any time," I said. "But we'll be the only girls going east, and if the rumors are true, Narcyz and his friends are coming with us. This won't be the last time we have to deal with drunk fools."

"Glad I'm not alone, then," she replied. "And if they get the wrong idea, I can always send an arrow through their head."

"Not if I get to them first."

19

Wacław

Why is war inevitable?

WITH THE VILLAGE ASLEEP, I walked in my soul-form to the place I had taken little Nevenka on the bank of the Wyzra River. The last thing I wanted ahead of the next day's travels was to encounter another demon, so I kept to the familiar parts of the forest. Clouds blocked the light of the moon and stars, but I had traveled these trails hundreds of times. Each one was etched in my mind like the veins on my arms and hands. They were part of me, and I would miss them.

The river's waters were calm as I sat along the muddy shore and stared at the island. It seemed like it had been far longer than a day and a half before that I had promised Nevenka I would climb across the chain of rocks to the island with her. Now, as I awaited my first trek beyond our territory, I feared I wouldn't keep my promise.

Before the spring equinox, I had dreamed of traveling to the beautiful places of the world. This felt different, though. Deep in my gut, I knew something was about to go terribly wrong. We were marching into the unknown, not just into clan lands but also through the Mangled Woods, where more demons lurked.

I had no idea what Marzanna had planned. I had no idea if we could even convince the nomads to accept our offer of peace. Worst of all, I was trapped between powers far greater than me—both the chiefs' battles for power and the eternal struggles among the gods. *What am I supposed to do?* I didn't know who I was asking. It could have been Perun or Weles, Jaryło or Dziewanna, or maybe even Marzanna. Had Strzybóg gifted me control over the winds, or was my power apart from even the gods? It had been hard enough to figure out who I was before I knew I was a płanetnik. Now, I also needed to figure out *what* I was.

That row of rocks called to me, tempted me to cross. I refused. It felt right to have another small thing to come back to. Though I promised myself I would return to Mom and protect her the rest of her life, there was something special in a promise given to a child. Nevenka wouldn't forget, so I wouldn't either.

A shiver ran down my back, like an icy fingernail tracing my spine. I spun and peered into the dark woods. Nothing met me besides the *huhuhuhooo* of a tawny owl, but my hair stood on end. I let out a sharp breath and stared up at the bird, perched in the pine tree above. Its unblinking stare bore into me. *Not a good sign.*

All my childhood, I'd heard the elders tell tales of owls bringing omens of death. The day before our journey was to begin, that was hardly reassuring.

A *crunch* came from the river. The cold closed in, and I struggled to breathe as I forced myself to turn around.

The gaze of a pale woman met me. Sleek hair like the night flowed over her shoulders, spilling down her black gown along with necklaces of both gold and jewels. Her eyes were a misty gray, her cheeks hollow, and claws as long as my forearm stretched from the tips of her fingers.

Marzanna…

The goddess stood ankle deep in the water. Around her feet, the river creaked and moaned as it froze—a frost that hardened the mud between us and turned the blood in my veins to ice. Even the winds seemed to keep their distance as a show of respect to the blizzard queen.

I dropped to my knees, head bowed. "My goddess," I stammered. "I—"

"Do not speak," Marzanna hissed, white crystals from her breath suspending in the air as she ran the tip of her sharp claws along my cheek. Her motions were that of a ghost, drifting through the air yet never leaving the ground. Everywhere she stepped cracked and snapped. "You have disappointed me, Wacław. I offer you power, the woman you adore, and the freedom to fly wherever you please, yet, despite taking my Frostmark, you plot against me."

I froze in fear, not daring to look up at her as she circled me. There were endless stories of the horrors Marzanna brought against her enemies. I was next. *How did she know?*

"I was pleased to hear you finally found your abilities when my zmora reached you," she continued with a sinister edge to her voice. "The golden egg is quite powerful, and it would have been shameful for a boy with so much potential to be nothing more than food for my pet to feast upon. One must hope it was enough to make you grasp the weight of your error. Do you understand now, my little Frostmarked servant, or must I pull your father deeper into his illness? What about your mother?"

Anger burned the frost from my heart, and I clenched my fists against the dirt. "What must I do?" I pleaded.

"Look at me."

I snapped my gaze up, meeting her sharp gray eyes as she prowled forward. In her extended hand she held a black blade—the dagger I had lost in the swamp. I took it in my shaking hands and gripped its hilt, feeling the cold metal in my palm before drawing it from its sheath. Little moonlight slipped through the clouds, but it was enough for me to see my own reflection in the dagger's flat. *Who am I to confront a goddess?*

Marzanna's lip curled as she paced to a willow and dragged her claws across its bark, leaving behind a line of decay. "You disobeyed my commands, young płanetnik, speaking against war and then seeking the szeptucha of my wild sister. That was not a wise decision, but I have need of you still. A greater war than any other lies ahead, fought by men full of greed and pride—one that we can stop together."

"Dariusz says horsemen will come from the east and burn our lands. Is that because of you?"

She scoffed as something rustled behind me. Two wolves burst forth from the brush, snarling and bolting to their place by her side. "Warlords and the men that follow them act like sheep on their own accord, but I have been known to whisper in their ears, bending them to my will. These nomads move west, joining my Frostmarked Horde in search of food and new people to conquer. Winters have been harsh on them; though, I could end their suffering and halt their attacks before they begin."

I shook my head, confused. "What does this have to do with me?"

She held a finger to her lips, the vicious claw at the end of it arcing across her face. "You will soon encounter my former lover. When you do, you will drive that dagger into his chest and steal his seven Moonblades."

"Who? Why me?"

"Your priests have forgotten the truth. How convenient," she snarled. "You know Jaryło as my twin, but there was a time when we were married—an *unfortunate* aftermath of Weles kidnapping him from Perun. When my brother returned from Nawia many years later, I did not recognize him. We fell in love, and as Jaryło now considered Weles his father, Perun saw our relationship as an opportunity to end his war with Weles. So, we were wed—I as a goddess of nature and Jaryło as that of agriculture."

She stopped and glared at the sky. "I gave him everything, but Jaryło desired more than me. He bedded another, breaking the sacred bond we held over the world and transforming me into a creature of decay. I killed him. Yet, he returned. Ever since, Dziewanna helps him slay me in the spring, and I tear him apart in the autumn."

Her eyes gleamed, ravenous as she stalked closer. "The cycle traps both us and the world, and I wish to be free. You see, he cannot die as long as he holds his Moonblades. Each is crafted from a Moonstone, granting him the strength to return during the corresponding moon and reign over it."

She lowered to lock her gaze with mine. One of her hands clasped my shoulder, a gesture that would have been motherly if her claws weren't piercing through my tunic. "Kill him, Wacław, and take the Moonblades for me. Only then can I protect nature and become whole. The Frostmarked Horde will not come, your father will not perish, and your people will no longer suffer the death of winter."

As she spoke, visions flashed before me of Marzanna as a beautiful goddess, running her hands through golden grasses and lifting her face to the sky. Her blonde hair was wrapped as a married woman, and Jaryło stood alongside her, as radiant as the sun. I sensed her joy, her love. Nature itself felt whole.

When the visions faded, I found it difficult to believe the frigid goddess of death in front of me could have been so *alive*. Her once full body and bright face were now frail and twisted, her hope replaced by dread.

All of it hit me at once, and I understood her pain and hatred. We worshiped Jaryło, hailing him as a hero as we burned Marzanna's effigy. *Why would the priests hide this?* I resented all the lives Marzanna had taken, but I pitied her suffering.

"I understand now," I said, "but why must it be me? Why do you threaten my family?"

"You rejected my call. For that, there are consequences." She sighed and reached down to pet one of the wolves. "I needed someone who would both feel my pain and be strong enough to face Jaryło. Though you only possess your power when your body rests, you will be able to earn his trust and get close enough to him." Her gaze rose the dagger in my hand. "Perun gifted me that blade when Jaryło and I were wed. It was molded from his Thunderstone and crafted by Swaróg himself, capable of killing any god. Steal the Moonblades, and the dagger will do the rest."

My stomach churned. Everything about this felt wrong, but if I could believe her, my decision would determine whether Father lived or died. That weight was too much to bear. "What will you do once you have the swords?" I asked.

She gestured to the wolves at her flanks. They growled, gnashing their teeth as they approached. "Without Jaryło interfering, I can reunite all the Moonstones under my control. No longer will I only rule winter. Nature's cycle can be mended." She extended her hand to me, a mix of rage and wanting in her eyes. "You will do as I ask, Wacław, son of Jacek, or I will consider you no better than him."

"I—"

She forced my hand shut around the dagger's hilt. "Your time to choose will come. It would be a pity if your father and tribe suffered because you did so poorly."

She turned and glided away as I stammered, lost for words. Then, she vanished in a flash of frozen air, stinging my face and covering me in a layer of frost. Once again, I was left with nothing but the owl's calls to keep me company.

As I knelt, paralyzed next to the Wyzra, I felt more alone than ever. The journey ahead was daunting, but Marzanna had left my mind spinning. I didn't know what or who to believe. She and Otylia had placed the weight of the entire tribe on my shoulders—a weight I didn't wish to bear.

I stared down at the dagger and wished the laughs and sneers of the others were all I had to deal with. I wished I could throw the blade beneath the waters and forget the last two days had ever happened, but they had. Things had been set in motion. Gods clashed, and in my hands, I held the key to their fates.

Part Two

The Path East

20

Wacław

Why is leaving so hard?

MY HEART ACHED as I strapped my dark blue wooden shield and spear to my back, taking in a breath of the cool morning air. Dew hung on the grass as the sun crept above the horizon. It would be a long journey, and Father had insisted that we leave at first light. Still, the fog from last night's encounter with Marzanna filled my head.

I shivered, remembering how the chill pricked at my skin as her eyes tore into my soul. The goddess of death, of disease, of winter, demanded I obey.

What choice do I have?

Marzanna had confirmed the diviners' visions of the Frostmarked Horde who'd invaded the Anshayman Steppe—men who would destroy our tribe if I did not betray Jaryło. How powerful was this advancing army if it drove fear into the warlords of the eastern clans? Would we face them or Marzanna's followers?

I sighed and nervously thumbed Marzanna's mark. It didn't matter what awaited us in the east. Everything was dragging me there, whether I liked it or not.

As Mom pulled me into her warm embrace, I already dreaded what was to come. Marzanna had torn away any sense of adventure and replaced it with cold, suffocating terror. No way forward seemed right, but in Mom's arms I was safe, if only for a moment.

"You have no idea how much I'll miss you," Mom said, taking my hands as tears wetted her cheeks. "Every day—" her voice caught as she pressed the words out, "Every day I shall pray to Perun for your strength, Mokosz for your heart, and Dadźbóg for light to show you the way."

And to Dziewanna that her servant doesn't strangle me. After last night, though, Otylia seemed tame compared to Marzanna's wickedness. I wrapped my arms around Mom again, unwilling to let go. "I don't want to leave."

A calm washed over me as she rubbed my back. "Your destiny awaits you out there, not on this farm with your old mother. You'll make me proud, as you do every day."

"I'll return. I promise." The words seemed truthful, but doubt made them bitter on my tongue.

"I know you will," she said as I cried myself. "If you didn't, who would ensure Tanek is given his treats and that the grain grows strong?"

I clutched her hands and forced a chuckle. No matter how distraught I was, she could always make me laugh. I would miss that more than anything. "I love you, Mom."

She smiled, not allowing her pain to show. "I love you too. Here…" Reaching back, she pulled the string band of her necklace over her head and wrapped it over mine. "My mother gave this amulet to me, and now, I'm giving it to you so that the Great Mother protects you when I cannot."

I cradled the round wooden amulet in my palm, admiring the carved Mothermark of Mokosz I had seen around Mom's neck so many times: four red diamonds, each in a quadrant formed by a matching X pattern. The amulet was warm against my chest, as it had spent much of its life against the heart of both my mother and grandmother.

"Thank you," was all I could think to whisper.

"You're welcome," she replied, nodding to the trail and adjusting my hooded wool cloak over my tunic. "It's time. Your father is not a patient man. You should hurry, or we will both never hear the end of it."

Sorrow filled me as I backed away, both unwilling and unable to let her go. She was more than just my mother—she was my friend, one of my only confidants. But she was right. My future lay in the east, far beyond our village, and it was finally time for me to face it.

With my mind lost in the clouds, I avoided the trails, instead wandering among the trees on my way to the village center. The forest felt like an escape during the day. At night, though, it appeared that Marzanna wished for me to have no rest. I still didn't understand how she expected me to find Jaryło, let alone earn his trust and take his Moonblades.

Focus on what you can control right now, I told myself as I smelled the damp bark of the oak and birch trees. Peace with the eastern clans was needed no matter what Marzanna planned. We had a long march ahead of the negotiations. I couldn't lose my head thinking of the gods' quarrels.

Father was talking with Xobas when I entered the village center. Taking a deep breath and faking a smile, I joined the group that had gathered around Perun's Oak. Each of the warriors was armed with their own weapons—mostly spears and wood-carved javelins—along with their round shields.

Kuba skipped toward me, beaming with his shield in his hand and five javelins strapped to his back.

A year ago, we had decided to paint our shields together: white spirals cut through the dark blue, spinning from the iron boss in the center that guarded our hands. Both shields had dents and chips scattered across them, but they connected us. He would guard my back in battle, and I would guard his.

"Glad you finally showed up," he said, glancing back at Father and whispering, "Your dad has been *loudly* calling for you."

"Am I the last one to arrive?"

"We're still waiting for Marek and a couple others."

"Marek is coming?" I asked with a groan. "Between him, Kajetan, Narcyz, and Otylia, we will have quite the band."

He chuckled. "I doubt he's even sober after last night. He's gotta have a massive headache."

I wish a headache was all I had.

I smirked as I remembered Kuba's own drinking. "Do you not?" His nose wrinkled as he shoved me with his shield, faking a fighting stance. With a chuckle, I raised my hands and stepped back. "Might want to save your strength for the raiders and demons."

Ara and Otylia were standing only a few paces away, and Ara turned toward us with curiosity in her eyes. The Zurgowie huntress wore a rough-spun sleeved tunic and leather trousers like our own hunters. With a short bow and quiver hung over her shoulder, she looked more threatening than some of the boys in the group. "You think the stories about the Mangled Woods are true?" she asked.

"Probably," I said. "Especially since we've already seen demons here, I would guess the Mangled Woods will have even more. And there'll be no cottages to protect us out there."

Kuba smacked my arm with a smile, startling me as he quipped, "Don't worry. Wacław the Nightchief will kill 'em like that zmora."

"Nightchief?"

"Yeah, I made it up after you killed that thing. Like it?"

I shook my head as Otylia grabbed Ara. "I think you have too much time on your hands," she said.

Kuba furrowed his brow and sauntered toward Father, mumbling, "Nobody asked you, Otylia."

I chuckled before following Kuba. The nickname felt odd, but everything Kuba did was, so I let it go. "Did you get the guts to tell Maja how you feel?" I asked as we reached the tree.

His cheeks flushed as he strapped his shield to his back. "Maybe…"

At least something is going right. I grabbed him in a quick hug. "You deserve to be happy, but ruin it with her and I doubt you'll ever sleep again."

"Ironic coming from the one who is sneaking off with the witch."

I winced, aware of Otylia still standing nearby. Before I came up with a witty reply, Father snatched my arm. "You're late."

"I'm earlier than Marek," I replied with a shrug as Marzanna's threat lurked in my mind. Father's frost-like face and quivering hands exposed his illness, even if he wished to hide it. "Why did you allow him to come?"

His grip tightened around my upper arm. "Marek is a chieftain, and you will respect him as one. It was on my recommendation that he is part of the mission. He is young for a chief, but it would be beneficial for the clans to see that one is present at the negotiations."

All I could do was nod. "Yes, my high chief."

Though I didn't agree that Marek would be a suitable representative, I knew Father would not appreciate my objections, especially after yesterday. Still, Marek's pride would make quite the distraction. I only hoped his skill with an ax would make up for that flaw.

Kajetan took Father's side and placed a hand on his shoulder. In the early morning breeze, the ambassador's long hair blew into his mouth—streaks of gray clashing with black—and he scowled as he batted it away. "All are present except for Chief Marek. How much longer must we wait for the boy?"

"Patience, my friend," Father replied sternly. "He will be here. We must only hope he did not shame himself and all of us last night."

I huffed. *Drunk chiefs get patience but not boys saying bye to their mothers?* Not that I had ever been given the benefit of the doubt.

"We have delayed long enough," Kajetan said, straightening his off-white and red-lined tunic. "I will address the others without him, but he better show his face soon."

Father sighed. "Very well."

Kajetan clapped his hands and waited for the warriors to turn their attention to him, exactly where he wanted it at all times. "Though we will march imminently, I want to issue a warning to each of you. The future of our tribe is on each of our shoulders. If any of us were to provoke the clans, the consequences would fall upon all of our families, so when you are tempted by battle, food, or women, keep your head about you. I would hate to have to remove it."

181

Otylia rolled her eyes at the mention of women being temptations. When I looked back at Kajetan, though, he was glaring directly at Kuba and me. "While in foreign lands," he continued, "never stray from the group, and if you must, bring two partners. Raiders and beasts may lurk in the forests and plains we are about to traverse, so be vigilant and keep your wits. Ah, Chieftain..."

Kuba scoffed. "If it ain't the chief of alcohol."

Marek scrambled toward us, still pulling on his boots as he ran. "My apologies for being late, there were important—"

"The reasons are irrelevant," Father interrupted. "Join the rest of the group so you may be off."

With a swift bow of the head, Marek mumbled, "Yes, High Chief."

Father turned his attention back to Kajetan. "The remaining instructions can be given on the trail. It is time for you to leave."

Without another word to me or anyone else, he left, coughing once more before disappearing into the longhouse. My hopes sunk watching him go. *Bye, Dad.* I tried to push away all the sorrow I had of leaving home and focus on the adventure. It didn't work. I would be gone for more than a moon, yet Father didn't care.

As Kajetan, Marek, and Xobas mounted their horses and led us down the trail east, Kuba patted my shoulder. "Don't worry. You'll come back on the horse, dragging Kajetan on his butt."

That forced a smile to my face. I was glad Kuba was coming. If he hadn't, I would have felt completely alone. Xobas may have been my mentor and Otylia an ally against Marzanna's threats, but neither of them brought the simple joy of Kuba.

As we walked in the back, the winding trails past the eastern gate felt further than they should have. I wished I could say farewell to each tree I had dashed between or climbed for so many years. Though I had promised Mom I would return soon, I didn't know if I believed that. After Marzanna's appearance last night, I faced a decision that would anger a god no matter what I chose. An ache in my chest told me either would mean my demise.

When the village gave way to the true wilds. I stopped, watching the trees sway in the breeze and the birds flutter among the pines. I missed it already. We had yet to even step foot beyond Dwie Rzeki, but my heart called me home.

To save it, I have to leave.

I sighed and turned ahead, where Kuba smiled back at me. "C'mon, the crops will still be there when we get back."

"Gods willing," I whispered to myself, following him into the trees.

21

Otylia

I'm going to kill them.

ARA AND I WALKED AT THE FRONT, just behind Kajetan and the other riders. Dadźbóg's light had nearly faded, but after eight hours of walking the trails east of Dwie Rzeki, Narcyz's gang of boys still kept staring at us and whispering. My fingers twitched every time I heard that dirt-haired idiot's snicker. *Genowefa would thank me for shutting him up.*

We stopped at a leaf-covered clearing as the sun reached the horizon. Our march had been slow with the storm on the equinox muddying the ground, and Kajetan complained to Xobas about the lack of progress. Barely listening, the Simuk nodded and went to work ordering the boys to build a fire.

Wacław, Kuba, and Narcyz pulled the cooking equipment from the pack horses across the clearing while the others laid out their gear to claim sleeping spots. Kajetan and Marek had the luxury of furs. The rest of us had to rely on woolen cloaks and simple bedrolls to keep us warm on the ground during the chilly early spring nights. The boys grumbled about the cold as the light faded, but lying in the dirt meant nothing to me. This was Dziewanna's land. At least it wasn't muck like the lowland trails.

I inspected my herb bag for anything useful for supper. I'd found some edible mushrooms, mint, and wolf cherries—what Narcyz's channeler-hating cult called deadly nightshade. Sprinkling the poisonous fruit in the idiot's meal was tempting.

"You think Kajetan is upset?" Ara quipped, rolling her eyes.

"His life is a constant search for the next thing to complain about," I replied. "Father rants about him endlessly."

"I can see why," Ara said before leaving to feed the horses.

I studied Wacław as he pulled his shield off his back and placed the pots on top of it. *He's starting to look like a warrior.* I shook my head. *Stop that. He's a demon who abandoned you for years.* Still, something tugged me toward him.

"Perhaps you're not a fool," I said, taking the mint from my bag and sprinkling it into the pots. At least now the meal would have some flavor.

"Trying to poison those who stare?" he asked with his brow raised.

"It's mint," I corrected. "If women poisoned every man whose eyes wandered, there'd be none of you left. The world would be quieter and less violent, but the end of our people isn't very advantageous."

His cheeks flushed as the boys in charge of cooking carried over the water they had collected from a nearby stream. I looked from them to Wacław, but he was gone. The crackle of twigs underfoot gave him away, heading out of camp. For a second, I waited. He obviously wanted to be alone. Curiosity got the better of me, though, and I followed him into the shadows.

I hid behind an oak and watched him step into the branches of a pine, its needles engulfing him. Smirking, I crept to the edge of the tree. "And where are you going?"

Wacław yelped and fell into the pine. The branches nipped at his exposed skin, but his hand caught the trunk and finally stopped his fall. He groaned as the sticky sap coated his fingers. "Can I not pee in peace?" he fumed, glaring at me through the needles.

I crossed my arms. "You're avoiding me."

"Did you divine that?" He stumbled his way back out of the tree, trying to wipe the sap onto his pants to no avail.

"No, you're just incredibly obvious."

"Wonderful!" he growled. "You have exposed my secret desire for a moment of peace. It was impossible to think about what's coming when Narcyz and the others yapped about their prowess with both of their spears the whole day. Are a few minutes too much to ask for?"

"Fine. Have your rest."

As I turned to leave, he sighed. "Wait."

"Well?"

"We need... We need to talk about Marzanna."

"I'm listening."

He glanced toward the camp, hesitant, then nodded deeper into the woods. I sighed, my stomach grumbling as I cursed his secrecy, but if he was this worried, whatever he wanted to say was important. Wacław always stuttered when he was nervous. From his wide eyes to the way he was grabbing the ends of his sleeves, something was eating him from the inside out.

The little remaining light was enough for us to spot two downed trees. He tapped his foot restlessly on one as I sat on the other, stretching my legs out in front of me, eager to take my weight off them for the first time in hours. The bark was damp against my butt and wetted my ashen travel dress, but the relief of finding a seat far outweighed my discomfort.

When he waited too long to speak, I did first, "I can't stop wondering why Dziewanna guided me to you and that leszy."

His lip twitched. "Probably to keep it from saying what I discovered last night."

"Did it return?"

"No, but when I wandered to the Wyzra, Marzanna met me."

I froze in fear. *She's alive?* I hadn't wanted to believe it before, but if he saw her... "It can't be true. Dziewanna and Jaryło should've banished her to Nawia."

"I saw her, Otylia, claws and all." He shuddered. "She told me of her marriage to Jaryło, how she had been a goddess of nature before he bedded another woman."

"What are you talking about? Father has never spoken about a marriage between them. They're twins, not lovers."

He huffed and stared into the forest. "I *saw* it. She showed me."

I shot to my feet. "What she showed you was lies! Dziewanna would have told me if this was true."

"How do you know? You said yourself that we can never truly understand the gods, and Dziewanna is no different. When Marzanna showed me the vision, I felt her pain, her loss. Whatever this fight is between them, it runs deeper than the seasons."

Scowling, I gripped my braid and picked at one of the bone amulets. "She is the goddess of death, Wacław. She cannot be trusted. But since she visited you in person, she must have asked you to do something for her. A goddess doesn't just appear." I stormed forward, fists clenched at my side. "What did she ask?"

His hand drifted to the sheath at his hip. When he drew the black blade, all I could do was back away and whisper to my goddesses under my breath, "Great Mother save us."

"She claimed Swaróg crafted it out of Thunderstone," he said. "You were right. It's powerful enough to kill a god, but the hard part is preventing him from returning."

I whispered in the old tongue as I leaned against a willow, trying to wrap my head around what was happening. Sure, Wacław was a płanetnik, but why would Marzanna ask *him* to kill Jaryło? What could he do that no other demon or loyal szeptucha could? Unless…

"She wants you to take Jaryło's Moonblades."

"How do you—"

"You can't listen to her! I don't know if what Marzanna says is true, but you can't do it. Without Jaryło, spring will never come, crops will never grow—the tribe will starve."

He gave a grim grin. "I thought you said you didn't care about the people of the tribe."

I snatched his forearm before circling away as I clutched

Dziewanna's amulet. "How can you make jokes while actively considering the death of a god?"

"There's more…"

"I don't need to hear more!" I snapped. "If she let you go, then you already said yes. She would've killed you otherwise." I gritted my teeth as I paced, staring at the ground. Every bit of resentment I'd felt toward him burned in my veins. "I should've never trusted you. Your word meant nothing before. Why would it now?"

He hesitated. Only my sharp breaths and the wind rustling the branches overhead broke the silence. Why had I convinced him to let me come on this trip? Was revenge for Mother's death and the poisoning of Dziewanna's altar really worth it? And who was I to defeat a goddess after I'd trusted a demon? My chest seared, and when I looked up at Wacław, his mouth hung open like I'd slid the dagger between his ribs. His eyes were glass.

"My father's illness is because of her," he stammered, averting his gaze, "and so are the dark riders of the east—the Frostmarked Horde. She claimed that Jaryło's death will allow her to retake her position as the goddess of nature. If I don't do as she commands, Father will die, and she'll command the Horde to conquer our lands."

I groaned and gripped my head. "And if you do what she says, the tribe will suffer anyway! Do you not see that she is using you, tempting you with lies?"

"What if it's the truth?"

"Even if Jaryło did bed another woman, that isn't proof Marzanna would end her reign over winter. Think about it. If people had burned your effigy year after year and praised the god you despised, would you suddenly act as if everything was fine?"

He stuttered, lost. I couldn't understand his hesitation.

Every time Wacław had showed up with a bruised cheek or a long-sleeved tunic in the heat of summer, I'd known what Jacek had done to him. When we were kids, he'd never stopped talking about how much he wished for his father's approval and how often he saw Lubena's pain. But now, when Marzanna threatened the man who had never cared about him as anything more than an asset for political power, he gave in. Why?

"There must be some hope to save the tribe, my father," he said with slumped shoulders. "I can't let her destroy what Father has built. The tribe—"

"Is more than Jacek," I interrupted. Dadźbóg's light disappeared completely, and the moonlight sent a heavy shadow over his face. For a moment, the same resentment I felt flashed in his eyes, and fear gripped me. Not fear of a boy who'd turned his back or one Mokosz had shown trying to kiss me. Fear of a demon.

Someone called our names from the camp. We'd been gone for too long, yet things were worse than before. Wacław's honesty hadn't fixed anything, and now more than ever, I wished Dziewanna would answer. Her voice had guided me for years. Its absence left me alone, isolated.

I leaned my head back. While the stars were barely visible, I found some hope in their twinkling as they cut through the night sky. *Maybe that's how it must be: little lights glimmering in a sea of darkness.*

With Wacław still standing there, looking at me like a wounded animal, exhaustion took over my body. "Your Father would not be the first chief to suffer the wrath of a god," I said, "but I will call to Dziewanna for guidance. She has to know more about her sister's plans."

"Then why hasn't she told you already?"

I took a long breath and started back toward the camp. His footsteps followed as I shook my head. "I don't know…"

The little patience I had was already running thin as we stopped on the bank of the Wyzra. We had hiked south of it until the river shallowed out to merely a stream. Now, it was time to cross.

Steep drops hugged the river's sides before giving way to a patch of grass. Of course, the boys had decided it was a perfect place to wrestle after they'd collected the day's wood for cooking. We'd been walking for five-and-a-half days now, and the soles of my leather boots felt like they'd merged with my feet. A sharp jab struck the ball of my foot with each step, replacing the ache when it was in the air. I didn't know which pain I preferred.

Ara and I sat in the shade. My back stung as I leaned against the trunk of a leafless ash tree, cringing at the memory of the utopiec's claws ripping through my dress. Despite my best efforts, the scrapes hadn't healed well. Mother had always said even her potions could rarely treat a strike from the undead. Wounds left by their claws and teeth had a bad habit of festering, but unless the cut was deep, they would heal in time. Unfortunately, time wasn't my friend.

"You look angrier than normal," Ara said, interrupting my thoughts as she rolled up the sleeves of her hunter's tunic. The brown thing was ragged, but from the way she looked at it, I knew she took pride in the wear.

"That's saying something," a boy snickered from nearby. I shot him a glare—enough to drive him away.

I swiped a stray hair from my face. Sweat had baked into my skin after hours of hiking in the day's sudden spurt of warmth. I had looked forward to the respite of the stream's cool water, but there was no way I would bathe with those oafs around.

"If only Dadźbóg could've held off the heat for a few more days," I finally replied as I removed my boots. A quick examination revealed a blister as large as an arrowhead on my foot. "That's great..." Though my herbs and channeling would be able to mend it, the last thing I wanted to do was waste my *žityje* on something so trivial.

Ara stretched out her legs and adjusted the long iron hunting knife strapped to her thigh. "You don't know what heat is until you've seen the Anshayman Steppe. Besides, isn't it *supposed* to be warm in spring?"

I glanced toward the boys to make sure no one was eavesdropping. "Marzanna's still alive," I whispered. "Wacław saw her."

"You mean..."

I nodded. "Marzanna claimed that she and Jaryło were married as a unity of nature gods or something. Apparently, he slept with someone else, and when she killed him, she broke that stability and became the goddess of winter. Wacław said she'll kill the high chief if he doesn't murder Jaryło and take the Moonblades that let him come back from Nawia."

"Teṇpa Āymaya," she whispered before noticing my raised eyebrows. "The nurturer. She's our Zurgowie goddess of nature and of, well, devotion. Perhaps it's not a coincidence Marzanna was a nature goddess who wanted to kill her cheating husband."

"Marzanna is not just a divorced woman. She's the goddess of death! She killed Mother. She poisoned Dziewanna's Willow. No matter how wrong Jaryło was, we can't let her win."

Ara gave a knowing smile.

Avoiding her stare, I rubbed an ointment on my blister as I whispered to Dziewanna. The pain faded. My temper didn't. I hated being so irritated, but I'd spent years despising Marzanna. The thought of having any sympathy for her made me want to vomit, and Ara's gaze jabbing at me wasn't helping.

"What?" I snapped, instantly regretting my aggression.

"We've known each other a few years now," she said, drawing her knife and driving it into the soft ground between us. "And if I've learned anything about you, it's that you like to throw your words around like javelins when you're scared."

"I'm not scared," I lied.

"Yes, you are, but considering the boy you were fond of for a decade is now a demon and your enemy is a death goddess, you'd be stupid not to be."

"I was *not* fond of him."

"And now?"

I pulled the knife from the dirt and spun, placing its edge at the peak of her throat. Our noses were so close I could feel her sharp breaths against my face, but she didn't even flinch. "Now," I began, "I don't want to talk about it. We need to figure out how to kill Marzanna, not worry about boys. My only job is to serve Dziewanna and

Mokosz. Making Jaryło pay for being like every stupid warrior that worships him won't bring Dziewanna back."

Ara's hands moved like lightning, and before I could react, she had me on my back with the knife backhanded against my throat. "There's a chance we can do both, but you need to be honest with me—and with him—if we're going to do this." She stepped back and offered me her hand. "Maybe he was stupid to turn away from you, or maybe there's more to the story—just like your ice goddess."

Scowling, I took her hand, and she pulled me to my feet. "Fine," I said, "I'm afraid we won't succeed. I'm afraid Dziewanna is gone, that I failed her somehow. And I'm afraid Wacław will give into Marzanna's demands. Happy?"

"Good enough." She slid the blade into its sheath and turned back toward the camp. "We should probably get back before the boys—"

"Demon!" Kuba shouted from the ridge by the river. His voice was strained, and water dripped from his hair and clothes as we ran to him.

"What happened?" I asked, looking down into the valley, where the rest of the boys stared at the river with their mouths ajar. Narcyz stood in front. Blood rushed down his nose.

Kuba coughed and wheezed, his hands on his knees as he searched for air. "Wacław. Something pulled him into the river. We couldn't get there fast enough."

I stormed past him and down the slope. *Why does it always have to be me?*

22

Wacław

I should've ridden a horse instead.

EVERY MUSCLE IN MY BODY ACHED when we stopped at the Wyzra's southern bend and prepared the campfire for Borys to cook what would surely be a tasteless lunch at best. Once we finished, I freed myself of my boots and weapons by the trees and climbed down to the river.

The frigid water rushed between my toes, making my hair stand on end. All I cared about, though, was the relief it brought to the sores that had appeared on the bottom of my feet after the days of marching.

Kuba was less graceful. His head splashed into the water before the rest of his body, and I laughed as he scrambled to find his footing in the shallows. "Maja would have loved to see that," I said.

He wrinkled his nose and trudged toward me. "She woulda said I deserved it."

"You did, you idiot," Narcyz sneered, squatting along the bank with his fingers drifting through the current. "You're going to complain the rest of the hike about your sopping wet clothes. Lucky only Half-Chief will be there to hear it."

Kuba lunged from the river and grabbed him. Fear filled Narcyz's eyes as Kuba lifted him up and threw him beneath the water, holding him as he flailed.

I chuckled. While I knew we might get in trouble for messing around, I enjoyed the sight of Narcyz struggling too much.

The other boys cheered the sparring pair on from shore. At first, Kuba's advantage seemed insurmountable, but then Narcyz's head popped up again. "You'll die for that!" He swung at Kuba, catching him in the jaw and drawing blood.

Oh no... Fire burst to life in Kuba's eyes. This wasn't a game anymore, and before I could get between them, he had his hand around Narcyz's throat. Kuba tried to force his opponent's head beneath the surface, but Narcyz pulled him under with him.

"Kuba, he's not worth it," I called, climbing knee deep into the water. Kajetan wouldn't forgive this, and someone had to stop Kuba from doing something he would truly regret.

When Kuba's head appeared again, I held out my hand for him to take. "He punched me!" he said, spitting out his mouthful of water. Rage burned through his eyes as his drenched tunic stuck to his skin.

"And Kajetan will kill you."

He scowled, but I grabbed his forearm and pulled him up. "I had him," he muttered, then glanced back. "What's he doing? Narcyz, you brute, get up here!" His gaze flicked to me, panic replacing anger.

Without a thought, I tore off my tunic and dove.

The freezing water stung against my face and body as my hands brushed the rocky bed. The river was shallow, only waist high, but he was nowhere to be seen. *Where are you, Narcyz?*

A disturbance came from downstream—a torrent of bubbles followed by splashing from above. I shot up and examined the chaos ahead.

Narcyz shouted from less than ten strides away. His arms splashed around him, grasping desperately at the water with sheer terror on his face.

"What's going on?" one of the boys yelled to me.

"I don't know..."

I trudged through the current and called out to Narcyz, but before he could say anything, he disappeared. I dove after him.

For a few seconds, the froth from Narcyz's panic obscured my view, but I froze when it faded. A pale blonde girl stared back at me as her slender, naked body wrapped around Narcyz. She would've been beautiful if her face didn't turn twisted and grotesque the longer I looked—her hair turning the green of moss as it strangled him.

Rusałka.

Mom had told many stories about the tormented souls of women that had unjustly died in the rivers. The tales all returned to me as a terrifying smile crossed the creature's face, her jagged, uneven teeth coated in dried blood. A giggle slipped from her lips as she rushed away, catching me in her wake.

I rose to the surface and took a breath. In that few seconds above the frigid waters, cries and shouts filled the air. I didn't have time to care. Narcyz would soon drown, and I was the only one who could stop the rusałka before that happened.

All my fears faded as I dove again. For once, I was needed; I had a purpose. I wouldn't fail.

No matter how fast I swam, the demon was faster. She slipped out of sight, but her giggles echoed through the water. I followed the noise, wishing Otylia had been nearby. Dziewanna's powers would have helped in the river. I was alone, though, and my own powers were useless while I was awake.

Soon, I found the demon curled against the riverbed, still laughing as her deformed gaze remained fixed on me. She didn't resist my approach, so I cautiously took Narcyz's forearm, and he slid from her, floating toward the surface. *Maybe she'll let us escape.*

I followed, but the rusałka's smooth hands closed around my leg. Panic swelled within me. I swam as hard as I could and kicked at her, trying to break free from her grasp, but her hair tangled my ankles as she pulled me deeper.

My confidence plummeted. I called for the winds, desperate. They didn't answer, and my focus was swept away as the rusałka slid her hands to my waist.

The feeling of her skin against mine drew me in, begging for me to stop resisting. A beautiful face replaced her warped one. Her soft touch demanded that I drown in her embrace, and I surrendered to her will as she tickled my sides, drawing a laugh from my lungs. Horrified, I watched the bubbles of my remaining air drift above us.

My chest screamed for a breath. I needed to struggle, to fight, but my consciousness faded as the darkness overtook me. *Why won't you fight?*

A force threw me to the side. The creature shrieked—a girl crying for help. I knew her trick, but I believed it for a moment. It didn't matter. Soon, I would be another restless soul like her, lost in the Wyzra's flow.

My consciousness faded as Otylia appeared, the waters circling around her as she glowed with Dziewanna's power. All noises faded to a dull hum. The river wrapped me in its cold arms as my body refused to move. My mind felt light, as if air had replaced all my anxieties and fears. Above me, Dadźbóg's light glimmered against the water, and as my arms floated next to me, useless, I stared at the dancing beams. *What a beautiful last sight.*

The time between then and my head breaking the surface was a blur.

The world rushed back to me as I sputtered and gasped for air. It felt like Swaróg himself had taken his great hammer to my chest over and over again. My stomach turned. My teeth chattered. And every inch of my body shivered as Kuba helped Otylia drag me to shore.

"Than… yo…" I muttered as they set me on the ground.

"Thank the gods you're alive," Kuba cried, shaking me more than necessary.

Narcyz shoved him down. "The gods sent that demon to kill us."

"They did not," Otylia said as she rang out her soaked hair. "It's stupid men like you that create the rusałki by abusing women." Her dress clung to her radiant skin, and I blushed at how it curved with her body. I had never seen her channel so extensively in the daylight before. Dziewanna's power made her eyes shine the color of spring leaves and her hair as encompassing as the night.

"Stuff yourself with hay," Narcyz muttered.

Feeling had returned to my limbs, so I rolled over, pushing myself to a seated position and trying not to watch each of Otylia's movements like a fool as water dripped from my face and bare chest. "What took you so long?" I huffed. "I almost drowned."

"At least you enjoyed a woman's embrace for once," Otylia replied, eyes narrow and ready for a challenge. "Besides, it seemed a heroic death for the Half-Chief—rescuing his boyhood rival."

"What is Perun's name is going on down there?" Kajetan yelled from the ridge.

Otylia held up her glowing hand. "The boys squabbled, and a demon dragged them beneath the river. It won't do so again."

Kuba pointed at Narcyz. "He attacked me!"

"It doesn't matter who struck first," Kajetan said, shaking his head. "Get yourselves clothed and back to the group. You three boys will be cleaning the pots until we reach the clans."

He stormed away, and I let out a shaky breath. In a flash, Kuba and Narcyz's fight had turned into a life-or-death scramble. The rusałka had released Narcyz for me. *Why?* Had she sensed I was a płanetnik? I didn't know, but if Otylia hadn't saved me, I would have drowned in the creature's arms. When I should have fought for survival, I'd frozen and allowed her to tickle me to death—just like in Mom's stories. I shuddered.

"What happened down there?" Kuba asked, tossing me my tunic.

As I caught it, I remembered I was shirtless, and Otylia was staring at me. I tried to hide my embarrassment, but my whole face burned as I looked down at the jagged scars from the zmora's claws across my chest. I shouldn't have been so flustered. What happened in the river, though, had jarred me to my core.

"She... it... whatever... was choking Narcyz," I finally replied, pulling my tunic over my body, "but when I chased after her, she let him go and took me instead. It was like she enjoyed it, laughing as she tickled and suffocated me. I thought... I thought I was dead until Otylia showed up." I looked from the ground to her. "Thank you."

Narcyz scoffed as he climbed up the hill. "First girl ever fond of him—a naked demon."

I would have never guessed the first time I saw a woman naked would be a demon that wanted to kill me. After the last week, though, it just seemed like my luck—or lack thereof. I felt like a fool, letting her draw me in.

"You're welcome, Narcyz," I spat. "Maybe, I'll let you die next time so your soul can spend eternity with her."

"He'd need a soul for that," Kuba said, smirking. "What did she look like, the rusałka? I heard they're—"

Otylia groaned and stormed off before he could finish. I chuckled watching her go, not knowing why my chest twinged as she did. "She was disgusting and beautiful at the same time," I said, "like the most horrible thing you can imagine mixed with a goddess."

"Huh… Not my thing."

"I'd hope not. C'mon. Kajetan is already ready to kill us, and we haven't even made it past Borys's lunch—not that my stomach can handle his gruel after that."

He faked vomiting as we climbed back to our gear. "I don't think mine could anyway."

When we rejoined the rest of the group around the small cooking fire, everyone's eyes were on me, except Otylia's. I may have saved Narcyz, but I knew they were eager to pounce on my dance with the beast. The only question was who swung first.

Marek spun away from his gang of warriors near the horses. *Of course.* The corners of his mouth curled as he lumbered toward me, the head of his iron ax shining in the sunlight. "Give up on humans, did you?"

His goons laughed, but I resisted the irritation trickling through my veins as I grabbed my share of the food. Kajetan already had his eye on me and I was soaked. Igniting Marek's ego into a fury would only make matters worse for all of us.

"Did you hear me, Half-Chief?"

I sat with Kuba on a fallen log, scooping the bitter soup into my mouth. Though I still shook from the fight and the cold, I was hungrier than I'd thought. The long days had taken a toll on my body. I needed every bit of energy I could find.

Marek knocked the spoon from my grasp, and I gritted my teeth as it flew into the dirt. "I'm talking to you!" he snapped. "Your father wouldn't appreciate you ignoring one of his chiefs, would he?"

"He also wouldn't appreciate his chief acting like an immature boy unworthy of his title," Xobas said, grabbing his shoulder. "Warriors do not fight within the tribe. If the clans were watching, they'd see us as weak and divided. They don't make peace with those they see as easy opponents."

Shrugging him off, Marek shot me a glance and stormed away. I smiled up at Xobas, never more grateful for him than I was in that moment. "Thanks. Didn't want to pick another fight today."

He sat as I grabbed my spoon from the dirt and wiped it clean with my tunic. "Is it true?" he asked.

"Yeah!" Kuba exclaimed. "Narcyz was dead in the water until Wacław dove after him."

Xobas looked at me with concern as I sighed. "He's right," I said. "The rusałka would have killed Narcyz if I hadn't pulled him from her. That didn't stop her from trying to take me instead, though."

"Strange. Two demons have attacked you now."

Three...

He glanced at Otylia. "Does your whisperer know anything?"

"She's not *my* whisperer," I said.

"Then perhaps it's best to not disappear into the woods with her," he replied, patting me on the back before he stood. "We must be on watch for other monsters, both demonic and not." With one last scowl toward Marek's circle, he walked away.

I sighed as my eyes drifted to Otylia, leaning against a tree with Ara, as far away from the warriors as she could be. She held her cloak closed around her wet dress as she ate her soup. *Why do I care so much about what people think—what she thinks?*

Even after what we'd been through, I felt the resentment toward her that I had carried for years. She'd called me Half-Chief like everybody else, and her szeptucha spells still scared me. I couldn't shake something else, though, something completely different. Discomfort picked at me when she wasn't by my side, and when she was, anxiety strangled my chest.

"He has a point, you know," Kuba said, following my gaze to her.

"It's not like that between us. She's helping me with something."

"With what?"

I stared at my boots, their worn leather meshing with the dirt around them. "I can't tell you. I'm sorry…"

He clenched his jaw. "You'll tell the witch but not me? What happened on that egg hunt? You've been weird ever since."

"I promise I'll tell you when I can," I said, clutching my head. "The diviners' visions, the zmora, they have to do with Marzanna. She's planning something. Right now, though, I need you to trust that I'm trying to do what I can to protect the tribe from what's coming."

"I trust you, but I don't trust her." He nodded toward Otylia. "I'll stick with you. Just, don't forget that…"

He stomped away, leaving me sitting there, alone with nothing but my thoughts and my soup. I took a sip from my spoon. *Great, and now that's cold.* I knew I should've told Kuba, but part of me feared that he would abandon me—like everyone else—if he knew the truth. Who would want to be friends with a demon?

I dumped the contents of my bowl and joined Kuba and Narcyz to clean the cookware. Kuba wouldn't talk to me, and it was humiliating to be punished for saving Narcyz's life. Still, the menial work was a nice distraction from the growing fear in my chest. The more time that passed without us figuring out how to defeat Marzanna and free Father from her illness, the more hope I lost.

When we finished, I grabbed my gear and joined the group as we crossed a shallow, rocky section of the river. I watched the waters with each step, half-expecting to see a hand reach for my ankle. None came, though, and we entered the forest on the opposite side.

Why must it be so cold when I'm soaked?

The air lost its heat the further we went, odd for the midafternoon. Even when the trees parted into a seemingly endless plain, its high grasses and rolling hills replacing the sea of bark and dirt, the sun didn't bring its usual friendly warmth. Ahead of me, the riders guided the way through the brush. Kuba was avoiding me now, so I walked by myself in the back.

What little energy I had before had been drained by the clash with the rusałka and the glare of my best friend. At least with Kuba by my side, I had his ramblings to keep me entertained. I had never needed to talk because he'd never stopped—exactly as I'd wanted it. Alone, though, Marzanna's words returned to me.

Your time to choose will come. It would be a pity if your father and tribe suffered because you did so poorly.

What choice did I have? Whether it was Father or Marzanna, it felt as if everyone was warning me to make the right one when the decision had been made for me. And why was the responsibility even mine?

Father had never accepted me as his son, yet it was up to me to ensure he lived. He was the high chief, Dariusz our priest. The tribe's future should have been in their hands. Instead, Marzanna had handed me the dagger that could save the tribe or end it. Being a płanetnik that wandered at night didn't qualify me to play with fate. I may have jumped the fire, but more than ever, I felt like just another lost boy.

"Stare at your feet much longer and you'll be a hunchback." Otylia laughed, springing from the tall grasses.

I staggered back. "What was that for?" I asked, suddenly very self-aware.

"Thought it might be funny," she said as we continued behind the others. "And I was right. Did you think I was another demon?"

"Are you not one?"

She grinned and rolled her eyes as we reached the peak of a hill. From here, we could see everywhere Dadźbóg's light kissed the bloomless golden plains. My breaths were hard to find as I gasped in awe of it, unlike anything I had ever seen. The forests of our village gave way to some open lands, but they paled in comparison. Here, Perun's clouds darkened the massive blue sky as they plowed toward us from the east.

"It's beautiful..." was all I could think to say.

Otylia looked from the landscape to me, passion filling her eyes. Though her szeptucha aura had faded, there was something different about her.

I took in every inch of her face, from the three freckles alongside her left ear to the few stray hairs that had fled from her braid as if they feared the bones within. I'd never looked close enough to notice those marks before. For some reason, it brought me a sense of ease to know the szeptucha blessed by two goddesses had the same imperfections as me.

"It's what we must protect from those who mean to destroy it," she said.

"You mean Marzanna."

"Yes, among others." She marched down the hill, and the grasses parted around her before engulfing all but her head.

With one last look at the majesty around me, I followed. Blades of grass and brambles cut at my arms until the tall plants yielded to shorter grasses, finally allowing me to see a few strides ahead. Otylia didn't look back as her fingers slid through the tips of the grasses. I even caught the glimpse of a soft smile on her face when she glanced down at one flower that had decided it had waited long enough to bloom.

"If it gets any colder, it'll wish it was more patient," I said.

Her hands cupped the little pink flower as she whispered too quietly for me to hear. When she stopped, its stem stretched until the flower was wrapped in a bud.

The channeling still unsettled me, but I approached and examined the plant, now like all the others. "I thought you had to draw from your *żityje* to do that."

The ends of her mouth flicked up for a moment. "Some things are worth drawing from your own strength to save," she said before jogging after the group. They had crested the next hill, and we needed to catch up if we were going to avoid any more suspicions.

I cursed my tired legs but ran after her. The east wind whipped through my damp hair, sending a shiver down my spine as I focused and tried to fall into sync with it. It was odd that it was so strong—usually the storms came from the northern or northwest winds. Even with its strength, though, the breeze was as distant as ever, nothing like the feeling of it joining with me that first night.

I had practiced controlling the winds in my soul-form since we'd left, commanding the gales around the camp while the others slept. A calm connection with the air itself had replaced the full power of the winds' anger. I could sense every storm for many miles, the rain and thunder in the clouds as well as their direction. This storm hadn't been there the night before, but I wasn't worried. Storms came and went like, well, the wind.

"About time you caught up," Narcyz said with a glare as we reached the top of the hill.

I smirked. "I'm flattered that you missed me."

"Zmory, rusałki, and witches," he said, looking from Otylia to me. "You have a kink for the mysterious, Half-Chief?"

I clenched my fists. Most of the group had heard, and they saw the unease painted on my face.

Narcyz pushed my chest. "Not going to deny it? What's next? You going to bed a hedgehog?"

With a step back, I hung my head. *He's not worth it*, I told myself.

He punched my shoulder. "What's wrong, Half-Chief? Too worried Jacek will hit you again?"

I swung.

My fist struck just below his nose, sending him staggering and drawing cheers from the gathered boys. I winced as my knuckles throbbed. But for once, I regretted nothing.

Narcyz spat and wiped the blood from his chin. "Maybe your Father didn't raise a eunuch."

He readied a fighting stance and shuffled forward, but a horse plowed between us. I fell on my back as Kajetan yelled from upon it, "I swear on Perun's Ax that I will leave you both to die if I hear you bickering again. Your fathers will thank me for ridding them of you clods."

Narcyz curled his lip as I pushed myself to my feet. "It will not happen again," I said.

"Good." Kajetan pulled on the reins to steady his horse. It let out a snort and lowered its head in submission, still clacking its teeth against the bit. "Narcyz, you will march with Chief Marek in the front guard. Stray from his mount's side and you'll have the unfortunate honor of being beaten by the flat of Xobas's sword."

"But—" he appealed, frustration replacing his cockiness.

"Not another word, boy. You have much to learn." I chuckled, but Kajetan's sharp gaze turned to me. "This is not a game. Otylia will join us at the front while you remain at the rear. I don't care what fraternizing you two have been doing, but it ends now. The festivals are over, and it is our responsibility to prevent a war. Our honor and our tribe are on the line. You should understand that better than most."

With that, he rode off to the front, leaving me lost on what to do next. Kuba was bitter and distant, and while I normally preferred being alone to talking with most people, I was actually enjoying the time with Otylia. Even after knowing her for years growing up, something about her was fascinating, urging me to learn more. That was over, for now.

Narcyz spat at my feet before following Kajetan, and I met the gaze of Kuba among the crowd of faces staring at me. His mouth was stretched in a narrow line. *I'll tell him soon...*

When Otylia passed, she avoided eye contact. I watched her heels kick the back of her dress as she walked, leaving me with nothing but the fading crunches of her boots against the dirt and the rattle of her amulets.

23

Otylia

Why did I ever curse the warmth?

WE'D MADE CAMP ON TOP OF A HILL somewhere in the plains. Here, the sky seemed larger than possible in the forest. Stars painted the night alongside the godless moon—each a person's soul yet to die. When they did, the star would fall with their soul as they traveled to Nawia and Weles.

Without Dadźbóg's heat, the cold had worked its way through my thin wool cloak as I wrapped myself tight within it upon my bedroll. Storm clouds were approaching. My dress had dried since our encounter with the rusałka, but the cloak would be useless if I was soaked to the bone. Ara lay strides away, too far to provide warmth. Of course, she kept her distance the one time I wouldn't have complained about her invading my personal space.

I sighed and stared up at the stars. Sleep hadn't been my friend ever since Wacław had told me about Marzanna's plan. I couldn't stop thinking about Jaryło's alleged betrayal. Was it true? Even if it was, did it make what she'd done and what she was doing any less horrific? All of Jawia was caught in the middle of their marital dispute, and apparently it was up to us to fix it.

Great. Because relationship counseling is my strong point.

Instead of letting those thoughts tear me apart for another night, I tried to remember the stories Father and Mother used to tell. The first that came to my mind was that of Simargł, the god of unbridled fire.

I'd lain between Mother and Father in the grasses by our house. I had been no older than six, and the moon had been a thin crescent, making the stars seem even brighter.

"Simargł is angry tonight," Father said as he pointed to a large star in the north.

"To be chained like that... You would be furious too," Mother replied, transfixed by the glimmering light.

Father smiled, the kind of smile full of joy that I hadn't seen since Mother's death. "Maybe that's a story for when she's older."

"Tell me!" I demanded as I grabbed his hand.

He chuckled and took a deep sigh. "All right, I'll give you the short version of the story. Simargł is a fearsome god of fire, but not Swaróg's celestial fire. No, Simargł believes only in destruction. Despite that, he was allowed among the gods for some time, marrying Kupalnitsa, goddess of the night, and having twins: Kupalo and Kostroma. He loved his children, and they tamed his rage until Kupalo heard the song of the Sirin, a beautiful creature with the head of a woman and the body of a bird, and was carried away to Nawia. When the boy returned, Kostroma had made a wreath that she boasted could never be blown from her head."

"Then she would never marry," Mother added with a wink.

"Yes, but the gods heard the girl's pride. Perun called a storm, and Strzybóg's great winds blew the wreath into the river. It floated downstream to where Kupalo was waiting. He discovered the wreath, not knowing it was his twin's. When he found Kostroma and was struck by her beauty, he returned the wreath to her. By the traditions, they were wed."

"Eww," I said. "Why would the gods do that?"

Mother ran her fingers along my cheek. "The gods aren't keen to be tested."

"No," Father replied, "they aren't. But their punishment proved too harsh this time. Both twins killed themselves when they discovered the truth, and Kostroma became the first miawka. Simargł was outraged at what the gods had done to his children. They tried to make amends, turning Kupalo and Kostroma into a beautiful flower with golden and blue petals called the *Kupalo-da-Miawka*. Noc Kupały is a celebration named after the love they found."

"Mi-aw-ka?" I asked, sounding out each part.

Shadows seemed to cross his eyes. "A *założnye pokojniki*—one of the unquiet dead."

Mother wrapped her arm around me. "But there's no reason to worry about demons, right Dariusz? The gods protect us."

"They do, but Simargł's power proved too much, even for them. Their only answer was to chain him to the North Star, where Dadźbóg's daughters guard him to this day."

My mouth hung open. "What if he gets out?"

Father stood and brushed off his tunic. "That's enough for tonight."

Now, I understood why he hadn't wanted to tell me the truth. Simargł would burn the world to ash if he ever escaped. *What's worse, eternal winter or eternal flames?* Despite the depressing theme of the story, the distraction had slowly lulled me to sleep, and the last thing I saw when I closed my eyes was the bright North Star and the fire god trapped in its grasp.

"Otylia. Otylia, wake up. Something's wrong."

I woke with a start. "Wacław?" He knelt next to me in his soul-form. Snow fluttered through the air, the cold flakes falling against my face. "No…" I flung off my cloak and stood in the thin layer of white that covered the ground. "Marzanna has cursed us all."

"Oi!" one of the warriors on watch called over. "It's only snow, girl. Lay your head back down so I don't have to carry you come morn."

"Mind your own business or you'll be the one who needs carrying," I snapped back before storming into the plains.

Wacław ran to catch up with me. "What does this mean?" he asked.

"I literally just woke up. Give me a moment."

I stopped on the other side of the second hill, out of sight of the guards. The gusts blew my free, mangled hair wildly across my face, and I shut my eyes as I tried to clear my thoughts. If winter had returned, then what did that mean about Dziewanna? Jaryło? Obviously Marzanna had survived, but had she already finished off the spring gods? Dziewanna's power was distant. Our connection had never been so weak before. *Is she dying?*

The gusts intensified as the storm clouds grew darker and blocked out the moon's light. Snow turned to hail that whipped against my skin. Behind me, Wacław gasped. I spun in horror.

A shroud of darkness tore around him, pouring from his eyes and mouth, joining with the night. I sensed his spirit burn, and it seared at my soul when I reached for him. "Wacław!" If he heard me, he didn't care to reply.

I rushed into the winds, trying to get closer as lightning cracked and illuminated his bright hair in the black. A force snapped through the air. The blizzard merged Perun's fury with Marzanna's hate. It threatened to pull me away as the static arced across my skin. But I pushed on.

"Wacław!" I shouted into the deafening roar. "Wacław, you have to stop this!"

He spasmed. A cry escaped his lungs. He dropped to his knees, but the shroud wouldn't relent. Each gust became stronger, tearing my feet from the cold, slick ground and throwing me into the frost.

I dug my fingers into the snow as I watched my first friend surrender to the darkness. *Of course.* He was a demon. No matter how much he fought it, that was part of his soul. I had been a fool to believe it wouldn't take hold. Marzanna had seen the truth. I'd believed a lie.

But in the midst of Perun's crushing storm, Marzanna's chill, and

Wacław's winds, there was another power lingering around me. *"Don't give up on him,"* Mokosz's voice called in my mind.

The tether I'd felt between us demanded I keep going. I had no choice. I gritted my teeth and whispered a prayer in the old tongue that Mother had taught me on her death bed, "When the light disappears, give me strength."

I pulled on our connection with everything I had and clawed forward, even when my arms screamed and my shoulders throbbed. Each foot was an eternity. Every second stole air from my lungs as the wicked winds sought to suffocate me.

My fingers bled in the hard ground. My eyes stung from the gales. I thought of Mother, of her smile and the smell of her lilac perfume when she'd held me in her arms. Marzanna had taken her from me, and now she'd taken Dziewanna. I wouldn't let Wacław be next. I couldn't.

A whirlwind had formed around him, stronger than the one he'd summoned with the golden egg. I shoved away my fear and lunged toward it with the little energy I had left. The winds screamed, but I broke through the barrier and stumbled into Wacław as he levitated off the ground. His eyes were black and distant, his skin cold.

"Wacław," my voice croaked as I held his face in my hands.

The darkness flickered from his eyes for only a second. "Otylia?" he mumbled.

"I'm here," I whispered with my remaining breath. "Fight it."

Then my air was gone. I collapsed at his feet, writhing in pain. I reached for Dziewanna's power, but it fled my grasp. All that remained was a cold void that even Mokosz's presence couldn't destroy. I needed Dziewanna. I needed my goddess. But I was alone.

My consciousness faded. The darkness danced around me, excited for the kill, but just as my vision slipped and I drifted like a leaf among the gales, Wacław's eyes shot open. He cried out, and a blast blew apart the whirlwind.

For a second, I could breathe as the moonlight crept over us. Wacław heaved, shaking and glaring into the night. Then the darkness returned.

The winds crashed down with the power of a thousand horses, battering my body as tears streamed down my cheeks. Wacław stood over me. A shroud swept around him, and with each wave, he fought back harder and protected me from its attacks. Then, he clenched his fists against his chest and loosed a shout.

The winds broke and turned against the darkness. Screeching filled the air, tearing at my ears, but Wacław threw out his arms. "Cease!" he yelled.

They listened.

All around us, the winds stilled. Moonlight cut through the darkness as the storm clouds dissipated and took the hail with it. Wacław fell into me, and for a moment, we knelt there, holding each other out of the frost as he shivered.

"You all right?" he asked, his breaths heavy against my neck.

"I should ask you that. What in Weles just happened?"

"I... I'm not sure." He took a raspy breath, slowly raking his hair out of his eyes, as if he didn't trust his own body. "When I reached out for the winds, it felt like they were tearing me apart. There was an old man wearing a wide-brimmed hat in the gale. He demanded that I embrace my power and push the storm west, to prove Marzanna's strength to the tribe. It was intoxicating, like I'd never felt what it meant to be alive before, but when you stepped through the whirlwind, I realized what was happening. I tried to stop it..."

A twinge of anguish crossed his face. "Marzanna will know I disobeyed her," he whispered. "She'll kill Father, then Mom and—"

"Then we have to get to her first," I interrupted, clutching his hand. "That man must have been another płanetnik." Father had told me stories of hundreds of demons. Only one fit that description. "But if Marzanna's alive, why would she need demons to call a storm?"

"I don't know..." He stared down at his palm, where the light from Marzanna's Frostmark glowed through his hand-wrap, but there was something else. He pulled back, his eyes wide as black lines crept their way across his forearms and neck. "What's happening to me?" he asked, trembling.

No... My heart stopped as I traced the blackened veins. I'd never seen anything like this before, but there had always been rumors of what happened when a demon drained someone's life force. "You used up your *žityje* to save me... Wacław, you're dying."

24

Wacław

I'm dying?

JUST MINUTES BEFORE, I had been more alive than ever with the winds rushing through me. The entire world had been at my fingertips as I sensed the storm rushing against the trees and Otylia's free hair. If I'd listened to the płanetnik, I would have blanketed the tribe in a blizzard and shown Mikołaj he was wrong about me. It frightened me how tempting the offer was.

But now my muscles burned as if the winds had seared my veins. My power was killing me, sucking away every drop of energy I had. The pain was too much, and all my senses were numb except for the ash that singed my soul itself.

I stared up at Otylia as she held me in her arms, protecting me from the frost. Though her words were lost to my ears, I knew she pleaded for my life as rivers flowed down her cheeks and strands of her dark hair covered her face. My fading mind realized this was the first time I had seen her hair unbraided since we were children. Only women with no intention of marrying ever wore their hair down when awake. Seeing her like that should've been an invasion of her privacy, but instead, she looked free.

Another figure appeared next to her. "Kuba?" It all became a blur as they clashed, sending me into the frigid earth, but the chill against my skull grounded my mind and pulled me back to reality.

Kuba smiled uncomfortably, looking at the spot on the ground he probably thought I was. "What has the witch gotten you into?" he asked with his usual dose of sarcasm.

"There's no time to explain," Otylia growled as she grabbed my forearm and helped me up. Still holding my arm, she wrapped both of our hands in the twine usually tied in her hair. "Fighting the płanetnik drained your soul. I need to transfer my *żityje* to you. No matter what you see during the ritual, don't let go."

"Don't let go," I muttered to myself, my mind fleeting.

Through her quick breaths, Otylia whispered in the old tongue. The bond between us glowed, and as her eyes met mine, a flash blinded me. Whispers overtook the air and circled us on the winds. The chill faded. Energy flooded back into me. I felt her heartbeat not in our grip but in my chest, as if our hearts raced together in the gale of light.

What is happening?

A tide of emotions hit me at once—Otylia's thoughts and fears, joys and sorrows. I saw the world through her eyes and experienced her connection to her goddesses and nature around us. Our souls danced together as one, our hopes and desires swirling as whispers in Perun's mightiest storm. I'd thought the winds coursing through my veins had been the first time I'd truly lived. But I'd been wrong. That strength, that brutal craving for more power, was nothing compared to the purity of the ritual. Our eyes never broke from each other, and though I sensed her pain, there was something else that burned like the heat of the summer sun.

Reality came crashing back.

I gasped as the freezing of my skin and burning of my insides struck simultaneously. When I looked down at my hands, the black lines had disappeared, and it no longer felt like my body had given up on life itself. The world seemed different, though, incomplete.

Otylia's bold green eyes hadn't left me, but for once, they were soft. In them was everything I had seen, everything I knew she'd experienced. The flood of experiences and emotions was too much to comprehend with my exhausted mind.

As we continued our grip, though, either too jarred or too afraid to let go, I understood her more than ever. My heart broke knowing the pain she carried and the suffering I'd caused her. Her soul had hit me in a flash, yet all I wanted was to know more. I wanted to know *her* more.

Kuba stood alongside us, his jaw hanging open. "How? What? Why?"

Otylia ripped away the twine and averted her gaze. Her cheeks were red from more than the snow. *What did she see?* "Wacław can tell you. I've done my part."

"But—" I started.

Her glare returned as she wrapped the twine around her hand like a fighter protecting their knuckles. "I've done enough. We can figure out what to do about Marzanna in the morning." With her hair flowing behind her, she stormed over the crest of the hill, leaving me with a lonely ache in my heart.

Watching her go hurt almost as much as the *żiłyje* draining from my veins. I had wondered for so long what she thought of my power, of me. It shouldn't have mattered, but it had gnawed at my mind. While I never questioned how Kuba, Narcyz, or Xobas felt, there was always an aura of mystery around Otylia. Even when she was direct, she somehow never said everything, and after connecting with what I assumed was her soul, I had so many questions.

"I don't have any clue what just happened," Kuba said. "Are you still here, or am I talking to myself while you already ran off after the girl who was making lovey eyes at you?"

I took a deep breath and revealed my soul-form to him, as I'd only done for Otylia before. "If you think she was making 'lovey eyes' at me, you really do have no idea what is going on," I said.

Creeping around me in a circle, he examined my soul-form from an arm's length away. "Maybe I do. When were you going to tell me you were a demon? When you were done bedding your little witch?"

I winced. Even in the dim moonlight, the scowl on his face was obvious, but I was weary. A fight with him would fix nothing. "I'm sorry. I should've told you."

"Ha! So you are with her. I knew it."

"No, you idiot. She still hates me for abandoning her like Father demanded. I meant that I should have told you I was a demon sooner."

He stopped, digging his boot into the snow. "How long?"

"What?"

"How long have you known?" he snapped. "Since when do we keep secrets from each other?"

I looked away and muttered, "Since the night of the Drowning of Marzanna."

"You've known for that long and you haven't told me until now?" His voice escalated as he stomped toward me, grabbing my tunic with a wild look in his eyes. "We've been friends for years, but you tell *her* first? A witch?"

Calmly, I guided his hands away. "She's not a witch, and I didn't want you to get hurt. We're dealing with things even Otylia doesn't completely understand, but she's my only hope of figuring all of this out."

I told him everything that had happened. As I repeated the stories, it was hard to believe how quickly things had changed. Between learning the truth about my wanderings, meeting Marzanna, and barely surviving multiple demon encounters, a quiet farm life seemed a distant dream.

"This is crazy," Kuba said when I finished. "So that storm and all that weird dark stuff… That was you?"

I stared down at Marzanna's Frostmark, uncovered for now. The glow had faded, but a dull throb lingered. "Not exactly. Another płanetnik was there, sent by Marzanna to convince me to blanket the tribal lands in a blizzard. I managed to repel his attack when I refused, but you saw what that did. He's still out there, and I think he might be the key to finding her in the Mangled Woods."

"You're going to just abandon your dad?"

"I don't know if I have a choice. Continuing east is our only hope to end this before whatever she's building becomes too strong to stop."

"Who are you anymore?" Kuba asked, the gusts blowing his hair across his face. "The Wacław I know would never abandon his family and lie to his best friend."

The winds flowed with me as I strode toward him. "The Wacław you knew didn't have the world thrown onto his shoulders after being told he's a demon." Tears welled in my eyes as I clenched and unclenched my fists. "I'm sorry, Kuba, but if we stand any chance of saving Father and the tribe, we have to keep going. No one else can know until we figure out a plan. It would only put them in danger."

Kuba threw up his arms and walked backwards, shaking his head. "Fine! You and Otylia have fun with your secrets. You don't need me anyway."

I watched him go. As much as I wanted to chase after him and fix it, there were more pressing matters, and if I knew anything about Kuba, it was that he was both curious and loyal to a fault. Tomorrow he would ask more questions with bright eyes as he thought of fighting demons and cultists. I hoped.

When I climbed the hill, I headed toward my sleeping body, but something held me back as I passed where Otylia was curled up under her soaked cloak. Her eyes were closed. If she'd had the same experience during the ritual, though, it was unlikely she was asleep. The array of emotions still ran through my mind. Any semblance of privacy we'd had vanished in that moment, and my heart pounded as I wondered what whispers she'd heard from my soul. *I get why she fled.*

"What are you doing, Half-Chief?" Otylia hissed, staring up at me with her brows furrowed.

Sweat coated my palms. *Why is she scarier than a demon?* She shouldn't have been, yet it was one thing to connect with someone. It was something different entirely to have experienced *everything* about them. "I'm sorry," I finally replied, crouching by her side.

"For what?"

"When most people would see me as a Frostmarked demon, you

gave me a chance. This thing inside of me, all of this… I would be lost if you hadn't been there—if you weren't here—but all I've done for years is push you away. Father—"

"I know," she said as sorrow seemed to creep into her eyes. "But maybe even demons and witches can change." She rolled over, facing away from me. "Night, Half-Chief."

I let the grin cross my face as I turned away and stared at the stars for a moment. Despite Kuba's anger, Father's fate hanging on a string, and the fact I had come so close to dying yet again, that small concession helped my soul feel calm for a minute. Words couldn't fix the years of distance between us, but it was a start.

The winds all but ceased once I returned to my body. They were light on my fingers, despite the demon's attack only minutes before. Somehow, I had pushed him away for now, but Marzanna would make me pay for disobeying her once again. That meant the planet-nik would be back. I hoped I would be ready when the time came.

25

Otylia

I'm living a nightmare.

WHEN DADŹBÓG CREPT THROUGH THE GRAY CLOUDS overhead
and rudely interrupted the little sleep I'd managed to find, I already
knew it was going to be a bad day. It wasn't just the burning of my
skin from the cold, the ache in my heart from Dziewanna's absence,
or the knowledge that Wacław had seen my soul. Those were terrible
enough. But there was something else.

My affinity for Mokosz's divination occasionally granted me a
sense of the immediate future, if the goddess was feeling generous.
Today, dread loomed over me the moment I opened my eyes.

The last thing I needed was another problem. With Marzanna's
presence, Dziewanna's silence, and Wacław's power, I had enough
to deal with. Last night's snowfall had revealed something was wrong
with the gods of spring. Winter had returned.

"Where'd you go last night?" Ara asked as we joined the march
behind Kajetan, Xobas, and Marek's horses.

"I'll tell you when we make camp." I glanced at the always snickering boys, but Narcyz wasn't among them for once. He walked by
himself, kicking the thin layer of snow that had remained overnight.

I smirked at the bruising on his lip. Wacław rarely retaliated, and it felt good to know he'd partly done it for me.

Wacław still marched alongside Kuba at the back, despite what I had to assume was a fight between them after the ritual. Ara would've put an arrow in my chest for keeping a secret like that. Apparently Kuba was more forgiving.

I had enjoyed the few minutes with Wacław in the plains yesterday—just like before—but now, I was thankful that Kajetan had forced us apart. That ritual had shown both of us too much.

I'd felt Wacław's anxieties, his fear. I'd experienced the pain of Jacek's fist striking him when he'd begged to see me and the longing in his heart when he saw me from a distance. Most importantly, I'd learned the truth. For years, Wacław had hated himself for turning away from me, but because of him, Jacek hadn't banished me to the Mangled Woods. How was I supposed to handle that?

An annoying smirk crossed Ara's face. "So, it's about *him*."

I swallowed my apprehension, but it was impossible to forget the darkness curling out of Wacław and everything I'd felt when I'd given him my *żitje*. "No, it's about *her*," I said, leaning in closer. "Marzanna sent another płanetnik to sway him to send a blizzard over the tribe. The demon almost killed me in the process."

"That's been happening a lot around Wacław lately."

I groaned. "This is serious. Winter obviously didn't end, so something happened to Dziewanna. But she must be alive if Marzanna is relying on demons to call the blizzards. Marzanna is probably draining her power or holding her hostage to lure in Jaryło."

Ara placed a hand on my shoulder as concern filled her deep brown eyes. I was more desperate for answers than I was willing to admit, but of course, she saw through me. "I know you want to find your goddess," she said, "but you can't do that right now. If it's just you, me, Wacław, and a couple warriors stupid enough to help us against Marzanna, we'll wind up dead."

"We have to do something. Even if we can't kill her, she told Wacław that we'd find Jaryło, so that's what we'll do. We'll figure out where he is, and he'll have some idea how to stop this."

She cocked her head to the side, either staring up at the graying back of Kajetan's head or thinking. "He'd already have done it if he knew how, don't you think?"

"I don't know. Maybe he's weakened like her," I growled as I cursed the sting of the cold air against my face. It was freezing, but I wouldn't raise my hood or clutch my cloak around me like the boys. They needed to understand I was a szeptucha of Dziewanna, immune to her sister's frost. Not that proving it would make them like me any more. "All that matters is stopping Marzanna before she destroys the cycle and Dziewanna's lands."

"Admit it. You care about the tribe and *him*."

"Says the girl who the tribe spits at."

"We're in the same herd there."

I grinned. "Then any more would be a crowd."

The crunching of snow under our boots and the chirping birds were the only sounds for a few minutes. Ara studied the dead grasslands. As much as I wouldn't have admitted it, the conversation had been a nice distraction from my thoughts. Ara was one of the few people who knew exactly what I was thinking, even when I didn't. That was both comforting and incredibly irritating. I needed her. It hurt to know I depended on anyone other than Dziewanna and Mokosz, but she'd kept me sane more times than I could count.

At midday, Kajetan turned his muddy-brown horse and slowed the march. His forehead wrinkled as he surveyed the boys behind us, and he snatched his eyes away the second they landed on me. *Good choice.* The ambassador had rarely agreed with Father. Neither had I, but even being near the musty old man made my skin crawl.

"We will march through the day without rest," he said, sparking groans from the boys. "And none of you will moan about it. The clouds remain ominous, and it is our best option to reach Bustelintin before dark to restock our supplies and wait out the snow. Besides, we're low on food."

His lip curled as he looked at Ara out of the corner of his eye. She was supposed to be our hunter, but even with Dziewanna's dwindling power helping me guide her, there'd been little game to catch.

"There will be plenty for all to eat when we arrive," Kajetan finished.

Bustelintin was the last village west of the Mangled Woods. My stomach rumbled at the thought of missing lunch, but he was right about the clouds. They'd been ominous for hours, and getting stuck in a blizzard after what we'd seen last night didn't sound enticing. If another day of sore legs without a break got me closer to Marzanna, then it was worth it.

Not everyone thought the same.

"You want our feet to bleed?" Narcyz asked as he pushed past the other boys, his wooden shield clattering into theirs along the way. "We'll march hard after we rest."

Kajetan furrowed his brow. "For a warrior who speaks often of his prowess in sparring, you're quite soft. Do you not agree, Xobas?"

"Da," Xobas replied. "He squawks like a boy. A warrior marches until his general tells him to stop. Unless Narcyz believes the high chief chose the wrong men to lead us?"

With wide eyes, Narcyz shuffled back. "No."

Xobas nodded sharply. "Good. Let's go. The sooner we arrive, the sooner I can warm my hands." He pressed his horse forward into a walk, leading the way as Kajetan and Marek fell in behind.

I smirked back at Narcyz. "If your feet bleed, I'm sure a *real* channeler might've been able to make a potion for you," I said, grabbing Ara and following the horses.

"That was wonderful," she giggled. "There's more brains in his shield than his head. Why do girls like Genowefa fawn over him and Marek?"

"Does it matter? You can put an arrow through both of their heads from fifty strides. Better for them to fear you than be fond of you."

"Does Wacław?"

"Of course."

Last night's ritual had proved that. Arleta had once said in her divination lessons that there was nothing more intimate than gifting someone your *žityje*. No matter which end of the ritual you were on, you saw into the other's soul as they merged. It was dangerous. As

221

far as I was aware, no szeptucha had ever tried it with a demon, but I'd had no choice. Demon or not, Wacław's connection to Marzanna was the key to defeating her.

I hadn't realized the fear Wacław carried with him. In the ritual, I'd sensed so much of it beyond just fear of Marzanna or who he was. Why? It was easy to understand his grappling with being a płanetnik, but when he looked at me, I felt it, like he was afraid of *me*. Was that because of Jacek? Or was there something else?

I groaned. Mother always said boys' minds were simple, but with Wacław, nothing was. Despite his fear, I had felt his joy in the connection. Joy of being around me? I couldn't understand how he avoided me yet had so much passion in his eyes when I caught him looking my direction. Mother would've known what to do.

As we walked, I fought the urge to look over my shoulder again and find Wacław in the back of the line. But no matter how hard I tried, I couldn't ignore the pang in my chest—the tether that kept pulling me to him. We were linked one way or another. That meant I couldn't avoid him forever, but for at least a few more hours it was just Ara, me, and Dziewanna's wilds. Nothing could ruin that.

26

Wacław

Why do I feel empty away from her now?

WHEN I HAD RETURNED TO MY PLACE IN THE BACK with Kuba that morning, a hundred questions still haunted my mind.

Everything had changed last night—with both Otylia and him. Though I had been scared to trust Kuba with the truth of my powers, I was glad I didn't have to lie to him anymore. His agitation had been obvious all morning, especially after Kajetan had announced we weren't getting lunch, but Xobas's rebuke of Narcyz had brought a smile to both of our faces.

The snow returned by the afternoon, blanketing everything in a layer deep enough to cover the toes of my boots with each step. Our cloaks did little to protect us from the freeze. I shivered as I pulled the ends of my sleeves over my fingers, the pain making me wish I couldn't feel them.

"Could you tell your friend, the goddess of the stupid winter, to maybe lay off?" Kuba asked, his teeth chattering.

"I doubt she would bother listening, and after seeing her once, I would be happy never to speak with her again."

He cocked his head to the side and stared at nothing. "She's a goddess. Isn't she supposed to be, you know…" His voice trailed off as he cupped his hands over his chest.

"Attractive?" I asked, rolling my eyes, relieved that at least he wasn't too mad to make his stupid jokes.

"Yeah. Like, when I picture goddesses, they're always—"

I held up my arms to stop him. "Knowing where your mind goes scares me more than fighting another zmora. Shouldn't you be missing Maja?"

His head dropped. "I do. Just hurts thinking about her."

"I understand," I said as we stepped from the plains into a forest, the shade enough to block the sun's limited warmth on our backs. I wished for my heavy wool coat, but spring was supposed to have come. If each warrior had brought one, it would have forced us to bring at least a couple more pack horses. It was hard enough to forage for the ones we had already on top of twenty-five people.

"I don't think you do," he replied, his voice sharp. "Leaving her behind right after telling her how I feel sucks. My chest feels like it's being crushed."

Smirking, I elbowed him in the side. "The great and mighty warrior Kuba, son of Piotr the Iron Fist, has fallen in love."

He blushed, his cheeks as red as corn poppies. Despite my joking, I envied him. He had been flirting with Maja for moons now, and since they had been friends for years, their relationship had seemed all but inevitable. There was something pure in that, something I had always dreamed of. After last night's ritual with Otylia, though, the thought of love was unsettling.

"You know they don't call Dad that because he's tough, right?" he said.

"Of course, but I thought it sounded better than 'Piotr the iron miner with anger issues.' It's all right to miss home, gods know I do."

He looked from the ground to me. "Thanks. I always acted confident about her and, well, everything, but this trek has made me think that maybe it's fine to be an iron miner. There's a lot less monsters trying to kill you, and I could see myself happy just returning to her every day. I'm kinda okay with being normal, finding bog iron for the rest of my life, and not having a demon best friend who fights goddesses."

My chest tightened, and I rested a hand on his shoulder. "I'm sorry I didn't tell you sooner. I thought... I thought I was protecting you from everything I'm facing, but I was wrong. Don't give up on your dream of being a warrior because of me." I couldn't blame him for missing home, though. After only a week away, my heart longed to return to the safety of the farm and Mom's warm soup.

His feet dragged in the snow, creating two lines alongside my footprints. "Warriors aren't afraid."

That comment hung in the air for a long while. In all the stories of great battles and warriors, Father and the other chiefs spoke of bravery, honor, and loyalty to the tribe—never fear. Yet, the first thing I'd felt when the monsters had appeared was exactly that. I was scared for not only my life but for Kuba's, for Otylia's, and even for Narcyz's. The risk of them dying if I failed terrified me to my soul, and knowing that the tribe, everyone I had ever known, might perish if I made one wrong decision was paralyzing. All I could do was march on, hoping peace and wiser minds would prevail. *Is that bravery or foolish hope?*

A rustling came from off to our right and pulled me from my thoughts. A little brown rabbit hopped along through the underbrush, apparently without a care in the world. Then came the sound of daggers sliding from sheaths. I had hunted my fair share. For some reason, though, I willed that rabbit to run, to hop off to safety.

It was too late. Before the rabbit knew what happened, an arrow was struck straight through it.

Red tainted the snow. The warriors all cheered for the additional bit of meat that would bring welcomed flavor to our next meal—whenever that was. I just stared at that splatter of blood, transfixed, until Ara looked up from her kill with shock in her eyes. "There's footprints."

Kajetan turned in a flash, and his horse trotted through the snow like it wasn't even there. "Bustelintin is not far. It would not surprise me if they had hunting parties sent out within the day."

"There's more," Xobas replied, jumping down from his horse and examining the tracks. "At least twenty, maybe more, and the prints are fresh. Keep your eyes open and one hand on your weapon."

"Until we see anything more suspicious," Kajetan said, turning his horse down the trail, "we march on."

As he rode to the front with Xobas, Otylia joined Ara to examine the prints. She glanced up at me, and I looked away quickly, my heart feeling ready to explode in my chest. There had been a hint of worry on her face. That was enough to put me on alert.

"Shoulda saw it sooner," Kuba muttered to himself as we marched once again. "That rabbit was a good shot to use Marzanna's dagger."

I held my finger to my lips. "Keep it quiet! No one can know about the dagger, about any of it. Father didn't believe any of the warnings. Imagine if he heard whispers of his son having demonic powers and conspiring with the goddess of death."

"I mean... They're not lies."

"But that doesn't mean everyone needs to know."

"Can I see it?"

"No."

He reached for the hilt at my belt. "Please, you owe me."

"No," I repeated with a chuckle, swatting his hand.

"Okay, fine." He furrowed his brow and stared forward, obviously thinking way too hard about something. It was never good when he did that. "Let's play a game."

"You know how much I dislike your games."

He grinned, giddiness washing away his anger—at least for now. "That's why they're so fun. There's only one rule: you get to ask me anything, and then I get to ask you anything. Whatever it is, we have to answer it."

A touch of curiosity filled me. *Maybe this could be fun.* I wiggled my numb fingers in my sleeves. "Fine, as long as I can ask the first question."

"Of course, *bies*," he said, using the formal word for a demon.

"Thanks for that."

"Any time. Ask."

I pursed my lips, trying to think of something I didn't know about Kuba. There wasn't much. When I was growing up, my time away from working on the farm or obeying Father's whims was spent with either him or Otylia. We had explored the woods, wrestled, and found ourselves in endless trouble so often that I had seen every side of him, so I decided on a less personal question. "If you could change one thing about the tribe, what would it be?"

He smacked his face with his hand, shaking his head as he did. "You could ask anything and you chose *that?*"

"Doesn't matter if you approve of the question, oh chief of games."

"Fine, I would create a tournament. Mud wrestling."

I laughed. Though I hadn't known what he would say, with Kuba, it was impossible to set the expectations too low. "What would the winner of your tournament receive? Weapons? A rare gem? A woman?"

Sticking his nose into the air, he wagged his finger. "No! The victor of the greatest tournament in all the tribes will be rewarded by the gods themselves. They'll make him the god of... uh... mud wrestling?"

"Only the most creative of rewards, huh?"

"Immortality and control over the best event ever sounds like a good deal to me, but whatever, it's my turn." He pretended to think for a moment, but I knew what was coming. "Show me the dagger."

I grinned. "That isn't a question."

"Will you *please* show me the dagger?" he begged.

I grabbed the hilt, barely feeling its chilled metal against my numb hands. Even now, it hummed in my grasp, as if it were excited to draw the blood of a god, and when I slid the blade from its sheath, Kuba's jaw dropped. No letters were etched in its flat this time, but its very essence seemed to scream death—a dark mark in a sea of white.

"That's awesome," he finally said. "Can I touch it?"

"Last time I did that it absorbed my blood, so I don't recommend it."

He drew back as curiosity, not disgust, filled his eyes. "That thing can kill a god?"

"If you believe Marzanna, then that's the idea."

"Do you?"

I shut my eyes and took in a breath of the frigid air, feeling it burn my nostrils as the sound of our boots crunching against the snow surrounded me. "I'm not sure what I believe anymore."

He offered a smile. "You may be a demon, and I may be mad at you for lying to me, but I believe in you. Not many of us would have rescued an idiot like Narcyz from a rusałka by sacrificing ourselves."

He makes me sound like some kind of hero. What I'd done wasn't heroic. A hero, a warrior, would have brought a blade or sorcery and slain the rusałka, like Otylia had. Whenever I acted hastily, things went wrong. "It's my turn to ask," I said, avoiding the topic.

Though he raised his brow, he allowed my diversion, like any good friend would. "All right, ask away."

"What was Maja's actual reaction when you told her, and did you get the approval of her father first?"

"Oh Weles…" he mumbled. "I'm gonna come back to her angry dad clutching a scythe."

"Why would you not talk to him after she said she felt the same way?" I laughed. "She did say that, right?"

He sighed. "Yeah, she said she's always been fond of me 'despite my boyish qualities.' What does that even mean? And we didn't have time. There was the vote and the festival."

I nodded toward Marek, who rode his horse with an ax still slung over his shoulder as he laughed at a joke. "You could have afforded a few extra minutes."

"I'm not the powerful chief of a village of ten."

"It's more like twenty, I think."

"Gods, he's been busy."

"Kuba! You can't talk about a chief like that."

He cackled. "Oh come on! Have you not heard the chiefs and warriors in the corners of the longhouse?"

"Because you're in all the chiefs' favors." I grabbed the leather canteen at my side and took a swig of the water. Only a trickle came out. "Hopefully Bustelintin has a river without tormented souls lurking in it."

"Yeah, it would be terrible if Otylia got jealous of you spending time with even more naked dead girls."

"Why am I friends with you?"

He clapped me on the shoulder, grinning. With a glance toward the front of the group, where Otylia would be walking with the horses, he said, "I get another question. You had two."

"All right, but last one." I knew he would ask about Otylia, but I had agreed to the rules of the game. As we walked, I kept looking forward. I couldn't see her, and that constantly itched at the back of my mind. *She's fine. You're better off back here, not arguing with her anyway.*

He slowed down to put more distance between us and the warriors ahead. His fingers drummed his leg as he waited until they were completely out of earshot. I dreaded each second, but soon, he seemed appeased, and a wicked smile crossed his face. "I know you'll reject it until you're with Weles, but you can't tell me nothing is going on between you and the witch."

"She's a szeptucha," I said. My cheeks flushed. Every time someone said that, I felt obligated to defend her, yet I had been calling her one myself just a week ago. "I'm not fond of her," I said once I recovered, "and I'm certain that feeling is mutual." The ritual had confirmed how much I had scarred her. Despite my inability to stop thinking about our connection last night, I doubted she would ever forgive me.

"Huh." He considered that for too long, sticking his tongue in his cheek as he thought. "Is that why you're always staring at her?"

I dropped my gaze to my boots. The racing of my heart told me he was right, but he couldn't be. Though Otylia may have been my ally now, she could never be anything more. Father's order for us to stay apart would remain upon our return. "She's a mystery I can't quite figure out, and don't pretend I've been the only one watching her closer than I should be."

"You're trying to change the topic."

I clenched my jaw, but I wasn't sure it was because he was persistent or right. Maybe both. "I don't know!" I snapped. "All right? Ever since Father forced me away from Otylia, I don't know what to do around her anymore. Maybe there's something between us, but it can never happen. I can't let him exile her because of me." My voice came out sharper than I had wanted. I couldn't help it. Everyone's constant prodding about Otylia made me feel like a caged animal.

"I'll accept that as a real answer."

"Thanks," I muttered, uncomfortable with my admission.

"You know you made the right choice, staying away from her, right?"

I let out a deep breath, fogging up the air ahead of us. "At this point, does it really matter if it was? Either way, we're marching to war and Father manipulated me. He'll probably marry me off to some chief's eighth daughter when we return, but how could I ever love someone who I'm forced to be with? Who is using me for her own political gain?"

"Has Otylia?"

I shook my head, confused. "What do you mean?"

He nodded toward the group again. "Has she ever used you? Because it seems like she's tried to save your life repeatedly, even when she's putting herself in danger. I still don't get what you two did last night, but giving part of your life force or whatever to someone else sounds pretty sacrificial."

"She needs me if she's going to protect Dziewanna's wilds. That's it." Those words left my mouth with a bitter taste, like I knew I was lying.

"And you just need her to help figure out your powers and beat Marzanna?"

"Exactly."

With a huff, he shook his head. "I don't think you believe that."

230

Shouts echoed ahead, and Xobas cantered toward us. "Weapons out, now!" he barked.

"What's going on?" I asked, pulling my shield and spear from my back.

He stopped his horse alongside me, his brown eyes narrow as he clutched his cavalry sword. "We found bodies. The blood's fresh."

27

Otylia

I don't like this.

THE MORNING'S TRICKLE OF DREAD TURNED INTO A FLOOD as we reached a crossroad not far from Bustelintin.

Bodies were sprawled across the dirt everywhere we looked, eight of them, their throats and torsos cut with brutality. I gagged and turned away, but the sights stuck as the horrific smell of rotting entrails choked me. *Who would do this?*

From somewhere ahead, Marek called back, "Guys, there's more."

Xobas and Wacław traded glances. The general's face was stone cold, and when Wacław averted his gaze, Xobas snatched his arm. "If you're going to be a warrior, you need to see death."

Wacław swallowed and forced himself to look at the bodies, shaking as he did. I felt no better.

These weren't the first corpses I'd seen, but someone who died from illness was nothing like this. Each of the villagers had been killed brutally, their blood warm enough to melt the snow around them as they all lay in the pool of red. No weapons were in sight. Every sense I had, both channeler and not, told me to run, but if these people had been murdered, we needed to know why.

"They... They slaughtered unarmed people," Wacław said, looking from the corpses to Xobas. "Who could have done this?"

"Marzanna," I said, trying to swallow my fear. It had to be. We knew her cultists were lurking in the Mangled Woods, and if they knew we were coming...

Xobas shook his head. "Now isn't the time for wild speculation, Otylia. We need to find the village."

As he ran ahead, Narcyz scowled down at the bodies. "*Your* people did this," he said, turning to Ara.

"Back off, Narcyz," I spat as I reached into Dziewanna's power, but it was distant, and I wavered at the attempt. Wacław had taken too much of my *żityje* last night. "I can sense Marzanna's presence. It's faint, but it's definitely here."

Ara knelt next to the corpses and examined the wounds. "And this was *not* the clans. Our people use arrows and horses—there's no evidence of either. If anything, this looks like the work of your weapons: spears and axes."

Narcyz pulled his spear and shield, curled his lip, and followed Xobas without another word. I was glad to see the snake go.

Kuba smirked at him before he scanned the forest, one of his javelins held tight in his hand. "Whoever it was, think they're still out there?"

"The tracks are fresh," Ara said. "The attack couldn't have been any more than a few hours ago—after the snow had started."

"Then we should stick together," Xobas said.

Wacław nodded. He had his own spear and shield ready, and there was a new edge in his eye. Between that, his weapons, and his puffed-up chest, he actually made a half-way convincing warrior.

He and I led the group down the trail as Kuba shuffled behind, never looking away from the woods. "You're right, Ara," Kuba said. "There's footprints everywhere. Whoever did this—"

"Could be anywhere," she finished, her bow ready as she nodded to me. She was trying not to panic, but I knew that look.

We neared a collection of smoldering wooden houses. Smoke still billowed from where they used to stand, and between them were at least twenty bodies: men, women, and children alike.

I stopped at the sight of the naked, ripped corpses. A little boy's decapitated head lay at my feet a few strides from his torso, his spine sliced jaggedly, like it took more than one try for the attacker to take it off. I slammed my eyes closed, trying to escape as images of Mother's cold body flashed through my mind.

My breaths quickened. Every part of me burned with rage. Marzanna had done this, slaughtered these people just like she had Mother. I'd ensure she paid.

As the others inspected the cottages, Wacław dropped to his knees in the snow and vomited. I winced as pain shot through my gut. *Is that Wacław's pain? Arleta said...*

No. I shook my head. While he had the privilege of weeping, I had to be strong for Mother and my goddesses. The pain had only been a moment of weakness. Nothing more.

"Get up, boy!" Kajetan yanked Wacław to his feet, and Kuba caught him when his legs wobbled. "If you don't want to end up like them, pick up your spear and be a man."

Xobas marched through the group, ordering them to scout the tree line in squads. His gaze fell on me. "Where is Ara?"

I scanned the crowd, but her long, dark hair wasn't anywhere among the worried boys. "I'll go find her," I offered. "She probably went to study the tracks in the woods."

"Take Wacław with you."

"No!" I said far too quickly. "I'll be able to search quicker on my own. Besides, the woods are Dziewanna's realm." My sanity required distance between Wacław and me—especially after that shooting pain that still throbbed in my heart. *What is happening?*

Xobas sighed but waved me on. "Go and bring her back. We can't have stray people wandering when enemy raiders could be near."

I ran to the forest. Once the shadows covered me, I slid behind a black alder tree, gripping its cracked gray bark as panic took over. Mokosz's warning and the swarming alien emotions clouded my thoughts. Was this because of the ritual? Was I still feeling Wacław's pain?

I groaned. There was no time for this. I needed to find Ara. I needed to figure out what had happened here. But all I could do was force myself to breathe as my fingers dug deeper into the tree.

After too long, I pulled myself away and stared down at my bloodied fingertips. "Please come back, my goddess. I need you."

There was a stir, and my hope returned as I turned toward the noise. But Dziewanna's voice did not greet me.

A warrior stood before me. Donning a wolf pelt on his head, he readied his spear as my stomach turned—Marzanna's Frostmark was branded on his bare chest. "If it isn't Dziewanna's little one," he said, inching forward as three others appeared from behind the trees. "The goddess will be pleased to see you."

28

Wacław

How could anyone slaughter innocents like this?

THE WORLD FELT DISTANT as I stood with Kajetan and Xobas, surveying the dead villagers as the others scouted the buildings nearby.
All I saw was red, all I smelled guts and smoke.

"Why?" I whispered.

Kajetan overheard, and he furrowed his brow as he scratched his
gray beard. "Raiders and warlords care little for the lives of common
folk. It may have been the clans, or it could have merely been ban-
dits."

"Kuba saw fresh footprints in the snow," I said, pointing my
spear back to the trail. "Whoever did this could be close."

Marek surged toward me, jaw clenched. I wavered as he raised his
ax and held it to my throat. "Half-Chief wants to play hero and run
down the raiders? Any of them would be worth three of you in a
fight."

"We can stop them!" I growled, matching his glare. My veins
burned as I shoved him and swiped his ax away. *Coward.* "We came
here for peace! Not that you'd know anything about that."

He scoffed and lowered his gaze, a smirk crossing his face as he
shook his head, enough to stoke the flames between us. "No such

thing as good or bad people. Everything we do is for honor since it's for our tribe. Everything they do is savagery since it's against us." With that, he walked away and disappeared into the ruins of what had used to be a cluster of cottages.

I clutched my spear so tight my fingers ached. "If he's right, what did they gain from razing a village of farmers?"

"Food, women…" Kajetan replied with a shrug. "Welcome to war. This is why we fight for peace and destroy those who disturb its fragility."

Xobas crossed his arms. "Regardless, the clans' armies would have left hoofprints. I see none."

"They would have conducted the raid by foot," Kajetan said. "It is quite difficult to bring cavalry through the Mangled Woods."

A warrior approached, out of breath. "They burned the grain, but it appears no one was taken."

"Burned the grain?" Xobas sighed. "Something's wrong. Be aler—"

A chorus of shouts came from every direction. Javelins sailed through the air, striking the warrior in the head and chest. By the time I turned to see the bare-chested raiders rushing from the woods, axes and spears ready, three more of our men were already down. Kuba quivered behind his shield, tucked between two burning buildings no more than twenty strides before them.

"Shield wall!" Xobas shouted, grabbing Narcyz and the boy-warriors around him to protect Kajetan. Only Marek, Ara, and Otylia were missing.

I looked from Xobas's gathered warriors to Kuba. The fool wasn't retreating, and he would be overwhelmed if I didn't help him. Xobas's gaze met mine. Fear filled his eyes as he ordered me to join the shield wall, but I sprinted to my friend.

Kuba stumbled into me as I took his side. He steadied himself and launched a javelin straight through the chest of the nearest raider. "You good?" he huffed, locking his shield with mine.

"Where's Otylia?" I yelled as three raiders closed in.

He threw another javelin, sending it through another raider's head. "Wasn't my job to stare at her."

Where is she? I groaned, but there was no time to look for her.

Two raiders slammed into us at full speed. Their axes smacked against our shields, battering my arm as I thrust my spear forward but found nothing but wood, iron, and air. As they pushed, we dug our feet into the hard dirt beneath the snow. But soon, my footing failed and my shield slammed into my ribs.

The raider before me growled and charged. The impact forced me to one knee as he swung his ax again and again. My shield-arm ached, but I waited for my moment. When his shield's peak dipped to his collar, I shouted and stabbed him through his neck.

Blood spewed over me. The raider's eyes rolled back, and with one last gasp, he dropped to the ground. My breaths sounded raspy and distant as I watched him collapse. *My first kill.* My stomach churned, but I firmed myself as Kuba cried out, tearing me from my trance. *I hate this.*

The second raider's ax was stuck in Kuba's shield. As I hesitated, the raider swung his shield around and battered him in the temple.

"No!" I lunged. Before the raider could react, my spear was through his torso.

He fell to the dirt as I dropped my shield and clutched Kuba. He moaned, gripping his head as blood seeped from a deep cut above his ear. "Go," he muttered. "Find her and make sure we don't all die. I'll hide behind the house."

"I'm sorry."

He pushed me. "Go! I'll be fine!"

I peeled away but stopped. *There's nowhere to run.* Warriors and raiders fell everywhere. Screams rang throughout the entire village. Xobas fought alongside Narcyz, their shield locked with the remaining warriors as they blocked the raiders from reaching Kajetan. Otylia wasn't with them.

My throat squeezed tighter. *Where is she?* Had the raiders caught her in the forest with Ara? I forced away my panic and bolted through the chaos, trying to catch some sight of her.

Then it hit me, a tug on my soul and then a sharp pain in my cheek. I chased it at full sprint as it pulled me toward the woods. *Perun protect her.*

I was just strides from the tree line when a javelin whooshed past me. As I spun, the raider slid another from his back, a grin on his weathered face. Anger washed away my panic. He loosed the javelin, and I charged with a yell.

Time seemed to slow as the projectile raced toward my head. I tried to dodge, but it was too fast. It struck my shield, piercing through the wood with a horrific *crack*. The force stopped me in my tracks, and the javelin's tip hovered a finger length from my shoulder—too close for comfort.

Keep going. Out of javelins, the raider pulled a short sword and charged as I yanked the javelin free. His shield clashed with mine, and my muscles screamed as we stabbed and spun. Wood creaked against the weight of iron, sending splinters flying through my vision and into my arms, but I didn't have time to think about the pain.

We circled each other, our breaths strained. My shield was in my hand, but I held it up—the only things stopping his sword from striking my heart.

The raider shouted and charged. This time, I stepped to the side and allowed his shield to crash into the edge of mine. I released it, and with no brace, it tumbled to the ground, pulling him down with his momentum. He let out a sharp cry as I drove the spear through the back of his neck.

I looked away from the kill as my stomach flipped again. The third was easier than the first and second—not by much. My whole body felt vile. But the pain in my cheek leaped through my chest as a force pulled me to the woods. *Go!*

Grabbing my shield, I surged through the tree line. "Otylia!" I shouted. Everywhere I turned, I could hear the sounds of battle, but she was nowhere to be seen. "Otylia!"

"Over here!"

Her voice came from near the trail we'd entered from. I darted toward it, each breath harder than the one before. *Please be okay...*

29

Otylia

You picked the wrong witch…

THE FIRST CULTIST GRINNED as he staggered forward with his ax ready. "Come nicely and Queen Marzanna won't pluck you limb from limb."

"Queen, huh?" I smirked. Despite Dziewanna's distance, I stretched my soul into the depths of her power and stepped toward the cultist. "Your *queen* obviously knows nothing about me, because if she did, she'd know I don't come nicely."

With one flick of the wrist, I sent the branches of an alder tree shooting through his stomach. Then his neck. Then his head.

The other three scrambled back as they stared up at their ally. He hung a foot off the ground—my first *human* kill. Blood flowed from where I'd impaled him, and his mouth gaped in horror as his ax slid to the snow. I regretted nothing.

"Who's next?" I heard myself say to the cultists as my pulse pounded through my veins, each breath feeding my anger.

They charged together, making easy targets as I knelt and dug my hand into the soil. "*Žńi*," I whispered. Reap.

Dziewanna's power was fleeting, but her wilds were not. Just as the cultists passed their dead comrade, the roots obeyed. One by one the attackers dropped, entangled in the unearthed thicket as it grew and wrapped each of their torsos.

"Where is she?" I stalked toward them as they writhed, failing to break from the roots. No response came, and I tightened their hold with a curl of my fingers. "Where is the winter queen?" I repeated, my voice laced with a feral edge.

"You'll... never... find..."

I closed my fist.

The cracking of ribs filled the air, and soon, they went limp. Blood seeped over the snow. Shocked, I stopped channeling and stepped back, staring at the death I'd sowed. *What've I done?*

Shouting rang out from the village. They needed my help, but I sensed the near-empty pit of *žityje* in my chest. By reaching so far for Dziewanna, I'd used too much. I didn't care. They had slaughtered a village of innocents—vengeance felt good.

But as I turned to run to the village, whispers called from deeper in the forest. At first, they were muffled and weak, but with each gust of the winds, their call in the old tongue became clearer, "*Spěji, malo dětę.*" Hurry, little child.

Child? Little one? Why do they keep saying that?

I sensed a power in the voices. The others needed me, but if there was a demon lurking, then the cultists would be the least of our problems. With one last glance toward the village, I clenched my fists and ran after the whispers, chasing them through the trees. They grew louder as I ran, and by the time I stopped in a grove, they were nearly deafening.

Then the voices ceased. The winds stilled. A shiver slid down my back like melting snow, and a puff of fog met me when I exhaled. *Szeptucha.*

A crackling alerted me to the channeler, but before I could react, an icicle sliced across my cheek. I spun with a growl and met her pure white eyes. "It's you..." I muttered. My cheek stung, but I refused to look away from Yuliya as steaming blood trickled down my chin and dripped into the snow below. Her first attack had been inches from killing me. If I slipped up again, the second would surely be lethal.

Dziewanna's power danced between my fingertips as Yuliya grinned and held her glowing, pale hand in front of her face, staring at me through her open fingers. A white cloak draped over her right shoulder and flowed with her layered white dress before joining with the snow. Beneath her hood, a few strands of her bright blonde hair crept into the light. She was a huntress. And when five more cultists emerged from the woods around us, I knew I'd fallen into her trap.

"I should've killed you the second I sensed your darkness," I growled.

"Queen Marzanna has plans for the boy," she said in the old tongue, her voice sharp, "yet you consistently have interfered. The goddess is not pleased."

"Good," I snarled, reaching out for every tree around me, poised to strike her and her minions down. Nothing answered.

The warriors laughed as Yuliya dropped a finger.

One. At first, I felt nothing but my heart hammering my chest, but then came the creeping death.

Two. The trees nearest to us groaned. Strips of black coated their bark.

Three. The darkness consumed them until they withered into nothing.

Four. The circle of disease grew, seeping deeper into the forest and sapping what little power I had left.

Five. She closed her fist, and a blast shook the air. Trees for a hundred strides cracked and died in an instant, each death like a dagger in my side.

I dropped to my knees. *How powerful is she?*

"Dziewanna is gone, taken by the Frostmarked," Yuliya snarled, sweeping her way to the grove's center. "And you're next."

"No!" Every breath burned my throat. *She's lying*, I told myself. *She can't be gone.* But my soul felt her cold absence in the void she'd left behind. If she wasn't dead, she was fading. *Who am I without her?*

"I'll burn you at the stake," I spat.

"Unlikely." She waved to the cultists. "You can have your fun with her. She is the goddess's gift to the one who slays Dziewanna's

first and final szeptucha. I'm going to enjoy a dance with her płanetnik."

She turned away as the men advanced with spears and axes ready.
I knew I needed to stand, to fight. But dread weighed on my shoulders. Dziewanna was gone, and I was nothing. It didn't matter that I
still served Mokosz. She would never need me when so many others
followed her divinations. I lowered my head. *Let me go to her.*

"Otylia!"

"Wacław?" I looked up at the advancing raiders as I dug my
hands into the snow. *Roots.* She'd poisoned the trees, but I sensed
their roots clinging to life. "Over here!" I finally shouted back as I
staggered to my feet.

A cultist loomed over me. He jabbed his spear toward my head
as I dove to the right, grabbing hold of the array of roots beneath
our feet and calling them to the surface. They shot from the ground
and entangled his legs. But more cultists closed in as my *żityje* faded.
They laughed as I scrambled away from the tips of their spears, and
when a root caught my foot, I fell face first into the ground.

Frost burned at my arms as the cultists pushed each other out of
the way, trying to take me as their claim. The distraction was enough.
When a large bearded one turned and pointed his spear at me, I whispered to the earth. He laughed. "I've always wanted to h—"

The root shot up through his groin, holding him still long enough
for me to pull my dagger and lunge. His shield dropped as he
screamed, but the iron blade silenced him as it slid across his neck.

I smirked down at him while he choked on his own blood. Pride
swelled within me for only a second. The three remaining cultists
shuffled closer, each eager to take their prize. I could see it in their
lost gray eyes as Yuliya watched from the edge of the grove. Her
mouth split into a wicked grin. *I'll kill you someday.*

I held my hands to my chest, feeling the race of my heart as it
fought to keep my body alive. Each command drained more *żityje*
from my soul, and dreariness had already begun to take hold. But as
I gulped down each breath, I promised myself that either all of them

would leave that grove dead or I would. A death fighting for Dziewanna was worth it.

The biggest of the cultists charged first with his spear held high. I readied one last spell, but a shout tore through the clearing.

The cultist wheezed. His eyes flicked to his stomach, where a blood-coated spearhead had split straight through his body, as he dropped to his knees.

Wacław was covered in blood as he pulled his spear from the cultist. Determination filled his eyes. He met my gaze, softening before he lunged toward me and raised his shield. A cultist's ax crashed into it, sending splinters tearing through my arms and chest as I fell. Above, Wacław growled and pushed back the attacker.

The snow crunched behind me. I spun as the final cultist stabbed at my chest, missing me by inches as my feet slid on the ice. I stumbled into Wacław's back. He groaned in pain, still clashing with the axman while the other cultist smiled with his few remaining teeth.

Anticipation filled the cultist's eyes as I searched for an answer. I was too weak to reach for the roots, but I remembered what lay beneath the snow.

When his spear raced toward my side, I called to the leaves. They spiraled around us in a flash, blinding the cultist as I threw aside his spear. He charged anyway, and air fled my lungs as his shield collided with my chest. The world spun. A dagger appeared in his hand as I gripped my own. We jabbed and dodged as I reached for Dziewanna, for Mokosz, for any bit of power in my grasp, but my arms trembled with the leaves swarming, useless.

Then the cold leather handle met my hand.

Shock filled me as I held Wacław's wooden shield. Wacław had left himself defenseless to protect me as the cultist rushed forward, his dagger cracking against the wide rim of the shield. Before he could recover, I lunged and drove my blade into his throat.

My hand slipped from the hilt as he gurgled, choking on his blood. Rage filled his eyes, and he collapsed into the pool of red at our feet.

But we weren't done. Wacław had spun away, shield-less as the last cultist closed in. His spear gave him a longer reach, but each of his stabs met air or the cultist's defense. He was losing ground fast and was retreating right toward Yuliya, who watched the whole fight with a cruel grin.

My power had waned, but the leaves still circled my feet. *Better than nothing.*

With a sharp breath, I swept the foliage across the grove and into the cultist's face. He scowled and shot me a glare. *Good. Keep your eyes on me.* Every pass of the leaves irritated him more, and soon, his stance faltered as he growled.

Wacław bided his time, his face focused as he waited for his opponent to give him an opening. Every swing of the cultist's ax was wilder than the one before it. Wacław slipped his spear passed the cultist's shield in quick succession, but the strikes only skimmed his tunic.

I groaned in frustration. With my remaining *žityje*, I reached for every fallen leaf, twig, and shrub around us and whispered into the winds, "*Stridzi.*" Slice.

Nothing happened.

Exhaustion washed over me, and my legs gave way as Wacław stumbled on the exposed roots. The cultist laughed, sensing his opportunity. But when he raised his ax, it never came down. The leaves shot through the air and cut at his arm and face. Blood poured down the cultist's cheeks as he tried to drive his ax toward Wacław, but his shield was lowered. He was too slow. Wacław slid his spear through the cultist's sternum with ease.

The cultist gasped, but before he had the chance to fall, Wacław drew the Thunderstone dagger and drove it into his heart.

Yuliya stepped back into the clearing as Wacław pulled his weapons from the cultist's corpse. Spatters of blood streaked across his face and dark green tunic. His breaths were heavy and his shoulders hunched. This wasn't the calm, hesitant Wacław I'd grown up with, but from the care in his eyes when he looked to me, he was no demon either. *If only it mattered...*

"Well done," Yuliya said with a cackle, switching to our Krowikie tongue. "The queen thought you would resist, but the two of you together are quite something to watch. Unfortunate."

I charged as she swept out her arm. My dagger arced toward her chest, but pillars of ice grew from the ground, snatching my legs mid-air. I fought as they climbed my torso and reached my neck. It was no use. My *żityje* was drained. And soon, the ice covered my face, each breath becoming a struggle as my mind slipped.

The last thing I saw was Wacław kneeling by my side before everything went black.

30

Wacław

How could I let this happen?

"RELEASE HER!" I SNAPPED, fire burning through my veins as I looked from Otylia's frozen body to the witch. "Release her, or I swear to Perun, I will kill you."

Marzanna's Frostmark shone on Yuliya's neck as she glided through the snow. Beyond her pupils, there was no color in her eyes, and I shivered when she stopped before me. "After all the compliments you gave me during the festival, you're making threats now?"

In one swift motion, I drew Marzanna's dagger and grabbed her thin throat. My hands shook as I held its point to her ribs, right above her heart, and pressed just enough to draw blood. "Let her go!"

Her eyes dropped to the dagger as she smiled again, her teeth far too white to be natural. "You would do well to remember that you are Marzanna's Frostmarked servant, whether you believe so or not, storm summoner. You have failed Queen Marzanna many times, but she will be pleased to hear you have not lost her dagger."

"I imagine if it's able to kill Jaryło, then it'll do much worse to you," I snarled, my voice hoarse as desperation took over.

She held open her hand. Magic emanated from it, casting a glow over the grove as Dadźbóg's light dipped beneath the treetops. "Perhaps I will let the girl live, but that's up to you."

"What do you mean?"

"Let go of my throat."

"Why would I do that?"

"Because it would be quite simple for me to kill both of you before you even blinked, and it would be a shame to ruin your fair szeptucha's face."

Is she telling the truth? Though I tried to fight it, my cheeks burned under her knowing gaze. I couldn't risk her killing Otylia, so I let go, wincing at the red line I had left on her neck. A fury had taken over the moment I had seen the cultists surrounding Otylia. Only now did I examine my tunic and realize I was covered in blood—blood of my kills.

Yuliya danced her fingers through the air as she smirked. "Good little demon. A promise is a promise, so I will give you a chance to keep her alive."

I swallowed. Dread swelled in my chest as sweat beaded on my brow, but when I looked at Otylia, I knew I would do whatever it took to save her. "Say it."

"Oh, how bold." Yuliya approached me and drew back her hood, allowing her long, unbraided hair to flow down from her shoulders to her waist. "Marzanna has seen your failures. You rejected the call of your płanetnik brother to serve her, but our queen is ever so forgiving to those who disobey. Just this time, you get to choose who dies and who lives—your father or the girl."

No...

My heart stopped. I dropped to my knees, tears stinging my eyes as I stared at Otylia's frozen face. I had prepared for Father's death, but did that mean I could sacrifice him for Otylia? Perhaps the answer should have been simple, yet as I knelt there, picturing the ghastly faces of the man who was the tribe's only hope of unity and the girl who had saved my life more than once, my heart gave the wrong one.

I looked up, and the words came without thought. "Let her live."

Yuliya rocked back on her heels with a smirk. "Well, isn't that adorable. The demon child chooses a girl over his tribe." She waved her hand, and Otylia fell into me, her skin chilled against mine as I cradled her head against my chest. "Fine then, take her, but next—"

An arrow flashed across the grove and embedded itself deep in Yuliya's shoulder. She reeled back in shock, but as she raised her hands to channel, a streak of fur crashed into her, yipping and snarling with its teeth tearing into her jugular.

Yuliya clutched her neck. Blood poured through the gaps in her fingers as a red fox stood between her and us, ready to fight.

"Don't move," Ara said, emerging from the trees with her bow raised and an iron arrow nocked.

Yuliya spat at her. "It doesn't matter. The deed is done." Her glare flicked to me, and I shuddered knowing what chaos I had wrought for the tribe. "Betray the queen again and there'll be no saving anyone you love. We'll start with your lonely mother, and then maybe that cute little sister of yours. Ack… Kill Jaryło, or you'll watch them all suffer.'"

Ara fired, but a spiral of frost encompassed Yuliya. When the arrow passed through, the szeptucha was already gone, and we were left huddled in the snow.

I tried to steady my breathing as the world spun around me. Though Ara and the fox had driven away Yuliya, it was too late. Father was dead, and his blood was on my hands.

The little auburn creature nuzzled Otylia as she shivered in my arms. Bustelintin was supposed to have been our place to recuperate and restock our supplies before the rest of the journey. Instead, everything had fallen apart. The cultists had attacked us out of nowhere, and I had *felt* their souls drifting away, stealing part of me with them.

I wiped the tears from my eyes and petted the fox, suspiciously tame seconds after tearing a hole in Yuliya's neck. *Where do we go from here?*

Ara scanned the forest one last time before scampering to us. "You okay?"

Otylia shook her head and coughed into my chest. "I feel like I just got frozen to death."

"Who was that? She looked like that girl Wacław danced with during the festival."

"Yuliya," Otylia replied. "I've never met a szeptucha that powerful. She... She poisoned all of the forest with one spell."

"And froze you solid," I added, gritting my teeth. "That's not all. Father... He's dead. She said this was punishment for me disobeying Marzanna's płanetnik, and if I fail her again, she'll kill everyone else I love."

Silence hung over us as the winds stirred the trees and a flock of birds took flight. It was just a relief to hold Otylia and hear her breaths. I couldn't bring myself to tell her the truth about my choice—not when I was already so close to losing her.

Eventually, Otylia uncurled herself from my arms and stumbled as she tried to stand. Ara reached out to help, but she was greeted by a scowl that was sharp enough to drive even the huntress away. *At least the shock hasn't changed her.*

When Otylia finally had her footing, she looked from the fox to the way back to the village. "I'm sorry, Wacław, but we can figure out Marzanna and Jacek later. First, we need to find the others."

"You're right..." I forced my sore limbs to push me to my feet. My spear still stuck out of the final cultist's stomach, and I winced at the noise of it sliding out before I picked up my shield from where Otylia had dropped it. Though neither were in great shape, they were better than nothing. I had no idea what we would be walking into when we returned to the village, and I didn't want to be unarmed when we did.

Ara gripped Otylia's arm. "Go. I'll watch your backs and make sure no one is following. Meet you back at the village."

Otylia nodded, and we crept back to the tree line with the fox on our heels. Kneeling, we peered into the village. Bodies were everywhere. Where there should have been a few families of farmers preparing for the spring planting, warriors and cultists had joined the corpses of the villagers. Despite the snow, more red coated the ground than white.

"It's a nightmare," I said more to myself than Otylia.

She shuddered and dropped her gaze to her feet, her breaths raspy. "They're all dead." Tears welled in her eyes as she clenched her fists in the snow. "Your father, this village… I failed them."

"This isn't your fault."

"I'm a diviner!" she spat, letting the torrent stream down her face. "I should have seen this coming. But I didn't. Now they're dead, and all of this was for nothing!"

Her body trembled as she glared into the opening. I had never seen her like this, and I found myself lost on what to do or say. My heart yelled at me to comfort her, but I couldn't even figure out how I felt. My insides were on fire. Everything seemed like another world, like a dream. Except I didn't dream. All of this was horrifyingly real, and there was no waking up from it.

"Say something!" Otylia screamed, her pained eyes fixed on me before her voice softened. "For once, I need you to say something."

"I don't know what I can say," I said. The void in my chest made each word painful. "But we need to figure out who else is alive. Kuba is injured and hiding out behind one of the houses. He needs your help, and maybe the others do too."

"Okay," she whispered, her eyes distant.

I limped into the village. My legs were heavy as iron as Otylia followed with the fox, but when we reached the area where I had left Kuba, a rush of relief hit me. Xobas knelt by his side, bloodied but very much alive. Narcyz paced behind them as he held his face in his blood-splattered hands.

Xobas's face remained unbroken when he looked up, his mouth in a narrow line. "Thank the gods you're alive."

"Yours or mine?" I quipped, unable to laugh at my own joke. My soul ached. *I want to go home.*

He glanced from me to the fox that had curled itself around Otylia's calf. "My people have no gods. Did you find anyone else?"

I hung my head as Otylia replied for me, "Just Ara. She's sweeping the forest."

"Then it's only the six of us and the fox. Where'd it come from?"

Kajetan's gone? I surveyed the field of bodies. Too many had died with him.

Otylia wiped her eyes with her sleeve. Her mask had returned, but it was too weak to hold. "I'm not sure, but it helped chase off the szeptucha that attacked me."

Xobas's eyes widened as a cry came from behind the burning houses. He and I exchanged glances. "Narcyz with me," he said. "Wacław, protect these two in case any more raiders show up."

Otylia frowned, and amusement replaced my sorrow for only a moment. *Around her, Kuba and I are the ones that need protecting.* Now wasn't the time for laughter, though. I nodded, and the two of them crossed the sea of corpses to the still smoldering houses, their shields and weapons ready.

"Who you think did this?" Kuba asked, still holding his head. The fox approached and nuzzled him before hopping back with a yip. Kuba grinned at the creature. "I like him."

"Her," Otylia corrected. "We should wait until they get back to talk. Just let me see your wound."

Kuba looked to me for help, but I shrugged. "Let her try."

He winced as he uncovered his head. Blood seeped from the deep cut on his temple, and he swallowed as Otylia pulled a variety of herbs from her bag and whispered to the gods. Seconds later, a few of the herbs withered and died as the rest turned to a dark liquid, which she rubbed over the wound.

"Gah!" Kuba shouted, snatching at her hand.

"Knock it off if you want to live," she shot back. "This is going to keep bleeding if I don't help it heal. You wouldn't shut up around Maja about being the toughest warrior."

As she went about her work, I thought about Yuliya's omen. "Marzanna won't stop until I give her what she wants."

Kuba looked up. "Why you think—ow!"

"Keep moving and I'll stab you myself," Otylia sneered.

At least we're all back to our usual bickering. I sighed. "That channeler in the woods served Marzanna, and—"

"The Half-Chief lives!"

Marek... I scowled as he emerged from the smoke alongside Xobas and Narcyz. Although he was gripping his arm and nearly twenty allies lay dead around him, that cocky smirk hadn't left his face.

"And a fox!" the young chief said, surveying those of us who remained. When his quick count was done, his shoulders slumped. "Kajetan?"

"Took a javelin through the back," Xobas said with a slow shake of his head. "They flanked us."

Narcyz just stared at the ground. He had been by Xobas's side, defending Kajetan. For once, I felt for him.

Otylia finished with Kuba and stepped around me to inspect Marek's injury. He growled with each touch, but she ignored his complaints. "It's badly bruised," she said, "but you're an infamous chief, right? You'll be fine."

That wiped what remained of the smirk off his face as Ara returned from the forest with her bow still nocked. "What now?" Narcyz muttered. "We're out of food and there's no way I'm going into the Mangled Woods with most of us dead."

"Considering the footprints we saw by the rabbit and now the ambush," I said, "this must have been a trap set specifically for us."

"What makes you think that?"

I glanced at Otylia, but her eyes told me this wasn't the time to tell them everything. "One of them recognized me, and their channeler—"

"Lured me into a grove," Otylia stepped in, apparently not trusting me to hide the important information. "They knew we were coming, and each of them bore Marzanna's mark."

Marek held up a silver necklace. "And I doubt any raiders would've left jewelry behind."

"Dariusz always believed her Frostmarked cultists had fled to the Mangled Woods after being exiled," I said with a nod. "Perhaps he was right."

Xobas crossed his arms. "If this is true, then we must send word to the high chief. We can't let an army raze our settlements. It doesn't matter who they serve."

Otylia's glare warned me once again not to reveal anything as she replied, "How do you expect to do that? There are seven of us left. If we have any hope of reaching the clans, it's together."

"Especially if those ice bastards are coming after us," Kuba said, slowly pushing himself to his feet. I threw his arm over my shoulder to help him stand.

"We cannot allow Jacek to be uninformed of his ambassador's death along with almost twenty of his warriors," Xobas said.

"Send Marek," Narcyz quipped. "Nobody likes him anyway."

Marek growled and stormed forward, but Xobas stepped between them and placed a hand on his chest. The general's glare was enough to send a shiver down my spine. "We're done fighting among ourselves. Tensions are high, but we stick together, no matter what." He turned to face the rest of us. "That means all your squabbles end today. I don't care who mocked who, or who stole your woman. We're all each other has."

At least part of that was directed at me, so I bowed my head. "Yes, General."

"I hope that goes for all of you," he finished as he turned back to face the field of corpses. "We will burn the bodies before dusk and camp east of here with what supplies we have left. The horses fled, but we will carry enough."

He sauntered toward the buildings with the others in tow, leaving Kuba, Otylia, and me behind.

Kuba took his arm from around my shoulder. "Are you going to be okay to walk?" I asked as he stepped forward.

He took a long breath. "It's hard to know what okay is after that." Head hung, he shuffled after the others.

The fragility of life shook me as I stood there, staring at the bodies of over fifty people who had been alive when Dadźbóg had guided the sun over the horizon that morning. They were gone, and so was

Father. An endless stream of ways I might have done things differently raced through my mind—with Marzanna, with Father, with the footprints. *I could have prevented all of this.*

"Why do I have a feeling you're thinking the same thing I did in the woods?" Otylia asked. Beside me, she stared into the sky, the fading light enough to show an arcing scrape that graced her cheekbone, joining with the chilled red of her cheeks.

"Because I am," I finally said as I dropped my gaze. I couldn't stand to see the bodies or smell the blood any longer, but we still had to cremate them to prevent them returning as demons. The nightmare wasn't over, not even close. "How can we ensure peace when chiefs and kings, gods and goddesses want nothing but war, and daring to care for those around you leads to the death of a village?"

Otylia considered that before looking at me. Something was different about her in that moment, as if she lacked the energy to maintain the veil that covered her emotions. Where I had once seen nothing but the hard, jagged exterior of a witch ostracized by her people, I now saw a girl so devoted to serving her goddess that she sacrificed herself every day to defend Dziewanna's wilds. She was hard because she had to be when no one bothered to care.

"When all the world wants is war," she said, barely louder than a whisper, "then we must be the ones to protect the fragile things— no matter the cost."

31

Otylia

He's not telling me something.

MOST GIRLS THOUGHT WACŁAW WAS SIMPLE. He was anything but, yet after years spent with him growing up, I could still see past his lies. Yuliya had frozen me for a reason. I intended to find out why.

The work of cremating bodies was never easy nor enjoyable, but it had to be done. And as the closest thing to a priest in the group, it had been my responsibility to provide the final rituals while the light fled the earth. Not that their souls' journeys were over.

If given a proper cremation, souls wandered Jawia for forty days before they flowed with the rivers to Nawia. I'd never liked most of the foolish boys who had marched with us, but they deserved for their souls to be free, not trapped in their body as a demon. Soon, Nawia would greet them with its rolling plains of cattle and grain. Never again would they have to fight or toil.

I'd thought often of Mother's forty days and wondered if she'd visited me as a bird during that time—if she'd been proud. As we burned the warriors, I recited the same words that Father had said during her funeral, "May your souls fly like the raven through the skies of Jawia. May you soar to Prawia's edge and glimpse the glory of the gods, if only for a moment. May you taste the bountiful fruits of the south, smell the salted oceans of the north, hear the thunderous mountains of the east, and feel the kind western winds as you set with the sun. Then, when your forty days have passed, may you visit us one last time before you follow the waters to paradise."

Tears stung my eyes when I finished. Whether they were for Mother or the dead warriors didn't matter. I swore I would make Marzanna pay for all she'd taken from me. For Mother. For Dziewanna. And for my tribe.

No one else spoke as the fires burned away the bodies. Only Xobas didn't flee from the smell of burning flesh. He just stood with his hands behind his back and his eyes fixed on the flames. Every now and then, his thumb would rub the scar on his forearm, but no emotion showed on his face.

I didn't know what terrors the Simukie general had seen in his life. But if that day's events had left him unfazed, I decided it was best if I never found out.

When I finished the ritual, we grabbed the gear we could in makeshift packs: our sleeping cloaks, spare clothes, a hatchet to chop wood, a pot for soup, as much water as our canteens could hold, and what little remained of our food.

The night's chill hung over us as we entered the woods, nothing but the crunching of our boots in the snow to distract us from the destruction we left behind. Xobas picked a spot for us to camp once we reached a safe distance from the village and declared he would take first watch.

As he walked away, Wacław snatched his arm. I was too far to hear, but even in the moonlight, Xobas's irritation was obvious. Still, he offered a small nod before marching off with his hand on the hilt of his sword.

With his mentor gone, Wacław turned back toward the group and caught me staring. I wanted to look away more than anything. I couldn't.

The pain in his eyes reflected my own. Whatever he'd done to convince Yuliya to free me had taken its toll—the whole night had.

We'd had a dozen problems on our hands before we'd lost Kajetan and the rest of the group, but now, it all felt petty, childish. I'd avoided talking with him about last night's *žityje* ritual. I'd avoided telling him about Mokosz's vision the morning of the spring equinox. And I'd avoided admitting to him how much it hurt to see him mourn Jacek.

Gods, I'm pathetic.

Only a couple hours ago, I'd walked alongside the slaughtered boys. That should've ruled my mind. Instead, thinking about the things left unsaid made my breaths weak. What if it had been me instead of Jacek? What if Wacław had died trying to save me?

It had all happened too fast. I should've been stronger, but Dziewanna's power had felt so far that just searching for it had drained much of my *žityje*. Though Yuliya had claimed she was gone, I still sensed Dziewanna's presence. She was alive. She had to be.

"Two weeks ago, you couldn't look at him without a scowl," Ara said as she skinned the rabbit with ease. "Now you're drooling. Not my culture's custom after a funeral, but our clans are different."

I tore my gaze from Wacław and glared at her instead. "It's not what you think."

"Okay then, tell me," she said with a wicked grin.

"Did you hear anything Yuliya said before you shot her?"

"I don't see how—"

I slid my knife from its sheath and drove it into the rabbit. "It's important. Marzanna wouldn't have allowed Yuliya to just let me go if she wasn't toying with Wacław."

When Ara hesitated, I knew she was about to lie before her lips even moved. "No, nothing," she claimed. "The fox led me there just as she unfroze you."

"Fine." I stood. My body and soul alike were drained, and fighting with her wouldn't make the terrible day any better.

Before I could leave, she grabbed my arm. Her eyes were stern like Father's. "You need to tell the others. They deserve to know."

"Tomorrow. I need to talk to Wacław first. About today… about everything."

She nodded. "I trust you. Just... This isn't about you and him, Otylia. People are dying."

"I know!" I snapped. "That doesn't make it any easier."

"Father always said the most difficult, most elusive hunt is always worthwhile. Facing a goddess was never going to be simple, but since when have you liked simple?"

32

Wacław

How much death has he seen?

WHEN XOBAS WALKED AWAY, it hurt to watch him go. He'd kept a strong face, but the exhaustion in his eyes and pain in his heart had been obvious—the heart of a general who had lost his men. Despite his resistance to the idea, I would join him on guard while the others rested. I couldn't let him suffer the night alone.

Hope fled my soul as we went about making camp. It had been hours since the raid, yet my hands still trembled. With only seven of us left and the long journey through the Mangled Woods remaining, what lay ahead seemed more impossible a task than ever. Demons, the Frostmarked Horde, Marzanna, and now her cultists all wanted us dead. I just wished for my boring old life back.

I looked to Otylia. That wound arcing from her thin cheek to her eyes was as striking and dangerous as the godless moon itself. For her, I had lost my father. Yet, because of her, my heart still beat in my chest. I owed Otylia my life, but everything unsaid between us crushed me every time I saw her.

I warmed my hands by the fire as she wandered over, her ears bright red from the cold. "I doubt any of us are going to sleep tonight," she said, quiet enough for the others not to hear.

"I know. That's why I'm standing watch with Xobas."

"We're safer with you guarding us asleep."

I flexed my Frostmarked palm as the burning chill faded into a dull throb. "It's not about that. Someone's got to keep him company, and I know him better than you, Ara, and Kuba."

"What about the others?"

"Marek's hurt, and I don't trust Narcyz watching you... I mean us... while we sleep." I rubbed the back of my neck, aware of my slip up. "Besides, like you said, I doubt I could rest if I tried."

She sighed and looked at Kuba, who had already wrapped himself in his cloak. *If he's skipping dinner, he's really in a bad place.* Her gaze returned to me, the ferocity in it fading. "You didn't cause this. Even if Marzanna wants you on her side, you're not that important."

A chuckle forced its way past my sadness, and I found myself staring at my boots again. Her pity just made my heart ache more as I longed to fix what had broken. "You had me worried. Thought you were about to say something nice for once."

"It'll take more than an ambush and mass slaughter for that to happen."

"Then I hope to never see that day."

Otylia smirked, but when I met her eyes, she looked away quickly. My stomach fluttered. Though the sun had set, the ever-fading moon was enough to cast shadows across her face. *Why can't I tell you everything?*

"We should probably talk about next steps," she finally said, wincing.

I rubbed my arms as the winds picked up and blew through the tears in my tunic. "I know what I have to do, and that scares me more than it should."

"We can't hide it from them any longer. Maybe we were wrong to in the first place." Sorrow filled her eyes in the flickering of the fire. "Wacław, I should've said it before, but I'm sorry about Jacek. He was a good—"

"No," I interjected, "he wasn't, and that's the problem. My heart burns—for what? Father never cared about me as his son, never bothered to raise me unless it suited his purposes. All that mattered to him was pride and his power over the tribe, yet I mourn him anyway. My father is dead because of me. Mikołaj will be high chief now, and unlike Father, I doubt he'll be able to keep the chiefs' loyalties. The tribe will fall apart because I failed to heed Marzanna's warning."

She opened her mouth to reply, but Ara wandered over, casting a suspicious glance in our direction as she checked the pot. "It's ready."

"For anyone who can eat without vomiting after today," Narcyz muttered as he sat away from everyone else with his back to a tree.

I turned to leave, but Otylia snatched my hand. "We'll figure this out," she said. "We'll find the płanetnik and kill as many of Marzanna's cultists as we can—avenge Jacek's death and then return with the clans united behind you. It won't end this, but it'll be enough to weaken Marzanna and solidify the tribe."

"I thought you didn't care about the tribe."

"If we're going to survive what's to come, I'd rather not be caught in the middle of a civil war."

I clutched her hand as memories of the *żityje* ritual flashed before me. "Okay," was all I could muster.

"What are you two whispering about?" Narcyz said, coughing as the smoke drifted over him. "Don't you care about everyone we lost, Half-Chief, or are you too busy rolling around in the woods with a witch?"

Anger took over. Before I knew what happened, I jumped through the fire and pinned Narcyz to the ground, Marzanna's dagger at his neck. "Say it again," I hissed, but fear gripped my chest. My voice didn't seem like mine. Neither did the rage. Yet there I was, holding a blade to my rival's throat because of a petty insult.

Marek just laughed as he emerged from the woods and scooped his share of the stew into his bowl. "Half-Chief grew a pair! Well done, Otylia."

"If you don't want to be next, you'll shut up," she snapped. "Wacław, get off him."

I pulled back the dagger and stood, offering Narcyz my hand. He ignored it as he staggered to his feet. "What are you playing at? Not enough of us dead already?"

I sputtered, unable to find the right words, as Narcyz filled his bowl and stormed off.

Since when do I attack people? The stench of death hung over me, and blood still coated my tunic. Beneath the terror of killing had been the thrill of the fight, of revenge—though I fought it, something was changing in me. Whether it was the demonic part of my soul or something else didn't matter. It was frightening.

Otylia grinned through the smoke when I turned back to her. *What does she think of me now, after this, after our ritual?* Why did I even care? I was a demon, and nothing would change that.

She kicked the snow and joined Ara away from the others. As I watched her go, her eerie gray dress swaying and amulets clanking, I regretted not revealing the truth about Father's death. There was so much I wanted to say, that I needed to say. Why was it so hard?

I realized I was staring and quickly tore my gaze from her. *What is wrong with me?* We had lost so many people only hours before, yet here I was, fighting with Narcyz and gawking at a girl.

Shaking my head, I joined Xobas deeper in the trees. The mangled mess of black curls on his head looked like a creature of its own in the dim light, reaching out to attack whatever came near.

He didn't speak when I took his side. It was nice, actually, to have a moment of silence that was mutual. When it happened around Otylia, or any girl really, it felt like I had to fill the gaps, to ramble on. Xobas, though, expected silence at times, almost demanding it. I wished more people were like that.

I studied the stars as the birds stopped their songs, sleeping with Dadźbóg until morning. Even the winds seemed to rest for the night, leaving us alone with our thoughts.

The faces of each warrior we'd lost cycled through my mind. When we reached the clans, it would be up to me to negotiate in Kajetan's stead and make sure their deaths were not in vain. We could ensure the tribe's safety and unity with their help, at least for now. Marzanna would pay in time—I promised myself that. Whether all of this was because of my actions or not, I would do whatever I could to fix it, but as my hand drifted to the dagger at my side, a shiver tickled my palm.

Can I sacrifice a god to save the people I love?

It scared me that my heart pulled for me to say yes—to save Otylia, Mother, Nevenka, and so many more—but a seed of doubt had been planted in my mind. I had experienced Marzanna's horrors firsthand. With Jaryło's death, would she retake her position as a nature goddess or send us into an endless winter, allowing the tribe to be destroyed by starvation before the Horde even reached us?

I shook my head. Otylia was right. I couldn't trust the winter goddess, but something told me I didn't have a choice.

It was a long time before Xobas spoke. "You're often quiet," he said as clouds rolled over the moon and left us in a few minutes of darkness, "but you're also a boy. Something troubles you."

What doesn't trouble me?

I looked from the trees to him. "A week ago, I jumped the fire, foolishly hoping for love and a purpose. Now, I'm freezing in a random forest after most of our warriors died in a raid that was probably my fault. With Kajetan dead, I'll likely have to negotiate, because gods help us if Marek talks to the clans' warlords, but at this point, I don't even know if we'll make it."

He patted my shoulder with the look in his eye that Father used to give me when he talked of my future. "You asked the gods for a purpose. Just because you don't like their answer doesn't mean it's not yours."

"But what if I've already failed?"

He shook his head. "I don't understand."

Tears filled my eyes as I took a breath of the dry, chilled air. "Father is gone, and it's because of me."

I told him everything that had happened since the Drowning of Marzanna, including my choice to save Otylia. My throat burned as if it rejected every word, but I needed to admit it to him. Xobas had looked out for me for years. If anything, he was the closest thing I had left to a father.

His face remained expressionless the entire time, and the only sound he made was the occasional grunt until I finished. Even then, he stood in silence for a few minutes before he pulled his sword and ran his finger along its edge. "I had feared the worst when I saw Jacek's condition. No warrior wishes to die by anything but the blade, but there are forces I will never understand."

"How do I live knowing his blood is on my hands?"

Sheathing his sword, he placed a hand on my shoulder. "You were never given a choice."

I looked up at him. "What do you mean?"

"Your goddess forced you to choose between the man who never loved you and the girl he tore you from." He smiled as my jaw dropped. "Yes, I know about that, and whether you are a demon or not, you are a good man, Wacław. There are few people I've met who care like you. Stop blushing. Your father may have separated you two, but I know Otylia still means something to you. Deny it all you want."

But I couldn't stop blushing. Everything within me was being ripped in a million directions, and Xobas's calm demeanor surprised me. "It doesn't matter how I feel if the tribe collapses. Mikołaj won't be able to unify the chiefs alone."

He shrugged. "To the Simukie, the world is a cycle. Clans rise, armies come, clans fall. Empires and tribes are forgotten to the winds when there is no one left to remember. We are no different. Things will change when we return, but if all you say is true, we must deliver a strike to Marzanna's forces before they can gather."

"*We?*" I asked. "Have you finally accepted you are Krowikie at heart?"

A spark struck in his eyes. "Your heart never leaves your home. With my people, all the Anshayman Steppe was ours, until now."

He had told me many times of the endless steppes of the east, where his nomadic Simukie clan roamed. I didn't know exactly how old he was, but age had weathered his face. Even ten years with our tribe wasn't enough to replace his time with his people.

"Take me to your homeland sometime, beyond the clans' camp?"

I asked, picturing me riding across the grasslands on Tanek's back. "Maybe you could teach me how to shoot a bow on horseback like your people do."

"You can't even shoot a bow standing still."

I cursed my terrible aim, but considering I apparently could control the winds, an arrow seemed like nothing. "Then we'll race to the great sea you spoke of in the south and swim to the lands beyond, where we won't have to worry about the scuffles of chiefs, priests, kings, and gods."

One end of his mouth curled. "I forget how young you are."

"What's that supposed to mean?"

"It means you have a lot to learn about the 'scuffles of chiefs, priests, kings, and gods.' Our people are not unique and neither are the clans or even this Frostmarked Horde. Anywhere you travel, boys who believe themselves great leaders and old men who seek something to be remembered for lead their people to war." He sighed. "It all ends the same."

"So, you think everything we're doing is hopeless?"

"No, just temporary. Like you, me, and every warrior who was in that village."

He glanced toward the others, who had all bundled up in their cloaks. The fox lay next to Otylia and observed us. Apparently, it had joined the group, and with Otylia by its side, none of us were going to question it. "Sleep, even if it's only your physical body. Your honesty is appreciated, but we will discuss more with the rest of the group in the morning. If you're desperate to stand guard, you can do so when my eyes tire."

I hesitated, unwilling to leave the brief respite our talk had been, before sauntering to my pack.

Closer to the fire, I could finally feel my limbs again—I wished I couldn't. Everything burned or throbbed. My fingers were slow, and when I tried to wrap my cloak around me, it slipped from them. I groaned and stared down at my only hope of warmth, now covered in snow. *Just my luck.*

The frost hugged me as I lay by the fire. My feet were happy to be free of their boots, though, and my muscles relaxed after days of hiking. I shivered and nestled my head onto my shield. Sleep pulled me away faster than I expected, and one thought filled my mind as my consciousness faded.

I wish I could actually dream.

I spent most of that night sitting by the fire in my soul-form, desperately trying to keep warm as the temperatures dropped.

How does Xobas do it? The steppes were supposed to be warmer than here, yet he didn't so much as shiver when the breeze brought another gust of cold air through the camp.

I glanced at Otylia. She slept with her hair loose again, draped over the mark on her cheek, and I wondered if she only braided it to please her father. Knowing Dariusz, he would want his only daughter to find a man, not be known as a single witch her entire life, but she admired Dziewanna above anyone else.

The priests' stories claimed the goddess had only married Weles when Perun forced her to. Even then, she never wore the headscarf of a wife. Otylia seemed to carry that same spirit in her, and seeing her only a night before with her hair down had made me realize how free she'd seemed.

Across the fire, Narcyz had pretended to sleep for hours, but from his constant shifting, I could tell he hadn't reached its embrace. I hadn't been in that shield wall. Based on how much I hurt after barely protecting Kuba and Otylia, though, I knew Kajetan's death would haunt him. He was a warrior who'd failed to complete his mission. Seeing him suffer made me forget all the times he'd played his mind games and embarrassed me, if only for a moment.

Pitying bullies and gawking at the girl I'm forbidden to see. What would Father think of me?

It was late when Xobas quietly tried to wake me up. I smiled and returned to my body. All the soreness and fatigue rushed back to me as I shot awake with his hands clutching my arms.

"You ready?" he asked, a touch of concern in his voice.

"Yeah."

With a nod, he took his place next to the fire and held his cloak tight. It was odd seeing a warrior like him asleep and vulnerable. Legendary generals had to sleep like the rest of us, but at times, it seemed the world could never pick past his tough exterior. Today had been rough on all of us, though, even him.

My mood was sour as I kept watch, leaning against a tree and gazing at the moon, less than half full. Our time was running short, and if we failed to reach an agreement with the clans, all of this would have been for nothing, all their deaths for nothing.

Time passed with the speed of the still night wind. Eventually, though, Dadźbóg rose through the gate of his morning daughter, Zorza Poranna. When his light appeared, I prayed to them both that they would give us a better day than the one before it. *It would be hard for it to be any worse.*

33

Otylia

We've lost nearly everyone, and we haven't even reached the Mangled Woods...

I AWOKE THE NEXT MORNING to a ball of fur next to me and the smell of smoke, ash, and cooked mushrooms as I resisted opening my eyes. But curiosity got the better of me. With a groan, I pushed myself up and surveyed the camp, petting the fox as she nuzzled my cut cheek.

Wacław watched over a pot, his eyes dreary as Narcyz stood. "Morning," Wacław said, faking a smile at him.

"Since when do you cook?" Narcyz mumbled as he stretched.

"I'm not," Wacław sniffled from the cold, "but half of us didn't eat last night. It's up to you whether you trust it more than Borys's elixir."

"That's a generous way to describe his manure-meal."

Across the fire, Kuba yawned. "Please tell me it was a nightmare."

"I wish," Wacław replied. "I made soup, if that'll help you feel better."

Disgust crossed Kuba's face. "This must be another nightmare then."

"Good thing I didn't make any for you," Wacław quipped, grabbing a bowl and scooping some into it with a ladle.

Narcyz folded his arms and sniffed the pot. "I'll eat if you don't die from the first few spoonfuls."

"We left the spoons with the horses to save space. You'll have to settle for a few slurps." Narcyz rolled his eyes as Wacław held the bowl to his lips and sipped the liquid. "It doesn't taste like much, but at least it doesn't feel like my insides are burning."

Kuba leaped to his feet. "Good enough."

I chuckled as Narcyz and Kuba knocked each other over in a fight to get the next serving. Wacław heard and turned toward me, a smile flicking across his face. "Morning," he said. "There's halfway edible food."

"That's half more than Borys's gruel," I replied, sliding out of my cloak. A shiver trickled through my body away from its warmth, and I wrapped it over my shoulders.

Marek awoke to the noise of the boys' scuffle, holding his injured arm gingerly as he stood. "Are we actually at the point where we're fighting over Half-Chief's food?"

"Desperate times," Narcyz muttered before sipping on his soup. "You going to be of any use with your sword-arm like that?"

Marek's lip twitched, but a smirk quickly replaced it. "I could defeat you with just my off-hand, but I doubt Xobas would allow it."

Narcyz scowled but turned away to keep drinking his soup.

I braided my hair as the others ate. Soon, Ara and Xobas rose and took their share much quieter than the others, exhaustion covering their faces. Yesterday's losses hung over us like a cloud. I doubted that would fade soon, but we needed to move quickly. Marzanna could strike again at any time, and the clans would march at the new moon.

When everyone was finished eating, Wacław cleared his throat, his eyes fixed on the frozen earth. "Before we leave, there's something we need to discuss."

I wrapped my cloak tighter around me as I shook for an entirely different reason now. Narcyz, especially, wouldn't react well, but we couldn't afford another fight like last night. Wacław had a new anger in him. It had been frightening to see him jump Narcyz last night, even if it was deserved, but I hoped both of them were feeling more level-headed this morning.

Surprisingly, Wacław told them all of it. His face was flushed red and his leg shaking, but he left out almost nothing—almost. He didn't mention our *żityje* transfer ritual, and I silently thanked him. That was the last thing I wanted to explain.

When he finished, Narcyz and Marek were silent for what seemed an eternity. Based on Xobas's lack of reaction, Wacław must've told him last night.

Wacław glanced at me, but I looked away, linking my hands in front of me as I stared at the hem of my dress. I sighed. This had been my secret too.

"Never thought you'd actually be a demon, Half-Chief," Narcyz eventually said as he paced, his brow furrowed. "Maybe you really are the reason this trip has gone to Weles."

Wacław rubbed his thumb across Marzanna's Frostmark, still covered on his palm, and hung his head. "Neither did I. Nor did I expect to face so many of them within a moon of jumping the flames. You can blame me all you wish, but it won't solve the problem."

Narcyz scoffed. "I definitely blame you, but it's also *her* fault." He pointed at me without looking away from Wacław.

"This explains all your whisperings with the witch," Marek said with a nod.

"I'm right here!" I shot a glare at them, enough to make both flinch.

Xobas held up a hand to silence us. "It's reasonable to be upset for Wacław and Otylia hiding this, but it's also understandable that they did so. Many among us, including Jacek, would not have reacted well."

"But it doesn't matter, considering he's dead!" Narcyz spat. "You killed your own dad, Half-Chief. Congrats."

I clenched my fists and reached out to Mokosz as the fox nuzzled my leg. *Help me, Great Mother.* "Don't you think he knows that?" I said. "Marzanna would've killed Jacek no matter what he did. We've seen what one powerful płanetnik can do. If Wacław were to join with her, the whole tribe would be doomed."

"As would the plains and forests that sustain us," Wacław added, smiling at me.

I nodded. "Exactly. With Jaryło dead and Dziewanna missing, neither crops nor the wilds would grow. Dadźbóg may bring some warmth, but we would still starve, and Marzanna would be unstoppable with an army of demons. I hardly see how Wacław refusing to destroy the world as we know it is worthy of criticism."

Narcyz yanked his spear out of the ground and stormed toward me. "How do we know you're not in on it?"

"That's an incredibly foolish question," I replied, unfazed. "Marzanna has poisoned Dziewanna's altar and taken her away. It's my responsibility to bring her back, but I understand if your little cult can't understand how the gods work."

"Says the girl whose best friend is a foreigner!"

Ara cocked her head to the side. "Then why can I see Marzanna's threat better than you?"

"Enough!" Xobas exclaimed, stepping between them. "We are a day away from entering the Mangled Woods. We must agree on a path forward before then, and all of you fighting like children will not fix it."

Narcyz scowled and stepped back as Marek stared into the fire. "Marzanna seriously wants us to kill a god?"

Wacław pulled the Thunderstone dagger from its sheath, and Marek gasped as he held it in the light. "Apparently," Wacław continued, "but I have no idea how I'll find Jaryło, let alone stab him in the chest and take his Moonblades. If we can find him, though, he may be our best chance to defeat Marzanna or at least weaken her."

Kuba shook his head. "How do we know Marzanna would even spare your family if you followed through?"

"She won't," I said. "Why would she when there's no one left to stop her?"

"What about that goddess of yours—Dziewanna?" Marek replied. "Do you not claim she kills Marzanna?"

I grabbed a fistful of snow. "Does it look like she succeeded? Things warmed for a few days, but now she's either dead or trapped. Without Jaryło, Marzanna would have an endless reign, and *all* of Jawia would wither."

Wacław sheathed the dagger again. "And that's why we must stop her." I could *feel* his heart break through our connection as the words left his mouth, but we both knew what we had to do. The choice had never been real.

"Is there anyone you wouldn't let die?" Narcyz asked. "We're warriors. It's our job to protect the high chief and our people, and we already failed at one of those."

My hands burned from the snow, so I stood and warmed them by the fire. "This is about more than any chief or king. Whether Jaryło was unfaithful to Marzanna or not isn't our concern. He's punished every year by her, and if we allow her to kill him permanently, no one but Marzanna's chosen will remain."

Xobas stepped into the center of the circle we'd made. "If all of this is true, and I have no reason to believe it's not, then there is nothing else we can do except complete our mission. That means we must prepare for the off-chance that not all of us reach the clans. Ara and I will teach the rest of you as much of our language as possible in such a short time. Few of them will understand the Krowikie tongue."

"You expect Narcyz to negotiate?" Kuba quipped.

Narcyz spat at his feet. "Shut it."

Xobas raised a hand to quiet them. "Wacław, you suggested that Marzanna's cultists are hiding in the woods with this other weather demon?"

"That's our best guess," Wacław replied. "How many days do we have left until we reach the clans' camp?"

"March quickly and it'll be five days, maybe more, maybe less."

I remembered the waning gibbous from last night. "That gives us another five days at most to find the płanetnik and her cultists."

"And hopefully Jaryło along the way," Wacław added.

Narcyz looked around the circle. "Are we really going to trust a witch and a demon? Marek? Kuba?"

Kuba threw his shield over his shoulder. "I'd trust Wacław through Nawia and back. I saw that storm demon attack him and Otylia. It's real."

My stomach growled, but with the fight ahead, I couldn't handle even the thought of eating.

Next to me, Ara's brown eyes seemed to burn. "I may be just a foreigner to you, Narcyz, but I trust them too. That channeler in the woods killed a ring of trees a hundred strides wide. Whether Marzanna is your goddess or mine doesn't matter. She slaughtered a village, drove my people from our homeland, and is threatening my friends. That's enough for me to fight for."

I offered her a smile as Wacław grabbed his own weapons and looked to Dadźbóg's light. "If there weren't so few of us, I would say we should split up, but I don't think we have another choice than to stick together. We have a chance if we're quick. Though, that's assuming we make it through this."

"Appreciate the positive spirit, Demon-Chief," Marek quipped as he finished gulping down his bowl of soup.

Besides Narcyz's grumbling, silence took over as we packed up our gear and continued our eastward march. Without Kajetan's directions, we were far less familiar with the territory, but Xobas had seen much of the east. I hoped his memory served us well as storm clouds approached overhead, signaling another snowfall.

Marzanna's grip had not let up. Whatever hope we had of Dziewanna or Jaryło ridding the land of winter slowly chipped away the longer we walked. With my feet throbbing, skin freezing, and heart broken, spite and desperation were my only company.

"You see them too? Their faces." Kuba asked Wacław as we entered a small plain.

Xobas had given up his lessons on the clans' tongue for a few minutes, and I let the breeze wash over me while I took a breath of air. Kuba's question was a stupid one. Of course we saw the faces of the dead. If Mother's death had taught me anything, it was that pain that deep never left.

"Every one of them," Wacław replied. "Even Kajetan's. It's weird how you never think you'll miss someone when they're alive, and then they're gone like a crack of lightning that leaves you burned to the core."

"Especially when you don't see it coming," I said.

Pity filled his eyes. I thought I didn't want it, but seeing he cared calmed my soul, if only a little.

"You'd miss me, right?" Kuba asked.

Wacław chuckled. "If you were in Nawia, then I doubt I'd be far behind." His smile slid away as quickly as it had come, and I knew he was thinking of his father.

Xobas hung back and glanced over his shoulder. "Keep your eye out for any wildlife or edible plants. We've got some more mushrooms. That's it."

"There's always the orange ball of fur," Narcyz sneered before jumping away as the fox yipped at him. "See, it isn't even friendly."

"*She* saved our lives," I said, furrowing my brow.

Marek huffed. "Meat is meat."

"And your people call *me* barbaric," Ara said.

Kuba nearly leaped out of his boots. "We need to name her!"

"Well," Wacław began. "She's Dziewanna's creature, so it seems right for Otylia to grant her a name."

"Sosna," I said without hesitation. The name had quickly come to my mind, but it seemed right, like a gift from Dziewanna.

Scoffing, Narcyz slapped the snow from the tips of the grasses as he walked. "You want to name a fox 'pine'?"

Ara shrugged. "Makes sense to me. She appeared to me as she rushed through a pine."

Sosna nuzzled my calf, and I bent down to scratch her head, which she seemed to like. I had to admit that I enjoyed her presence. Most animals I'd called never stayed long, but she had come without my asking.

"I think she likes the name," Ara said.

Kuba chuckled. "For a wild thing, she's nicer than our cat."

"The cat might've liked you if you'd bothered to name her," Wacław said.

Kuba rubbed the back of his neck. "I was getting around to it."

Suddenly, Marek shouted from ahead. We exchanged glances before running through the tall grasses after him.

The chief knelt on the other side of a hill, his large body amazingly well hidden in the brush, and Wacław tripped right over him, landing hard on his shoulder. I smirked, amused as Wacław struggled to his feet. Then the pain hit my own shoulder. *Why didn't Arleta tell me how the ritual would connect us?*

Marek shushed us. "There's a deer."

I knelt and peered through the prickles of the grasses against my face. Sure enough, he was right. A doe grazed only thirty strides away. "Ara?" I whispered.

She grinned and pulled an arrow from her quiver. "It's mine."

"I want it," Kuba replied, pushing down her bow. "My javelins don't have the same range, but I can take it down in one throw. Don't waste your arrows."

Ara looked to Xobas for support, but he nodded to Kuba. "Go, but Ara will down it if you fail."

"Great," Narcyz said with a scoff. "It's down to the clumsy son of an iron miner to ensure we don't starve."

Ignoring him, Kuba swallowed and crept through the tall grass. It swayed in the wind, obscuring his movements while we waited. With each gust, the doe scanned the area before returning to its grazing among the shorter vegetation.

"What's taking him so long?" Marek whispered.

"Would you rather he run and startle it?" Wacław asked, shooting him a glare. "Kuba knows what he's doing, I hope."

A twig snapped in Kuba's direction. The deer looked up, startled, and we groaned as it darted toward the forest.

Kuba shot forward and launched the javelin—far too short. I cursed the fool under my breath, but Ara jumped to her feet. She pulled her bow's string back to her chin, loosing an arrow before nocking another. The first struck the doe in the hindquarters. As it limped away, the second went straight through its head.

I smiled and wrapped my arms around her. "That's my master huntress!" It was a small victory, but we practically skipped toward what felt like our first bit of luck since the start of the journey.

Xobas patted Kuba on the shoulder as we approached the deer. "Your aim will improve in time."

Without a reply, Kuba sauntered over to his javelin while Xobas pulled his knife and started skinning the deer.

It would take a good amount of time for him to finish, so I pushed my way through the grasses, heading to the forest. We would need more herbs, and after a morning of stupid arguments, I needed time alone. Sosna followed close behind. *At least she's somewhat quiet.*

"Where are you going?" Wacław called after me.

I took a sharp breath, trying not to snap back at him. "None of you will know where to find the edible plants. I'll return by the time he's finished."

Wacław looked from me to Xobas, who let out a sigh. "Go with her," Xobas said. "Who knows if there's more cultists out there? We'll pack everything from this we can while you're gone. The rest can feed her goddess's animals."

Wacław nodded and jogged after me.

I gritted my teeth but let him follow. I needed to pick the mushrooms and herbs whether he came along or not, and I had a feeling we needed the chance to talk in private. But, just as much, I needed space to think.

Apparently, he got the idea from my glare and kept his distance as we entered the woods. My frustration took over anyway. Not because of him, but because the snow covered most of the useful fungi, making it difficult to find what I needed.

Sosna, on the other hand, was ecstatic. After a few minutes of aimless running, she charged into the snow with a leap.

Wacław chuckled when she emerged with a bloodied mouse in her teeth, dropping it at his feet. "Good job, girl," he said as she devoured her catch.

"It's a wild fox, not a child," I replied, kneeling and picking burnet-saxifrage from the base of an oak. The plant was well known for its usage in healing potions—both for illnesses and wounds. Considering we faced the goddess of pestilence, I hoped it could help.

"She acts more like a hunting dog than anything," Wacław said as Sosna placed the remaining bits of the mouse at my feet, her paws tapping in the snow as she stared up at me. "Adorable, she wants to share her kill with you."

I crouched and picked through the bones. "Actually, these could be useful. Good girl."

Sosna yipped and took off into the woods at full sprint. I watched her go, letting myself smile.

"Do the animals you summon ever stay this long?" Wacław asked.

I spun away and searched for more herbs as my amulets jangled through the otherwise quiet woods. "It's a call, not a summon. Usually, Dziewanna's creatures leave within hours, but to be honest, I haven't called many. I didn't call her either."

"Why don't you call them often? If I could call foxes and wolves whenever I wanted, I would have an army."

"Exactly why Dziewanna only allows me to channel her powers. Besides," I continued, picking a brown bit of fungus that would also be good for a healing salve from the bark of a downed tree, "my powers as a szeptucha only work when the goddess I'm channeling decides to answer. That's why I became drained so quickly against Yuliya's cultists. Dziewanna is there but distant. It takes so much to reach her."

Wacław ran his fingertips along the oak's bark. "I never asked: Why can you channel more than one goddess?"

My hand drifted to Mokosz's amulet on my wrist. Even while Dziewanna was distant, the Great Mother's warmth was always with me. "The gods choose which szeptuchy can channel their powers. I not sure why Mokosz chose me too, besides that I'm Dziewanna's first channeler and they are mother and daughter." Thinking of parental relationships among the gods was mind bending. All of them were so powerful and ancient.

"Then why can't you channel Perun or her siblings?"

"You seem to know Marzanna so well, why don't you ask?" I snapped. "I don't know about Perun. Perhaps, he judged me unworthy—just like he judged his daughter."

Wacław stepped back, his eyes wide. My anger was misplaced, but as I gripped Dziewanna's Bowmark amulet, I missed her as much as Mother. It was hard to accept how much I'd used the goddess to fill the void Mother's death had left.

When Wacław finally replied, he clutched his own amulet to Mokosz in his hand, "Yet, two gods did choose you. That's better than being born a demon and forced to choose between your father and Jaryło. I see now, though, why you're hesitant to hurt him."

"My duty is to serve Dziewanna, and as far as I'm aware, she does not wish for the death of her brother."

"And I didn't wish for the death of my father..."

Silence cut through our debate. My heart ached knowing the pain he felt. I'd felt it too during the ritual—how badly he wished to please his father and prove his worth. Now he'd never have the chance. Like me, he only had one parent remaining, and no matter how much Jacek beat him, that would always leave a scar.

"I'm sorry," I said, setting aside my herb bag and stepping toward him.

He didn't reply. Tears wetted his cheeks, and he held his fist to his forehead as he shut his eyes. Whatever tension had restrained me before faded as I hugged him. After all that had happened, I couldn't blame him for crying, and soon, tears welled in my own eyes.

"Father was wrong," he finally said, accepting my embrace.

"What do you mean?"

"When he told me never to see you again, when he punched me over and over because I begged him not to make me leave you. He said you would ruin me and that he would banish you to the Mangled Woods if I ever saw you again. I was foolish to give in. I... I don't know what happened during that ritual, but I get it now. For so long I didn't understand how much I hurt you, how alone I left you." His raspy breaths were warm against my neck as he struggled to find the words. "Otylia, I'm so sorry."

I buried my face in his shoulder, trying not to lose my composure as we both quivered, but the sorrow came too fast. Mother's face and the little blond boy I'd known for years flashed through my mind.

Everything had gone wrong so quickly. I'd despised Wacław for turning away, yet the ritual had shown me how much it had hurt him too, how much pain he'd felt every time he saw me. But there in that still forest, holding each other in our arms, things were right for a few minutes.

When Xobas's call came for us to return, I had lost track of time. I felt like an idiot, unable to do anything but sob when we finally had a moment alone.

Wacław stepped back and wiped the tears from his cheeks. "I understand if you can't forgive me."

As he turned to leave, I caught his hand. "Wacław, wait."

He hesitated, but I forced him to look back at me. It took everything in my soul not to look away from his eyes as blue as the sky. "What Jacek did to you will never be your fault," I said. "A lot has happened since then, and wounds take time to heal, but I'm willing to start again if you are."

He smiled as he raised my hand to his lips and kissed it. My stomach flipped. My instincts told me to run, to leave him behind, but my heart never wanted him to let go. "Then it's a pleasure to meet you, Otylia, daughter of the wilds."

34

Wacław

What I wouldn't give for my furs.

WHEN THE NEXT SNOWFALL HIT, Strzybóg's eight winds joined in the storm, slamming us from every direction as we blindly stumbled toward what we could only hope was east at this point. I tried to raise my head, to see what lay ahead of Xobas's brown tunic, but the snow whipped through my vision. I was blind.

A dull throbbing battered my fingers as I tucked them hopelessly into my sleeves. Like the others, I had wrapped my cloak around me to protect myself, yet my face stung with each blast of frigid wind.

In the fight forward, I had lost track of time long ago. It could have been hours or mere minutes since the storm had begun.

"We can't go on like this," Narcyz yelled from ahead of me.

"Be a man," Marek replied. He glanced at Otylia, who hadn't said a word since our talk in the woods. "If the witch can handle it, so can you."

She's not a witch. I didn't have the energy to say it. All I focused on was the next step. Though I had no clue where it would take me, anywhere was better than the forest of death we found ourselves in.

Narcyz coughed as he leaned against a birch tree. His breaths were long and hard, but he still managed to snap his glare to Marek.

"She can probably summon heat or something. It could've been her who called the blizzard!"

Silent, Otylia walked close by my side, her cloak tied tight around her as she stared into the storm with her sharp green eyes narrowed. The bite in Narcyz's voice was harsher than normal, as if he actually meant it. Though he knew the truth about Marzanna's płanetnik, it was easier to blame Otylia.

"She doesn't even deny it!" he spat.

Sosna yapped as he scowled at Otylia, but when she whistled, the fox returned to her side. Otylia slipped passed Narcyz, stopping at the last second. Without meeting his gaze, she spoke barely louder than a whisper through the winds, "If I wanted you dead, I'd have more fun with it," before stomping off.

A smirk crept across my face as I stepped past Narcyz. Seeing him disarmed so quickly was satisfying. He muttered something as he dropped behind with Marek, who clapped him on his back. "The boy who wishes for war but can't handle a woman."

Kuba called out from ahead of us, but he was too far away to understand. Moments later, though, he appeared, hopping more than running through the snow. His face was as red as Sosna. I doubted mine looked much better. "Xobas thinks he knows of a cave," he huffed as he held his knees. "It's not far, I think."

Marek chuckled. "First time I've heard something I like come out of your mouth."

"Is that what the women say when you're leaving?" Kuba quipped back, taking off ahead. Marek frowned, but with his injury, there wasn't much he could have done if he'd caught Kuba anyway.

We followed Kuba's footprints more than him as the winds picked up again. I wished I could use even a bit of my power to quiet them, but in the day, they felt as alien as always.

My legs were heavy by the time we reached Xobas. He surveyed us before pointing ahead. "The cave is just over that ridge. It should provide space for us to rest until the storm passes."

I followed his finger yet saw nothing but the endless sea of white, rushing over the hills like a great flood. Every gust of wind tore through my cloak and tunic, despite me wearing my spare, unripped one. *Why does Marzanna curse us so?*

My teeth chattered as I studied Otylia. Determination filled her eyes, her cloak fluttering behind her as she held the ends of it together with one hand at her chest, the other glowing with what I assumed to be Dziewanna's power. Though my skin stung and exhaustion gripped every inch of my body, I couldn't help but be in awe of her.

Xobas led the way down the first slope, and as it steepened, my balance waned. The snow disguised the true location of the ground and threatened to slide out beneath my feet if I took one wrong step.

We soon reached the middle of the valley and stared up at the snow cascading over the top of the next hill. My heart sunk just looking at it. "Only a couple hundred more strides," I whispered to myself.

"Easier than the pines we used to climb," Kuba said, out of breath.

Both of us were lying. We seemed no closer to the ridge as snow slid through the gap between my boot and pants, but my toes were already numb. For once, that was a gift, relieving me of the pain. But everywhere else hurt more, and doubt crept into my chest as I struggled.

Somehow, Xobas charged on, unfazed, with Narcyz and Marek not far behind. They disappeared into the snow, and I cursed them for leaving the rest of us.

When I neared the peak, a young tree gripped the side of the hill no more than ten strides ahead—a resting spot. My legs ached with each step toward it. The winds carried the creaking of its trunk as I reached for its lowest branches, but the icy wind sliced at my fingers.

Two more steps. You can make it...

Ara and Kuba helped each other over the peak as I lunged forward and wrapped my arms around the branch, begging for it to hold my weight as the gusts demanded I fall. *Where's Otylia?* I glanced over my shoulder, but the snow obscured my vision. She was nowhere to be seen, and my strength was failing me with each passing second. *Come on, Otylia… Where are you?*

The branch snapped.

I dropped into the deep snow, shivering as whatever hope I had left fled my body. My frozen fingers clutched Mokosz's amulet, but for once, it provided no relief. Then, something nudged my side. "Sosna?" I asked as the ball of fur rammed her head into me once more and hopped down the hill. When I didn't follow, she yipped and fixed her dark eyes on me.

"Otylia…"

I forced my legs to stand. At first, I stumbled, yet the winds drove me on as Sosna barked and disappeared. I rushed after her. "Otylia!" I shouted. "Otylia!"

Sosna nuzzled something halfway down the hill. I drew nearer, and Otylia's shivering figure appeared, huddled in the snow. Relief and dread clashed in my heart as I stumbled to her side. "Otylia? Talk to me."

A layer of white slid from her head as she met my gaze with pain in her eyes. "You came back…"

I smirked and clutched her hand—colder than ice. "Considering the number of times you've saved me, this doesn't make us even. C'mon, let's get to the cave."

She trembled in my arms as I helped her to her feet. Every muscle in my body was drained, every bit of my skin numb or searing, but hope kept my heart beating with her hand in mine. My will to keep her alive was enough, even while my strength failed.

Blind and beaten, we forced our way forward. Our fight to the peak became a climb against the winds more than elevation. I led the way, trying to block as much of its power as possible, but it came from every direction. East swirled. South pounded. North slashed. Together they overwhelmed us. *Strzybóg, calm your grandchildren!*

"Marzanna won't let us rest!" Otylia yelled over the rush of the gales. "Why has Dziewanna failed us?"

"We can worry about her when we're not freezing to death," I said, trying to stay positive as I pulled her forward. The ridgeline appeared just a few strides ahead. "We're almost there. Look, Sosna already made it!"

The little red fox hopped around, her eyes eagerly watching us. Otylia stumbled into me, and I caught her, wrapping my cloak over her shoulders. Through its open sliver, her eyes were like daggers as another frigid gust froze my skin. The pain didn't matter. If she died, I didn't know what I would do. My heart ached at just the thought of going on without her, lost in the fight against the threats we faced from gods and demons alike.

When we staggered over the ridge, Sosna yapped and wagged her tail as Xobas grabbed hold of Otylia. "This way," he said.

We made quick progress clear of the climb. Though the winds still fought us every step of the way, I could see the cave, and energy rushed through me, driving me to the end. *Less than fifty strides. Almost there.*

That's when I heard the cries.

I craned my head as the gales carried another round of shouts from the woods to our right. I looked from the trees to Xobas and Otylia. *I could pretend not to have heard.* My body was in no condition for another rescue mission, but someone was out there, begging for help. I knew what Mom would want me to do.

"Xobas!" I yelled. "There's someone calling from the woods."

He stopped and glanced over his shoulder. "It's just the blizzard."

I wanted to believe him, but the shouts returned. This time, he heard them too. "We can't just let them die!" I said, desperation flooding my voice.

He paused, looking from his boots to me. "Go, I'll take Otylia to the cave and then find you."

They continued toward the cave as I turned to the forest, my pulse pounding. With what little energy I had left, I tucked my hands back into my sleeves and took off into the trees. They broke the wind as I wound through them in search of the source of the cry. I couldn't see anything, and the shouts had ceased. "Hello?" I called. "Is anyone out there?"

"Over here!"

The voice came from deeper into the woods. I followed it, ignoring the nagging feeling in the back of my head. Mom had always warned me about the voices, but we had almost died in the storm. If I could save another life, I had to at least try.

As I reached a ridgeline, a horse as white as winter itself burst from a ditch ahead. It rounded me with a wild look in its eye, and I watched it flee before looking back to the ditch, where the ice-blue eyes of two wolves met me.

I yelped and stumbled, grasping for my weapons as they snarled. *Why does it always have to be wolves?* Shield and spear in hand, I crouched and slowly stepped back as the cold, lifeless air stung my knuckles. "Can't we all be friends?"

They lunged, one on each side. I blocked the first's blow and stuck my spear through its throat. The second was too quick. As its jaws closed around my left forearm, I cried out with the pain arcing up my entire arm. My shield slid from my grasp.

The beast latched on as I kicked at it, its teeth ripping through flesh and muscle alike. Red replaced white. A scream escaped my lungs, and in a clash of flailing limbs and gnashing jaws, I dislodged it.

The wolf scampered back with a whimper, but its teeth had left a gruesome mark on my arm. I struggled to grip my spear as blood coated my sleeve and dripped from the wolf's fangs. "It's over," I told it as I staggered forward, my footing unstable in the loose snow.

More growls came from behind me, and I clenched my jaw as the noises closed in, their paws crunching the snow.

Don't follow the voices. How hard was that to understand?

The first wolf charged. I readied my stance as it lunged toward me. Iron met flesh, coating the snow in red as it dropped. I turned to meet the others, and my hands trembled on my spear as the ten wolves encircled me. "Perun save me," I whispered.

I readied myself for the feeling of their teeth ripping me apart, but they waited, their numbers pinning me in place as their circle closed in. Each moment was an eternity. My arm throbbed. My head spun. My heart pounded so hard it hurt to breathe. Part of me wished they would lunge and finish me off—another refused to surrender.

Then, with one unified howl, they attacked. My spear found the first's neck. I spun for the second, its jaws racing toward me, but I was too slow.

A blade ripped through the air. The wolf whined and dropped as a figure spun, striking down another in a blink. I could only stand there, stunned at the elegance of the figure's silver sword as it danced through the falling snow and sliced down the wolves. *That's not Xobas...*

"You fancy to help?" the man yelled over his shoulder, his long blond hair whipping behind him as he seemed to dance more than fight.

I shook myself from the daze and scrambled for my shield. With my throbbing forearm, I struggled to hold it up, but four wolves remained, and more crawled their way out of the ditch. With them drawing nearer, I didn't have a choice. "Did you have to anger the entire pack?" I said to the man.

"This pack is the least of my concerns."

The beasts leaped together, growling and biting at my shield as I stabbed one's chest. The man struck down another and darted to my side, but even with the two of us, there were too many. They just kept coming.

With each wave, we clashed in a desperate fury, blind in the endless snow. A second wind drove me on as his blade and my spear cut through the mass of fur. Then, all went still.

Fifteen wolves lay scattered at our feet. Blood carpeted the snow. For a moment, the rest relented, and everywhere I looked, their teeth met me. *I should've just died in the valley...*

A yell broke through the chorus of growls. I turned as Xobas appeared from the woods, slashing his curved sword across a wolf's jugular and downing a second with a swift strike. There was blood in his eyes. But another wolf lurked at his back.

"Behind you!" I shouted.

An arrow loosed from somewhere in the trees as the beast lunged. The tip struck home, and the wolf dropped into the snow. Ara grinned as she stepped from the shadows and toward the pack of wolves. Then they attacked.

Arrows rained and blades sliced. The harsh odor of blood stung my nose as I stabbed at every patch of fur I saw. Desperation surged through me, burning away my pain. All that remained was instinct and rage.

When the last wolf fell, I dropped to my knees, my arms trembling. Blood seeped from the wound on my forearm and scrapes across my torso, but I felt nothing. It was hard to know if that was a blessing or a curse.

I raised my head and met the gaze of the mysterious man, his fair hair blowing against his shoulders as he strapped his sleek sword to his back. For such a skilled fighter, it seemed odd he had no shield, especially since he spoke our tongue. No Krowikie warrior would ever willingly fight without one.

"Who are you?" my voice said.

"Juri," he replied, surveying the killing field with a grin as though he were admiring his work. There was a youthfulness to his sharp face and movements, but his eyes were those of an experienced warrior. After a few moments, he offered me his hand. "And if I remember correctly, you're Wacław Lubiewicz, son of the high chief."

"How—"

"Your help was appreciated, but we should all find somewhere to ride out this storm. Marzanna seems in quite the mood today."

Xobas nodded back toward the cave. "Our group is nearby. Come."

Juri whistled, and the horse I had seen before stormed through the snow, stopping in front of its master with its head bowed. He patted its side. "Couldn't go anywhere without my girl Zofia," he said as he twirled and cracked another smile at Ara.

With a white layer of snow coating her black hair, Ara rolled her eyes and slid into the woods.

35

Otylia

Why do I fear so much for him?

MY FINGERS NO LONGER MOVED by the time we limped into the dark and damp cave. Xobas dropped me into Ara's arms before taking off after Wacław, but as Narcyz, Marek, and Kuba just stood around like idiots, Ara grabbed her bow and ran after him. "Start a fire if you want to live."

"Where are you going?" I asked her.

"I'm not sure, but a feeling in my gut tells me they'll need my help."

In the crawling minutes that followed, I pulled Wacław's cloak tighter while the boys fiddled with the wet wood, flint, and an iron dagger in hopes of making fire. The frost felt as if it had joined with my skin, my bones. I gritted my teeth. Wacław had come back to save me, but now he was out there, chasing some stupid voice in the woods and drawing away another two members of our group while we slowly froze to death. If he didn't return...

A sharp pain ripped through my forearm. I bit my cheek to stop from crying out as Marek continued his futile attempts to light the fire. *What's happening out there?* Worry threatened to overtake me, so I focused on the failing boys. "You're doing it wrong," I growled.

Marek crossed his arms. "Says the witch who's curled up in the corner."

I unfurled the cloaks and launched them deeper into the cave. My eyes never broke from him in the process, and as I stomped toward their measly pile of wood, he stepped back. *Coward.*

"Wood's wet," Narcyz said, slapping the stones they'd collected into my hand. "But you're a witch, so it should be easy."

My *žityje* was all but gone after yesterday's fight. It had made me weak during the climb, but I tapped into the little I had left. With a whisper to Dziewanna, I pulled the moisture from the wood, striking the stones and showering the tinder with sparks. There was nothing at first, but then the smallest twigs caught. Kuba and Narcyz both winced as I smirked up at them. "You're welcome."

They rolled their eyes while I looked around the cave. Now that I had recovered, I studied its jagged, rocky walls and ground. The space was no wider than eight strides, but its depths stretched beyond the light emitted by the fire.

Soon, the sound of a horse's hooves in the snow came from outside. I shot to my feet, weak as I reached out blindly for Dziewanna's power.

A pure white mare with a mane as long as my arm galloped through the haze of snow. Its lean, tall rider wore a silver sword slung over his back, and his hair as golden as a field of wheat stretched down to cover its hilt.

Narcyz leaped for his spear as the horse jumped the woodpile and stopped with its head held high. "Who are you?" Narcyz asked, his voice shaking too much to be threatening.

The rider bowed before sliding off the horse and striding toward us in one fluid motion. Just by the way he raised his chin like the arrogant chiefs, I knew I wasn't going to like him. "Juri," he said as he stopped in front of Narcyz, sizing up the shorter boy.

"And what in Perun's name are you doing in our cave?" Marek said with his ax ready.

More steps came from outside. My heart raced. *Please be him.* I cursed that thought. Ara was my best friend, so I should've been hoping for her return, but when she emerged from the blizzard, disappointment hung over me.

"We saved him from a massive pack of wolves," Ara said. "Father would've gawked at the number of them. Come daylight, we can skin them for their furs."

"Where's Wacław?" I said too fast to play off as mere curiosity.

She grinned and joined me by the smoldering fire. "He and Xobas are coming, but he's in rough shape. We showed up just in time to save both him and Juri."

Relief filled me, but I looked away, trying to hide it as I turned my attention back to the rider. He wore a fur coat over his tunic, so he must have been on his journey since before the equinox. "What were you doing in the woods in the middle of a blizzard?" I asked.

"I could ask the same of you," Juri quipped.

The snow beyond the cave crunched once again. I held my breath and only let it go when Wacław appeared with his arm slung over Xobas's shoulder. A new layer of blood covered their already tattered tunics, and Wacław's shield arm had a gouge in it that could only have been a serious bite from a wolf.

Kuba rushed to them. "Thank the gods!" He helped Wacław to his knees in front of the fire as Wacław reached out for its little flames, desperate for its warmth. "Why are you bleeding?" Kuba asked. "And who's this guy?"

"As I said before, you can call me Juri," the rider replied with an odd smile on his face. "I was traveling through the woods when this storm hit. Zofia and I were making good time too, until those wolves appeared and ruined the trip. Luckily, young Wacław emerged just in time to distract them while I took out the rest... with some help."

Wacław shivered and looked up at me through the smoke. Pain filled his eyes. *What happened out there?*

Kuba winced when he saw Wacław's arm. "That looks really bad. Otylia, do you have any more of that stuff you put on my head?"

I reached into my bag without a reply and pulled out the herbs I'd collected. Wacław's skin was ice cold as I rolled back his sleeve to expose the purple and red teeth marks across his forearm. I traced the wound with my trembling hands. I'd treated plenty of injuries. This shouldn't have been any different. But seeing Wacław's pain—*feeling* his pain—and the blood covering his tunic was enough to force me to hesitate. *He's making me weak...*

"You're lucky it didn't grab a better hold," I said. "You'll be all right, but this will hurt."

"Just do it," he muttered before looking at Juri. "The wolves, their eyes were like ice. Why would Marzanna send them to attack you?"

"Your guess would be as good as mine," Juri replied as he strode across the narrow cave. He stopped pacing for a moment at one of the walls before flicking his gaze to me. "Why don't we ask the szeptucha?"

I raised my brow. "How do you—"

"I've traveled through nearly every village in your tribe, seen all types of people. I hope I would know a whisperer when I see one, especially one as rare as a follower of Dziewanna." He nodded to my necklace before pulling his own from under his tunic. Two symbols hung at his collarbone: Perun's Thundermark and Weles's Serpentmark.

"I doubt Perun appreciates you wearing Weles's mark alongside his own," Wacław said as I began whispering, turning the herbs into the dark healing ointment I'd used many times before. "Perhaps it wasn't Marzanna that sent the storm after all."

The ends of Juri's mouth twitched as he knelt next to the fire, his fingers running along his thumb as he thought. "No, this must be her work. Winter's grip has not loosened since the burning of her effigies."

As Wacław stared at him, I took advantage of the distraction to apply the potion, but the second it touched the bite, Wacław cried out. I kept going. The whole wound had to be covered in the ointment, and since the wolves were under Marzanna's influence, I added a blessing of Dziewanna. That took time—time he wasn't tolerating well.

When I finished, I held his wrist and met his gaze. "You're fine," I whispered softly, gripping his shaking hand. "It'll pass."

Nothing but his heavy breaths filled the cave for almost a minute. Despite the cold, sweat poured down his face. I could see him struggling to even stay on his knees, but the whole time, he never looked away from me. "Thank you," he finally said.

Marek faked a cough as he stepped behind Juri. "How do you know all this? And how did you know who Wacław was? I've never seen you before, and I know I would've remembered a sword like *that.*"

Juri chuckled.

"How's this funny?" Narcyz snapped, emerging from the shadows, his fists clenched. "Too many of us were slaughtered yesterday. I'm not in the mood for jokes."

Xobas sighed as he placed a hand on Narcyz's shoulder. "What he means is we're tired and have taken heavy losses. We risked a lot to find you."

"And for that, you have my eternal gratitude," Juri said, that cocky tone lingering in his voice.

Narcyz growled, but before he said something rash, Wacław intervened, "You said you've traveled throughout our tribe, and obviously you speak our tongue, so why are you this far east when we're about to march to war?"

Juri popped to his feet and pointed at him with a smile. "Now that is a good question. The answer is not so simple, though."

"I'm getting the feeling it never is with you," I said.

Juri ignored me. "My father told me I was to ride to the Mangled Woods but gave me no further instructions. I've been traveling for quite a while, as I assume all of you have, based on the state of you." He spun and locked his eyes on Narcyz. "You say you lost members of your party?"

"Eighteen," Ara answered for him. "Marzanna's cultists attacked from the woods after burning Buşte—How's that pronounced? Your tongue has some odd pronunciations."

Marek huffed. "Bustelintin."

Juri tapped a finger against his chin. "Hmm. I had gotten word of increased raids and the gathering of the clans near the Mangled Woods. Inopportune timing with the march against the Solgawi."

"Exactly why we're traveling to the clans," Wacław said as he made a move to stand. "Father sent us to make peace."

"Stay still," I muttered as I tore a strip of wool from my cloak and used it to wrap his arm. It was ugly but would do the job. With how poorly the last two days had gone, I was willing to settle.

Juri's eyes lit up. "Then consider me another sword along the way, especially after your assistance with the wolves."

"Wait," Ara replied, crossing the cave and pushing him back against the wall. Juri's cocky grin slid from his face as she glared at him. "You stride in here, don't answer any of our questions, and what? You expect to just ride alongside us with your perfect white horse? Narcyz is right. We still don't know who you really are."

Juri cracked an unconvincing smile. "I'm Juri, a traveling swordsman who solves problems and slays demons. Though I'm unsure what my father sent me here for, I can only assume that these storms have something to do with it."

Wacław and I traded glances. *Did you come to slay him?*

I shuddered as the thought of his silver sword slicing Wacław's throat ran through my mind. Ara had a point—he was hiding something. Behind the smile and the waving of his hands, there was a secret he didn't want to say.

"Slay demons, huh," Marek said, nodding to Wacław. "Half-Chief over there already killed a zmora, and both he and Narcyz had a run-in with a rusałka a few days ago. You saying there's more out there?"

"As long as men are fickle beings full of wickedness and deceit, there will always be demons," Juri said.

Ara released him. "I hope you're better with that shiny sword than you are at answering questions."

"If he fights demons like he does wolves," Xobas replied, "then we'll be just fine. Juri can join us. We could use the extra hand."

Narcyz scowled and threw himself down next to the fire. "I don't like it and neither would've Kajetan."

"He's dead," Marek said. "If we don't want to end up like him, it's about time we learn to work together, all of us."

Kuba raised his brow. "That's the most mature thing I've ever heard you say. You sure the storm didn't get to your head?"

"I'm a chief. It's my responsibility to ensure this mission succeeds for the good of the tribe."

"It's all of our responsibilities," Wacław replied, raising his gaze from the fire to Marek. For the first time since he'd stumbled into the cave, he didn't look on the edge of death. "We all have our reasons for being here, even if it was because Father requested us to be."

Narcyz scoffed. "Says the guy that caused his death."

"Narcyz!" I spat. *He's going to expose us to a stranger...*

"His what?" Juri asked. He'd stopped his pacing as shock broke through his smirk.

Wacław offered me a nod as Kuba helped him to his feet. He still wobbled, but with Kuba's support, he looked across the fire at Juri and Narcyz. "My father is dead from Marzanna's Curse. I failed to stop it, and I'll live with that the rest of my life. What's in the past won't fix what's coming, though, and if Marzanna lives, then we need each other if we're going to make it through."

I returned the remaining herbs to my bag as Wacław spoke. The pain in his words weighed on my heart, and when he finished and looked to me, I saw that same burden in his eyes.

He took a raspy breath and stepped away from Kuba, surveying the group as he continued, "It doesn't matter if you're a chief, half-chief, witch, demon hunter, foreign general, huntress, or the son of an iron smelter or miner. We are heading into lands that are not our own, facing forces we don't understand. Each of us has our grievances with the others in this cave, but right now, it's time to leave them behind if we wish to preserve our tribe's honor."

"Spoken like a true warrior," Juri said as Wacław's eyes lingered on me. *Why is there so much more I need to say to him?*

"No," Xobas said. "Those were the words of a chief."

36

Wacław

Will spring ever return?

THE LITTLE PILE OF WOOD DWINDLED as I stared into the embers in my soul-form.

Narcyz had taken first watch this time. Leaning against the cave wall, he glared at Juri, who slept covered in his own furs across the fire. I should've been jealous of the swordsman's warmth, having risked my life to save him from the wolves, but exhaustion dulled my mind.

Darkness loomed over me. It felt as if a year had passed since I had seen Mom's warm smile and Nevenka's silly dancing. I couldn't see the moon from that cave, but I sensed its slow crawl toward the end of its cycle, when the clans would march on the tribe's eastern lands. On top of the imminent attack, Marzanna's threats seemed closer than ever—the dagger at my side constantly reminded me of that. Though I had saved both Otylia and Juri, the moment Yuliya had forced me to choose kept running through my head. It scared me knowing that would probably never change.

I glanced down at Otylia, curled up in her cloak alongside what remained of the fire. The slice on her cheekbone had begun to heal, but it was deep, and it seemed safe to assume that red line would leave a scar behind. Most girls would've had a panic attack. I doubted she would wear it as anything other than a badge of pride.

For the first time, she'd chosen to sleep near the group—right next to me. Something fluttered in my stomach at that thought.

There was so much unsaid, too much to address in the few minutes we'd ever had to speak alone. She'd said she wanted to start new and forget the years of distance between us, and as I sat there in the flickering darkness, I promised myself I wouldn't abandon her again. No matter what, I would be by her side.

Smoke hung in the air as Juri stretched and climbed out of his furs.

Narcyz's lip curled. "Go back to sleep."

"Why do you distrust me so?" Juri asked without a hint of exhaustion in his eyes.

"Tell me who you really are."

"Have I not?"

Narcyz scoffed and ground his heel into the dirt. "I don't know who you are, but I hated having a witch with us enough. Demon hunter doesn't sound any friendlier."

"Are you a demon?"

"Do I look like a demon to you?"

"I've seen prettier demons," Juri said, striding toward the mouth of the cave. Though I was invisible in my soul-form, his gaze lingered in my direction for a moment longer than was comforting.

Narcyz reached for his spear. "Where you think you're going?"

With a raised eyebrow, Juri looked over his shoulder. "Unless you're curious whether this swordsman's cock is any different than yours, I would prefer to piss without an escort."

Narcyz's cheeks burned red in the flicker of the flames as he huffed and returned to the wall. I chuckled before covering my mouth. My heart stopped as I watched Narcyz, ready for him to grip his spear and charge, but he only crossed his arms and stared at the roof of the cave.

Juri's footsteps crunched against the snow. I hesitated, questioning whether it was a good idea to follow the stranger. If something went wrong and I used my power, Marzanna's płanetnik could return, and Otylia wouldn't be there to save me this time. But curiosity defeated fear. I snuck out after him, careful to not create any more footprints in his wake.

In the light of the moon's waning gibbous, Juri's blond hair seemed to glow against the darkness of the forest as he wound through its trees. As I followed, I couldn't help but wonder how his brown tunic showed no signs of blood after our clash with the wolves. Surely *something* should have gotten on him?

He was returning to the place we'd met before.

The hours of snowfall since had covered our tracks, but I recognized the ditch he'd emerged from, and soon, the bloodstained ground appeared. Having been in shock from the bite and the overwhelming chill, I hadn't counted the number of wolves we'd faced. Now, though, the winds were gone, and at least forty of them lay dead, maybe more. I had never heard of a pack that large nor that aggressive.

Juri climbed into the ditch with one leap, landing softly in the snow before bending down and picking up a wide-brimmed hat. He examined it, then glanced up at me. "Do you know what this means?"

I staggered back, falling into the snow as my heart pounded. *He sees me?*

A laugh full of joy escaped his lungs. He bounded up the hill to my side, grabbing my good forearm and hoisting me to my feet. "You're odd for a demon," he said as he gave me a look up and down. "Rare for you to be so…" His voice trailed off as he searched for the word.

"Alive?" I finished for him.

"No, that's not it. Oh, right! Charismatic, that's the word I was looking for."

"Oh… uh, thanks?"

He grinned and wiped the snow off the straw hat in his grasp. "I wouldn't take it as too much of a compliment. Charisma is subjective, and the vast majority of your kind just screeches and grunts."

My mind spun, and his ramblings were making it worse. "How can you see me? And why are you out here looking for a hat?"

"You don't think I would look good with this on?" he asked, plopping the hat on his head. It was far too big, but considering how well he could swing a sword, I faked a smile. He sighed and ripped it off. "A shame, but to answer your first question, your szeptucha in there isn't the only one who can see spirits, souls, and demons. Others of us receive the gift from the gods."

I groaned. "Why must everyone call her 'mine'?"

"Is she not?" He clapped me on the shoulder, then walked over to a tree and knocked on its bark, as though he expected a reply. When none came, he twirled back toward me and tossed the hat, which I fumbled. "Based on all the tender care and lovey eyes you two were giving each other, I thought it a safe assumption. But you asked a second question, did you not?"

My mouth hung open, and I stuttered as I tried to find an answer. *Lovey eyes?* I didn't love her. At least I didn't think I did. If we were going to stop Marzanna from killing Father and destroying the tribe, I needed Otylia. *Is that it?*

"Right!" Juri said when I failed to reply. "You asked about the hat." He took it from my grasp again and spun, studying it in the dim moonlight. "Oh, you blasted godless moon, why must you make it so difficult to see? There!"

"What?" I asked, completely lost.

"Don't you see it?" he tapped the inside rim of the hat, and I narrowed my eyes, trying to figure out what he was pointing at. After a few seconds, he let out a deep sigh. "It's blood! Black demon blood. That explains it…"

I shuddered at the memory of the zmora lying mangled against the fence. Its blood had spilled out black, on top of everything else that had seeped out of its orifices. What that had to do with the hat, Juri, or the blizzard, though, I didn't know. "What, exactly, does a drop of demon blood on a hat explain?"

"You really don't know much about demons, do you?"

I winced. "Considering I found out I was one less than two weeks ago, not really…"

He fiddled with the hat as he looked to the stars. With the storm clouds gone, they shone through the barren branches of the trees. "You're a *ziemski* płanetnik, right?"

An earthly płanetnik? Are there others like me? A jolt of excitement hit my chest at the thought of not being the only person alive with the same abilities. "Otylia believes I'm a płanetnik. Though, I don't know what an earthly one is."

"Simple, you're breathing, the others aren't. Like the one that wore this hat."

Then it clicked in my mind. "I knew that hat looked familiar… A płanetnik serving Marzanna attacked me wearing a hat like that and tried to recruit me into her army. But how can you be certain it's not another type of demon?"

"Trust me. When you've been doing this as long as I have, you know the difference between a płanetnik and a chała."

"A what?"

"It's not important." He paced back and forth, drumming his fingers on his thighs like a madman. "Just trust me that the demons like you, they wear these hats to protect them from the terrible weather they cause. If you've already encountered one, then that sounds like our culprit." He strode back toward where we came from, muttering to himself as he went.

"We knew that he might attack us again," I said as I ran to keep up. "Otylia thinks Marzanna is using his power to make it winter in this region. We're trying to find him on the way to the clans, but why would he come after you?"

"Your szeptucha was correct. A chief płanetnik leading a band of lower order płanetnikami could control a region's weather and put many tribes under Marzanna's grip. Defeating them would at least end these storms and delay winter's advance. Marzanna is still too weak to bring blizzards without her minions, so a demon hunter like me is as much a threat as you are."

"Why did the płanetnik need me, then?"

He stopped, and I crashed into him, forcing him to catch me as I fell. "Undead demons are tied to where they died. If they stray too far, their power wanes. To bring winter across all Krowikie lands, he needed your help, so this płanetnik was quite likely from east of the Wyzra. That is good for us. We need to strike Marzanna now, when she's weakest. I'll need you and the girl. Gods know the world could use more of Dziewanna's spirit."

"Then you'll help us find the płanetnik?"

Laughing, he threw up his arms. "I'll do one better—I'll help you kill him." He paused, and the ends of his mouth flicked up as he eyed me. "Just tell me one thing first: What's the real reason the high chief is dead?"

I hesitated.

"You have no need to fear me, Wacław. I already knew the truth about you, and if I wanted to harm you, I would have done it."

A shiver raced through my whole body. Father's ghastly white skin met me every time I blinked. "Marzanna demanded I kill Jaryło and steal his seven Moonblades. I resisted, and she punished me by killing Father. If we don't stop her in time, the Frostmarked Horde in the east will burn our tribe, and she'll kill everyone I care about."

His shoulders slumped. He nodded back toward the cave. "Including the girl?"

"Yes, including her."

"You made the right choice to defy her, Wacław. If Marzanna and her allies are allowed to gather their strength, then it won't matter if your father lived or died, and it won't matter if you prevent a war or not. Winter would never end, crops would wither, and the people you love would slowly die around you anyway from starvation and pestilence. Don't you wish to prevent that, so people can stop calling you the Half-Chief?"

How does he know so much about me? I stared at my boots, feeling even more exhausted than when we'd left the cave. "When they discover I'm a demon, nothing else will matter."

An understanding smile crossed his face as he patted my shoulder. "It took me a long while to figure out who I was, but I realized in time it wasn't who others believed me to be but who I chose to be."

"What if you're left with no choice?"

"Then you're defined by your decision to keep going."

With that, he pushed the hat into my chest and strode away, leaving me standing there in the snow. I stared down at the hunk of straw and string in my shaking hands. *What now?*

37

Otylia

This is going to be a terrible day.

I KNEW IT FROM THE MOMENT Dadźbóg's light broke through the mouth of the cave. It wasn't the dread of Mokosz's warning but distant whispers.

They'd spoken to me all night. I'd thought them only products of my drowsy mind, but as we collected our packs, they didn't disappear. It wasn't Dziewanna's call either. There were so many voices that they merged—a mass of unintelligible mush that hammered my brain—as Ara tried to explain how to take down a bear and Sosna yapped at me endlessly.

What I wouldn't do for a few more minutes of sleep.

The boys weren't helping. They fought over the hat I had seen Wacław bring back after he'd crept off with Juri last night. Against my instincts, I'd pretended to sleep, letting him follow. Juri had been hiding something, and if anyone could coax the truth out of him, it was Wacław.

"Where'd you get the hat?" Kuba exclaimed, snatching it from Wacław's hands. He beamed as he held it in the light of the fire. It was similar to the ones many farmers in the village wore to keep the sun off their faces, but this one was wider. I sensed the remnants of demonic power on it, and when Wacław nodded to me, I winced.

"The son of an iron miner wants a farm boy's hat?" Wacław asked with a smirk. "Planning to join my mom and me in our fields?"

Kuba laughed. "I would never."

With the flick of his wrist, he tossed the hat back to Wacław, who caught it by its brim. "That's probably for the best. Who knows how many innocent crops would have suffered at your hand? And besides, I doubt Maja would appreciate this thing ruining your perfect hair."

Narcyz gagged as he stomped out the embers of the fire, sending ash and smoke hurtling through the space. "She might have to worry more about you stealing her man. Are boys who you finally settled on, Half-Chief, or just witches?"

"The płanetnik struck again," I said, not bothering to acknowledge Narcyz. Some of the ashes had landed on my skin, but I wasn't going to give him the pleasure of causing me pain, even if the whispers were already causing a headache. "How did you find it?"

Wacław blushed as he stuffed the hat into his bag with one arm protecting his face from the ash. When he was done, he looked to Juri, who was busy fixing Zofia's bags. "I followed him."

"I knew he was a liar," Narcyz muttered.

"Quiet Narcyz," Xobas ordered before stepping toward Juri. "How did you know where the demon's hat was?"

Juri smiled. "Simple. I'm a demon hunter… and I saw him amidst the storm. I had already sensed that Wacław is a demon. It was my hope that he would follow, and he told me about your plan to hunt down Marzanna's chief płanetnik and his minions. This must be the creature Father sent me here to kill."

Marek huffed. "Seems convenient for you."

"How do we know you're not working with her?" Narcyz asked. "You could be luring us into a trap."

"I don't intend to alter your path at all," Juri replied, his eyes challenging, but that smirk never left his face. "It is in all of our interests to eliminate the demon and end this winter blight—for now. Hunting these creatures is what I do. Let me help you."

Sosna nuzzled my side as I glared at Wacław. He hadn't asked any of us before exposing everything to a stranger, and if Juri had already known about Wacław's power, it made him a threat to all of us. It also confirmed he was hiding something. No ordinary demon hunter could've sensed Wacław's demonic soul. Even Mokosz hadn't allowed me to do that, and every time Juri's dark blue eyes looked in my direction, a voice in my mind screamed for me to run. *Who are you really?*

"We need him," Wacław said when no one else spoke. "I've seen the other płanetnik's power, we all have. Even if I can keep training and improve, we need all the help we can get to fight him and whatever cultists and demons that Marzanna is sure to have protecting him."

Xobas nodded. "I agree. Our numbers are thin, and our experience against demonic forces is even thinner."

"One by one we fall to the sword, but many by many we are an unbreakable herd," Ara said in her Zurgowie tongue, standing and looking from me to Juri.

Kuba shrugged. "I have no idea what Ara just said, but I'm good with it. Better to have a sleek sword like that with us than against us."

"You can say that again," Marek replied.

Wacław's gaze fell on Narcyz and me. "Either of you object?"

Narcyz grumbled under his breath but voiced no complaint. I looked to Juri and studied him, hoping to see some reason for my distrust, yet all I had was a gut feeling and the hissing of the voices in my ear. *What do you want from me?* Their source was alien, but I knew Mokosz's senses. The Great Mother had never failed me before. "There's something you're not telling us," I finally blurted out.

"And there is quite a lot you haven't told me," Juri replied.

"We saved your life. You owe us the truth."

He raised a brow. "Perhaps I saved yours."

I rolled my eyes, but I had nothing. No evidence. No rationale. No reason to doubt his word.

But doubt was all I felt.

"That settles it," Xobas said. "Juri will join us. Be ready, everyone. This was our last night outside the Mangled Woods."

"Gods save us all," Narcyz muttered.

Before heading further east, Ara insisted we stop to skin the dead wolves. It took hours with the sheer number of them, but when we were done, each of us had a crucial extra layer to line our cloaks and hoods. The stench of death lingered on the furs. The warmth, though, was worth my nose's suffering.

I walked ahead of the group the rest of the morning. Ara and Sosna joined me, and we didn't look back at Juri as he trailed us on Zofia. I couldn't trust him.

The whispers swirled like the angry winds with Juri around, but when I looked into Dziewanna's power and Mokosz's, there was nothing about his soul that would make him anything but a man with an incredibly pristine silver sword. Yet he'd seen Wacław. *How?*

Near midday, Wacław jogged to my side. I wrinkled my nose as he whispered, "We need to talk about Juri and Marzanna."

"I assume it has something to do with the hat and you revealing of all our secrets without bothering to ask first?"

He winced. "In fact, it does, but—"

Marek slapped his back and laughed as Wacław stumbled. "What are you two always whispering about? I hope not me."

Wacław's cheeks reddened as I stared down at my boots, now covered in the shin deep snow. I clenched my fists so hard my fingernails broke the skin. *Why am I so embarrassed? We weren't even...* There were a hundred more important things than worrying about Wacław and the way the sunlight acted like a crown on his head.

When Wacław recovered, he faked a smile at the boy chief. "I would never speak ill of you, chieftain, especially after you were injured defending us from the raiders."

With a glance down at his bruised arm, Marek grinned. "I did, didn't I?"

"You ran off behind the houses and got caught," Narcyz spat. "Just like Half-Chief fled into the woods while me and Xobas fought beside the others. We followed orders to protect Kajetan. You hid like a coward."

A *crack* filled the air.

Narcyz stumbled back, clutching his cheek as Marek roared and stormed toward him again. Before Narcyz could even reach for his shield, the chief had him pinned to a tree with one hand around his throat and his other wielding his battle-ax. "You were saying?" Marek growled.

"You abandoned all of us!"

Marek squeezed. "How many raiders did you kill? Huh?"

"Coward..." Narcyz croaked.

"That's enough!" Xobas shouted as he grabbed the ax. "We all fought to protect our friends, our allies. Too many have died."

The two didn't stop their glaring match, but Marek released Narcyz's neck, wincing at the use of his injured arm. "You'll never be a warrior, you scrawny boy. Run back to your furnace and make sure the real men have spears."

Narcyz snapped his fist into Marek's jaw. The birds nesting nearby took flight, the beating of their wings filling the air as Narcyz gripped his bloody knuckles. "Kajetan should've lived instead of you."

Xobas threw Narcyz to the ground and pulled his sword. The veins on his forearms bulged as he stared down Marek. "I will not hesitate."

Marek stepped back, a smile popping to his face as he did. "No need for swords. We were just wrestling, you know, like boys."

"You're a chief. If we fail, I will ensure the others know why." Without giving Marek a chance to reply, Xobas joined Juri at the front of the group.

Kuba nudged Wacław's arm. "How long you think 'til he sends his ax through Narcyz's neck?"

I groaned and turned to follow Xobas. "The question should be how long until all of you use up my patience." Between the boys' petty squabbles and my pounding head, I was sick of everything. We faced a goddess, a powerful demon, and the most dangerous szeptucha that I'd ever seen, yet they would rather size each other up.

"You have patience?" Kuba replied as they walked alongside me.

"I do," I said, shooting a glare at him. I never understood what Wacław saw in Kuba as a friend or person. He was boisterous, immature, and no less annoying than any other boy, yet the two of them had been inseparable ever since Jacek had forced Wacław away from me. "In fact, I'm using it right now."

He smirked and leaned over to Wacław. "I think she's mad," he whispered loud enough for me to hear.

Without thought, I grabbed hold of the roots beneath our feet and called them to the surface. They flung through the snow, snagging his ankle. I didn't stop walking, and all I heard was Kuba's yelp as his face smacked into the snow. I let myself smirk. *Worth it.*

Something gripped my chest. The little burst of power had felt different, wrong, like it had when I'd dispersed the whirlwind and then again when I'd fought the utopiec.

My channeling had always involved reaching through Dziewanna's power, but in that flash, it had almost seemed like the roots had listened to *me.* It was impossible. All sorcery was channeled, whether it was through a god, spirit, or demon. That didn't stop the fear from creeping through my whole body, especially with the whispers becoming ever more deafening with each step we took toward the Mangled Woods. When I'd called those roots, they had been pleased. *What game are you playing, Marzanna?*

Approaching footsteps cut me from my thoughts. "Everything all right?" Wacław asked, catching my arm. "You seem a little...off..."

I snapped my gaze to him but hesitated when I saw the care in his eyes. "I'm fine. Just leave me alone, okay?"

He was right that we still needed to talk about Juri and how we were going to find the płanetnik, let alone kill him, but I couldn't handle the thought of it right now. All I wanted was to grip Dziewanna's nature and force everything back to normal. I'd been fine being the village's witch of the wilds. It had been easier. My powers had made sense and so did the world. But now, everything I'd thought I'd known had fallen apart.

Wacław released my arm. Pain covered his face, and for a moment, I wished he hadn't. I wished he would've fought and demanded that I give him an answer.

But that wasn't him. Wacław was too soft to force my words—to force me to tell him the truth of everything. We'd experienced so much in that ritual together. I didn't know how to handle that or how to reveal that, ever since he'd told me why he'd left me, I couldn't stop thinking about him. I was a szeptucha. I needed no one but my goddesses. I served no one but my goddesses.

I needed *him*.

Nothing scared me more. Not Marzanna. Not Yuliya. Not the Mangled Woods' most dangerous demon. I needed the boy who'd turned away from me so I wouldn't be exiled, so I could live, even if it meant us being apart. He'd never abandoned me.

As I strode away from him with the voices shrieking in my ears, I remembered the feeling of his heart beating in sync with mine. I had felt his care as our souls danced as one. Though frustration and fear threatened to strangle me, that moment of wholeness gave me hope in the face of the oncoming storm.

Part Three

The Mangled Woods

38

Wacław

When will she strike?

FOR THREE DAYS WE WALKED AMONG the warped, blackened trees of the Mangled Woods. They devoured Dadźbóg's power and replaced it with a darkness that seemed to breathe and lurk with a life of its own. All familiar creatures and flora faded in the shadows of their branches. Nothing remained but a layer of snow so gray it appeared like ash.

Few had ever dared to cross the woods, and Dariusz's tales had ensured we had no doubts of why that was. Though even he didn't know the full truth of why the purity of the forest had become tainted, every variation of the story began with a powerful witch willing to do anything to protect what she believed to be hers. Great empires had tried to capture the wide expanse and its many resources for themselves.

They had all failed.

The witch had called upon spirits and demons, using the bountiful life force within the forest to repel the attackers. Warriors and channelers alike had fallen by the thousands. In time, the chiefs and kings had abandoned the Mangled Woods, and countless years later, still no tribe dared to take it for themselves.

Now, no one knew the witch's identity or whether she lived. We didn't need to, and it likely didn't matter. Alive or not, the horrors she'd left behind were enough to keep ambitious leaders out.

Yet there we were, amid the creaking trees as the air stung my nostrils and the winds stabbed at my raw fingers.

Even if we hadn't wished to chase the płanetnik, the route around the woods would've been too long to reach the clans in time. The mountain range we called Perun's Crown arced from the south until it met the Mangled Woods. Only the Narrow Pass in Astiwie lands split the peaks. That was the path all the eastern refugees had taken, safe from the legends of demons and witches. We weren't so lucky.

I had harnessed the winds each night in the woods. The płanetnik had created powerful blizzards, and Juri believed that he was a chief of an entire band of demons. If I was to defeat him, I needed to strengthen my grip on my power. More importantly, I needed to do it soon.

Here, though, the winds were strange. An alien force seemed to fight me with each command of the gales, but I was slowly gaining confidence. By now, I could identify each of Strzybóg's grandchildren—the eight winds—and use their *unique* personalities against the made-up targets I had created. Cervenko's eastern wind raced like a stallion, Dogoda's western twirled like a gleeful child, and Chorna's northern black brought the storms of the frigid seas. They were starting to be familiar friends, distant but helpful. It was impossible to know if it would be enough against Marzanna's Frostmarked płanetnik.

Ever since the morning in the cave, Otylia had been increasingly irritated. She'd paced away from the group whenever we'd stopped, and though she'd hiked alongside Ara at first, now only Sosna was at her side.

I had tried more than once to talk with her, but her glare had been enough to drive me away. Every time she left, I could only stand there and watch her go—too weak to know what to say. A hole had opened in my heart, aching as her amulets rattled with each sway of her hips.

314

After yet another failed approach, Kuba threw his arm over my shoulder, sending a trickle of snow down my back. "You're doing it again," he said.

"What?" I muttered, shuddering from the chill.

"Oh boy, she's got you good."

She did. So, I let Kuba lead me along, my feet dragging in the snow as we climbed yet another hill.

I tried to untangle the thoughts in my mind. Otylia's abrasiveness had never mattered before, yet now it felt like she had driven a dagger into my chest. I had been bitten by a wolf days ago—why did this hurt so much more?

Only Juri seemed to be enjoying the day as we trekked through the endless forest. At point, he held his chin high, trotting on Zofia.

Otylia always kept as far from the demon hunter as possible. Sosna never left her side, except to occasionally leap into the depths in hopes of catching a meal. So far, though, she was as disappointed with the Mangled Woods as the rest of us.

Kuba and I positioned ourselves between Marek and Narcyz in case they broke out into another fight. They glared and spat, but even with Marek having only one good arm, I doubted Narcyz would come out of a second brawl with his face intact. Though he and I had our differences, I didn't want to see him mutilated by a prideful brute.

The thought of Father's death hung over me, only making the dread of the forest worse. Killing the płanetnik would delay Marzanna's storms, but unless we found Jaryło soon, I feared Mother or Nevenka would be next. There had been no sign of the god, though, and it had become apparent that whatever we did would be without him.

Dadźbóg was racing toward the horizon when Ara stopped and looked through a gap in the trees. "There's a trail."

Xobas marched back with one hand on the hilt of his sword. After our last encounter with a village, I couldn't blame him. "Why would there be a path here?" he asked.

"Many reasons are possible," Juri said returning at a trot. "Before the woods were abandoned, there were a few small settlements. If I remember correctly, this trail may lead to a hunter's cabin."

"We following it?" Marek asked. "I could use a bed for a night, and if it's a village, maybe a woman."

"It might go anywhere," Xobas said.

Ara crossed her arms. "The only woman you'd find would be a witch or decaying. There's no reason to risk it when we have no idea where we're headed."

I stared down the trail, watching it wander east before cutting south. "It at least doesn't go the *wrong* direction, and if there is a cabin, gods know we could use the rest."

Narcyz threw up his arms. "No more risks! That's exactly where the demons would be."

"We can't afford to keep going this slow," Marek replied. "At this rate, the clans will have swarmed half the tribe before we cross the forest."

"The chief's right," Juri replied as he guided Zofia through the trees. "We will need to make haste if you all want to stop the płanetnik and prevent this war."

In one motion, Ara nocked an arrow and pulled back the string, aiming at Juri. "I don't trust you. Otylia started hearing voices when you showed up. You claimed you could lead us to the cultists and płanetnik, but we're just wandering in the woods. What's next? You take us down this trail into a trap?"

Voices? I glanced at Otylia, but she diverted her gaze. By the dark rings under her eyes, she hadn't been sleeping. Was it the forest, Juri, or something else bothering her? *At least it's not because of me this time.*

Xobas pushed away her bow. "Let's not put an arrow through our new friend so soon," he said, approaching Zofia and patting her neck. "Your horse is unlike any I've ever seen, here or in the steppes. Where did you acquire her?"

"Why does that matter?" Narcyz asked.

With a pat on his shoulder, Xobas quieted him and looked Juri straight in the eye. "You can tell a lot about a warrior by how he treats his horse. I don't know why, but I believe you, Juri. You're hiding something—that doesn't make you a liar."

"Doesn't it?" Otylia finally said.

Marek huffed. "Ironic coming from the girl who hid so much from us. I say we follow the trail."

"What about the rest of us?" Narcyz asked. "Are we really going to trust a stranger and a demon to find the cultists?"

Juri offered him a smile. "You can't know who to trust, but you need me regardless, just like you need Wacław. No one else can find the demon."

"Apparently you can't either."

Without bothering to reply, Juri looked through the trees. "There is a *special* lake a couple days east from here. The girl can use its connection to spirits beyond this realm to help Wacław find the source of his power. Hopefully, that will be enough to allow him to locate his brethren."

"Her name is Otylia," I said, crossing my arms as she clenched her fists.

"Right, of course. *Otylia's* sorcery will help you find your power, and my experience will help you slay the demon."

"What if it doesn't work? What if I can't find him?"

Juri grinned and patted Zofia. "Then we must make him come to us. Are we following the trail or not? My dear friend's light is soon to fade."

We all looked to Xobas, who leaned against a tree, cracking his knuckles as he stared at the dirt. Father's death had hit him hard. The two of them had fought side-by-side for years, and I wondered if he'd known my father better than me.

After a minute of silence, Xobas nodded. "It's not a good option, but it's what we have. Until Wacław identifies the demon's location, we should follow the path. Time is shorter than ever."

"Agreed," I replied as I tucked my hands into the wolf fur along my cloak's edge. "Let's hope whatever lies at the end of it is kinder than Bustelintin's cultists."

"Can't get worse," Narcyz muttered, pushing past me and storming down the trail. After a few moments, he looked back with a frown. "You coming?"

Kuba and I traded glances before following with the others. *Or we can just hope they're nicer than him...*

"What does it feel like to control the winds?" Marek asked as Dadźbóg dipped below the trees.

I was too caught in my mind to respond. We had been following the trail eastward for hours, and I'd given up hope of finding a cabin anytime soon. Where was this lake Juri had spoken of? Why did he know of a ritual to help me find the heart of my power? Would it even be enough? I groaned. I didn't want an extra weight on my shoulders, yet that's all each new obstacle seemed to add.

"Hey, Demon-Chief, you hear me? Demon-Chief?"

Shaking my head, I broke myself out of the daze. "It...uh..." I looked to Otylia, and though the sharpness hadn't left her glare, she offered me a small smile and nodded. That was enough. I took a shaky breath and recovered. "If you at the very least go back to calling me Half-Chief, then I'll answer your questions."

"You're still a demon and very much not a chief," Marek said.

"Then what is secret will remain so."

"Fine, Half-Chief."

I bowed my head, oddly grateful that the old insult had returned. "Sometimes it's like a fifth limb, like I'm touching everything the winds are, experiencing their every twist and gust. Other times it almost seems like they're part of my soul..." A shiver ran down my spine as I remembered my clash with the płanetnik's storm, its fury whipping around me and then into me.

"Can you fly?"

Kuba's eyes lit up. "That'd be awesome!"

I chuckled—it hurt with the ache in my chest. "I don't know.

Unfortunately, I didn't exactly get sent through demon training. Though I can kind of control them, the winds have a bit of their own minds."

"Nature always will," Otylia replied. "Dziewanna always will…"

"I can't believe you're still acting like this is normal," Narcyz said to Marek. "We're supposed to fight demons and witches, not work with them."

"Would you rather die in an eternal winter?" Kuba asked. "Because I kinda like food and the spring."

"Not that you could grow any if you tried," I quipped.

Ara glanced over her shoulder. "Or hunt."

He blushed and held his head in his hands.

I've missed this. Ever since the night of the Drowning of Marzanna, Kuba and I had been disconnected, even after he'd known about my powers. We had only spoken a few times in recent days. He was my best friend, and though I needed time to be alone and think, I also needed his lightheartedness.

"I think I remember you tripping quite a bit before letting that javelin fly," I said. "Then you still missed."

"It was a distraction," he said. "You're welcome, Ara."

"You're lucky I've had tougher shots," she replied.

Marek sighed. "Are you sure there's no way to stop the storms or the Horde? What if Marzanna is telling the truth?"

"Those two questions may have different answers," I said. "We're dealing with the realm of the gods, and I don't think we were meant to know unless they choose us."

"And even then, they're not very talkative," Otylia muttered.

"How long until we get to this cabin?" Narcyz asked.

Xobas shrugged. "Remember, you're a warrior. We march until our feet bleed."

"So, we could be walking toward nothing? Great."

I nodded toward the mangled trees. "Would you rather be winding your way through there again?"

He didn't reply as he sped up, putting distance between us that I was happy to have. Though I could sense the hesitation of Ara and

Otylia to follow Juri, Narcyz's anger scared me. We would need him on our side when we faced the demon, and I wasn't sure he would be keen to protect us. Considering my physical body would lie defenseless while I fought in my soul-form, that concerned me even more.

"How'd you start hunting demons?" Kuba asked Juri, his eyes wide as he looked up at the rider.

Juri considered that for a moment. "My father... He has always been a protector, and I suppose I hoped to be like him, unafraid of Jawia's terrors."

"You must fear something," I said, looking to the moonlight as it hung over the naked branches of the trees, exposing each twist and knot where they didn't belong.

"Nothing but the godless moon," Juri replied. "Even the gods fear the moon."

Before I could say anything else, he trotted ahead. I slowed and glanced back at Otylia. While I wanted to understand these voices that had her so upset, I feared another rebuke. When she winced and stopped to lean against a tree, though, I rushed to her side.

Her breaths were weak as she clutched her head. "What are you doing?" she asked, furrowing her brow.

"Ensuring you're okay," I said.

"Why?"

"Is it wrong for me to say I care?"

Her eyes softened for a moment. Then she groaned and caught her shoulder on the trunk of the tree. I stepped toward her, offering my hand. But she pulled back. "Please, just stay away. I'll be fine."

My heart panged as I struggled to find words. She was obviously hurting. Why didn't she want help? "You don't look fine."

"Maybe that's because a hundred voices are screaming in my head!" she snapped.

"What are they saying?"

Her eyes became distant, her body limp. I caught her as she fell into the tree, and seconds later, Sosna was at my side, whining as she stared down at her master.

39

Wacław

Gods save her.

"OTYLIA!" I CRIED, shaking with her in my arms. "Otylia, wake up!"

My chest seized as the rest of the group continued on, oblivious. I called out for Ara and Xobas before turning back to Otylia's lost gaze. Whispers began creeping from her lips, too quiet to understand, but I sensed the swell of power around me.

"What happened?" Ara asked as she and Xobas rushed to my side.

I shook my head. "She said she heard a hundred voices. Then she just collapsed."

Xobas narrowed his eyes. "What's she saying?"

"I don't know, but I can feel *something*."

"We have to find that cabin, wherever it is," Ara said.

"It doesn't seem like rest will be the solution," Juri said, pushing his way into the circle we'd made around Otylia.

Anger flooded through me as I stared down at her increasingly pale skin. "Unless you have a better idea, Ara is right. We need to get her out of the cold."

Narcyz ran into the forest and tore at the snow. "What are you doing?" Kuba asked.

Without a reply, Narcyz pulled two branches as tall as me from the ground and dragged them toward us. "You're not going to be able to carry her the entire way," he said, tying his cloak around each of the sticks and making something resembling a cot. "Help me lay her down on this."

I nodded and held Otylia's torso as he guided her legs onto the cloak. Her whispers continued, but at least now we had a way to carry her. As Narcyz and I grabbed opposite sides of the branches, Ara whipped her head around, scanning the forest. "Has anyone seen Marek?"

"Who cares if the brute got lost?" Narcyz quipped.

Singing came from far off in the forest, lofting on the winds, as if it were part of a joyous dance. That single voice became a chorus, and the chords pulled on the strings of my soul in a demand that I come. My hands loosened on the branches.

No.

I shook my head, trying to focus. Around me, everyone but Ara seemed lost in the tune, their legs beginning to shuffle toward the darkness of the forest. Ara and I traded glances. Fear paralyzed me, but then I realized. "Demon..." I muttered to myself as I met Otylia's glazed eyes. "They're demons! Don't listen to it!"

Xobas shook himself free of his daze and drew his sword. "Then we know who has Marek."

"Let him die if he fell for their spells," Narcyz said.

"Did you not a moment ago?" I asked, turning to Juri. "Do you have any idea what they could be?"

His mouth gaped. "It... It couldn't be. But it is? Unless..." He scrambled toward me and grabbed my wrist. "Tell me you didn't do it."

I tore my arm from his grasp, trying to keep Otylia raised. "What are you talking about?"

"Put the girl down! Did you give the dagger what it asked for? Did you?"

"Back off!" Ara commanded as she nocked an arrow.

My breaths quickened. The visions and whispers demanding I

give the dagger my blood flooded my mind. *Was Dziewanna's blessing not enough?* I nodded to Narcyz, and we slowly set the branches on the ground. At least the cloak and furs were enough to protect Otylia's body from the snow.

Juri snatched my wrist again and tore away the cover—revealing Marzanna's Frostmark. "You did…"

I glanced at Otylia. "But she called Dziewanna's blessing. Shouldn't that have stopped it from affecting me?"

"The longer we wait, the longer whatever demons are out there have to kill Marek," Xobas said. "This better be important."

Juri released me and stepped back, shaking his head and mumbling. The only words I caught were, "The goddess of death shall exert her wrath."

I froze. With Otylia lying, lost, at our feet and Marek wandering toward a trap, I didn't know what to do. Then I figured out what Juri was saying. "Are the demons in the woods doing this to her?" I asked.

He gave a solemn nod, and a fury ignited within me. I felt the passion of the winds in my soul, their wild edge demanding I attack, even if I couldn't wield them while awake.

You've gone too far this time, Marzanna.

I took off toward the woods at full sprint, only turning back for a moment to tell Kuba to protect Otylia. He was the only one I could truly trust.

My injured arm throbbed as I pulled my shield and spear. The blood in my veins was alight, burning away the chill that arrived in Dadźbóg's absence. I had no idea where I was headed. All I could do was run toward the sound of the demons' song and hope the others caught up.

The moon's dim light guided me through the trees, barely enough to see a few strides ahead. From every direction, the demons' calls swarmed around me, trying to lull the weapons from my hand. But my rage was stronger. I saw Otylia's collapse each time I blinked. It crushed my heart. *I can't lose her.*

I stumbled into an opening in the woods where no trees nor underbrush grew. The moon hung high above, illuminating the clearing and the twelve dancing women within.

Flowing, translucent dresses swept down their bodies with their long black hair as they hopped and flew through the sky, their music almost carrying them along. Flowers draped from their head, and wings fluttered at their back. They sang with their eyes fixed on Marek, dancing in the center of it all with his mouth ajar and his eyes glazed over.

"Marek!" I ran toward him, but when I approached, he scowled and threw me to the ground.

The dancing continued around me as Xobas arrived with Narcyz and Ara. *Where's Juri?* They looked as lost as me, though Narcyz apparently couldn't resist smirking at the giant of a chief dancing like a fairy.

Then it all stopped at once. Nothing filled the air but the breeze, the fluttering of the demons' wings, and the sound of Marek still dancing along to the nonexistent music.

I stumbled back in fear when I realized the demons' eyes were fixed on me. I tried to steady my breaths as one of them flew down and landed, studying me the entire time. As she approached, the warm smell of flowers in spring washed over me, but her teeth were jagged and black. "You have failed her, boy of Jacek. Another must die."

It took everything I had not to turn and run. I didn't know where I would flee to, but anywhere seemed better than face to face with that creature. "How could I have failed the goddess when we haven't even found Jaryło?"

She hissed and stepped closer. "You are Frostmarked. She's sensed him in your midst, yet he lives. Now, you must pay for your betrayal."

In our midst? What does that mean?

A *crack* came from behind her, and my heart stopped as Marek flailed on the ground, his arm bent and broken. I struggled to breathe. The mark seared. "I swear that I don't know where Jaryło is. What do I need to do to save Marek, to save Otylia? Tell me!"

She snapped her fingers, and in a flash, Marek screamed for help. I dropped my weapons and rushed to him while the demons let out a high-pitched note. He spasmed as Xobas and I knelt by his side, trying to hold him still. But the screeching hammered at my ears. I clutched my head and begged for it to stop.

After an eternity of huddling on the frigid ground, silence struck. I dared to look up, and Xobas's gaze met mine. Between us lay the motionless body of Marek, his neck broken and twisted.

I whimpered, gripping the snow in my hands until they went numb. Another chief was dead because of my failure. He had never been my friend, but he had fought with us, survived with us. Though he was a fool, I couldn't claim to be any different as I blindly stumbled toward what I hoped was right. *May Weles treat you well in the next life, Chieftain.*

A shout of rage rang out behind me, and I turned to see Narcyz charging the creature. "Narcyz, no!"

I was too late. The demon swooped at him, lifting him high in the air and launching him into a tree as if it were no effort. He dropped to the ground and let out a muffled groan before falling limp. As the demons turned their gaze back to me, all I could do was be thankful he was alive.

"You have not learned your lesson," the leader said, flying toward me as I trembled. "The goddess warned you what would happen if you disobeyed her."

I dropped to my knees. "Then kill me! Leave my friends alone. This was not their choice."

"Don't do it, Wacław," Ara said, approaching with her bow aimed at the demon.

The fairy giggled as she lifted my chin. Just the touch of her cold finger was enough to make my stomach churn. "They chose their side when they learned the truth." With a hiss, she landed next to Xobas and shook her head before returning her gaze to me. "None are innocent, but lucky for you, Marzanna needs demons to win the war to come. She does not have use for chiefs and szeptuchy who worship her sister."

"No..." My whole body shook as I looked back into the trees, where Kuba would be guarding a dying Otylia.

"She must die for you to learn," the demon whispered. "First her, then your poor cast-aside mother, then perhaps the little girl."

My breaths came so quick my lungs hurt. My heart pounded as I cried, holding my face in my hands with no clue what to do. Without my power, I was useless with so many of the demons around us. I couldn't stop them.

"Stop!" A voice yelled.

I gasped as Juri emerged on Zofia. He rode toward us, his silver blade in one hand, a golden shield in the other, and seven colored swords—each unlike any I'd ever seen—strapped to his back.

"How..." I mumbled.

"Let them free, wiły," he roared, sweeping down from his horse. "I am Jaryło, god of spring, and that boy right there is *my* demon."

40

Wacław

Gods, what have I gotten myself into?

HISSING FILLED THE SKY as the wiły took flight, their thin wings battering the air like an insect swarm attacking a field of crops.

I looked from Juri's golden shield to demons' shocked faces, unsure what to believe. They seemed convinced, though, and I was relieved their attention was no longer on me.

"The unfaithful one has shown his face," the leader said, letting out a giggle that felt wrong coming from such a hideous mouth.

"Yet one of us is a demon and the other is a god, worshipped by tribes across the lands," Juri quipped. "How ironic for you."

"Your presence changes nothing. The whisperer suffers the queen's curse. She will die."

Juri's eyes landed on me, a solemn look on his face. "Let the girl and all my friends go free," he said, turning back to the wiły, "or I'll slaughter each of you. My swords haven't tasted demon blood for too long." He tapped a bright red hilt and at the center of his back. "Lipiec is quite reddened enough already, but I'm not sure whether to bloody Wrzesień or my silver sword."

The swords representing the seventh and ninth moons shimmered in the moonlight as he drew Wrzesień, its blade the deep violet of early autumn. I glanced at my weapons, unsure if I would be any help but eager to take the chance to save Otylia's life. Father was gone. I couldn't lose her too.

"Go," Xobas whispered.

I sprinted with all the rage that flowed within me. The wiły shrieked and dove as Juri—or Jaryło or whoever he was—launched himself at their leader.

The battle rang out above as I grabbed my weapons. When my hand closed around my shield, a wiła swooped toward me. Her talons stretched for my torso, but I spun just in time to throw her aside. She took off again, hovering above me and loosing a screech that pounded at my ears. Before I could recover, she slammed me to the ground.

A squeal came from far above, and seconds later, the leader's lifeless body crashed to the earth just strides away.

The wiła ahead cried out. I took advantage of her hesitation, pushing her away with my shield and stabbing her from my back. Her claws grabbed at my spear-arm, but she was too late. Black blood poured from her stomach.

"Wacław!"

I rose to see Xobas backing down as two demons attacked him— one from the air, the other from the ground. He slashed and fought, but with every one of their screeches, he stumbled back further. I looked to Ara, but she was too far. In the air, wiły clashed with the god in a supernatural fight I would have loved to watch if everyone I cared for wasn't on the line. *Kuba would've been ecstatic.*

I charged to Xobas's aid. The demon on the ground didn't see me coming, and as she turned, I drove my spear through her back. The other hissed and screeched, forcing us to retreat as she dove, striking Xobas's shield.

Xobas smirked and leaped to one side. She followed—a mistake I'd made too many times to count. When he spun back around, even her wings weren't quick enough to make up for her error. His curved blade sliced clean through her neck.

I caught my breath as we exchanged nods. Xobas had taught me everything I knew. It was good to finally show him I wasn't a complete waste as a student.

"Wacław, look out!" Ara yelled.

The claws grabbed hold of me before I could react, and a wiła pulled me off the ground. I flailed, uselessly trying to break free. But she was too strong. We climbed through the air, and horror filled me as we reached the peaks of the trees. I called for the winds, begging for them to break what would surely be a fatal meeting with the earth, but there was no reply.

Then the creature shrieked. I was falling. The ground raced toward me as the air burned past my ears. *This is how I die. A demon of the wind who couldn't even fly.* One last time, I cried out for the winds, but they didn't catch me.

Xobas did.

The impact could've killed me, but Xobas broke my fall, sending us both into the snow. For a moment, I caught my breath and examined the dead wiła next to me, an arrow stuck through her head. I staggered to my feet and helped Xobas up before offering Ara a smile. "Thanks for that."

She just nodded and nocked another arrow.

Before she fired, the last three fairies dropped from the sky and landed in a pool of black blood. Jaryło grinned down at us. *At least his personality is the same...*

When his feet returned to the ground, the god wobbled for a second, then caught himself and dusted off his tunic. "Well, that was splendid! I haven't had a good fight with wiły in too many moons."

My mind was a flood of emotions. I didn't know whether to pick anger, shock, or sorrow, so I just blurted out, "Wha..."

"Well stated," he replied. "We can talk more when we return to the others, but I think it best to keep moving. Marzanna will know what happened here and send more of her minions."

"You owe us *something!*" I yelled. "Where were you when they killed Marek and threw Narcyz into a tree?"

"When I realized what was happening, I had to scramble to get my weapons out of Zofia's bag. And as you can see, I have quite a few of them. Besides, it doesn't matter what I did. Otylia is going to die anyway."

I took a shuddered breath and stared through the trees. *Otylia...*

Xobas huffed and stepped toward him. His forearm was bloodied, and the red mixed with the black ink in his skin, making the horse seem to be a warrior itself. "You could have made do with your silver blade."

The god shrugged. "Would've ruined the entrance." He looked to the woods as Narcyz let out another groan and struggled to his feet. "Ah, yes. We should check on the angry one."

As they met up with him, I stared back at Marek's twisted corpse. I couldn't shake the feeling that I could've prevented all of this. Another one of our allies was gone because of Marzanna. *What could I have done?*

"Half-Chief!"

I raised my gaze to Narcyz as I tried to push back tears. He clutched his chest but seemed to be walking fine. I sighed. *At least there's some good news.*

"I get it," Narcyz continued as he stumbled toward me. "You're a demon, just like them. Why would you care that I almost *died?*"

"Part of me wishes I didn't," I said. "We need to burn Marek's body. He deserves for his soul to be free to travel to Nawia."

Jaryło patted me on the shoulder. "There's no time, but worry not. I'll ensure his soul gets on its way."

I glanced at him, not feeling very grateful after he'd let us suffer, and ran toward the forest. The cold crept into me as I ran. Each step brought back the aching of my muscles and the stabbing pain of the bite on my forearm—enough to distract me from Marek's death, if only for a moment—but nothing could take the wiła's words from my mind.

She must die for you to learn.

When we returned to the trail, Kuba's head shot up, and relief covered his face. "Thank the gods," he said, rushing to hug me. I didn't return it, and when he stepped back, his smile was wiped from his face. "Where's Marek?"

I hung my head as Xobas stepped in for me. "The demons killed him with some type of sorcery."

"They danced him to death," Jaryło clarified. "As the undead wiły are girls who were unable to dance at their own weddings, they apparently believe the rest of us should suffer too. Not sure what's got the ones born as fairies so riled up."

Kuba's jaw dropped. "Those swords... You..."

The god chuckled as I knelt by Otylia's side. "That's not all," I muttered. "Marzanna has cursed Otylia with the same illness that took Father."

"What?" Kuba asked.

"Marzanna knew I was with you," Jaryło said, a scowl creeping across his face. "That Frostmark on Wacław's hand led them right to us."

Fear washed over me as I studied Otylia, remembering my choice. In the moment where I could have chosen her or Father, I'd picked her—the girl who'd fought with me for years. Now she was dying anyway, and the sight of her suffering tore at my heart. *What would I give up to save her?*

That question haunted me as Xobas laid his hand on my back. "The high chief would've been proud, had he seen you slaying those beasts."

Would he have been proud of my failure? Sosna yipped and whimpered at my side as she looked from me to Otylia. Her whispering had stopped. "How is she?" I asked, my voice shaking. *Please be alive.*

It took a moment for Kuba to clear the shock from his eyes. "She stopped chanting a while ago, but she's still breathing."

"Is that a good thing?" I asked.

"Of course it's good," Ara snapped, pushing me away. Tears streamed down her cheeks as she felt Otylia's neck for a pulse. "She's alive at least, but not for long because of Jaryło."

Jaryło crouched next to me, tapping his chin. "It's starting to all make sense now."

"What is?" I asked.

"Everything with Marzanna. The two of us are diametrically opposed, so as long as one of us lives, the other can never be close to their true power. She must be weaker than I thought if she is relying on demons to conduct storms and even curses."

I held Otylia's cold hand. Her lips had turned as pale as the snow, and even the scar on her cheek had lost its reddish tint. "So those wiły did this to her with Marzanna's power? Aren't the szeptuchy the only people who can connect with the gods' abilities?"

He let out a single laugh. "Of course not! They are our closest followers, so they are often given the widest access to our power, but we are gods. We choose who may channel our gifts. It seems Marzanna has recruited an army of demons to do exactly that."

"How do we fix this? The wiła said—"

"We slayed the demons that gave her this illness, but it's Marzanna's power that attacked her. If she survives will depend on how far the attack pierced into her soul."

Kuba shook his head. "I don't get it."

Jaryło gave an understanding smile. "She was whispering to Dziewanna and Mokosz, using their power to hold off the illness and protect her soul. We must hope that defense was enough."

"There's nothing we can do?" I asked, my lungs burning.

"No," he said. "My sister is nothing if not vengeful, and her curse's bite is no less potent."

"How far is the cabin?" Ara asked.

Xobas shook his head, but Jaryło nodded down the trail. "It's no further than another hour. If you have it in you to continue, we can make it."

"No way!" Narcyz said as he leaned against a tree, still holding his side. "If there's someone there, I don't want to find out who when we're injured."

Ara stood and shot a glare as sharp as Otylia's at him. "It doesn't matter. For her sake and all of ours, we need a safe place to rest."

I ran my thumb along my Frostmark. "Ara's right. If we're to face the płanetnik soon, we need to be ready, not exhausted."

"Fine," Narcyz muttered. "But you're going in first."

Xobas nodded. "Then it's decided. We find the cabin tonight and leave early in the morning."

With that, Kuba and I took the ends of Otylia's stretcher and lifted her off the ground. I smiled across at Kuba as I realized he must have laid his cloak over her to keep her warm, but he was too busy staring at Jaryło to notice. Though his gawking was understandable, I couldn't replicate his awe. My chest was tied in a tight knot. I just didn't have the words to express my anger at the god yet.

"Why'd you pretend to be Juri?" Kuba asked.

"When an army of demons and your angry former lover who happens to be a goddess are hunting you down, it is usually best to take on an alias," Jaryło said, sliding his Moonblades back into the bags at Zofia's side. He snapped his fingers, and the golden shield shrunk to the size of his palm before he placed it in with the swords. "I apologize that Marek's life was lost because of my hesitation. There's so much I truly regret." He flashed a smile that I could only assume was fake. "But that is life as an immortal."

The thatched-roof cabin was quiet when I spotted it among the vines and trees. They had become one with its structure over decades of decay, but underneath, it was similar to our own village's houses, reminding me of home just enough for a pang to strike my chest. It appeared to have been unoccupied for a long time, so Kuba and I carried Otylia through the wooden door as Xobas held it open.

At first, it seemed all that filled the cabin's interior was a dark, dead hearth lined in stone. Light spewed through holes in the ceiling, though, and provided enough light to expose another room.

A tattered piece of cloth covered its entrance. When we pushed it aside, we found a bed made of rotting wood and a mattress so torn that tuffs of straw stuck out of it.

"It's not the nicest, but at least she isn't sleeping in the snow another night," Kuba said as we laid Otylia down. Even the fur cloaks beneath her would be better than the itchy straw—not that comfort was the greatest concern.

Once Kuba had joined the others back in the main room, I knelt next to Otylia, eager to rest my feet for even a moment.

My heart twisted as I studied her face. For so long I had never paid attention to the details. Now, though, I saw everything from the little bumps and scratches dotting her skin to the way the rogue hairs refused to cooperate with her braid. *Fitting.*

Otylia's flower wreath and flowing dress had made her seem as harmless as a princess on the night of the equinox, but that wasn't who she was in her soul. She was the witch of the wilds that could tear my heart out with one sharp look. She was vengeful, improper, uncompromising, imperfect… beautifully imperfect—like that early blooming flower in the plains. She was unbound, free.

And I couldn't live without her.

Clutching her limp hand in mine, I whispered a prayer to Mokosz. The Great Mother's amulet burned at my chest as I wept. Sorrow flooded my heart and mind.

Admitting how much I needed her felt like a knife driven between my ribs after our years of separation. But choosing between her and Father had made me accept how much she meant to me. Marzanna had almost taken her once. I couldn't let that happen again.

After a long time of kneeling by her side, I rose and felt the dagger's hilt at my hip.

Marzanna had demanded that I help her kill Jaryło, yet either by chance or fate I had become his ally. I didn't have a choice now. She had killed Father, Marek, Kajetan, and so many others, but she wouldn't win. She couldn't. I would find the goddess of death, drive the dagger into her heart, and ensure she never touched the lives of anyone else I loved. Not Mom. Not Nevenka. Not Kuba. *Not Otylia…*

"Dziewanna protect her," I whispered before joining the others in the main room.

Jaryło was pacing, his fingers almost dancing through the air as he spoke, "And *that*, my friends, is why it's good to be a god."

Kuba gawked and Ara groaned as I joined Xobas near the stoked furnace in the corner, radiating warmth that I hadn't felt since I was back with Mom. *Was I in there that long?* A small pile of wood sat in the dark opposite corner as the others talked.

Xobas glanced at Jaryło over his shoulder and nudged me. "Is he how you expected?"

"Who expects to ever meet a god?"

"And now you've met two."

I shuddered. "I'd rather not remember the first encounter. I can't believe I walked into Marzanna's trap. All of this... Father, Otylia, Marek, Kajetan... It's my fault."

"The blame is neither entirely on your shoulders nor entirely off any of ours. How is Otylia? You spent some time in there."

My heart throbbed as I stared into the fires of the hearth, its light radiating across the stone and casting a dull glow on Xobas's sullen face. I shook my head. "Nothing's changed. I... I can't lose her. It's selfish, I know, but I can't."

He wrapped an arm around my shoulders and pulled me to his side. *Like a real father would.* Without looking from the flames, he said, "I have met no one, man or woman, more determined than that girl. Time will tell if she is strong enough to defy death herself."

"What if we don't have time?"

His eyes fell on me. Sorrow filled them. "I don't know, but I would not deny you another moment at her side. Tonight may be all you have left."

I couldn't sleep. I didn't want to sleep. My body was exhausted, but the sight of Marek's snapped neck and Otylia's cold body haunted me. For hours I had sat by her before trying to rest, yet instead of fading away, all I could do was listen to the others breathe.

The warmth that remained from the fire wafted through the room, and for the first time since the snow hit, I felt everything. Each bruise and slice stung. My heart was cold, vacant. Perhaps it was better than sitting there in my soul-form and waiting for daybreak. Not that I had a choice.

I rolled up the sleeves of my tunic, examining the wolf's bite and then, higher up, the crisscrossed lines from the zmora's claws. I winced as I traced them with my finger. They had stung as the scars had slowly turned from red to gray—permanent marks of my first encounter with a demon. After so many days of travel, I seemed no closer to truly understanding the power that had saved me that night or who I really was.

Further down the wall, Jaryło lay under his cloak. I wondered if a god needed sleep. *Apparently so.*

The tug on my soul returned, calling me to Otylia's room. She'd been in danger the last time I'd felt it, and my breaths quickened as I jumped to my feet. *Please, no.*

Otylia's chest rose and fell beneath her cloak as I pushed through the curtain. Nuzzled by her side, Sosna locked eyes with me. I offered the fox a smile as I approached the bed and petted her head, unsure what I was doing.

White blanketed Otylia's face and her every breath sounded raspy, weak. I sensed a power around her, and a chill tickled my spine. As I stood there, useless, anger at Marzanna—and myself—boiled within me. I wished Marzanna would've killed me and spared Father, spared her. This was all because I'd taken that stupid dagger. The goddess's promises had been enticing, but all that had followed was pain and regret.

"I'm sorry," I whispered to Otylia. "But I'll fix this, I promise you."

"Take her hand. Give her your strength."

I stumbled away as the whispers swirled in my head. "I'm not listening to you ever again, Marzanna."

"Do not mistake me for my sister."

I looked to the bed, where Sosna stared back at me. "Dziewanna?"

The fox seemed to smile. *"Sosna has been a good servant of mine, but she is not me. Unlike my brother, I am not so much a fan of disguises."*

"My goddess," I stammered, dropping to my knees. "Otylia said you haven't spoken to her. Why would you ignore your most loyal priestess?"

"I am fading, Wacław. Marzanna has entrapped me somewhere that I do not know. It takes all of my strength to even contact you now. For days I have drifted, and when I awoke, I poured much of the power I had left into protecting Otylia from my sister's illness. I cannot hold on for long. Take her hand and purge Marzanna's Curse from her."

My chest tightened. "How? I'm not a healer."

"Marzanna's Frostmark remains on your skin. Use that connection. I—"

"Dziewanna?" I grabbed Sosna, holding the fox and begging for the goddess to return. But there was only silence. I shook as I looked from her to Otylia. "What can I do?"

As if giving an answer, Sosna nudged Otylia's hand, which stuck out from underneath the covers. I traced the Frostmark on my palm. *Use my connection with the goddess that wishes to kill everyone I care for?* My mark's phantom pain returned for a moment, and I shuddered at the thought of Marzanna staring me down as her wolves snarled. *Will this always be a part of me?*

Otylia's fingers were frigid when I slid my hand into hers. Her weak breaths filled the room as I held my own. Through our palms, I could barely feel the faint beat of her heart.

I searched for the connection Dziewanna had said was inside of me, but instead of the winds, I called Marzanna's power, demanding it release Otylia. Though its frost hid at the corners of my mind, I pushed harder. I thought of our adventures in the woods as children, of the time our souls had danced together, and of the moment I had turned my back on her.

The power surged through my veins—ice searing like fire. A thousand daggers sliced my soul and heart to pieces. My knees buckled under me.

I threw my free hand over my mouth to muffle my cry. The mark scorched my palm and tore through me. I clutched Otylia's hand, willing the power into her. *Take it away. Save her.* The freeze writhed as it fought against my command, but I wouldn't let it win.

Save her!

A sharp chill replaced the burn, and I watched in horror as my fingertips turned black, the frost seeping the life from within me. I wheezed. My body screamed for me to release Otylia, but I *felt* the power rushing into her. So, I willed it to continue, even as my fingers continued to die before my eyes.

Just as Otylia's breaths seemed to strengthen, darkness grabbed me, pulling me to its depths. I groaned and fought it, but it was too much. My consciousness slipped, my grip weakened, and my legs failed as I lost hold of the light.

41

Otylia

I failed.

THE WHISPERS HAD SWARMED MY MIND as I'd grown sicker and sicker. Each day we'd wandered further into the Mangled Woods, the illness had progressed through me. I'd thought I could fight it. But I'd been foolish.

No woman or man could defy Marzanna's Curse. It came in the longest days of winter, a creeping fog that swelled over a village and stole its victims. Weak or strong. Child or warrior. It never mattered. The curse took who it pleased. It had taken Mother years ago, and now it had come for me.

Dreams pulled me deeper as I awaited death. Though my heart screamed for freedom, to return and enact my vengeance on Marzanna, I felt tranquil as I floated in an endless void. *Maybe death isn't so bad.*

I jolted awake.

My throat burned with each breath as I gasped for air. The world's cold sting returned to my skin, and each ache in my body reminded me of life's brutality. *How am I alive?* I coughed and scanned the room in a panic, but Sosna hopped onto me, whining with glee.

Then someone groaned.

"Wacław?" I asked as I examined the figure sprawled on the floor—motionless.

Wincing, he pushed himself to his knees. The room's dark glow was enough to see the red in his eyes and the exhaustion weighing on his cheeks. But a relieved smile crossed his face when he saw me. "I'm here, Otylia… and so is Sosna," he choked, gripping my hand as the fox yipped and dug her head into my side.

My jaw hung open as I looked down at his hands holding mine. "What… What did you do?"

"I had to channel Marzanna's power to save you." He wiggled the fingers on his left hand, still emblazoned with Marzanna's Frostmark. Everything beyond the last knuckles was dead and black. "You said there's always a cost to sorcery."

My words caught in my throat. "I… I can't fix it. Marzanna rejected your call, but you used her power anyway… Wacław, you drained the *žiłyje* from your body. That can never be healed."

"If that's the cost to bring you back, then it was worth it," he said as tears streamed down his face. "Nothing else matters right now."

"Maybe you *are* more of an idiot than most boys. Channeling her power could've killed you."

He grinned through his sobs and wiped the tears from his eyes. "Glad to see your illness didn't change you a bit."

I wrinkled my nose. "What happened? Where are we?"

"For once, I know more than you. We're in a cabin Jaryło knew of in the woods. A lot has happened, so I'm not sure really where to start."

"Jaryło? You mean…"

"Juri is Jaryło, yes. We thought it was a risk to go to a house that may have been occupied, but you were dying. We didn't have a choice."

I gritted my teeth. "I knew he was hiding something."

"What do you remember before you passed out?"

"Not much. There were all these whispers flooding my head for days, and then I felt too weak to stand. Besides you trying to help me, that's the last thing I remember."

He nodded to the branches on either side of me. "Narcyz came up with the idea to make you that cot to carry you, but before we could take you here, Marek wandered off after some singing."

Singing in the darkness that lulled a brute like Marek away could've only been one thing. "Wiły," I groaned, laying my head back onto the bed. As much as it hurt to admit, I was too weak to even sit up for that long.

"How did you know?" he asked.

"If there was singing deep in the forest at dusk, it had to be. But most of them aren't dangerous."

"These ones were." He looked toward the doorway to another room, where I assumed the others slept. "Whatever sorcery was in their singing made Marek dance to death. We tried to stop them, but they threw Narcyz into a tree. They... They said you would die for my failures. I couldn't lose you too."

Silence hung around us as he dropped his head. I'd seen his care for me during the *żityje* ritual, and now I felt the pain in his heart like it was mine. All he'd wanted was to prove his father wrong about him and about me. Jacek had been brutal, but now that he was gone, that hope had left Wacław's face. Tears welled in my eyes. "Wacław, I—" I started.

"No, Otylia. This was *my* punishment for betraying Marzanna. I knew what would happen if I chose to fight her, but I couldn't let you suffer for my choice."

I swallowed and looked down at Sosna. "Just... I know how much it hurts. We've both lost a parent, and despite your father being the one who tore us apart, I'm sorry you've lost him. I'm sorry she's threatening your family, that you feel the need to protect me."

"You know, I always thought I understood your pain when you lost your mom," he said, sniffling. "But I really didn't until now. There's this hole—"

"That can't ever be filled," I whispered.

"Yeah."

I squeezed his blackened hand. "I'm sorry I acted like his death meant nothing before. After everything you've been through, it was brave for you to save me. Thank you."

"I thought it would take more than mass-murder for you to say something nice," he said with a forced chuckle.

I narrowed my eyes, but the ends of my mouth twitched in a moment of weakness. "How did Marzanna know you planned to betray her?"

He held open his hand. Her harsh blue Frostmark had been cut fresh over the scar. "Her mark is still there, and apparently she sensed Jaryło through it."

"Why did he hide for so long?"

Wacław tensed. "He made up some excuse that Marzanna was after him, so he had to be careful. Though he strode out of the forest and helped us kill the wiły, he was too late to save Marek. Jaryło didn't care about Marek's life."

"I couldn't tell the Frostmark's power remained or that a god was literally traveling with us?" I gripped his hand as my breaths became short. "I can't believe I was so blind. If Dziewanna's blessing hadn't failed, none of this would've happened."

He squeezed my hand back, softer than my death grip. "This isn't your fault. Everything that's been thrown at us since the Drowning of Marzanna has been far more than any of us were ready for. How were you supposed to know Dziewanna's power wouldn't be enough to destroy Marzanna's mark?"

A stray tear ran down my cheek, but I wiped it away. "I could've stopped this if she would only talk to me. Why has the goddess abandoned me?"

"She hasn't," he said, grinning.

"How do you know?"

"She spoke to me. The wiły said the illness would kill you, but Dziewanna showed me how to stop it."

With energy shooting through me, I pushed myself up and gripped my head. "She spoke to you? Why? This makes no sense."

He shook his head. "She said her power is fading in Marzanna's trap. For days she had lost consciousness, or whatever a god's equivalent of that is. Apparently, it took everything she had left to hold back Marzanna's illness long enough for her to tell me how to save you. She sent Sosna to protect us too."

I pulled in my knees and ran my thumb along Dziewanna's Bowmark on my neck. *She's alive. Trapped but alive.* "Why would she sacrifice so much to save me?"

"Probably for the same reason I did." His hand shook as he wound his blackened fingertips into mine. "She needs you…" He hesitated, and his unspoken words hung between us, *I need you.* Part of me wanted him to say it more than anything—that the throbbing of my heart wasn't only mine. But that was a foolish hope. Even if he felt the same, he was a demon. That wasn't enough to stifle the hope in my soul when he was near.

My thoughts returned to Dziewanna, and dread took over as I laid my head back against the cold wall. A chill trickled down my spine, reminding me of the problems we still face. "It should be a good thing to be needed by the goddess I serve, but I feel like a burden. I'm a diviner who couldn't foresee these attacks and a priestess who can't protect her goddess. What good am I?"

"You're also a sorceress who saved my life more than once and are the only reason I've had any hope to figure out what's happening to me, to everything."

Wacław stood and paced away. There were nerves in his voice, and with a sigh, he ran his fingers along the cracked boards on the wall opposite me. "I don't know why Dziewanna did what she did," he continued, "but I know the whole time we were fighting demons and trying to survive, the only thing pushing me forward was the thought of saving you. I need you, Otylia, and it scares me what I would do to protect you."

Silence filled the room once again as he stood there, frozen, staring at his feet. A tingle ran through my body, and I had to bite my cheek to stop from smiling as I clutched my legs. He'd said it. In his own roundabout way, he'd admitted how much he cared. Or at least

I thought he did. A boy's mind was a strange place, and Wacław was stranger than most.

"Wacław, look at me."

He didn't move.

"Look at me, Wašek."

Slowly, he raised his gaze to me. A mix of fear and longing filled his eyes, and I wondered what he saw in mine. "I haven't heard you use that name in a long time."

It seemed a different life. Otylka and Wašek, two foolish children running barefoot through the wilds. No one else had used those names, save our mothers, and just saying his brought memories flooding through my mind.

"I have no idea what we'll face tomorrow or the day after," I said. "Every day of this stupid trip has been a nightmare, but I'm glad Dziewanna guided me to you in that forest. After Mother died, nobody's bothered to care about anything but my sorcery. Father has never believed I could become a priestess. All he's ever wanted is for me to find a boy who could ensure he has power—power that I won't inherit."

He huffed. "That sounds familiar."

"But ever since we left Dwie Rzeki," I continued, "you've been there. During the raid, you left your best friend behind to protect me. When the storm threatened to swallow me whole, you came back to find me. And now, you scarred your hand to save me from Marzanna's grip. I... I don't know what to say to that. It shouldn't scare me to know how much I mean to you, but it does—maybe because I feel the same."

He failed to hold back his own smile, and his cheeks flushed as he rubbed the back of his neck. "You don't need to say anything more than that," he breathed.

His bright blue eyes fell on me, and my heart longed for him to keep talking, for him to commit to more than this half-admission we'd made. For a boy who so often failed to keep his mouth shut, why did he have to be frugal with his words now?

"We both should rest," he finally said, approaching and wrapping the wolf furs tighter around me. "Tomorrow will be another long day, and I'm sure all of us will have plenty of questions for our resident spring god."

He walked to the cloth hanging in the open doorway, but as he stepped out, I called after him, "Wašek, wait."

"Yes, Otylka?" he asked as he turned back. That giddy smile lingered on his face. He knew what saying that name meant to me.

My heart told me to ask him to stay, to spend one night lying next to him instead of drifting alone in sleep's cold embrace. But my heart was a fool, and I was a coward. "Thank you. For a demon, you're pretty great."

With a swift bow, he ducked through the cloth, leaving me with nothing but Sosna's little whines.

42

Wacław

She called me Wašek…

FOR THE FIRST TIME SINCE I HAD LEFT HOME, I slept with a smile that night. The chaos of my thoughts relented as I sat in my soul-form, staring at the fires in the stove and remembering Otylia's last gaze—a healing touch to my cracked heart.

There had been so much more I'd wanted to say—how much I would've given for her, how even being near her made my mind spin and my heart pound like an ironsmith's hammer against his anvil. I couldn't. Just the thought had caused my stomach to flip as a hundred doubts had swarmed me at once.

What would Father say if he were still alive? Would Dariusz kill me? What does this mean for us?

I had only been able to stand there and stare as desire had swelled within me. When she'd slept, I'd cried, but in that moment, I had been caught in a trance, taking in every inch of her—from the scar arcing from her eyes as stunning as nature itself to the hint of pink gracing her lips and the way her dress hugged her body. Father had said marrying Mom for love was an abandonment of his duty. *What does duty protect without love?*

Despite the warmth of the cabin, my frosted fingers still stung come morning. Ara had disappeared into Otylia's room a couple hours before, and I thought more than I should've about whether the two were talking about me. I needed to be focused on finding the płanetnik soon. Even in my soul-form, though, I couldn't sense his presence anywhere.

When the others woke, Ara emerged with Otylia, who flashed an unusually excited smile in my direction. The exhaustion was obvious on her face, but considering she'd been on her death bed last night, her swift recovery was impressive.

Jaryło's head popped up at the sight of her. "Dziewanna's chosen lives, wonderful!" He turned his attention to me. "A cure for Marzanna's Curse is unknown among the gods. What did you do?"

I held up my frostbitten hand. "Dziewanna spoke to me last night."

"You saw my sister?" he asked, raising a brow. "Of course she didn't want to talk to me. Ever since… Never mind. What did she say?"

"And what does this have to do with your hand?" Narcyz asked.

Sosna slid between Otylia's legs and looked up at me as I pondered my response. "I didn't *see* her, really," I said, "but she whispered to me through Sosna. Marzanna has entrapped her somehow, so while she protected Otylia from the curse, her strength was fading. The only way to cure the illness was for me to channel Marzanna's power."

Narcyz pulled at his hair. "This just keeps getting weirder."

"That was brave of you, Wacław," Xobas said before looking to Otylia. "Is there no cure?"

She shook her head. "No, unless *Jaryło* has something else he'd like to tell us."

The god shuddered at her glare. "He told you, huh?"

"Maybe Marzanna was right about you."

"If she were, then why do you bear my amulet at your waist?"

Without hesitation, she tore the amulet from her belt and threw it at his feet, burying it in the dirt floor. "You were saying?"

His lip curled as he reached for his silver sword, but I stepped between them. "Before anyone does anything rash, you do owe us some answers, Jaryło."

Though Otylia muttered quite a few curses behind me, Jaryło took his hand from his sword's hilt. "Very well. I will admit that I perhaps should've been more open with all of you sooner. However, from what I've heard, even you were not honest with your friends."

"I know," I said, lowering my head.

"But *you're* the reason Marek's dead," Narcyz said. "If you'd told the truth, he'd still be here."

"Marek's death was tragic but the least of our concerns," Jaryło said. "When I was taking Dziewanna to kill Marzanna, an army of demons came for us. With my twin alive, I was too weak to protect Dziewanna, and we were overrun. I awoke alone. Father did tell me to travel to the Mangled Woods—I did not lie about that. He said the key to stopping Marzanna would meet me along the way."

"Why didn't you tell us about Dziewanna's capture sooner?" Ara asked.

"And what about Strzybóg?" Otylia said. "He's supposed to help protect her."

Jaryło scoffed. "That old man hasn't participated or bothered to send his sons in years. And if I'd told you before, then you would've panicked like you are now. I have no inclination of where Dziewanna is, so the only plan of action is to kill the płanetnik. At the very least, that will be enough to delay Marzanna's attacks until we figure out how to find her."

Xobas scratched his beard. "Your father, Perun, why can't he help? I'm not exactly familiar with your gods."

Amusement replaced Jaryło's frown. "Ah yes, you're Simukie—horse worshippers. Perun has been too obsessed with fighting Weles ever since Weles kidnapped and then raised me. Besides, he considers my fight with Marzanna to be my fault entirely."

"Isn't it?" Otylia said. "Nature's peace was destroyed because you couldn't keep it in your trousers."

With a chuckle, Jaryło paced toward her and grabbed her Bow-mark necklace. "If you knew everything Dziewanna has done wrong, I doubt you would be so critical of me."

Otylia matched his gaze, not wavering a bit. "Your mistake threatens to destroy nature and every tribe that worships you. Was our mistake to believe you cared at all?"

"I knew there was a reason my sister chose you."

"And what's that?"

He smiled as he reached down and picked up the amulet she'd thrown. "You're exactly like her—all grit and determination. No understanding of flair."

Xobas grabbed his shoulder. "If we're going to kill that demon and still reach the clans in time to stop this, we need to move."

"You are right," Jaryło replied, drifting toward the door. "And that means Wacław must enter the Lake of Reflection and find the heart of his power. If you will allow me, I shall lead us there. It is no more than a few hours east if we move swiftly."

Otylia looked past them to me, her eyes lacking the softness from last night. "We don't have to like Jaryło," I said, "but we need him,"

"Fine, let's go then," she grumbled.

"Are you sure you're ready to walk?"

"I'm *fine.*"

As Otylia stomped out the door, Ara's gaze met mine, and she shrugged before following with a smirk. I sighed and grabbed my bag. *Nothing's simple.* Why would it be? I was a demon fighting a goddess. It seemed unlikely things would ever be simple again.

Kuba and I stepped out into the frigid air behind the girls. The winds slipping through the slices in my tunic instantly made me miss the cabin's warmth, but there was only one way forward—deeper into the woods.

Kuba nudged me. "You really think you can handle her?"

"I wouldn't dare to try," I said, watching the winds blow Otylia's talisman-lined braid. Everything with her was either wonderful or mysterious, and after she'd gone toe-to-toe with a god without flinching, I was more in awe of her than ever. I cursed my heart.

We'd all but admitted our feelings to each other last night, yet fear still lingered in my chest.

"Never wrong her if you want to keep your cock," he said.

"Why do I have a feeling she'd go straight for the jugular?"

"Just like a wild dog."

"If only she were that easy to understand."

He laughed and slapped me on the back as the others emerged from the cabin. Jaryło mounted Zofia and led the way down the trail with the rest of us strewn out behind. "If you two do, you know, what are you going to do about Mikołaj?" Kuba asked. "He'll probably be high chief when we get back, and I bet he'll try to wed you to some chief's ugly fifth daughter. Imagine what your dad would say about you being *with* Otylia."

Taking a deep breath, I looked from him to Otylia, who whispered with Ara ahead. "Miko is the least of my concerns. Father is gone, taking whatever alliances he hoped to build with him. I've spent so much of my life trying to please a man who never cared for me in hopes of finding happiness. What if the purpose I've been searching for has been in front of me my whole life?"

"Pshh. She's got you good."

She does. My heart twinged as I remembered her deathly pale face last night. I had almost lost her, and though Marzanna had threatened my family, Otylia consumed my mind like a pack of hungry wolves. When I should've been thinking of the fight ahead, I worried about her, about us. "A few weeks ago, we cared only about jumping the fire and finding girls. All of that seems so silly now, yet I still can't get her out of my head."

"I don't think it's silly," he said with a shrug. "We could die out here, but I'm longing to return to my girl and you're still drooling after one. Doesn't matter if the tribe is on the brink of destruction. Our minds still go back to them every time."

I chuckled and looked to Narcyz, who dragged his feet through the snow. "How about you? You miss Genowefa?"

He furrowed his brow. "Why? You hoping you can steal her when we get back?"

"*If* we get back," Kuba quipped.

"Your optimism is always appreciated," I said before returning my attention to Narcyz. "And no, I mean it. You two seemed to finally connect during the festival, and I know it can't be easy to leave her behind. It's tough enough for me to be away from my mom and the farm, especially with Father gone."

"Don't pretend to care," Narcyz said.

Kuba rolled his eyes. "Maybe if you weren't so stubborn."

"Kuba!" I interrupted. "Aren't you feeling the same way about home? You have Maja."

He muttered under his breath but nodded. "Just wanna get back to her, you know?"

"No, I don't miss her," Narcyz said, pulling his dagger and launching it into the trunk of a nearby tree. "She pushed me away after that night. Said I was too blunt."

"I see her point," Kuba said as Narcyz tore the blade from the tree.

"Shut it, bog boy."

"If we didn't bring your dad his bog iron, he'd be useless, just like you."

Narcyz grabbed Kuba's tunic and threw him to the ground, landing two punches square to his jaw before Xobas grabbed hold of him.

I looked down at my friend's bloodied face. "You know you deserved that," I whispered while I pulled him to his feet.

"Thanks for the back-up," he mumbled through his moans.

Across the trail, Xobas had a grip on Narcyz's shoulders. "If this were an army, you'd be flogged, boy!"

"And we'd be attacking instead of getting ambushed every day!" Narcyz spat.

"What would you have us do?" Xobas said. "A warrior knows when to fight and when to prepare. We cannot face the demon until we're ready."

Narcyz hung his head. "I'm sick of losing."

"As long as we continue our journey, we've yet to lose. Men fall in war. If you want to be a warrior, you'd best learn that lesson."

Jaryło rode toward us, that cocky smile back at its usual place. "If you boys are done arguing, there's a demon destroying spring out there just waiting for a band of heroes to slay him."

Narcyz tore himself from Xobas's grasp. "You're a god. Why don't you kill the demon yourself?"

"Were you not listening?" Jaryło replied with a sigh. "My power is weakened as long as Marzanna is alive. I could face the płanetnik on my own, but with the protection Marzanna surely has around her pet, I need your aid."

"That's not concerning at all," Ara said.

"What kind of protection we talking about here?" Kuba asked. "Scary demons? Guys with pointy sticks? Seductive women trying to dance us to death?"

Otylia groaned. "You'd like that, wouldn't you?"

"His lower order płanetnikami will surely be with him," Jaryło replied, "assisting his crafting of the storms. Marzanna may also have some of her loyal szeptuchy, cultists, and other demons nearby."

Kuba cocked his head to the side. "Where's your cult? I've never heard of 'em."

Jaryło chuckled and rubbed Zofia's neck. "There is no need for such a cult when all of the tribes worship you. That being said, I've sent my few channelers to search for Dziewanna, but none have succeeded."

"One step at a time," Xobas said.

I nodded. "Xobas is right. First, we kill the płanetnik and satisfy the clans, then we find Dziewanna."

"Don't forget the war *you're* running from," Narcyz said, rubbing his arms as another gust of frigid wind washed over us. "When this is over, I'm marching with the army. I'll kill the Solgawi for taking our western lands."

"Oh, big tough Narcyz is going to take down the entire Solgawi army," Kuba mocked.

I shot him a glare as Narcyz kicked the snow. "You wouldn't get it," he muttered and ran ahead.

Xobas watched him go, solemn. "Must you constantly bicker with him?"

"I'm trying to keep the peace at least," I said. "He hasn't exactly tried to do the same."

"This has been a rough time for everyone. I know neither of you have ever gotten along with him, but this is about more than each of us."

Kuba dropped his head. "I'm not used to the tribe relying on me."

Xobas smiled. "Even when you were helping your father find iron, the tribe was relying on you. Narcyz and his own father wouldn't be able to craft our warrior's weapons without that metal."

"This is so much different than finding the right rocks," Kuba said.

I chuckled. "Or planting the crops in spring."

"What spring?"

"Good point."

The trees shuddered around us as another cold breeze whipped through my hair. Xobas wrapped his cloak tighter and let out a deep sigh. "Oh, what I'd give to feel the steppe sun burning my neck."

Ara flashed him a smile. "You can say that again." She looked to Jaryło. "What's your strategy for facing Marzanna's forces? There are only seven of us, plus a fox. Hardly an army."

"And only Otylia, Jaryło, and I have any sorcery," I said, shrugging. "Well, if being a demon is sorcery."

Jaryło tossed his long hair over his shoulder. "Sorcery involves channeling a god's power. Demons draw from their own strength, like gods."

"So Wacław's like a god?" Kuba asked, his eyes alight. We'd caught up to Otylia and Narcyz again, and both of them seemed as intrigued as us with what the god had to say.

"Not quite. Being born a demon is a curse, one that Wacław will suffer his entire life." His smiled faded. "Gods recover in Nawia when we die, but no demonic soul, living or undead, can ever enter the underworld."

An ache deep in my chest stopped me in my place. "What are you saying?"

He sighed. "I am saying, son of Jacek, that your demonic soul feeds on your human one's *žityje*. With each use of your power, your human soul withers. Soon, you will be entirely a demon, living infinitely in this life until you're slain, and when you are, you shall disappear as Oblivion consumes you."

43

Otylia

He's immortal?

MY HEAD SPUN as I stared at Wacław. This changed everything. His human soul would slowly fade. *What part of him will it take with it?*

I searched for words, but fear choked me. I didn't want to believe it. He would live on forever, and the rest of us would be left behind—I would be left behind. "We can transfer *żityje* to his human soul," I finally blurted out. "I've done it before."

My cheeks burned as I remembered that moment between us. The thought of *needing* it to maintain his human soul was both enticing and frightening. Arleta had never told me the risks of conducting the ritual more than once, but something in me craved that connection to him. I despised that primal pull.

Jaryło shrugged. "Perhaps, but it has never been tried. A human soul unchosen by the gods never maintains much *żityje*, and if he has already drained himself once, he will have damaged the tether tying his soul to this world."

"Wait a second!" Wacław said, holding his hands up and stepping between us. "This is *my* future we're talking about here. Stop talking about me as if I were some animal."

His pained gaze met mine. I wanted nothing more than to grab his hand and give him some comfort, but not in front of the group. Instead, I gripped Mokosz's amulet so hard my fingers went numb. *Great Mother, give us your guidance.*

"How can you have two souls?" Kuba asked. His brow furrowed as he shuffled back and forth, digging a trench in the snow.

Wacław shook his head. "I don't know."

"Neither do I," I replied. "I'm sorry…"

Jaryło ignored me and looked to the sun as he said, "There are a plentiful number of possibilities for his having two souls. Blood moons, teeth from birth, being born the wrong direction—any of them could make you a demon—though it has been many years since I have seen a mortal born as a demon." He shrugged. "It is a surprise you have a human soul at all. A pity. You're a fine boy, and I would have enjoyed seeing you during my five moons down under."

I snatched his arm, my breaths becoming weak. "You're sure it's impossible for you to fix it?" Desperation cut through my voice, but for once, I didn't care. There had to be a way to stop Wacław from becoming fully a demon.

"There may be some, szeptucha, but even I cannot know the true contents of a soul. All I see is whether you're human, demon, or some other creature."

"Then who would know?" I insisted.

Jaryło stepped back. "Divination was always my mother's realm. Though, are you not a diviner yourself?"

"I'm far from an expert."

He grinned. "This appears to be a wonderful time to learn. The Lake of Reflection may explain more, but he'll need your sorcery to complete the ritual. Until then, my uncle's journey through the sky won't wait for our discussions."

"Easy for the one riding a horse to say," Narcyz mumbled.

Jaryło rode off, Zofia's strides kicking snow up onto our clothes. Wacław's eyes were lost, broken. I clenched and unclenched my fists as we continued down the trail in silence. *Is the lake our only chance?*

Wacław shuffled behind the rest of the group. Even when Kuba spotted a family of hedgehogs scooting along a log, Wacław only mustered a small smile at their spiny backs and tiny heads. Despite my own exhaustion, I worried for him. Whether the Lake of Reflection gave us answers or not, I promised myself I'd figure out a way to save his human soul. He had to live.

By midday, we reached the end of the trail, and Narcyz groaned as we stared at the thorny undergrowth ahead of us. He looked to me. "You're Dziewanna's witch. Any chance you can get her plants to back off?"

I rolled my eyes and shoved him out of the way. The thicket's thorns were abnormally long, but I expected nothing less from the Mangled Woods. Sosna darted through it with no hesitation. I wasn't far behind. Even when the thorns grazed my dress and sleeves, tearing a few fine threads from the fabric, I didn't stop. Considering the horrific stories Father and others had told, a few holes in my dress were the least of my concerns.

Soon, I reached the other side and looked over my shoulder at the gawking boys. "Coming?"

Narcyz clenched his jaw and charged forward, grabbing the branches and yanking them out of his way. Wacław's shoulders slumped, but he slid through the thicket with ease. Halfway through the patch, he glanced back to check on Kuba. He was still ten or so strides behind as he carefully tried to move each branch out of his way. One slipped from his grasp, though, and Wacław laughed as it smacked Kuba in the face. *At least he's not that depressed.*

"Graceful as always," Wacław quipped.

Kuba pawed at his cheek, checking for blood from the tiny pricks. "Hate this stuff."

Xobas pushed past him. "Stop talking and it'll be over faster."

"If you like this," Wacław said, "then you'll love the demons Marzanna sends after us now,"

"Think there'll be another zmora?" Kuba asked.

"Probably," I said as the boys slid out of the thicket. "They're well-known servants of Marzanna."

Wacław brushed himself off. "I just hope I can find some answers before then. The last thing I need is to end up killing what little piece of my soul that I have left."

"Both your human and demon souls are you, Wacław," Jaryło said, riding Zofia through the thorns with ease. When they made it through, there were no traces of red on her white coat.

Kuba smiled. "We'll figure it out together. Even if you're an immortal demon whose soul isn't human, you're still my friend."

Wacław chuckled. "I'm not sure whether to take that as a compliment."

"If me sticking by your side despite knowing you're a demon isn't a compliment, I don't know what is."

It was a few more hours until we stopped for food by a pair of downed trees. Little white fungi that I didn't recognize coated the pine Wacław, Kuba, and I sat on. Kuba gagged and wiped them away, scattering the fungi into the snow before I could inspect them. I shot him a glare, and he scampered to the other side of Wacław. *Sure, hide behind the demon.*

No one spoke as Ara and Xobas worked on the meal with what little meat remained from the deer. It should've given me time to think of a plan, but Kuba continuously bounced his leg, and the crunching of the snow under his foot was enough to drive all of us mad.

Wacław let out a raspy breath and shot to his feet. "I thought I saw a pond nearby when we passed over the hill. I'll fill up our canteens."

Xobas grabbed his and tossed it to him. "Good idea. Kuba, go with him."

"I'll be fine alone. It isn't far, and at least during the day, there shouldn't be any demons."

I raised my brow. "The last rusałka didn't care about the time of day."

"Those pesky ones never do," Jaryło said with a smirk, "but you are right, you shouldn't take Kuba."

Wacław bowed his head. "Tha—"

"You should take Otylia," he finished, flashing a smile at me. "That 'pond' is the Lake of Reflection, and you two must go alone if you're to complete the ritual. Divination is best conducted in private."

My chest tightened. Jaryło had given me no instructions for the ritual, and if I failed, we'd have no more answers and no way to find the płanetnik. I took a sharp breath and stood. *Dziewanna, guide my hand.*

Wacław glanced in my direction as he grabbed the canteens in his arms. "How long will the ritual take?"

"I've never swum in the lake myself, so I cannot answer that," Jaryło said. "But preferably you would finish before my sister sends her next round of demons to kill all of us."

Wacław nodded and led the way down the hill, his footsteps crunching in the snow as I followed close behind.

Only my whispers to Dziewanna and Mokosz broke the forest's eerie silence. I loved the woods when there were birds singing, flowers blooming, and an abundance of creatures scurrying across the forest floor, but the witch's magic seemed to have drained the very soul from the wilds. Even with Dziewanna's distance, the forests in Krowikie lands had brought some familiarity. Here, there was none.

The trees soon broke for a mostly unfrozen lake. With a shiver, I stripped down to my linen underdress as Wacław dropped the canteens and knelt on the shoreline. He pooled the water in his hands, splashing it over his face. The frigid droplets trickled through his hair and down his back, but he didn't flinch. "I can't explain why, but that water brought me back to life," he said.

A laugh escaped my lungs at the sight. He turned and smiled up at me before reeling away, noticing my lack of clothing. "Oh, uh..." His cheeks flushed from more than the cold.

"I fail to believe a boy who laughs at freezing water and blushes at a girl in her underdress has the soul of a demon," I said, amused at his embarrassment. The thin underdress revealed my shoulders, arms, and my chest just beneath my collar—apparently enough to excite him. "You may be foolish, but you're far from evil. Come on, we'll both have to undress if we don't want to freeze afterward."

He averted his gaze back to the lake, and his blackened fingers hung in the clear waters as Dadźbóg's light radiated against his bright blond hair like a halo.

How can he be a demon?

That question never left me. Though I'd seen the strength of his demonic soul, the Wacław before me was the same innocent boy who'd wandered the woods with me what seemed like an eternity ago. I wished for those days back. The time with him, with Mother. We'd always had our troubles, but still, life had felt right.

"Saving your life apparently earned me half-a-compliment," he said, tearing me from my thoughts.

"And not an extra pinch of kindness." I crouched next to him and stared into the depths. It was odd. The lake seemed perfectly clear, yet I could see no bottom, even less than a stride from shore. "Are you sure you're ready for this?"

"If I wasn't, would it matter? It's my duty to the tribe and my family to stop Marzanna. Finding the root of my power may be the key to defeating the płanetnik. I have to try, even if it's just to figure out who I am."

My shaky breaths fogged the air between us as I raised my gaze to him. He didn't meet it, and by the way he clenched his jaw, I knew he was more nervous than he was letting on. "You might not know who you are, but it's obvious to me."

"That's easy for a diviner to say. You have probably seen my future or destiny or something."

Don't remind me.

Mokosz's visions had never left my dreams. Each of them had come true, except for the last two, and my gut told me those were still ahead. These had been the most frightening of all—Wacław wielding lightning as anger flowed through him and then the moment in the plains when he would try to kiss me. I'd hoped they would never happen. But as I looked at the lanky sky-eyed boy in front of me, I knew they would. We needed his power to bring back spring, and with Dziewanna gone, I needed his embrace more than I wanted to admit.

But now wasn't the time. Reaching into my bag, I pulled out the deer's bones and scattered them between us. "Destiny is just an excuse for chiefs to throw warriors to their deaths. We choose who we are."

He eyed the bones. "Are those from the deer Ara caught?"

"Bones are powerful," I said with a nod. "They would've gone to waste if I hadn't collected them. Gods know I've never done this ritual, but they should be enough."

With a sigh, he looked up at me. The fear in his eyes was the same as the one in my heart. "You didn't deny seeing my future."

"I didn't confirm it either."

"Otylka, do you know something?"

More than I wish to.

A gust rattled the trees, snapping a branch somewhere in the forest. In our silence, I listened to it clatter against the lower branches before smacking into the ground. *Thank you, Strzybóg, for the convenient distraction.* I aligned the bones into the Mothermark of Mokosz. No matter how hard I tried, my hands trembled, but they were soon in position. "Rituals like this take both of us through. So, if there's anything... I just don't know what we'll see, okay?"

He took a deep breath. "A few weeks ago, I could've never anticipated saying this, but I trust you."

"A lot has changed," I said, gazing over the pond.

"Well, you're still a witch."

"And you're still a fool."

He raised a brow. "I expected you to say that I'm still the Half-Chief."

"That would be a lie."

"Why isn't that comforting?"

I offered him a smile. "Facing the unknown never is."

"Then I'm glad I have Dziewanna's chosen one to face it with."

Birds chirped from the trees above as he took my hands and linked his fingers with mine. My instincts told me to fight it, to pull back out of fear of what could come, but I let him.

I traced his frostbitten fingertips. "We should start the ritual. Take off your clothes and grab my hand."

His cheeks burned red again as he removed his tunic and trousers, revealing the scars across his arms and chest. He wasn't the strongest boy I'd seen, not that I'd ever cared, but I found myself studying him in his undertrousers. After years of training with Xobas and the weeks we'd spent traveling, he'd developed the muscles of a warrior. *Not so lanky after all.*

When he was done, I sat cross-legged and snatched his hands again—rough and calloused. His pulse raced against my fingers as I whispered to Mokosz and the spirits of the lake, calling out to them.

At first, there was nothing but the winds, but then the power swelled in my chest, spiraling through my veins and into him. The world's chill disappeared. Our heartbeats fell into sync once again, and a sense of calm washed over me as the spirits began to sing. We stood as they danced around the lake, beckoning us into its depths.

I released his hand and furrowed my brow. "Take off your undergarments and keep your gaze on the water. I swear to the gods…"

His eyes widened in fear as his entire face reddened. "I… uh… right…"

A laugh escaped my lungs. His embarrassment was too amusing, but I was more uncomfortable than I would let him know. "Don't make this worse than it needs to be."

We turned away from each other, and I cringed as I pulled my underdress over my head. *This would've been so much easier with anyone else.* I hated feeling so exposed. Wacław had experienced my soul's emotions during our last ritual, but I wasn't ready for this last barrier of privacy to drop. Not yet.

My pulse raced as I shivered and slowly faced the lake, extending my hand toward Wacław. "Take my hand when you're ready. Don't let go."

"Do I want to know what happens if I do?"

"You'll probably sever our connection and be trapped between the physical and spiritual worlds. Then we'll all die because you didn't find the płanetnik. Can we begin?"

"Fair enough," he said.

Out of the corner of my eye, I saw him holding his hand alongside his face to block his view. I blushed at that. *And anyone else would've looked.*

When Wacław's hand found mine, he squeezed it tight. "Ready?" he asked, his voice shaking.

"Ready," I confirmed, and together we approached the waters. *Mokosz protect us.*

As the surface broke around my feet, the waters shimmered with a reflection of me. But something was off.

Within the reflection, my dark hair strayed freely down my shoulders, meeting a silver dress made from a fabric more beautiful than I'd ever seen. The crescent scar on my cheek shone like the moon as swirls of power circled my fingers and roots crept up my legs. An intricate band of silver and wood wrapped my left forearm with symbols of the old tongue carved across it. Even my skin and eyes seemed to glow.

I lost my breath staring at the reflection. I never thought I could look like *that*, and I could've stood there forever. But the spirits called us further into the lake's depths. We followed, and the frigid waters engulfed us until we were entirely submerged. Then, everything went black.

44

Wacław

What am I doomed to become?

I FELL.

The winds screamed through my tunic as I twisted and grasped at the black air in a desperate fight to stop my descent. It didn't work.

Far below, the earth rushed toward me, and I was gaining speed, spiraling so fast that the sharp gusts of air cut my face and threatened to pull my hair from my head. I tried to scream, to call for help from Otylia, from Jaryło. But I was mute.

Something caught the corner of my eye. When I twisted my neck to catch a glimpse, I saw Otylia's ashen dress flowing through the darkness. Her now free hair meshed with the dark sky around us. Her eyes were shut.

Fear arced through my veins as I looked from her to the ground. *Call the winds!* I closed my mind and reached for them. But they fought.

West slid from my grasp.

North's bite stung my fingers.

South hissed like the sun against the summer sands.

East answered.

Cervenko, lord of the east wind, charged into me like a stampede of horses, sending his power around me and through me. A gust slowed my fall as his power arced between my fingers, but Otylia kept falling.

Save her.

Cervenko whirled, a wild horse screeching in defiance. I clenched my fist, grabbing his neck as he bucked, but I wrestled against his weight.

Save her!

I took control as he tossed his head. Otylia hurtled ever closer to the ground, and the other winds battered against me, slashing at my arms and face. I flew against them with Cervenko's force behind me. Though they swore and cursed, I broke through them and chased after Otylia.

She was seconds from the ground. My heart raced. My veins burned. I poured my energy into Cervenko, demanding he go faster. *I'm not going to make it.* I yelled and leaped from Cervenko's back.

The tips of the grasses scraped my arms as Otylia dropped into them. Relief washed over me. Her eyes were still shut, but she was alive. And—thank the gods—the ritual had clothed us both.

We rose with the wind, flying over the trees and out of the darkness. The frigid air stung my face and lungs as I commanded Cervenko's east wind to glide us over the lake.

As we flew, I gazed down at the surface and remembered my reflection in the lake the moment before we'd entered.

Dark lines had etched their way across my skin, dancing through my veins and meeting at the wolf bite on my left forearm. There, diagonal streaks of silver cut through a red circle with a downward crescent missing from within. The płanetnik's wide-brimmed hat covered my head, and the Thunderstone dagger hung from the tips of my fingers. Blood dripped from its point, and when the reflection drew a sword, Kwiecień—Jaryło's golden blade of the fourth moon—had shone in my hand.

What is it supposed to mean?

The winds swirled beneath us as we slowed and then hovered just above the pond's surface. Otylia's eyes fluttered open, and her brow furrowed as she stared up at me. "Why are you holding me?" She looked around us, eyes wide. "And why are we floating above the lake?"

I set her down so that she stood on the winds with me. "I was hoping you would know more than me. All I remember is falling and then catching you."

"Thanks for not letting me die, I guess." She ran her bare feet through the gusts. "Is this what it feels like when you use your power?"

"I'm not sure. I've never flown outside of visions."

Rolling her eyes, she waved across the pond. "Do you think that maybe your soul is telling you something?"

"Cervenko from the east is mean and the other seven winds hate me?"

"Or it's telling you that you can fly…"

The winds swirled up my arm, as if they awaited my next command. "How does this tell me what we need to know?"

"The ritual is meant to show you into your soul, and your connection to the winds must be part of that."

"Then what do we do now?" I asked, staring into the sky.

Then darkness dropped upon us, covering her in a shroud. The winds still danced at my fingers, but the chill and smell of algae were gone—a dull warmth replacing them.

Crackling echoed through the black, and Otylia grabbed my hand as flashes of lightning illuminated the void, disappearing as quickly as they had come. I felt nothing beneath me but the winds holding us up. With them, I searched for a bottom to whatever chasm we were in. They found only endless depths.

This isn't right.

The lightning returned, and with each bolt, I followed its source with the winds. Whatever summoned it, though, was too fast.

"What is it?" I said, knowing Otylia was with me only because of her sharp breaths and her hand clutching mine.

"I've never heard of anything like this."

A *crack* hammered my ears. Something slammed into my chest, and Otylia's hand slipped from mine as I tumbled from the winds' hold.

The gales rushed to follow, but I commanded them to protect her. This creature, this demon, was no friend, and there was no use for Otylia's nature sorcery here.

Only Cervenko's east wind fell with me, tethered to my body as a fifth limb. I controlled my fall and used his power to charge toward the bolt. For a moment, the lightning halted long enough to reveal a feminine figure crackling with energy, but she darted away before I could strike.

"Wašek!" Otylia shouted from above as the bolt raced toward her.

Anger surged through me. "I'm coming!"

The winds slashed at the demon, but her lightning broke through. As she reached toward Otylia, my heart burned. I fought closer with the might of the winds at my back while Otylia struggled against the creature's grasp. It was no use. The lightning cracked around them just as I slammed into the demon.

We tumbled through the sky. Lightning arced through the demon's entire body, illuminating her in a blinding electric blue. Her pure white eyes glared back at me as I reached for my dagger.

It wasn't there.

The demon grinned. My Frostmark seared as her glow intensified, and moments later, a surge of lightning threw me back. Spinning through the air, I called the winds to steady me before charging after Otylia.

But I was knocked away. The demon delivered a series of blows to my face and torso faster than I could comprehend. My breaths escaped my lungs. The winds slipped. I gasped and plummeted into the darkness. *What is happening?*

While the winds swept under me to slow my fall, the demon shot toward Otylia. *No!* I stormed after her with all of Cervenko's fury, desperate to stop her. The air burned my face, but still I pushed harder as the bolt of lightning shot beyond my grasp. The winds surged through my veins, joining with every inch of my body and soul.

I wasn't fast enough.

The demon's light closed around Otylia. Though I could see her struggle, she didn't stand a chance without her sorcery. The demon stared down at me and winked. Then, a flash of lightning blinded me as I passed through where Otylia had been a second before.

The winds stood still as the endless darkness returned. Silence hung over me—my short breaths the only sound in the vast void. I let out a whimper, then a cry.

She's gone.

It was impossible to keep track of time in the unending darkness. I had tried to fly to its depths, to search for Otylia and the demon, but after what seemed like hours, I stopped and just floated on the air. Otylia had mentioned that losing our connection could leave me trapped between the physical and spiritual worlds. Was this it?

And what was that lightning demon? She had appeared from nowhere in a literal flash. Right when I finally had some control over the winds, she'd proven my powers didn't make me invincible. She'd taken Otylia and left me alone with my thoughts and burdens. I didn't know if that was the intent of the ritual, but if it was, I had no more answers than before. If anything, I was only more confused.

I should've been mourning Father and Marek and fearing for my friends, my tribe—but the only thing filling my mind was a growing anger at the demon for taking Otylia from me.

Otylia had taken a risk conducting this ritual. I had failed her. I needed her for more than her power and her knowledge of demons and the gods. I needed her determination, her grit, the way she pushed me to be better, and her understanding of being the outsider. Most of all, I needed the feeling of my heart soaring when she was around.

I am a fool.

In the end, it didn't matter how I felt about her if I was to be trapped there for eternity. I needed to get out.

"Is anyone there?" I finally yelled, but my voice was swallowed by the void.

Then a noise came from the distance—faint, yet definitely there. I summoned the winds and made chase as the sound moved. Down and left it flowed, swinging behind and forcing me to flip around and drop to follow it.

If I hadn't been so consumed by desperation, it would've been fun to spin and hurtle through the air. This void wasn't air, though, and none of this was real.

Soon, I closed in on the noise as it stopped.

An orb hovered in front of me, pure white and radiant in its glow. At the sight of it, hope washed away my pain and fear like the warmth of Mom's hugs with a bowl of her soup steaming over the stove. I could smell the food and feel her soft hair as she rubbed my throbbing back. The image seemed so real. I was home, far from Marzanna's threats and our impending clash with the płanetnik. There were no worries but feeding the animals and caring for the fields.

The orb pulled away, and the vision disappeared with it, leaving behind the wide-brimmed straw hat of the płanetnik. All around me, the winds whispered, "You must accept the truth to save her. The chała awaits."

I took the hat in my hands. *Accept the truth?* My fingers traced the straw as I dreaded what that meant. Was I a demon? A human? Both? Neither?

"You know the answer," they whispered again.

Jaryło had said my human soul would whither, but until that happened, I refused to give up what part of me was human. I had not accepted the truth of my demonic soul, though. The fear of what lurked inside me was paralyzing. Had that reflection been my future? Or was my path my own?

"Otylia!" I shouted.

There was no reply as I stared down at the hat. *I am a demon.* There was no way to deny it anymore. No matter if my human soul remained or not, I was and would always be a demon, and to save Otylia, I had to accept I would live forever, never being truly human.

How can I live knowing that?

The glowing orb returned, illuminating the demon's hat and my frostbitten fingers. I shut my eyes to flee. It didn't work, and all that filled my mind was Otylia suffering on the bed in the cabin, her face deathly pale and my heart torn to shreds. The winds swirled around me, urging me to answer their call.

I have to save her.

A cold trickle crept down my spine as I raised the hat to my head. Nothing changed at first, but then frustration surged through me. I seized the winds and lashed out at the orb, at the void, at everything and nothing at the same time.

The harder I fought, the stronger my power became. I felt the vast emptiness surrounding me. I felt everything inside my heart. All the pain I'd denied, the anger I'd pushed away for the sake of pleasing Father, every brutal blow of his fist against my cheek when I'd disobeyed his command to leave Otylia, every insult thrown by Mikołaj and the others who looked down on me because of Mom, and every moment that the tribe had believed I was just the Half-Chief.

The memories burned through me as I dropped to my knees, crying out for help, for someone to hear. But there was no one. It was just the void—my black soul. "Come back to me, Otylka."

"Wašek."

The winds broke in an instant, dying to become barely enough to hold me afloat. It wasn't a voice I had heard but one that echoed through my mind—Otylia's voice. My breaths quickened and my heart raced as I scanned around me, yet she was nowhere in the orb's light. "Where are you?"

A tug on my soul was the only reply. That same pull I had sensed during the raid and then in the cabin. The call to her.

I dove as it summoned me deeper into the abyss. Whispers rattled my mind, but my only thought was the sight of her in the chała's grasp.

A ring of blue lightning soon appeared. Its cracking deafened my ears, and my hair stood on end as I stormed toward the circle with all the force of the winds. The lightning's glow wasn't enough to illuminate what lay within, but my heart knew it was Otylia.

I flipped and landed on a plane of energy, humming like the golden egg as it sparked. Otylia lay curled in a ball at its center. Her whispers were barely audible over the noise, but I knew she called to Dziewanna for protection as I rushed to her side and wrapped her in my arms. As she trembled, I swore to myself I would make the chała pay for hurting her. But where was the demon?

"I'm here," I breathed. "It's all right."

Otylia muttered as she turned her head to me, her eyes distant and lost, "It's a trap."

A bolt flashed through the darkness. Pain tore through me as I flew across the circle, landing hard at its edge.

I struggled to my feet, but before I could call the winds, the circle's hum became a roar. Lightning arced up my arms and seared at my skin. My muscles seized as I collapsed.

"The goddess told me to expect more from you," the chała sneered.

I forced myself to look up at the demon, the blue lightning dancing along her skin like a skin-tight dress that left little to the imagination. A wicked smile crossed her face as she zipped to Otylia. Her movements were faster than should've been possible, and all I could do was scowl and curse as the chała grabbed Otylia's throat.

"*This* is the girl you're sacrificing everything for?" the demon said, cackling. "Marzanna promised you endless power, and you picked a scrawny witch who's useless without her precious goddess? Pathetic."

I threw the winds at her from every angle, but she held out a fist toward me, sending another jolt through my body. A cry left my lungs as tears stung my eyes. "Let her go," I spat.

"No, you need to. She's holding you back, Wacław, keeping you human when you're meant to be powerful like us." Otylia kicked at her shin, but the demon furrowed her brow and squeezed her neck tighter. Sparks crawled up the chała's arm until they reached her hand. "Shall I just kill her now and make this easier? Or do I need to hold her hostage?"

Rage took over. I rose, lightning dancing at my fingertips as I embraced the anger and let it surge through me. My body buzzed with the lightning's power, every ounce of blood in my veins yearning for revenge. "I said, let her go!" I threw everything I had forward, commanding both wind and lightning.

Nothing happened, and the chała cackled, tightening her grip. "Your choice."

Otylia screamed.

A slash of pure light arced from my fingers and sliced the darkness. The *crack* tore at my ears as the demon staggered back, black coating her skin. I charged without thought.

Power swelled in my soul. I summoned a whirlwind around the chała, faster than either of the ones that had suffocated me, and the winds drew every breath from her lungs. I sensed her suffering—I *wanted* her to suffer. She gasped and dropped to her knees, clutching her neck as I pushed the winds harder.

"Wašek!"

I stepped through the gale and glared down at the chała with a wide grin as she wheezed. Her pain felt good, fueling a hunger in my soul. She'd tried to kill Otylia. She deserved pain. As my blackened hand closed around her throat, I pulled Marzanna's dagger, appearing once again at my side.

A hand grabbed my shoulder. "Wašek stop!"

I lashed out, pushing Otylia back. The winds slipped away as I watched her fall. My heart stopped, regret seizing my chest. "Otylka!" I scrambled after her.

Fear filled her eyes. "You're... You're glowing..." she stammered as I reached her side.

Streaks of blue raced up my arms beneath my tattered tunic, merging with my veins and crawling up my entire body as if I'd absorbed the lightning. My whole body shook with its power. "What is happening to me?" I took her hand. "Are you okay? I... I don't know what's going on. It was like something inside me demanded I make her suffer."

"I'm fine... I think," she said, rubbing her forehead before she ran her fingers along one of the bolts on my forearm. Her touch ignited my soul in a way far different than the anger. "I've never seen you like that, and I've definitely never seen this."

I watched her trace the lines through my torn sleeve up my arm and shoulder. The fascination in her eyes was pure awe, and that same feeling filled me as I sensed the power's dull throb, desperate to be called forth once again.

"I've never felt like this," I said as I looked back toward the chała, but she had dropped into the void. My breaths became short as I grabbed my head in my hands. "The winds said I need to accept the truth of who I am, but that couldn't have been me. The anger I felt... I enjoyed watching her suffocate."

That hurt to admit. I pulled back from her gentle touch as guilt overwhelmed me. There weren't words to explain to her how desperate I had become, how I would have done anything to protect her in that moment. My power scared me, but knowing that rage was inside me was worse. Would I lose myself every time her life was in danger?

Otylia sat cross-legged on the winds, staring down at her hands. "There's darkness in all of us. You just have a whole soul's worth of it." Strands of black hair wound their way down her cheeks as she shook her head. "I wish I could answer all the questions you have. I wish we didn't have the entire tribe and multiple gods relying on us. I wish all of this was simple. But it's not, and I doubt it'll get any easier for either of us."

Tears welled in my eyes. I wiped at them but failed to stop the onslaught that followed. "I want to go home," I mumbled. "I don't care if Jacek was a terrible father. I want to bury him and mourn like a son should."

There was silence. Then I felt her arms wrap around me, and for a few minutes, we just knelt there with the weight of the world on our shoulders. She was right. Nothing was simple anymore. But in that moment, with everything I knew crumbling, I felt a peace in her embrace—that was enough.

When she eventually pulled back, my heart twitched as I saw her wetted cheeks. "You'd never expect me to say it," she said, "but I miss Father, all the stupid girls' gossiping, and even the boredom of the village."

"The world seemed a lot smaller."

"I liked it that way."

"I didn't." I sighed. "Father wanted me to stay in the village, but I always dreamt—well, as close to dreaming as I could get—about exploring like we are now. The chiefs told stories of their great battles against armies and creatures, yet I never wanted that. I just wanted to see the world and other tribes, find ways to make peace. Instead, it seems like we've only found more strife."

The corner of her mouth ticked up. "We've also found Dziewanna's beauty: the forests, those stunning golden plains, and even this lake. I've always served her but never seen the true wilds. As horrible as this journey has been, I feel whole out here, away from everyone else."

I let myself smile. "You and I agree on something for once." I swallowed and reached for her hands, taking them in mine. "And maybe, we found something else too."

Her eyes met mine, softer than normal, before she spun away. I winced. For a moment, it had seemed like she felt the same as me, but her heart was behind a veil I couldn't pierce. Everything ached as I stood, unsure what to do now. I stared down at my hands. *At least the blue veins are gone.*

"We need to finish the ritual," she said, her voice sharp once again.

"How? Obviously, we found my soul."

"No, we didn't." Pushing past me, she examined the orb as its bright light illuminated her hair and the bones lining it. "We're somewhere between the physical world and the spiritual. That chała must've interfered with the ritual somehow."

Dread washed over me. "You're telling me we're still not done?

We found what we came for—I have command of the wind and apparently lightning. We can find the płanetnik and end this."

Her fingers drifted through the orb's aura as she replied, "The ritual shows us the true person within our soul—or souls. All we've discovered is that the power of your demonic one can leak into whatever realm this is. That's why she was able to follow us. But if we're going to figure out the source of your power, we need to keep going." She turned back and reached out her hand. "Trust me?"

With a deep breath, I took her hand and joined her alongside the orb. "Promise me that all of this remains between us. Besides Kuba, I'm not sure I want the others to know what just happened."

"Yet, you're okay with them seeing that horrific hat," she quipped with a deadly smirk.

I tried to resist grinning but failed. "You don't like it? Rumor is all the most powerful demons are wearing them now."

"Keep it up and I'll tear it from your head." There was a bite to her eyes, but the little smile on her face and her hand in mine were enough to make my heart skip a beat. She returned her gaze to the orb. "This will be our secret. I swear to Dziewanna."

"Good. Because apparently, she's quite fond of me, and I'll be sure to let her know if you go back on that promise."

With one swift stroke, she spun and pulled Marzanna's dagger from my side, holding its tip to my chest. "I'd drive this dagger through your heart before I betrayed her."

I looked from the dagger's frigid point to her eyes, just as sharp as the blade. This close to her, I could feel her short breaths against my neck and the pounding of her heart through her palm in mine. My soul ached. It didn't matter that she could've killed me with a flick of her wrist. The tether between us pulled me forward, but I resisted and took a step back.

"Then for both of our sakes," I said, "let's make sure that never has to happen. We'll stop whatever Marzanna is doing, together, and then we'll free Dziewanna."

A shadow draped over her face as she slid the dagger into her belt, adding it to her collection of amulets. "If we're too late…"

I squeezed her hand. "We've made it this far. Obviously, she trusted you with the last of her power before she faded, but you won't be alone. I promise you I won't rest until we bring her back."

"Thank you," she whispered, snapping her head back toward the orb. "But we have to complete the ritual before we can do that."

"How does this work?"

"I don't know, but this has to be your soul. Just follow my lead and don't let go."

As she raised her hand to the orb, I did so as well. A calm flowed through my fingers when I laid my palm against it. My pains and worries faded, and I closed my eyes, letting the feeling wash over me. Everything around us shifted. The world seemed to rush past us for minutes before it stopped and my feet met solid ground. When I opened my eyes again, I gasped.

Otylia huffed. "Well, you wished for home."

45

Wacław

Is it home if it never accepted me?

THE MOON BLED RED through the parted clouds. Well, most of it did. Only a thin crescent of white crowned the blood moon as it cast a dull glow over Perun's Oak.

We stood at the tree's base. Everywhere I looked, Dwie Rzeki stretched with all its trails, forests, and cottages—the warm sights of home. Even the bristling of the leaves in the summer winds brought back memories as they revealed their underbellies.

A storm is coming. Beyond just the leaves and the wind, I smelled it in the air, sensed it on my skin. Most of all, though, I knew it in my soul.

The storm's energy danced at my fingers, trickling up my arms and begging for me to take control. I felt the winds as they brushed against everything from the wild grasses to the curve of Otylia's collarbone, and I shivered at the excitement it brought me before pushing it away. We were there for a reason. That in itself was enough to scare me.

"We start at the beginning, I guess," Otylia said with a deep breath of the fresh air.

"The beginning?" I asked. "Mom always said I was born the

morning after you—and definitely not during a blood moon." I stared up at the full red moon above, remembering the stories some priests whispered about children born during eclipses. "Is this why I'm a demon?"

"We can only wait to find out. C'mon, let's go see baby Half-Chief." A smirk crossed her face as she pulled me toward the long-house, where a much younger version of Father stood on its porch.

Fear froze me to the spot. Every shred of truth I'd learned so far had only made things more complicated. Suddenly, I wasn't so sure I wanted to know more about my soul. "What if there's nothing for me but a lonely eternity? If I was born during a blood moon, then even my mom lied to me…"

She stopped and held my blackened hand between hers. "And what if there's nothing for me but the worship of a nature goddess who will never speak to me again? Fight for those you love, even if it's for an eternity with no one else."

Her last phrase felt like she'd driven a dagger into my chest, just like her threat. Before I could reply, Father shouted, his voice carrying across the village center. We exchanged glances and jogged toward him.

The moonlight glinted off the tip of his spear, and though his dirty blond hair was fuller, his muscles were larger, and the scars had yet to show on his face, he was still the father I knew—the father I had allowed to die. I shuddered as he fixed his jagged glare on his old village rival.

"Why is my father here?" Otylia asked.

The torch in Dariusz's hand cast a flickering light across his furrowed brow. "The gods have their way, Jacek," he said. "Do not defy them."

Father pointed his spear at the priest. "The gods gifted me this child, blood moon or not. You shall not lay a finger on him."

"The gods demand that children of the blood moon be sacrificed in their name!" Dariusz hissed. "If you do not follow their commands, we will all suffer the repercussions of your foolishness."

"What?" I asked, looking to Otylia for an answer. "Is that true?"

She staggered back, staring at her father with her lips separated and the flames reflected in her eyes. Her hand gripped mine so hard it went numb. "I... I don't know. Father always claimed the tales of living demons were lies."

Father stormed forward and grabbed the priest's robes. "The demons will not have my son. Though he may never be chief, Perun will protect him!"

"Perun's laws must be followed!" Dariusz sneered. "Only giving your son to the gods now can ensure he greets you in Nawia. Don't deny what's due to Swaróg, to Perun. Don't curse him to never see the afterlife! Oblivion will be all he knows if you let him live."

"You're a hypocrite! If your daughter hadn't been born mere hours before the eclipse, you would be hiding her just the same."

As Father towered over him, Dariusz's fearsome look—the same one I had seen far too many times from Otylia—faded. He lowered his torch. Without the flames to illuminate his face, his sleek black hair faded into his crimson robes, but I didn't need more than the moonlight to see the hatred in his glare. This wasn't where their rivalry had begun, yet I wondered if it was where Father's cynicism of the gods had.

Dariusz clenched his fists but bowed his head. "May the gods have mercy on us all," he said before he turned and slid into the darkness.

Otylia's eyes tracked him the whole way. Even when he disappeared down a trail, she stood on the tips of her toes, searching for where he'd gone. I sensed her urge to follow him, but Father had entered the longhouse. Whatever the vision meant to show us was inside.

"We need to go in," I said.

"Mother is down that path with newborn me." Years of pain weighed on her face, but she took a sharp breath and looked to the longhouse. "But you're right. We need to focus."

"Are you sure? Seeing Father, I understand."

"No, it's fine. Let's go."

Her grip crushed my hand as she charged through the door. We entered the torchlit longhouse, and a chill ran through my veins as Father knelt before Mom, obscuring the view of the baby in her arms.

Though it hurt to forget Otylia's sorrow, the baby's cries—my cries—filled the space. The exhaustion on Mom's face couldn't mask her smile, and I found myself struck by the beauty of her pure joy. The joy of holding me for the first time. Seeing her happy with Father brought back a sea of memories as he took the baby in his arms.

"Hello, Wacław," Father said with a rare smile. "Men fear what they do not understand, but I will protect you until the end, my son."

I couldn't help but weep as I watched him cradle me, my nearly bald head not any larger than the palm of his hand. Here, Father claimed to love me as his own, yet all he had done since that moment had proved the opposite. My ears rung with his words—the man who I could never please.

A creaking echoed through the room and tore me from my thoughts. Father's head rose from the baby, his joy washed away by dread as Natasza's voice came from behind us, "The child goes, and so does she. I won't have a demon or the woman that birthed it in our house."

"Fight for me again," I pled. "Fight for Mom…"

Father handed the baby to Mom and stood, his long, muscular frame suddenly hunched as he crossed the room to his first wife. "He is as much my son as Mikołaj is," he said. "I will not cast the boy out for a false curse of the moon."

My heart twitched as Natasza waltzed into his embrace and ran her fingers along his stubbled cheek. "You will lose the people and your fragile alliance with Mieczysław. If you will not listen to the priest and sacrifice it, then send it away."

It.

"Mieczysław will not know," Father replied. "The people will believe Wacław was born in the morning, when we will show him to the tribe."

I looked at Mom and the fear in her eyes as she clutched me

against her breast. I wanted to do *something*, anything, to stop the moment that I knew tore apart her heart. Yet all I could do was watch, my face burning in anger.

Father pushed against Natasza's hand, trying to catch a glance of Mom, but Natasza held him in place. "Do not force me to tear down your work," she said. "What will your chiefs and my brother believe when they hear the mighty Jacek is raising a demon?"

"You will do no such thing!"

She smirked. "The priest may keep his mouth shut, but the lips of women are known to gossip. You need me, Jacek. Your first-born is mine, and you stand no chance against the Solgawi without Boz's men."

"Enough!" Father tore himself from her arms and stared back at Mom and the baby. His lip quivered ever so slightly as he stood there for a long time, his yell echoing through the longhouse. Each of his breaths was shorter than the one before it, and I thought for a moment that he would throw Natasza out in our defense. But I knew what he would do. In Mom's eyes, I could tell she knew it too.

"Fight for me," I whispered.

His head dropped. "I'm sorry, Lubena. We will find you a—"

"Coward!" Mom's shriek tore through my soul. The room darkened and the torches extinguished as she rose, her teeth bared and her hair wild. "Your first words to your son were a promise that you would protect him, yet you throw him to the wolves before he has seen Dadźbóg's first light!" She glared up at the warrior chief, defiant as she covered her child's face. "My son has no Father. May Mokosz protect him from all of you." She slipped past him, avoiding Natasza's gaze.

I tried to follow, but Otylia held me back. "Wašek, look."

Through my tears, I saw the orb hovering in front of us. For once, its calming influence wasn't enough to still the storm in my heart. I wanted more than anything to comfort Mom as she ran alone into the night. Father hadn't sacrificed me like Dariusz had asked, but he'd cast out the woman who had done nothing but love him and a child that had only been born on the wrong day.

Why did Mom defend him? All my life, she had only blamed Natasza for our exile and never told me it was because of my birth. "They knew I was a demon," I muttered as we held the orb once again. "I tore my parents apart…"

The shock hadn't left Otylia's face either. She squeezed my hand as the memory faded around us, blurring the world along with my mind. "Lubena was right—Jacek was a coward and a fool to fall prey to Natasza's schemes."

"Why did they never tell me?"

"I wouldn't doubt he ignored it in blind hopes that nothing happened."

"And Mom loved me too much to admit it. She always said my wanderings were a gift from the gods, but I don't consider a demonic soul a gift." I groaned and stared into the swirl of colors ahead of us. "Why does every answer we find only bring more questions? How did this help me find the truth about my souls?"

One of her hands gripped the bow amulet at her chest as the other shook in mine. "To find who we are, we need to discover our past. Apparently, that includes the lies."

The winds escalated, and my mind spun as the world whipped around us. I dreaded what came next. Life had been easier before I knew the truth, when Father still lived and I hadn't known my parents' deceit. In the chała I had found only an inkling of my power's depth, and knowing I had two souls from the blood moon wouldn't help me defeat Marzanna.

When the whirlwind ceased, we were left in the still air of a spring morning. The sun shone in a cloudless sky and warmed my face as we stood beneath Perun's Oak once again. *Forever constant.* I ran my blackened fingers along its rough bark, and though I could no longer feel its texture, its presence reminded me Perun was watching from Prawia—even if he didn't bother to help.

"What's this day have for us?" I asked as I surveyed the bustling village center, trying to distract myself from the fact my last two memories of Father would be him abandoning me.

Women walked with baskets on their heads, carrying the reaps of their harvest to barter with the other villagers, both farmers and not. Men peddled their loot from last summer's war with the Solgawi: weapons, armor, and helmets made of iron and metals beyond our tribes' knowledge. Others sold wool, furs, and horses in addition to the rare bars of silver, jewels, and, most valuable of all, golden coins bearing the face of long dead Anvoran leaders from south of Perun's Crown. One of those coins could buy at least a moon's worth of grain or enough jewelry for a warrior's wife to be admired above all her friends. *The spoils of war.*

Otylia had her hands over her mouth. She probably hadn't even heard me because she was staring at the crowd gathered at the head of the trail to her family's house. Among them, a brunette woman with eyes like moss sold her pottery—Odeta.

"Mom?" Otylia whispered as though she was afraid the answer would be yes.

Her mother's beaming smile was unlike any I had seen on her daughter's face. As the crowd descended on Odeta to trade, she laughed and touted her potions as the most potent in the tribe. She wasn't lying either. Some had accused her of witchcraft. Others had believed she possessed a gift from the gods.

We slowly approached the crowd, and Otylia trembled worse than when we'd faced the demons and raiders. She had looked up to her mother as an idol, following at the hem of her dress whenever she wasn't wandering the woods with me, yet none of the boys or girls had consoled the little witch when Odeta had passed—none except me.

Otylia had wept endlessly the morning after, sitting on a fallen log in the midst of her goddess's forest. Mom had sent me out to collect wood, not unlike how our new journey had begun this year. When I'd seen Otylia, Father's fresh beatings and threats of her exile were enough to stop me from saying a word.

Hellebore flowers had blanketed the ground. They were so purple they almost appeared black, as if the forest itself mourned Odeta's death. I had never seen anything like them, but I picked one and placed it by her side as she held her head in her hands. She'd never looked up. It had been next to nothing, and I had questioned my decision not to speak every day since.

Now, my heart broke watching the tears stream down Otylia's face as she reached out for Odeta. But her hand passed right through.

"Mom!" she cried out, swiping her hand at every part of her mother, desperately trying to touch the woman who had raised her.

I didn't know what to say or even what I could say. For four years Otylia had never rested in her mom's embrace, and now that she could see her one last time, it seemed more a curse than a gift. No words would mend a wound that deep.

After a moment of hesitation, I wrapped her in my arms. She buried her face in my chest, her tears soaking my tunic and the sound of her cries piercing through the deathly still air.

It felt so wrong for the sun to be shining and the crowd to be joyous as her shattered heart lay in my arms. All my worries about my powers and Father were nothing compared to that pain. I wished more than anything I could help it disappear, but a mother holds a special place in her child's heart—an irreplaceable one. Who was I to patch that hole?

After a minute, she craned her neck to meet my gaze. Streaks of red clashed with her sharp green eyes—her mother's eyes—and though I could see her trying to fight the sorrow, it was a futile effort. "Why is it that the only times you're quiet are when I need you to say something the most?" she asked.

My head felt heavy. The pain in her eyes was too much. I looked away and instantly regretted doing so. "I don't know. Maybe I just don't want to say it wrong."

"For all the things you say wrong, my expectations aren't that high."

I swallowed and forced myself to look at her. From her reddened nose to her hair racing every which way, she was a disaster, yet I saw her heart more in that moment than ever before. I felt myself begin to cry. Not for Father. Not for my own pain. But for the beautiful, broken girl who stood in front of me who I would've given anything to fix. "Do you remember the black flowers?"

"You saw them?"

"I… I was the one who put the flower by you in the woods."

Her eyes widened. "That was you?" Her voice was weak as she held her free hand to her chest. "I'd always hoped it was Mother's spirit during her forty days of wandering. I've used Dziewanna's power to keep it alive in my room, to remember her."

I stared at my boots. "I'm sorry."

"For what?"

"For not knowing what to say then, or now."

She lifted my chin, squeezing my hand as she did. Though the pain still lingered in her eyes, along with the tears, there was something else now. They almost seemed to shine in Dadźbóg's light. "In the moment I felt the most alone, you bothered enough to care for the witch nobody loved. Father never looked at me the same when she left, but that stupid little flower gave me hope, even if it's deathly poisonous."

"Even more appropriate for you."

The ends of her mouth flicked up, only for a moment. "Maybe you can say the right things, even without words." She cleared the tears from her eyes and took a shaky breath. "Why would it show us this? It isn't even your memory."

I scanned the clearing, but she was right. I was nowhere to be seen.

Then a black-haired girl emerged from the forest behind Odeta, no older than twelve. With Dziewanna's Bowmark hanging from her neck and a wicked grin on her face, I could only chuckle at the sight of little Otylia.

Next to me, Otylia broke down again when Odeta set aside her wares and hugged the girl. I squeezed her hand and admired the joy of the pair enjoying each other's presence.

I miss Mom.

Despite her obvious anger with Father, I knew she would be taking his loss hard, and I regretted not being there for her or for my entire family. Seeing Odeta's love for her daughter reminded me of how much Mom had lost because of me. I cupped Mokosz's warm necklace in my hand—all I had left of her until we made it home. *I'll come home, Mom, I promise.*

Odeta smiled down at little Otylia. "Find anything exciting in the woods?"

The girl crossed her arms and shook her head. "Just a fox, but he ran away when he saw me. Even animals hate me."

A pang struck my chest. Spring was young. This must've been just after I had turned my back on her—not long before Odeta's death—and the wound was fresh. Despite suffering from Marzanna's Curse, Odeta had hidden her symptoms for weeks before she finally succumbed.

"Foxes have quite an independent spirit," Odeta said as she collected her things. "They remind me of someone else I know."

Both Otylias wrinkled their noses at that as their mother picked up her basket and began walking down the trail. Leaves had begun to cover the trees, and a few stray ones had slipped to the ground. I tried to hop on each as we followed, but my boots only passed through, stealing my dose of childish excitement.

Otylia smirked at my attempts as she sniffled. "What made you think that would work?"

"It did."

She raised an eyebrow.

"You're smiling, at least a little, so I consider that a success."

Blushing, she looked into the forest, where the spring's sea of green broke the barrenness of winter, making the trail feel like a warm escape from the reality we'd left. "You are aware that I still have your dagger, right?" she quipped when she snapped her eyes back to me, that devious edge returning to them. "I'd hate to find out what happens to a half-demon stabbed by Thunderstone."

I chuckled. "You're back to threatening me again, so at least I know my plan worked. The whole being nice thing really had me concerned."

We soon reached her family's house among a patch of trees near the eastern gate. Instead of crops, a small garden of herbs peeked

between the trees behind the cottage. It felt appropriate for the servant of Dziewanna to live in the woods, even if it was within Dwie
Rzeki's walls. Because of the prestige of Dariusz's position, their
house had multiple rooms. In our little cottage, I could only wish for
that much privacy.

Odeta stopped young Otylia at the steps down to the door.
"Would you like to find me some mint to bring the food some flavor
tonight? I forgot to gather some earlier."

"Thought you might want bellflower or another herb for your
potions," the girl replied, disappointed.

"I remember this," Otylia whispered at my side, as if her mother
would hear. "Why was this moment important?"

Odeta tapped her daughter's nose, making her wince. "Actually,
I could use more bellflower," she said. "I've heard of a few men suffering from consumption in the area, and they'll probably be wanting
a potion from me."

The girl grinned and scampered off into the woods as her mother
turned to enter the house. Otylia pulled me after the girl, but I held
her back. "Something tells me this isn't about what you saw," I said.

"What do you mean?"

"If you don't remember anything important about this moment,
then maybe it's because you didn't see it. The vision took us to Odeta
first."

She shook her head. "But why is the ritual showing us any of this?
It's supposed to be revealing the truth of your soul..."

I nodded toward the house. "Well, there's only one way to find
out. You okay to go in?"

Without a reply, she pulled me to the door, and when we passed
through it, my heart stopped. Odeta was looking right at us. "Hello,
Otylia. I knew this day would come soon." With a smile, she gestured
to a stool near the wooden table in the center of the room. "It's time
I told you the truth."

46

Otylia

It's actually her...

A HAMMER HAD SHATTERED MY HEART into a thousand pieces. "Mom?" I whimpered, staring across the room at her, just as I remembered.

Her hair like the color of willow bark peeked from under her forest green headscarf, and her eyes, the ones Father always said were mine, showed her joy. This memory was only days before her death. As she flowed around the room, I admired how strong and graceful she'd been. Anyone could have mistaken her for the fairest queen if she hadn't possessed the bite of a bear against those who wronged her.

I rushed toward her, and this time, her arms met me. She cradled my head to her chest and stroked my hair as she laughed with glee.

I forgot everything else. I had missed her more than anything, and here she was, waiting for me.

"You have grown into quite the little *žená*," she said, using the old tongue's word for woman. "I'm so sorry I wasn't there to see you jump the fire."

My fight against my tears failed, and they raced down my face as I struggled to speak, "Why'd you have to go?"

Mother pulled back to look at me. Red streaked through her eyes as she pursed her lips. "I had hoped I would have more time, but he found me."

I shook my head. "Who found you?"

"Your father," she said. As she rounded the table, I winced as she let out a deep cough. *Marzanna's Curse.*

"I don't understand…" I stepped back, trembling. "Who is my father?"

With a deep breath, Mother looked up. Her breaths were weak, and she leaned over the table to steady herself. "My true husband, Weles."

I froze. Panic tore away each coherent thought that formed. *Weles is my father?*

Wacław's footsteps approached when I failed to speak. "If Weles is your husband then…"

"You're Dziewanna," I finished, my eyes wide and my breaths fleeting.

A thousand memories ran through my mind. The hellebores. Both her and Mokosz's decision to choose me. Sosna's constant presence. Dziewanna's sacrifice to protect me from Marzanna's Curse. Father's secrecy around Mother's childhood. It all made sense now, but I couldn't understand why she would come here, fake a life with Dariusz, and lie to me for sixteen years.

I stared at Mother, at Dziewanna. My knees were weak. I should've knelt before the goddess, but all I could do was stammer, "What does that make me?"

Mother swept forward and clutched my hands. "Otylka, my *księżniczka*," she said, calling me the formal term for a princess, "you are my daughter, a goddess."

I tore myself from her grasp and circled the room. *This is a dream, a nightmare.* It had to be. My role was to serve the gods, not be one of them. I'd worshipped Dziewanna for years as I grieved Mother, but she'd been with me the entire time. Why wouldn't she tell me?

"I swore never to have a child with Weles after Perun forced me to wed him," she continued, "but in time, I foolishly gave into his comfort. When I discovered the pregnancy, I knew I couldn't let my

daughter grow up in Nawia. I wanted her to be free, like I never was."
She sighed. "I came here and married Dariusz in hopes Weles would
never find us. I even turned your hair black like Dariusz's, but Weles
came too close to finding you anyway. To keep you safe, I had no
choice but to return to him."

"And abandon me!" I shouted with my fists clenched. *How could
she leave me? My mother... my goddess...* Power swelled around my
hands, but I didn't fight it. She'd left me without a word. "Why?"

Her eyes dropped to the floor. "I was never meant to be a mother,
but when I had you, keeping you safe was all that mattered. The process of gaining your powers is slow at first. You may have started
feeling it already, wild and out of control, but soon you will face the
Trials of Ascension, grasp your own strength, and lose the ability to
channel. I couldn't risk you knowing before you were ready. Weles
would have sensed your power and come for you."

I dropped to my knees. "I'll lose my connection to you and Mokosz?" I asked, staring up at her. "I don't want this. All I wanted was
to serve you and protect your wilds."

"You will never lose your connection to me, my love. You are my
daughter. Even when you can no longer channel my power, we are
inseparable." She looked from Wacław to me. "You serve me every
day you work to become the woman you're meant to be."

"Who is that?" I spat. "How could I know who you wanted me
to be when you never told me the truth?"

She knelt in front of me and took my cheek in her hand. I leaned
into it, feeling the warmth of her love. "If you're here," she said,
"then Marzanna's plan has begun. My sister's sickness gave me a
convenient story to return to Nawia before, but when I go silent this
time, it is because I'm fighting with all I have to survive. It will be up
to you to free me from Marzanna." Sorrow filled her gaze as she
stepped away. "Our time here is short, but always remember, my
księżniczka, that I love you more than anything."

"Don't go!"

Her knowing smile met me. "Weles will come for you. He will try
to take you to Nawia, but it is *your* choice now whether or not to go

with him. Though he is not a gentle man, he is your father. Whatever you choose, I will be with you."

The world faded around us as I reached out, grasping at the fading wisps of her until nothing remained but darkness.

Tears poured down my face as I shut my eyes and screamed into the black. For years, I'd dreamed of seeing her face again. Now, she'd torn my heart to shreds. We'd entered the Lake of Reflection to find the truth of Wacław's souls, but as we left, I no longer knew who I was.

The chill of the northern wind sweeping across the lake met my wet, exposed skin as we burst from the water's depths. Stumbling and gasping for air, we quickly grabbed our undergarments and collapsed in the snow.

Was it real?

I knew Mokosz's rituals too well to doubt them. In the span of a few minutes, all that I'd known had been torn away. As I felt the snow's burn against my hands, I wished it had all been a dream, but it was the truth—the heart of his souls and mine.

Wacław's heavy breaths filled the air as I touched Dziewanna's mark on my neck and thought of the life-long pledge I'd given her during my initiation. *It was all a lie.* I winced at the cool water dripping down my face and neck, holding me to reality while only panic filled my mind.

With tears wetting his cheeks and water coating his bare torso, Wacław stumbled toward me and took me in his arms. The lightning no longer shattered his skin in his rage, but its power lingered in his eyes.

A demon and a goddess. Just our luck.

"What do we do now?" I whispered, clinging to him.

His chest heaved against mine with every breath as he repeated the words I'd said beneath Perun's Oak, "We fight for those we love, even if it's for an eternity."

"You forgot the last part." *With no one else.*

"It would be a lie."

"What are you saying?"

He hesitated, staring at the endless snow. *Say it.* Nothing in our lives made sense anymore. Nothing but him. *Please, don't hesitate just this once.* His bright blue eyes returned to me, and his voice cracked when he spoke, "Otylka, I—"

Footsteps approached from the woods. I cursed Kuba as he emerged from the tree line with his mouth wide open. He looked from me to Wacław, both of us only half-dressed, and muttered under his breath.

Heat rushed to my face as I pulled back and averted my gaze. *Why can we never have a simple moment alone?*

Wacław's own cheeks were bright red. He rose and reached for his tunic and trousers. "Kuba, my friend, you have impeccable timing as always."

Kuba smirked and hopped through the snow toward us. "The others sent me to see what was taking you two so long. Guess I found out."

I scoffed and pushed myself to my feet. In just my underdress, I was freezing, and I thanked Ara's insistence as I slid into my dress and wrapped myself in my fur-lined cloak. "You have no idea…"

"How dumb do you think I am?" Kuba asked, that smirk still stuck to his face as he ran his fingers through the water and shivered.

"You really want an answer to that?" I snapped.

Wacław sighed as he paced, clenching and unclenching his fists. "We conducted the ritual."

"It worked?" Kuba asked. "Or are we doomed to freeze to death out here?"

Wacław glanced at me, but I turned away with my cloak pulled tight. "We discovered that my parents lied to me my entire life and Father abandoned me at birth."

"Oh…"

"On the bright side," he continued with a shrug, "I can apparently fly and shoot lightning if I get mad enough. With a better control over the winds, I should be able to find the płanetnik."

Kuba's eyes lit up. "That's awesome! I mean, everything else sucked, but you can call lightning? You're lucky!"

"I wouldn't consider being a demon lucky. Besides, anything I can do, the other płanetnik can probably do with years of experience. Even if I can find him, it's going to take all of us to beat him and whatever else Marzanna has waiting for us."

"What about the Frostmark?"

Wacław shook his head. "Still there."

"Darn."

"Tell the others we'll be there soon," I interrupted, desperate to get rid of Kuba.

He raised his eyebrow at Wacław, probably expecting some type of signal from him, but when none came, he groaned. "All right, don't let me be part of all the fun. Just know Xobas is cleaning his blade."

Wacław chuckled. "Then we'll be quick."

I let out a deep breath as Kuba sprinted into the woods with an obnoxiously loud laugh. After everything we'd just seen, I couldn't handle his lightheartedness. It felt like the day had lasted weeks, but it was only the early afternoon. I needed an hour to just sit at the edge of the lake to think about life with my feet in the water. But that was a luxury for someone who wasn't fighting a winter goddess.

We just stood there for another minute, silent as Wacław stared down at his blackened hand. Despite me being a goddess, he really had saved my life. Mother had said my powers would come slowly, and until then, I assumed I was as vulnerable as anyone.

Just weeks ago, I had worried about Father's judgements and smiled about dresses with Ara. The Drowning of Marzanna was supposed to have been our official leap into adulthood, but I didn't want the responsibility of saving the tribe. I liked being the witch of the woods. No one bothered me—especially not Marzanna.

"Do you believe in it now?" Wacław asked, stray hairs of his blond hair peeking from beneath his hood as he shivered. "Destiny?"

I walked toward him. "What got us here was not destiny. There's no agreement of the gods to choose each of our lives."

"Then how do you explain a demon and a goddess being born in the same village—only hours apart—and that ritual showing us both of our souls? It's hard not to think someone out there is trying to tell us *something*."

"Souls and rituals work in strange ways," I grumbled, looking up at the demon who'd given me hope when no one else did.

A grin crossed his face as he took my hands. I wanted him to pull me close again, to help me forget about Mother's lies, but he moved no closer. "You don't think it's destiny you and I are here, together, after everything that has happened?" he asked. There was an allure in his gaze, different from when he'd seen me in my underdress.

I shook my head. "I don't know. It's hard to know what to believe anymore."

When I looked at him again, a new fear gripped me. Not fear of his power but of how much I needed him. Wacław had been there for me when no one else was, and as I stood there, I couldn't imagine life without him. That made me vulnerable.

I stepped away and glanced back toward camp. "We need to meet up with the others."

"Are we going to talk about what happened in there?" he asked, disappointed. "This changes everything."

"You don't think I know that?" I gritted my teeth. "I... I just need time to think. Okay?"

I was gone before he could reply. Tears burned my eyes, but I pushed them away as the camp came into view. Kuba had already seen too much, and the last thing I wanted was the others knowing something was wrong. It was hard enough to comprehend what had happened without an audience.

Xobas was still cleaning his blade when I joined the others around the ashes of what used to be the fire. *How long have we been gone?* The food appeared to have been cooked and packed up some time ago. My stomach rumbled, but I didn't think I could handle the meal anyway.

Every time I closed my eyes, I saw Mother, her voice ringing in my ears. I should've been happy that she was alive, but instead, it felt like she'd torn open a wound that had barely healed.

For years, I'd held myself together without her. I'd grown from that little girl into a woman without the only woman I loved. How could she have thought that one conversation would fix all that her absence had broken in my heart? It had been hard enough to accept her death, let alone both her and my immortality. Now I was alone again, left to pick up the pieces I'd spent four years trying to put back together.

"Find what you were looking for?" Ara asked as she strapped her bow to her back.

I grabbed my bag in silence, and Wacław answered for me as he arrived with the filled canteens in hand, "I'm not sure what we found, but I have a better grasp on my power now. Hopefully it'll be enough to find the demon."

She grinned. "Good. I don't want to waste all my arrows shooting at an air demon when the cultists are running at us. Not sure arrows could wound a beast like that anyway."

"Leave the cultists to Xobas and me," Narcyz replied with a jab of his spear.

Jaryło rubbed Zofia's side and slid his silver sword into its sheath on his back. There was something in his eye, a curiosity I hadn't seen before, and unease stirred within me—the same dark feeling as I'd felt seeing Yuliya. *What are you hiding?*

Before I could wonder further, Xobas patted Wacław on the back. "Glad to hear your ritual was a success, but time is running out. We must be swift if we are to defeat the demon and still reach the clans."

"Wacław will search for the demon tomorrow morning and summon it to us," Jaryło said. He took a swig of water before strapping his canteen to Zofia's bags. "Until then, we must continue our trek to the east. The ritual stole valuable daylight hours."

Narcyz took to the woods without hesitation, and Xobas let out a chuckle as the rest of us followed. I hung at the back.

The chatter of the group surrounded me, but I was deaf to their words and numb to their joy. Even when Ara tried to ask for the ritual's details, I could only force myself to mutter, "Everything I knew was uprooted."

What other words could explain the turmoil in my soul?

I had been one of Dziewanna's willows, stretching my roots deep into the earth in search of water and nutrients, only to find I'd been encircled with bedrock. My search for growth had been for nothing. Every bit of freedom I'd thought I had was nothing but a mirage in the dry heat of the summer—a false hope. The woman who'd raised me was the goddess who'd chosen me and given me purpose. My father wasn't the cunning priest who'd dared to challenge Jacek's rule but the god who'd dared to challenge Perun's. It had never mattered what I did or who I chose to be.

Only one thing was true: My life was a lie.

47

Wacław

Secrets have ruled both of our lives. Is that destiny or a cruel trick?

MY TWO SOULS WERE AS HEAVY as my legs when we made camp on a ridge near the edge of a small meadow. It was dark now, but Otylia hadn't spoken to me since we'd left the lake.

I had come so close to admitting everything I felt for her on that shore. Though Kuba had ruined the moment, the sight of her exposed chest as she wore only her underdress still had my mind buzzing. Dziewanna's Bowmark and Mokosz's Mothermark had shone at her neck as she'd clung to me, desperate. There was nowhere else I would've rather been.

Gods, I'm thinking like Kuba now. I couldn't help it. After all we'd experienced in the ritual, I felt closer to Otylia than ever.

As Kuba had joked and bickered with Narcyz on the afternoon hike, I'd walked silently by Otylia's side with Ara. There were a thousand words I wanted to say to her, that I needed to say to her. But I was mute, and every moment of silence panged at my heart.

I looked to the last bit of Dadźbóg's light and sighed. There was a time not long ago that I had wished for adventure. Now, I cursed that child. Kuba was right about the attraction of a simple life, but he could return home to Maja and his bog iron once we were finished. As I watched Otylia fight her sorrow, I knew I wouldn't have the same chance. She'd claimed not to believe in destiny, but it was hard for me to believe I had any choice in who I had to become.

"We need to discuss our plan," Ara said as she stoked the fire.

Xobas leaned against a birch tree and stared out into the fields with one hand on his sword's hilt. The moon hung in the clear sky, only a slim crescent remaining. "We must act quickly. The high chief is dead, and Mikołaj will not survive a war with the Solgawi if we don't bring our clans' cavalry."

I watched the flicker of the flames. I wished I could laugh at Mikołaj, but my entire family was suffering because of my failure to save Father. Now that I could fly and find the płanetnik, tomorrow would likely be the day we were forced to face him. If I failed again, then Mom and Nevenka would be next—they could be anyway. My focus should have been on that fight, yet my thoughts lingered on everything that had gone wrong. *How can I defeat an army of demons when I can't even protect my family?*

"We need to know what we're up against," Ara replied, pacing. Her brown cloak skimmed the top layer of the snow as she tightened it around her. "Beyond the płanetnik, how many cultists and demons can we expect, and will Marzanna appear?"

Instead of his usual smile, Jaryło's mouth was a thin line. "No, she is far too calculating to risk her life in a battle at this point, but there is no way to be certain how many spirits and star gazing fools she's recruited to her side. The only thing I'm sure of is that Wacław must find the weather demon. If he is nearby, he can draw Marzanna's forces here, where we'll have the defensive advantage of the ridge and forest."

He is a war god. I scanned the twisted trees scattered below the steep drop, most of them barely visible in the moonlight. The cultists could climb the shallower backside, but it was a narrow path—perfect for a small shield wall. The płanetnik, on the other hand, could reach us no matter how high the climb.

Narcyz nodded. "Defending the forests is what we do."

"It'll make for a tight shot," Ara said, eyeing the gaps between the trees, "but I'm always up for a challenge. Not much difference between a buck and a demon, right?"

"Otylia's sorcery will work better in the woods too," Narcyz murmured as he whittled a stick. When he looked up, we were all staring at him, shocked that he bothered to call her something other than a witch. "What? I don't need to like her witchcraft to know it's useful."

Kuba nudged him, throwing off his cutting. "Someone's getting soft on us."

Narcyz scowled but didn't reply as Ara placed the pot over the fire. "More soup," she said. "You can thank Otylia for gathering enough mushrooms for me to make anything worth eating." She smiled in Otylia's direction, but Otylia only stared at her knees as she huddled against a tree. Lowering her voice, Ara asked me, "What happened to her?"

I swallowed and looked through the smoke at Otylia, the flames dancing across her body. I couldn't imagine how lost she felt. A goddess without her power. A priestess without a purpose. A daughter without her mother.

"The truth," I whispered.

"Kuba, Narcyz, and I will form a shield wall on top of this ridge," Xobas said, ignoring our side conversation as he paced toward the steep, rocky slope dropping into the woods.

"Agreed," Jaryło replied. "The three of you shall guard Wacław's sleeping body at the peak of the ridge. With the elevation, Ara and Otylia can stand behind you and launch ranged attacks."

"While you and I will slay the płanetnik," I said, glancing at the god as I thumbed my marked palm. The fact they had decided to guard my body without asking questions felt like an honor—one I didn't deserve.

Narcyz took a chunk out of the stick and spat. "Our plan is to sit there like prey while Half-Chief fights a demon? How will we even know if he's won if we can't see him?

Jaryło grinned and tapped a finger to his temple. "A *ziemski* płanetnik can choose who sees him, or her, while they're in their... What did you call it? Oh yes, soul-form."

"You're telling me we could've seen him the whole time?"

"Doesn't mean I wanted you to," I quipped, glancing at Otylia. Her eyes met mine for a moment before she looked away. "We should also account for the possibility that I fail. An agreement with the clans is still crucial, no matter what."

With a wave of his hand, Jaryło leaned his shoulder against an oak. "If we are defeated, peace or war will not matter. Marzanna's wrath will continue. Luckily, I will return from Nawia as long as I have my Moonblades, but all of you..."

Kuba sneered. "Your empathy is appreciated."

"I only state the truth. There are advantages to being a god."

When he said that, I could have sworn he looked past Kuba, right at Otylia. I pinched my nose and shook my head. *I'm seeing things now...*

Xobas sighed and sat next to me by the fire. "If we fail, then who-ever survives will finish the last few days of the journey. We've come this far. There must be peace if the tribe is to endure."

That daunting truth hung over us. We had two battles still to fight—one with the spear and the other with charisma. Even if we lost the first, we needed to win the second.

Ara grabbed the bowls from her pack. "Now that the planning is finished, let's eat!"

I smiled at her attempt to lighten the mood. It couldn't have been easy for her to be one of the few female huntresses on top of being a Zurgowie refugee, but somehow she did it with confidence and a grace even the strongest men lacked. As she distributed the food, I grabbed two bowls, took a deep breath, and walked over to Otylia.

"I'm not hungry," she said without looking up.

"Hmm." I stared down at the steam rising from the liquid. "To be honest, neither am I, but if we're going to starve, would you at least join me for a moonlit stroll in the meadow?" Her glare met me, but I wasn't going to give up that easily. "If you come with me, I promise I'll leave you alone for the rest of the night."

She wrinkled her nose, like little Otylia had done during the ritual. It would've been cute if her sorrow weren't so potent.

I set down the bowls and offered her my hand, and though rebellion hardened her face, she took it, following me into the grasses. They tickled the tips of my fingers that still had feeling as the *huhuhuhooo* of tawny owls echoed through the open space. Memories of the owl's call before Marzanna's appearance sent a shiver through my body. *Is it an omen?*

The moon's dull aura cascaded over the tree-covered hills beyond the small meadow. Each of the bone talismans in Otylia's braid reflected the light as she fiddled with Mokosz's amulet on her wrist. My heart screamed for me to say something, anything, but I knew she would speak when she was ready.

Of all the questions the ritual raised, one wouldn't leave my mind. *Can a demon and a goddess ever be together?* It was a childish thought on the eve of a fight for our lives, yet I couldn't help but wonder. After being forced away from her for years, I wanted to spend each moment by her side and never leave her again. So much of the journey had forced me to become numb to the pain and suffering of myself and others. But everything that hurt her tore me apart. If I was an immortal demon and she an immortal goddess…

I bit my cheek. What would Father have thought of me obsessing over his rival's daughter instead of preparing for battle? *Does it matter? He's gone.*

I had lost track of how long we'd been walking by the time Otylia crouched and cupped a small corn poppy in her hands before letting the plant rest. "Father used to say these flowers blanketed fields after the worst battles," she said. "When he was tending to the dead in Jacek's wars, he believed the warriors' blood stained them red."

Father's wars. How many lives had he sacrificed for his dream of uniting the Krowikie tribes and expanding our lands? How much had he surrendered for glory and duty?

"I thought it just a stupid story, but Mother…" she said, hesitating. "Mother used them in her potions. I always helped her find what she needed, and she would teach me how to make them. She called me her *mała dziką,* little wildling, when I never wanted to leave the woods."

Tears wetted her cheeks as I knelt next to her and placed a hand on her back. *What am I doing?* I didn't know, but it was all I had.

Otylia looked to me, her eyes wanting. "Was she ever who I thought she was? Or was she lying about everything?"

I remembered young Otylia smiling with Odeta and the pride on her mother's face. It had been a familiar sight. Before Father had torn me away from Otylia, Odeta had fed us both many times when we'd returned from our adventures in the woods. No matter how covered in dirt Otylia was, Odeta had always seemed to adore each moment with her.

"She loved you more than life," I said. "Your mom left everything she knew to raise you apart from Weles. That takes bravery, even if she lied to keep you safe."

"So, you don't blame your parents for lying to you?"

The irony struck me, and I sighed as I gripped the amulet of Mokosz that Mom had given me. "While Father let his pride push me away, despite everything, Mom loved me enough to leave behind the man she fell for. She's lived her life as the chief's disgraced former concubine, even though she knew I would likely be a demon. It's hard to blame her for that."

Otylia rose and stared over the plains as the winds brushed across the tops of the grasses. One finger traced the Bowmark at her collar. "Mother has spoken to me so many times since then. She could've told me the truth."

"It seemed like she knew you would come. Maybe, that was what she had always planned."

"Then she chose the worst way possible…"

Her voice hung in the air before the breeze pulled it away. I didn't know what to say, so I just pulled her into a hug, half-expecting her to stab me when I did, but she accepted it, and we stood there in each other's embrace for a long time. Neither of us spoke. Only our breaths and the pounding of my heart filled the silence as I felt the rise and fall of her chest against mine.

"You know," I finally said. "Before this journey, before Marzanna, all I really wanted was a purpose. I was the hesitant Half-Chief, never the warrior Father wanted me to be. But tomorrow... tomorrow I'll have to face a płanetnik just like me, and to be honest, I'm scared. I'm scared of Marzanna and her demons. I'm scared of the power inside me, of what I can see it doing to me already. I'm scared of losing Kuba or Xobas or even Narcyz because I grabbed that stupid dagger."

I stepped back and slid my hands into hers. My voice was rough, cracked, but I needed to say it as I looked into her eyes—her beautiful green eyes that stole my breath.

"But most of all," I continued, "I'm scared of losing you. You gave me a purpose, Otylka. When Father looked down on me and Marzanna tried to use me, you risked your life to save mine and gave me hope to stop the goddess. It doesn't matter to me whether you're a witch, a szeptucha, a *księżniczka*, a goddess, or just the girl who bothered to care about the demonic son of a concubine. I know who you are and what your mom saw in you. You're the untamable, unstoppable, and unbelievable girl who I can't get out of my head."

Catching my breath, I looked away, blushing. *I really am an idiot.* I hadn't known what to say, so I'd said all of it, not knowing if it made any sense.

"Look at me, Wašek," she said, her voice soft.

I couldn't. My heart ached. More than anything, I wanted to tell her how I truly felt, but even I didn't know how to put that into words. I felt insane, irrational. But Mom always said that's why the heart was in control of love.

Her hand touched my cheek. It was warm against my skin, a rare respite from the chill around us, and when she forced me to meet her gaze, her face seemed to shine in the moonlight as all else faded into darkness. I studied her scar—that beautiful flaw that dared to scratch the face of a goddess—hugging her cheekbone before it curved toward her lips. The smallest of grins graced them.

"Thank you," she whispered.

"For what?"

"For being the first person since Mother died to see me as more than a witch or even a szeptucha. You might still be that foolish boy from the woods, but you're the kindest demon I've ever met."

I failed to stop the smile from creeping onto my face. "And of the goddesses I've met, you're by far my favorite, though, you've probably threatened to kill me as often as Marzanna."

"I've also saved your life plenty of times," she said, raising her brow as she slid her hand down my cheek. Her tender touch only brought more mystery, stealing my breath. "Ara told me about Yuliya, about how you chose me over Jacek."

"Oh…" My chest tightened.

"I don't know how to thank you for that. You sacrificed your father and the ends of your fingers to save me." She held her fingertips to my blackened ones. Though they had become numb from the frostbite, I swore I felt her warm touch.

I forced away the tears that threatened to come. "She would've killed Father no matter what I did."

"Did you know that at the time?" she asked, taking my hands.

"Would it matter if I did? He's gone because of me."

"And I'm here because of you. Why'd you do it?"

"Can you even die if you're a goddess?"

She furrowed her brow. "You're deflecting."

"Maybe I don't know what to say," I whispered, pursing my lips as I looked from my boots to her.

"Tell me the truth."

"All the truth has gotten us is more pain."

"The truth has shown us a way out of the lies."

I smiled. "You're starting to sound like me."

"Answer the question or I'll leave." She pulled away only slightly.

When I caught her waist, she didn't resist. "I don't remember what it was," I mumbled as she bit her lip and stared into my eyes. Every beat of my heart hammered my mind. I had no idea what I was doing.

She wrapped her arms around me and stepped so close that I

could feel her warm breaths against my neck and her hips against mine. "You really are a fool," she whispered.

"Can I kiss you?"

"Are you really asking for permission?"

"I figured it was better than a dagger in my chest."

Our lips met. I didn't know whether I kissed her or she kissed me, but it didn't matter in the moment. With each slow press of her soft lips to mine, I felt her passion, her desire as our souls danced again. Our minds spun and hearts soared in each other's arms. She was the world—a goddess among men—and for once, there was nothing keeping us apart.

When we parted, heat rushed to my cheeks as I smiled. It hadn't lasted long. For those few seconds, though, all I'd felt was her lips and her body pressed against me as our emotions joined. It was intoxicating. I could've held her forever, forgetting all the pain and struggle of the world with hearts racing together.

"You're beautiful, even if you're a witch," I whispered as my blackened fingers lightly traced the scar on her cheek, glowing as if she were channeling.

Her palm rested on the back of mine. "And you're still a demon, even if you're charming." She stepped back, and my hand hung in the air longer than it should've. "We should head back before the others get the wrong idea."

I beamed when I replied, "What idea would that be?"

With a raise of an eyebrow and a little smile, she turned and strode back toward the camp.

For a moment, I watched her go—the winds blowing her braid and each swing of her hips tugging on my heart. The taste of her lips lingered on mine, and I wished we didn't have to return. I wished we could've spent eternity in that field. No demons or gods battling for supremacy. Just her, me, and the night. But that was too much to ask for a demon and a goddess.

48

Otylia

He kissed me…

THE HESITANT BOY WHO'D DANCED AND EXPLORED with me in the woods for so many years had actually kissed me. And I'd let it happen. No, I'd *invited* it.

When I'd stepped back and threatened to leave, I hadn't realized how much I wanted Wacław to catch me. He had, and I'd given into the desire that pulled me to him.

I'd felt every bit of his excitement and eagerness as we'd kissed. I didn't know why or how, but after experiencing the pure elation of our souls together, I didn't care. It had been the most confusing and exciting moment in my life—I'd loved it more than anything.

It didn't that matter Wacław wasn't a warrior or chief or powerful priest. In his eyes, I saw the boy who'd taken beating after beating to see me one more time. The care in his heart was stronger than any ax and meant more than any chiefdom or army.

I had feared Mokosz's vision, but now my heart raced with glee underneath the pain of Mother's lies. It had taken every bit of my strength not to giggle and sprint to Ara. I was the witch of the wilds, not some foolish girl from old women's tales of true love, yet for the first time since we'd left Dwie Rzeki, at least one thing felt right.

A part of me had wanted to linger with Wacław in the plains as we held each other. It had been a glimpse of what our lives could've been, he my Wašek and I his Otylka, but there was an ache that lingered in that embrace.

Loss.

We'd both sensed it. Jacek had never been a true father to him, but he'd wept regardless. Though I wished I could understand Wacław's pain like he tried to understand mine, I resented Jacek tearing him away from me when I'd needed him most.

Father and the other priests would conduct a funeral in the high chief's honor. He would spend his forty days traveling Jawia one last time before he descended to the paradise of Nawia—to Weles. It was better than he deserved. I was just glad he was gone.

Weles...

My real father was in Nawia, not Dwie Rzeki. My real mother was the goddess I'd served since I was twelve, and she was trapped by Marzanna. When Mother had told me the truth, I'd never felt more lost in my life. Wacław had wept for me despite everyone he loved being at risk. It hurt to see him suffer for me, but I had no clue what to do about Mother's entrapment or me being a goddess. At least I knew whatever happened, I wouldn't be alone.

That stupid, foolish, rash, amazing kiss had made me forget everything.

I still felt Wacław's arms pulling me tight against him and the passion in the kiss itself, like he hadn't been able to hold himself back any longer. It was just a moment. Fleeting. Our souls had connected in the *żityje* ritual in a passionate dance, but knowing that he *wanted* me was a bliss that no ritual could match.

The boy that doubted himself and hesitated at every turn had cast that all aside in defiance of his father and the very nature of our souls. He'd kissed me despite the risks, despite every word I knew Kuba and Narcyz had whispered into his ear. More than anything, Wacław wanted peace. But I'd seen it in his eyes. For me, he'd go to war.

I should've stayed.

As I walked back to the camp, regret gripped me. Wacław had

been full of nerves, yet he'd professed that I'd given him a purpose. Should I have said something more, complimented his overgrown golden hair or the lean muscles he'd built on our trip? Ara would've known what to do. Any girl with a semblance of romantic skill would've.

But I'd just walked away. In a day, we'd be fighting for our lives, and I had left him standing in the meadow with nothing but a quip about him being a charming demon. Had that hurt him? Was he watching me leave?

I considered glancing back for a second but pushed away the thought. He was a boy, of course he was watching.

Good. I didn't know why, but I took immense pleasure in knowing his eyes were on me. Not Genowefa. Not Yuliya. Me.

After bounding up the slope to the ridge, I joined Ara alongside the fire. Her gaze snapped from the tip of an arrow to me. *I'm doomed.* Somehow, she'd read my mind every step of the way, and I had no doubt she had her idea of what had happened in the meadow.

"Feeling better?" she asked with a touch of sarcasm.

"It would've been hard for me to feel any worse." I glanced around at the others. Only Kuba seemed keenly aware of my presence, but whispers were never secret in our quiet camp. "Do you want to—"

Ara snatched my hand and yanked me into the sea of broken and scarred trees. Between the smirk on her face and the ferocity of her pull, I feared I'd been right about her observations.

"Don't stray too far," Xobas called after us. But it was half-hearted. He'd learned by now that we weren't warriors who waited to follow his commands.

We stopped running when the slope shallowed. The moonlight wound through the trees, splitting Ara's face between darkness and light as she giggled. "Tell me everything!"

I grinned and slid my hand across the hilt of the Thunderstone dagger, still at my belt. "How do you know there's anything to tell?"

"Because you've been distant ever since you entered the Lake of Reflection, but now you're smiling like a girl riding her first horse."

"Am I that transparent?" I said with a groan. "If you say anything to the others—"

She shook her head rapidly. "I promise I won't."

"Fine." I took a deep breath and failed to hold in my smile. "Wacław took me out into the meadow, and we talked about everything that has happened. Then... Then he told me that more than anything, he was scared of losing me. He said he can't get me out of his head, and when I confronted him about sacrificing Jacek and his fingers to save me, he dodged the question and kissed me instead."

Her eyes were wide when I finished. She squeezed my hand so hard it hurt. "I knew it!" she squealed.

I blushed. "There's more."

"Oh! Did you—"

"Gods, no!" I exclaimed. "Just the kiss, but something happened to us during the *żityje* ritual. We told you how our souls seemed to merge and I felt everything he did. Ever since, it's been happening whenever one of us is in danger. And when we kissed, it happened again."

She giggled. "You felt everything he did when you kissed? Wow. Never had that happen before."

I fiddled with my braid, trying to tell myself this was all normal, but I knew better. "Everyone always talks about their first kiss, but no one ever told me it would be like *that*. It was overwhelming and incredible and ugh... Why can nothing be simple?"

"Maybe it's simpler than you think," she said with a smile.

My shoulders slumped. *If only you knew.* But I couldn't tell her about Weles, not yet. We had enough problems without me burdening her with the truth of my birth. So soon, the elation from my kiss had already passed, and reality's snarling teeth met me. Between Mother, Weles, Wacław, and Marzanna, my head was spinning. "Tonight was a dream, but unless we kill the płanetnik tomorrow, it doesn't matter how I feel about Wacław."

"You're such a romantic."

With a deep sigh, I looked back toward the camp. "What am I supposed to do, forget that Marzanna has captured Dziewanna? If

409

we fail, the wilds will wither and the tribe will starve. The last thing that matters right now is how fond of a boy I am."

"Oh, Otylia," she said mockingly. "You'd be right if he was just some boy, like the one I ignored after the festival, but he isn't. You know I'm right."

"With Jacek gone, is it really that simple?"

"Does it matter? You're a powerful channeler, I'm pretty sure you can choose who you want."

I clutched Mother's amulet. "What if all I wanted was to serve Dziewanna and Mokosz? I didn't ask to fight Marzanna. I didn't ask to fall for a boy who's a demon. Why couldn't I just serve my goddesses well and be seen as more than a witch?"

She cocked her head to the side, giving a smile that told me I was being foolish. "He sees you as more than that, and so do I. Everything you've done to protect the wilds doesn't need to change. We'll find Dziewanna whether you're kissing demons or not."

"One demon is enough," I said with a little laugh.

"Then one fair-haired, blue-eyed demon it is," she quipped. "C'mon, we should make sure the boys haven't burned down the forest." For a moment, she started walking back but stopped sharply. "You two aren't going to be making-out all the time now, are you?" I rolled my eyes. "If we survive another day, we can worry then about how much I'm kissing him."

49

Wacław

What does this mean for us?

WHILE THE REST OF THE GROUP WRESTLED WITH SLEEP, I sat against a tree in my soul-form, spinning Mokosz's amulet in my fingers and wishing morning would come sooner.

Otylia was wrapped in her cloak alongside the fire, her hair free once again as she slept less than a stride away from my body. Those few inches felt like miles as I yearned to rest with her in my arms. She'd seemed calmer when we returned from the meadow. Still, the truth she faced wasn't something so easily fixed.

My hand drifted to my lips, and I grinned boyishly as I remembered our time in the moonlight. I didn't know what to believe about us or the future, but a giddiness had my heart racing. Though she hadn't admitted much, she'd kissed me—that was enough.

Across the fire, Narcyz and Xobas slept near their weapons. The two of them, along with Otylia and Kuba, would guard my sleeping body tomorrow. They each had their own reasons for fighting Marzanna, whether it be revenge for Father's death or a dedication to save the tribe.

I admired their will and loyalty. Without them, it didn't matter if I was strong enough to fight the płanetnik. My body would be defenseless, and the sheer number of cultists and demons would be too much. Only Otylia had sorcery among them, but they were the ones who could turn the battle in our favor.

Kuba let out a yawn. When he saw my soul-form, he slid from his cloak and scampered over. "You willing to talk about it now?

"Hush," I said, grabbing his arm. "Wake up Narcyz and we'll all regret it."

"Sorry..."

"Can't sleep?"

He nodded to my body. "Obviously you couldn't either."

"Technically, I am asleep."

"You're also *technically* demonic."

I jabbed him in the side. "Careful, you're almost starting to sound like Narcyz."

"How dare you?" he said with a quiet chuckle. "What'd you talk about on your romantic walk through the meadow? You tried to hide it earlier. That means it's good."

I grinned as I laid my head back against the tree. "Nothing."

"You really suck at secrets—probably bad for negotiations. So, are you two, like, you know?"

Running my thumb over my frostbitten fingers, I glanced at Otylia to check she was still sleeping. The thought of her overhearing this frightened me to my core. "I don't know... maybe? We kissed, but—"

"What ya mean, *maybe*? You kissed the witch who can strangle any of us with just her eyes. Obviously she likes you—we'd both be dead if she didn't—and I assume you like her too if you were dumb enough to try it."

"You've just been trying to get me to admit it, haven't you?"

"You still haven't." That stupid smirk was growing, and I smiled with him.

"I do," I admitted. "Despite everything, I can't get her out of my mind. We're so different, but it's like our souls are connected. I know it sounds stupid. Around her, though, I feel like I can be myself, and away from her, I feel lost."

Kuba tucked in his legs as his fingers dropped into the snow, the smirk fading from his face. "Before all of this, I would've called you insane—both for being fond of her and becoming so mushy. But I get it now. Maja's waiting for me back home, I hope. I haven't been right since we left. It's like a piece of me is missing." He looked to Otylia and patted me on the shoulder. "If anyone can deal with the demon Half-Chief, it's her. Just, don't mess it up. I'd rather not end up with a root through my head."

"The feeling is mutual." I stared at the stars through the trees. Mom had so many legends of great heroes who'd shone brightly among them before they had descended to Nawia. *I miss her stories.*

With a yawn, Kuba stretched and rustled up my hair as he did. "Demons don't need sleep, but I definitely do. You all right by yourself?"

I chuckled. "I've been alone in my soul-form for sixteen years. I'll be fine for the night."

"Maybe you won't be alone at night forever." He winked and hopped to his feet.

My smile returned as he stumbled more than walked back to his cloak and wrapped himself in it. Seconds later, his snoring pierced through the night, startling the owl. It took flight and hooted at us the whole way.

If it had been any other bird, I would've laughed, but its call reminded me of all we'd lost and everything we still had to face. Demons and cultists had brought death in the night and the day. Tomorrow, though, we would strike back against Marzanna for taking Father, for attacking Otylia, for threatening my family, and for slaughtering Bustelintin.

I looked at the group sleeping around me. Bullies, rivals, warriors, foreigners, witches, friends, deities, demons—none of it mattered anymore. We were united for the tribe, for our gods, and for our families. Together, we would stem Marzanna's frigid tide or die trying. That thought lingered with me, and I allowed myself to smile at the hair draped over Otylia's face.

I'm not alone.

Birdsongs floated on the breeze when the others stirred, squinting at the sunlight bursting through the naked trees. I had returned to my physical body already and had spent most of the morning scouting the ridge as Dadźbóg's light crawled over the horizon. As the little life left in that magic-strangled forest awoke to another frozen day, I hoped it wouldn't be my last.

Sosna was the only one who seemed excited to be awake. With the fox's yips and cries for attention echoing with the chorus of birds, Otylia groaned and sat up, her bleary eyes scanning the forest with contempt.

"Good morning," I said, pulling my cloak tighter around me. The winds brought an extra chill, and even after walking up and down the ridge my whole body was shivering.

She pushed her unruly hair from her face. "Your definition of *good* is flawed."

I offered a small smile, understanding. How could she sleep well the night after learning her mother was Dziewanna, her father was the god of the underworld, and she was a goddess who hadn't developed her powers yet? "Well, at least Sosna is happy to see the daylight," I said.

Her eyes flicked to Sosna and pain filled them as she watched Dziewanna's creature. "Life's easier as a fox," she mumbled.

"Dziewanna sent her to protect you. That fox saved my life and helped me save yours."

After pushing herself to her feet, she started braiding her hair—an intricate process that thoroughly confused me. Sosna noticed she was up and raced over, forcing her to quickly finish the braid and crouch to pet her fox. I smiled, and she shot me a glare. *Some things will never change.*

"You ready for this, Half-Chief, or you too busy flirting to fight?" Narcyz said as he gripped his shield and spear. Over the weeks of travel, the grime had become one with his hair, brown on brown. Unlike him, I'd actually bothered to use the grooming kit each of us had brought, but I doubted I looked much better.

It took everything I had not to glance at Otylia when I replied, "If you stop the zmory and cultists from sucking away my life, I'll do my job."

I hope.

Jaryło pulled his swords from the bag on Zofia's side and strapped them to his back. The Moonstone blades still amazed me, each pulsing with power. "Glad to hear it, because if you fail, we will all be caught in the planetnik's storms. I could slay him at a moment's notice if Marzanna's presence in Jawia didn't drain me of my power."

"I'm sure she thinks the same of you," I replied, preparing my own weapons—not that they'd be of much use in a battle in the sky.

"She probably thinks far worse, but I am quite honored that she still thinks of me at all after all these years."

Narcyz scowled and grabbed his arm. "You made this mess. Remember that."

The god raised his brow. "While I'm aware of my misdeeds, it isn't me who swore allegiance to Marzanna and chose a girl over the high chief."

I stammered, "How—"

"Though I may lack much of my power, I'm still a god," he replied, freeing himself from Narcyz's grasp before swiping at his sleeve as if Narcyz's hand had left grime on it. As he strode toward me, his golden shield grew to its full size and his glare struck me like the tip of his sword. "I'm also not blind."

The edge in his voice forced me back. Ever since we'd met, Jaryło had been cocky, even arrogant, but this anger was new.

"Half-Chief did what?" Narcyz snapped.

"He sacrificed his father's life for mine," Otylia replied for me. "But Jacek was dead either way. Marzanna couldn't be trusted."

Grateful for her support, I gave her a half-hearted smile. Her sharp edge had returned, and it felt good to have her defending me with it. "She speaks the truth," I said, fighting the mix of embarrass-ment and shame twisting my guts. "Though Marzanna would've killed Father anyway, I allowed him to die instead of Otylia, and even if I don't regret my decision, I... I'll never escape that guilt."

Narcyz growled and pointed his spear at me. "You could've saved him."

"How?" Ara asked, testing her bow's string. "Wacław barely saved Otylia, and she wasn't two weeks away."

"What son chooses a witch over his Father? Oh right, a demon."

Sosna snarled, and before I could reply, Otylia began whispering under her breath. Roots shot from the ground and wound around Narcyz's weapons as she clenched her fists and stormed forward. "And you're nothing but a boy obsessed with sizing up his cock."

"Otylia, stop," I said as the roots stretched up Narcyz's legs. He fought to free his spear, but it was no use.

She stopped inches away, her glare freezing him again. "If I was a witch, I would've cut it off already."

"What is this?" Xobas shouted as he climbed up the ridge with Kuba, returning from their scouting mission.

Narcyz let out a yell and tore his spear from the roots. He charged toward Otylia. But I got there first.

"Wait!" I said with one hand on his spear arm and the other grip-ping Otylia's wrist. *What am I doing?* My breaths were raspy as I stud-ied Narcyz's hazel eyes, swirling with rage. "I'm responsible for my decision, not her. If you need someone to blame besides Marzanna, then blame me."

Xobas reached us and placed a hand on my shoulder. "I feared this would happen."

"You knew?" Narcyz asked.

Xobas's head dropped. "Yes. Wacław told me after the cultists' raid. He made the choice he believed to be best. Put down the weapon, Narcyz."

Narcyz's glare remained fixed on me, but he lowered his spear. "You'll never be anything compared to him."

"And you'll never be anything, period," Kuba muttered.

"Perhaps not," I said, ignoring Kuba as I turned to Otylia. "Let Narcyz go. Though I appreciate the help, the consequences for this are mine to face."

For a moment, her gaze softened, but her lip curled as she commanded the roots to release his legs.

"You're crazy," Narcyz spat as he backed away. "You could've killed me!"

"I only kill threats," she quipped, squeezing my hand and stepping back.

By the fire, Jaryło grinned at us all. "We all make decisions others don't approve of. Do we not, Wacław?"

What game is he playing? We were about to go to battle against his enemy's demons, yet he was dividing the group. "The whole tribe worships you," I said, "yet you'll do anything to avoid taking blame for your affair."

"You have met her," he said with a laugh. "Would you want to spend eternity with that monster of a woman? Listen, what I was trying to show you is there is nothing any of us won't sacrifice for the right price, and at one time, I believed she was worth leaving behind for this *beautiful*—"

"Have you no loyalty?" Xobas asked.

The corner of Jaryło's mouth curled as he examined Kwiecień, the golden sword of the fourth moon that I had seen in my reflection. "When you've lived as long as I have, you realize there are few things that are permanent enough to deserve loyalty. My father is among them, as is my dedication to protecting the spring at all costs."

"You're not one of my gods, but I once admired the stories they told about you," Ara said with her arms crossed. "I thought you had bravery, honor, but you're just a coward."

Resting Kwiecień on his shoulder, Jaryło approached her. "All men are cowards for the sake of survival."

"Good thing I'm a woman," she quipped back.

He chuckled and circled toward us. Otylia's glare met him. "What actually happened to Dziewanna?" she asked as Sosna growled at him and wrapped herself around Otylia's ankle. "Did you bother to defend her, or did you run, fleeing with your tail between your legs?"

He knelt and held his fingers out for Sosna, but she only barked and yipped. "Dziewanna is essential for the coming of spring, and I happen to be quite fond of my sister. But if you must know, the demons overwhelmed us both."

He stood, exhaustion replacing pride on his face. "We became separated in the midst of the battle. I fought with all my strength to find her, but with Marzanna alive, it was not enough. Dziewanna had vanished by the time I reached her. Being a god isn't about being invincible, it is about using your power to fight for what matters. I've made my share of mistakes—as will every immortal, both deity and demon."

His gaze landed on me when he finished, and I shuddered at the idea of immortality. No matter how many times it was mentioned, the concept was impossible to wrap my mind around.

Narcyz dug his boot into the snow and Ara nocked and un-nocked an arrow nervously as I stared at the ground, not knowing how to respond. It was hard to know whether to believe him after all he'd hidden from us. In a way, I felt the weight of his immortal life, but did it excuse what he'd done?

Xobas eventually broke the silence as he stepped between Jaryło and me, "Your point has been made, but we cannot waste more time. The clans await."

"Then we best prepare to fight," Jaryło replied, turning back toward the fire.

I sighed as he went. *Am I ready?*

My cheeks burned. Each gust of the cold air stung more than the one before it as we stood at the peak of the ridge. I took a deep breath and watched the birds swoop through the twisted trees one last time before facing the group. As I handed Kuba the płanetnik's hat, I felt everyone's eyes on me.

"You sure you're okay with this?" Otylia asked, holding out a clay bowl.

I took it and stared down at the sappy liquid within. A sleeping potion—one her mom had taught her to make. She'd promised me it would last longer than the length of the battle, and I could only hope she was right. "It's just sleep?"

"I've heard it feels like you're drowning."

"That's… comforting? Luckily, I have some experience with that."

"The witch can't bail you out this time," Narcyz mumbled as he tapped his foot.

Otylia sneered at him before covering my hands with hers and pushing the bowl to my lips. "Drink."

I did. At first it tasted like oskoła, thick and sweet. I felt normal, and for a moment, I doubted whether the potion would work. Then its effects took hold.

This is wrong…

My mind became air, my muscles water. My throat spasmed as I fought to breathe, and a primal panic took over. Even the chill felt distant when my legs gave way and my face rested in the snow bed. I wanted to scream for help, to ask Otylia to make it stop, but when I opened my mouth, I couldn't speak. My vision blurred. The last thing I remembered was her green eyes staring at me against the endless sky.

Even my soul-form seemed distant when I rose. Whether it was the potion or the flood of sensation I received from the winds around me, I didn't know, but without leaving the ground, I already felt like I was flying. Each branch and blade of grass swayed at the tips of my fingers, and every breath from the others carried through me without any need of my ears.

"What was in that stuff?" I asked Otylia once I'd steadied myself, making myself visible to them.

She rolled her eyes as Xobas stepped forward and examined me with an entertained smile. "You are full of surprises."

"Let's hope the demons think the same thing," Ara replied.

Kuba smirked and shook a javelin. "We'll all show 'em."

The breeze blew Jaryło's long hair across his face as he stared over the ridge. "Best not to wait any longer. The płanetnik will sense the growth in your power when you reach out to him. He will follow it, and we will be prepared for his arrival."

"Wacław, are you ready?" Xobas asked, placing a hand on my shoulder.

I nodded to Kuba, signaling for him to bring me the hat. His body was tense as he walked toward me, and I pulled him into a hug. "Stay strong," I said. "For Maja, for the village, and for me."

"I'll kill you if you die," he quipped in response, sparking a laugh from both of us.

"Then I think it best we both live."

"Probably."

When I released him, he handed me the hat. I traced its wide straw brim and glanced at Otylia, who offered a smile as I placed it on my head.

I'm a demon.

There was no turning back now. My tribe needed me. My family needed me. My friends needed me. And Otylia needed me. I clenched my fists and felt the power of the winds within them. Every storm, every cloud was under my command, waiting for my order to strike.

"I'm ready," I said.

Jaryło began his descent down the ridge. "Then the płanetnik awaits. Once you lure him here, I will try to thin the cultists' numbers before joining you."

I hesitated, looking back at Otylia one more time, my heart aching as I did. Her eyes were soft, her lips parted, as if she were searching for words, and when I moved to follow Jaryło, her voice called out from behind me, "Wacław, wait!" She pulled the Thunderstone dagger from her belt as she approached and slid it into the sheath at my side. Her face hovered inches from mine and her fingers lingered for a moment as she whispered, "Survive, Wašek."

Everything in me told me to hug her, kiss her, anything. With the whole group watching us, though, I hesitated too long, and she turned away before I could move.

Cursing myself, I began my climb down the ridge. My boots kicked stones with each slow step, and by the time I reached the bottom, Jaryło was already on Zofia. "It's time," he said, his grin far too large for the occasion. "Call the demon. Feel the disruption in the winds to find him."

I closed my eyes and followed his instructions.

The eight winds touched everything for farther than I could ever see. They curved and shot their way through the mountains and valleys of the south, the plains of the north, and the forests all around. In the east, though, I felt them circling. The płanetnik upset them, and they demanded that I fix it, to stop the manipulation of their power. I focused on the center of the disruption and whispered into the breeze, "I'm here, and I have Jaryło."

A blast knocked me back. I took a sharp breath as I fell to my knees. In seconds, the sky darkened, and thunder drummed in the east as black clouds rolled overhead. A whirlwind circled the forest, throwing me into a tree as branches snapped and trunks creaked under the weight of the gale.

"I think that did the trick," Jaryło shouted, staring at the heart of the swirling storm.

"What do I do now?" I asked.

Kwiecień's golden blade cut through the darkness as the god charged toward the plains. "We fight!"

The ground creaked around me as screeching and hissing filled the air. *They're coming.*

I looked toward the storm, where a figure emerged from the

clouds. The cracks of lightning seemed to weave with his skin, giving it an eerie blue glow, and his beard stretched down his worn and tattered gray cloak. He clutched a wooden staff in one hand as his other gripped a cut cord of rope that entrapped his neck. On his head was a hat exactly like the one he'd left behind.

I called the winds under me and they obeyed, lifting me up through the trees. It took everything I had to not panic as the storm battered me from every side and the ground faded away. Soon, I flew as high as the płanetnik himself.

His eyes fell upon me, and when he raised his staff, a blast of wind slammed into my chest. The air fled my lungs as the demon cackled and flew toward me, bringing the winds with him.

This time I was ready. As another blast raced toward me, I grabbed hold of it in my hands. I stared down at the ball of winds and smiled as the energy of the gust shook within my grasp. Squeezing it tighter, I launched its power back at the płanetnik.

The ball tore toward him. Hope swelled in my chest, but at the last second, he swung his staff, knocking it away with no trouble.

My arms already trembled as he surged forward. His storm strengthened around us, its power growing far outside my control as thunder roared and lighting rained on the forest below. I wanted to look down, to check on my friends, but there was no time.

The płanetnik launched gust after gust at me. At first, I deflected them and even managed to launch a few in response. One struck him in the side, another in the chest. Then I saw the shadows emerging from the wall of clouds.

The deformed creatures swooped toward me with bat-like wings, snickering as they called wind blasts of their own. *Płanetnikami.* These were the demons under the command of the chief in front of me. Though their attacks were far weaker than his, there were at least ten of them, and I couldn't stop them all.

They circled me and sent a series of blasts into my chest. My grip on the winds slipped beneath me. I wheezed, losing my breath, and when another gust smacked my head, I dropped.

50

Otylia

We're doomed.

THE ICY WIND SEARED at the exposed skin beneath my cloak's hood as I stared up at Wacław's clash with the płanetnik. I'd feared for him from the second the demon had appeared in the eye of the massive storm. Wacław had grown increasingly powerful in recent days, but he'd never commanded anything like that.

Focus.

I forced myself to look away. If he was going to survive, we needed to protect his body from the cultists and demons on the ground.

Jaryło had claimed he would prevent as many as possible from reaching the ridge. But as Ara and I launched everything we had at the three-dozen ax and shield wielding cultists bursting through the tree line, I wondered whether he'd done nothing or if we'd underestimated the size of Marzanna's army.

The first cultists had already reached the base of the ridge. Sosna yipped by my side as I glared down at their pale, shirtless bodies. Gashes covered their backs and chests, like a whip had been taken to them, and blood stained their feet as Ara sent an arrow through the first's head.

"Why is game so much easier than people?" she called out as she nocked another arrow.

"Shields," I replied, crushing the legs of the next two with a batch of roots. They writhed on the ground as Sosna swept down the ridge and tore at their jugulars.

Ara loosed the arrow, sending it wide. "I meant why does this feel worse?"

Worse? Besides my fear for Wacław, I felt alive. Power coursed through me, and as I sent the branches of the highest tree shooting through another cultist's chest, nothing but the will to avenge Mother filled my heart.

"I don't know," I finally replied.

The remaining cultists glanced at their dead comrades before bolting each way around the hill—just like we'd planned.

"They're coming!" Ara yelled to Xobas, Narcyz, and Kuba, who'd formed a small shield wall on the narrow strip of grass ten strides behind us.

This better work. We continued to intercept as many of the cultists as possible, but at least half reached the covered backside of the hill. They charged toward the shield wall as Kuba's javelins, Ara's arrows, and my roots thinned their ranks. Moments later, the cultists crashed into the wall, outnumbering our line three-to-one. There were too many. But they would have to hold because a screeching tore at my ears.

Zmora.

The demon's ripped corpse gripped the rocks at the ridge's base. What remained of its hair had become nothing more than a mangled ball of gray, tangling with the rotting skin covering its body. A trail of black blood and pus followed it with each step as its cold, dead eyes stared up at me.

And it wasn't alone.

Two more zmory flanked the first, screeching and clawing their way up the ridge as I launched roots and branches at them with my trembling hands. A sea of vegetation blocked their advance, but when the demons touched the roots, they slipped from my grasp and retreated into the ground.

"What?" I staggered back as my hands stung. The trees and vast array of roots beneath the ground retreated when I reached for them again, like a wounded cat hiding in the corner. Ara loosed an arrow into the lead zmora's shoulder, doing little to slow its climb as Sosna bit at its arms.

Could the stories be true? The Mangled Woods had been manipulated by sorcery, by the witch. Most demons were supposed to be vulnerable in the sunlight, but they were unharmed as the wilds defied my call. Were they no longer Mother's realm?

"Otylia!" Ara shouted. "What are you doing?"

I stared down at my hands. "The forest won't touch the demons!"

She groaned and loosed another arrow. It struck the zmora in the eye, but the demon only screeched and increased its pace. "We need to figure something out *fast!*"

"Working on it!" I yelled, rushing to the edge as Sosna whimpered and scampered to me. The demons were closing in fast. Behind, the sound of axes crashing against shields filled the air as Xobas, Narcyz, and Kuba fought back the cultists. If we didn't stop the zmory soon, we were dead.

Ara kept shooting as I stared down at the zmory, trying to think of something. There was nothing but rocks and snow.

The rocks!

I leaped down from the ridge and skidded to a boulder as tall as my chin. Ara called down from above, but I couldn't hear her as I threw my whole body into the rock. All around me the storm raged, stinging my face as my muscles strained. It wouldn't budge.

"Mother, Weles, someone help me," I muttered as sweat dripped down my forehead and into my eyes. Sosna's growls forced me to look beyond the boulder. The zmory were only strides away now. Time was up.

Rocks slid around my feet. I turned as Ara skidded to my side along with Kuba. Together, they threw their weight into the boulder, and my heart skipped a beat as it shifted.

Kuba raised an eyebrow at me. "You gonna help or just daydream about dying?"

I shook myself out of the shock and joined them. The hissing of the zmory became deafening as they approached the boulder. Their bones cracked and their claws swiped at my arms as I groaned, pushing with all my strength.

It seemed the boulder had no will to roll, but as a zmora's claw reached around it toward Ara, the boulder's weight shifted. It gave way, and in a mess of tangled limbs and deathly screeching, the zmory fell with it, crushed between the stone's weight and the maze of dagger-pointed rocks below.

Relief washed over me for only a moment before the ground beneath my feet slipped away. In a flash, I was tumbling down the ridge. Those same jagged rocks sliced at my arms and torso as I covered myself, but each blow drew blood. And when my head struck the fallen boulder near the ridge's base, my vision faded.

"Otylia!"

Ara's voice was distant. My arms were numb, alien. Through my bleary eyes, I saw the zmory lying next to me in the snow, crushed into a gray and black mush.

My gaze drifted to the battle in the sky. Dizzying clouds crashed together as a dozen dark figures swarmed Wacław. The winds danced around them, every gust a lethal weapon lashing out among the demons. The chief płanetnik laughed as Wacław's body jolted back with each hit from what seemed to be balls made of the winds themselves. Then, with one *crack* that vibrated the entire sky, Wacław dropped.

"No!" I heard myself scream. The voice was mine, but I felt like an observer in my own body with the world spinning around me. My movements were slow and jolted as I pushed myself to my feet. Fear and desperation overwhelmed whatever pain I should've been feeling. I couldn't take my eyes off the boy who'd given me hope, and as I watched, useless, my heart shattered in my chest.

51

Wacław

I'm going to die...

"Jaryło! Help!" I shouted as I tumbled through the sky, grabbing at the air as if it would become solid enough to catch me.

No response came. My breaths quickened as I reached for the winds, but they evaded every grasp. "Listen," I commanded.

Nothing.

The air whistled past my ears as I shot toward the ground. I remembered the Lake of Reflection, when my only hope to save Otylia had been to command the winds to lift me. Sheer panic had saved me then, but with their power beyond my hold now, I needed control.

I shut my eyes and blocked out the sounds of the storm. I cleared my mind of all the fear and anger that threatened to choke me. All I let remain were my memories of Mom's smile, my promise to return to Nevenka, my childhood adventures with Otylia, and our kiss from the night before. As I hurtled toward my death, I remembered why I needed to live.

Then I let it go.

"Listen!" I screamed, clenching my fists and letting my rage, my desperation, flood through me. Seconds from the trees, I yelled and spun, grabbing hold of the throbbing power within me and releasing it in a burst.

The winds answered. They swirled beneath me, their excitement dancing at my fingertips as they shot me back toward the storm. I felt each of them individually, their powers and wills all aligned with mine. They hated the płanetnik's control and Marzanna's return. When I charged into the heart of the storm, they loosed themselves on the płanetnikami.

Screeching, the demons scrambled. Their chief scowled and launched another gust at me, but I pulled my shield, deflecting each attack and flying directly at him. He raised his staff as I readied my spear for a strike.

Lightning cracked around me. Pain arced up my spine. I spun through the air without direction, my mind fried as the bolt's energy surged through me.

All around, the płanetnikami had fallen, but their chief's staff glowed with power as he launched another bolt. Lightning shot toward me. I raised my arms, preparing for the shock.

But the pain never came. I stared down at my hands and the blue lines darting up my arms. The lightning raced through my veins, surging between my fingers as it crackled, waiting for my command. The płanetnik laughed as I focused the energy on the palm of my hand.

He swung his staff around his head and the storm roared, buzzing with the lightning dancing through it. My hair stood on end. The static shook me to the bone. An endless stream of lightning arced to his staff and shot toward me as I launched my own strike.

The currents met between us in a sphere of sparks that shot into the sky and blinded me. I called upon his storm, letting it feed my power as I sent all my strength into the bolts. Every moment of the clash burned my veins, and I screamed as I charged.

Sparks seared at my arms and face when I grabbed the sphere. My hands burned against it, but I couldn't stop. All its energy, all its power, coursed through me. My demonic soul demanded more.

The płanetnik's eyes widened as I tore through his bolts. He stumbled back, firing strike after strike and gust after gust. But they felt like little more than pin pricks on my skin. All around us, the winds hissed as I stormed toward him, the ball of light tearing through his darkness.

He tried to flee into the clouds, but I launched the sphere before he could. It arced through the sky, and when the sparks crashed into his back, his skin burned, turning as black as the tips of my frostbitten fingers. His mouth gaped open. No sound came out.

The płanetnik writhed amid the storm. I called a whirlwind, holding him in place as I marched forward on the air, lightning shooting through the clouds with each of my steps. Never before had I felt so much power. My soul craved it as I contemplated what to do with the demon.

In a flash of light, Jaryło appeared next to me and held the tip of Kwiecień to the płanetnik's head. "Deliver justice! He sided with Marzanna and helped kill the high chief. If he had his way, then Otylia would be dead."

A smirk crossed my face at the thought of returning to Dwie Rzeki with the head of Marzanna's płanetnik in my hand. The warriors would stomp their feet and tell stories of my victory, the chiefs would realize I was no weakling to walk away from, and the girls would no longer giggle and call me the Half-Chief. I imagined the shock on Mikołaj's face. What would he say then?

But when I pulled the Thunderstone dagger, doubt clenched my chest. Only moments before, I had seen the demon's power. Would it not be a waste to simply extinguish it, preventing its use for a better cause? After all, hadn't he helped bring the winter storms? And where had Jaryło gone? He hadn't fought with me as he'd claimed he would. Could I even trust his word?

The god scowled when I slid the blade back into its sheath. "What are you doing?" he snapped.

"Marzanna has an army even larger than the one my friends are fighting below," I replied. "If we're going to defeat her, we'll need powerful allies."

"He's a demon!"

I spun toward him, and his eyes seemed to burn as I spat, "So am

I! But the only reason he's following Marzanna is because of her Frostmark. It lets her speak to them, influence them." I raised my hand, watching the sparks dance between my fingers. "Maybe, I can do the same."

"The power always goes to your heads…" he muttered.

"I can't fight her alone. If there are orders of the płanetnikami, then why should I not be among them, leading them against the goddess that manipulated them? I need to accept who I am, and this is it."

He scowled. "Do what you want, but being a demon doesn't mean you need to act like one."

I opened my mouth to reply, but he dove away. *Then what does being a demon mean?* I turned back to the płanetnik. The Frostmark on his cheek glowed a harsh white as I crouched in front of him on the winds. "What was your name in life?"

"Eryk, son of Oskar," the płanetnik said.

"And who were you before you died?"

"I was a farmer, like my father and his father before him."

"I know the farmer's life. It's hard, hot, and unforgiving. Is it why you hung yourself?"

He shook his head.

"Then why did you?"

The demon's eyes narrowed. "A boy would not understand."

I chuckled and released the whirlwind from around him. "Then it's a good thing I'm no boy."

His head hung as he pushed himself to his feet. "I married my only daughter off to the village's strongest warrior," he replied, hushed. "She returned days later, bruised and suffering. I went to confront the man, but he beat me down. When I awoke, he had burned my farm and slaughtered the cattle. My wife… My wife hung from a tree, and the warrior said he'd do the same to my daughter if I wasn't hanging beside her by the next morning."

My heart twitched as I felt the man's—the demon's—pain. "Why have you not returned to your village and freed your daughter from this warrior?"

Sorrow filled Eryk's eyes. "I am lost in the wind, unable to find them. The goddess swore to free her if I were to help her defeat Jaryło."

"Marzanna manipulated many of us, promised us things she never intended to fulfill. I understand her sway, so I will give you a choice: You can perish for serving her, never having freed your daughter, or you can take up my mark. If you do so, I will do whatever I can to help your daughter, but then you must help me defeat Marzanna. We cannot let this continue."

"You would allow me to find her before joining you?"

I nodded. "I am not blind to a father's love, whether I've felt it myself or not. Once this battle is won and our journey to the clans finished, we will find your village."

The płanetnik dropped to his knees once again, the winds holding him aloft. "Gods bless you, Wacław, son of Jacek. I agree to your terms."

I swallowed as the lightning intensified in my palm. With no clue what I was doing, I placed my hand on his cheek, and he screamed as it burned into his flesh. Quickly, I pulled back, horrified at what I'd done.

The Frostmark was gone. Instead, emblazoned from his cheekbone to his jaw was a red circle with patterns of silver within. *The partial blood moon.* It was the same symbol I had seen in the Lake of Reflection—the uneclipsed crescent still bright near the mark's peak.

My hand shook as Eryk stood, clutching his side. "I must rest," he said.

I nodded. "Go. I'll call you when it's time to find your daughter." He bowed and flew into the clouds. I watched him go before dropping toward the woods. The winds followed me through the fog and into the daylight below, where the battle still raged.

52

Otylia

Gods save him.

ARA AND SOSNA HAD REACHED MY SIDE by the time Wacław caught himself on the winds. His recovery should've brought me some relief, but he was flying back into the literal heart of the storm. Nothing was comforting about that.

"You okay?" Ara asked as she winced at Sosna nudging a dead zmora.

"Alive is enough," I replied. The pain from my fall had become apparent, and from my bleeding and bruised arms to my tender head, I was a mess. Every slash in my dress showed skin of red, black, and blue. And as I tried to steady my breathing, blood trickled down my hands, dripping into the pool of it at my feet.

"C'mon. Let's get back up the ridge," she said, pulling my arm over her shoulder with no care for the crimson that ran onto her rough-spun tunic. In her free hand, she clutched her bow as she scanned the forest, her eyes fiercer than I'd ever seen. She wasn't the same girl who'd left Dwie Rzeki. Neither was I.

A pile of debris almost as tall as me had piled up at the base of the ridge. The boulder's fall must have set off a rockslide that had stripped the hill of much of its snow, revealing a solid shelf of bedrock beneath it. I was lucky to be alive. "We're not climbing that," I said.

"No, you're not," a voice said in the old tongue from behind us. My heart stopped. I knew that voice. *Yuliya.*

The szeptucha's bright blonde hair and icy glare met me when I turned back. She wore the same white dress and cloak as before, but now she gripped a staff of warped birchwood. "The goddess believed you were already in Weles's hands," she said, switching to the Krowikie tongue.

I stepped away from Ara. Though it took all my strength not to wobble, I couldn't show Yuliya my weakness. "Just another thing she got wrong."

Yuliya scoffed and waved her hand. A ring of ten cultists appeared, seemingly out of thin air. Three of them held nocked shortbows, their iron-tipped arrows reflecting the sunlight as the others advanced with axes and spears ready.

"It was a shame that I had to release you last time," she said, "but now that the demon-boy has failed, Queen Marzanna has bestowed the pleasure upon me to ensure your wild stench is eradicated."

She slammed her staff into the ground, but as the ice began creeping up my legs, Ara nocked an arrow and aimed in one swift motion. Yuliya was faster. She flicked her hand and sent Ara flying back into the ridge.

I gritted my teeth as Ara writhed on the ground. I was the szeptucha. I should've been able to help her. But I was useless, frozen without my power.

"You see, *mały dětę*," Yuliya sneered, calling me a child once again, "these are not your wilds, and they do not obey you." She swung her staff through the air, and the trees creaked as their branches shot toward me, wrapping around my torso and constricting as the ice entrapped me up to the waist. "These woods worship death herself, and she's very excited to meet you."

My lungs burned as the trees tightened around me. I reached for the wilds, for my goddesses, but I found nothing but taint and death. These were Marzanna's woods now, and we'd walked right in.

Ara wheezed as I struggled to look back, to see my friend one last time. The branches were too tight, but I heard her voice when she whispered, "I believe in you, my szeptucha."

Rage tore through me as I remembered all Marzanna had done. She'd killed Mother. She'd slaughtered the women and children in Bustelintin. She'd toyed with my life in exchange for Jacek's and had manipulated the only boy foolish enough to care for me. She'd taken Mother's power, stolen it from me as she entrapped the spring goddess.

She could kill me. But she wouldn't kill the little refugee girl who'd believed in me only moments after arriving in a village that wasn't her own. That huntress of the steppes had trusted the witch of the wilds without a second thought, and she'd placed her life in my hands coming on this journey.

Marzanna wouldn't take her.

A wave of energy washed over me as I yelled in desperation, throwing my arms out and tearing through the branches and ice. My lungs seared. A sharp pain tore at my core, as if a spear had been driven through my soul, and all my *žityje* burned away with the sorcery. I dropped to my knees as whispers swirled around me on the winds. Their voices were clear.

"Protect us from the creatures in the swamps and forests tonight."

"Father is gone. Please show him the way with your light. Let him find Nawia's embrace."

"Ease grandmother's suffering from Marzanna's Curse and breathe new life into her lungs."

They were an endless roar. Sons desperate to please their fathers. Wives fearing for their husband's safety during the war. Farmers pleading for protection from the demons lurking around them. All of them were praying... *to me.*

Shock flashed across Yuliya's face as she staggered back, but before I could pull myself from the whispers' grasps, she raised her staff once again and shot a row of spikes. The archers loosed their arrows. And as one, the cultists charged.

Time seemed to slow as I watched the projectiles slice through the air. I'd broken from the branches and ice, but it had used whatever *žityje* that had remained in my soul. The burst of energy had gone as quickly as it had come. There was nothing I could do, and as I knelt there, my body felt distant and heavy, the still air almost warm against my face. *Is this how I die?*

It wasn't.

A whirlwind struck the woods, sweeping up the arrows and ice and shooting them at the advancing cultists. Three dropped to the ground while the others gawked at the sky. I followed their gaze, and a cold laugh escaped my lungs as Wacław landed in front of me.

Streaks of blue had returned to his veins, and the Thunderstone dagger floated above his hand as he glared at Yuliya. Static hung around him, making my hair stand on end as each of his breaths seemed to give life to the swelling storm around us. I sensed his anger, his rage—his desire to save me.

"You don't get to take her," he said. "That's *my* witch."

53

Wacław

You're not taking her from me.

CULTISTS SURROUNDED US AT THE BASE OF THE RIDGE, their heavy furs and white face paint a sharp contrast to the dark and formless płanetnikami. As I helped Otylia off the ground, they smacked their axes against their shields and chanted in the old tongue.

"Are you okay?" I asked Otylia as she leaned her back against mine for support. Anger boiled within me at the sight of the blood coating her shredded sleeve and the deep cuts exposed across her ribs, stomach, and arms. Seconds later and I would've been too late.

She looked past me, fixing her sharp eyes on Yuliya as the scar on her cheek glowed with the radiance of a goddess. "Only when she's dead."

Lightning danced among my fingers as the winds and storm bent to my will. With each passing moment, the power grew in my soul, but I wanted more. I *needed* more. And they needed to pay.

A shout silenced the cultists. Yuliya spun a staff that appeared to be molded from the trees of the Mangled Woods. As she chanted, those very trees creaked and snapped.

"Look out!" Otylia yelled.

Branches broke through the whirlwind and wrapped my arms.

The winds slipped from my grasp in the shock, and when the gales crashed around us, the remaining cultists charged through the gap.

The first reached us in seconds as I fought against the branches, trying to regain a hold of the winds. But it was no use. While the storm raged above, the winds swirled around us in an uncontrolled frenzy, striking both us and the cultists in their madness.

"The lightning!" Otylia called from behind me. "Use the storm!"

Of course! I closed my eyes and reached for the heart of the storm, its power crackling with electricity ready to be freed. With all my strength, I embraced it, controlled it, let it surge through me and give me new life. Then, as the cultists' spears and axes streaked toward us, I called it down.

A deafening *boom* tore through the sky.

The air buzzed as a bolt of lightning struck before us, sending the cultists flying back on a shockwave that battered my chest. My heart stopped and started again, and I wavered back into Otylia as my whole body shook.

Surrounding us was the scorched earth from the strike. The charred, blacked bodies of the cultists lay dead everywhere I looked, and the smell of burning flesh filled the air as Yuliya staggered back to her feet. Bitterness and terror clashed on the szeptucha's face as her jaw hung open. "The queen believed you a chief of the planet-nikami, but this…" She shook her head and pointed her staff at us. "None of it matters anymore."

I tried to call to the winds and storm, but I was weak, drained. The burgeoning power I had felt moments before was replaced by emptiness. The whirlwind hissed and the thunder rolled, yet neither answered my call. Black coursed across my hands as the lightning faded, and I shook in fear as I remembered Jaryło's warnings of my soul's *żityje*. I had used too much. My human soul would suffer. And as I glared through the trees at Yuliya, I knew I would too.

She whispered one word in the old tongue, and I gripped Otylia's hand as the bolt of ice shot toward me, waiting for it to strike my chest.

A figure darted in front of us with a shout, his ripped brown cloak flapping against the single remaining javelin on his back. Kuba's expression was rigid, covered in both muck and blood. It was that of a warrior, and as the shard of ice sliced through his shield and into his stomach, he didn't even scream.

I did.

Blood spewed from his abdomen as he pulled his final javelin from his back. Though his hands trembled and my cries tore through the forest, he launched it in one swift motion. Yuliya loosed another strike of her own, but the javelin was already in the air.

Time felt impossibly slow as the projectiles flew toward their targets. Terror clutched my throat like a noose, choking my voice and body. It was because of me that Kuba was on the journey. It was because of me that he'd left Maja behind. And it was because of me he would never get to see the beautiful life with her that he'd dreamed of.

The missiles struck simultaneously.

For a moment, nothing broke the silence except for my whimpers and the sound of tearing flesh. Kuba staggered back, clutching his stomach as I rushed to his side.

Across the patch of snow, Yuliya stared down at the javelin that had struck through her heart. Anguish and rage covered her face, but when she looked up, all she could do was whisper, "My queen... I am yours..." and drop into the crimson snow.

Kuba curled his lip, glaring at her before his body convulsed. I cried out as he collapsed into my arms. Though tears filled my eyes, as he stared up at me, his were clear. "Guess I get to die a warrior after all," he said, coughing on blood.

I shook my head. "No!" I cried as I pled to Otylia, "Save him... Please, there has to be something..."

She pulled her jagged gaze from Yuliya and examined Kuba's bleeding abdomen with sorrow in her eyes. "I..." She stuttered and clenched her fists. "There's nothing, I'm sorry. My herbs are up the ridge, and I don't have the *żityje* left to mend a minor wound, let alone this."

Each of Kuba's breaths came weaker than the one before it. His hand closed around the fabric of my tunic, pulling weakly on it and forcing me to look at him. "Tell Maja…" he wheezed.

"I promise," I said with tears streaming down my cheeks. My heart shattered as I stared down at him, and I hated myself for letting him risk his life for me. This was my fight. I was the demon who'd given in to Marzanna's call. I was the one Yuliya had tried to kill. Kuba had stood by my side through it all, and now he had sacrificed his life for mine. "I'll tell her you loved her. That you died a hero. That I owe you my life…"

I held my forehead to his. He still didn't sob, and his mouth wore that ridiculous smile he'd never lost. "I'm sorry," I whispered. "I'm so sorry."

He wrapped his arms around me, trembling as he met my gaze. "I regret none of it, brother."

His fingers slid from my back as the life faded from his eyes. Anguish washed over me, and I shook him, screaming his name over and over.

But he was gone.

The one friend who'd followed me with no questions. The only one who could laugh and joke through anything. I had dragged him away from everything he loved and to his death in the forest of the damned. He deserved to be happy, living with Maja and a house full of kids to cause mayhem with him as he told stupid stories of heroic things he'd never done.

But Kuba had done them. He'd fought demons, sorceresses, and cultists, fought through endless blizzards and days with no food. His javelin had pierced the heart of the szeptucha that neither Otylia nor I had managed to defeat, and it was because of him that both my physical and soul bodies had lived. It didn't matter that he'd been goofy or clumsy, foolish or hopelessly optimistic. When trials had faced us, he'd never left my side—like a true friend. I wished I had done the same for him.

The snow crunched behind me. Ara limped toward us with her

bow dangling from her fingers. She scanned the trees as shouts echoed from the meadows. "More are com—" She stopped when she saw Kuba's body.

Otylia stepped toward me, her hand gripping Dziewanna's Bowmark as she whispered under her breath. When she was finished, she knelt next to me. "Ara's right. We must return to Xobas and Narcyz before the cultists reach us, and neither of us are in the condition to carry him."

"We can't just leave him!" I shouted.

"I can grant him a blessing that should help him on his way to Nawia, but then we need to go." She softened her voice as she laid a hand on my arm. Tears welled in her eyes. "I'm sorry, Wašek."

The *twang* of Ara's bow snapping drew me away from Otylia's scraped and dirtied face. Ara grimaced as she slid the bow back over her shoulder. "Can't pull the string with my arm." More shouts came from the tree line. "Hurry!"

I nodded to Otylia and let Kuba's body rest. My chest ached as I did, but they were right. We'd come this far. Kuba would've shamed me for crying like a child over his body as enemies loomed nearby— that didn't make it any easier to leave him.

As Otylia whispered over Kuba in the old tongue, I scanned the woods, waiting for the cultists to burst forth. All I had wanted was to protect my tribe and those I loved, yet after defeating the płanetnik all I felt was failure. If I couldn't save Kuba, how could I save Mom, Nevenka, and the entire tribe when Marzanna came?

Ara's head popped up as a twig snapped no more than twenty strides away. "They're here."

Before I could look down at Kuba one last time, Otylia's hand grasped my forearm, and she pulled me around the ridge. My tired legs dragged behind, slipping with each step as we made our way up the shallow slope.

I wanted to focus. I needed to focus. But all I thought of were those bolts of ice striking Kuba and how he'd stared up at me during his dying breaths. How had I gone from feeling invincible to helpless in mere moments? How could I have let my *żityje* sweep away so quickly once again?

Cultists' corpses littered the forest floor when we reached the narrow clearing up to the ridge's peak, coating the snow red and black as the chants from behind us seemed to flow over the woods in an endless hum. Xobas stormed through the trees with Narcyz not far behind. Blood dripped from Xobas's sword and cracks were scattered across his shield, but when I met his eyes, there was no damage, just the face of a warrior.

"Get behind us," he ordered.

"There's too many," I said. "Kuba…"

Otylia ignored my mumbling, hauling me past the duo as I glanced back at the army we still faced. No less than thirty cultists swarmed through the trees. They were an unending tide of axes, white-painted faces, and heavy furs. I'd defeated the płanetnikami, but it wasn't enough—I wasn't enough.

"No," I muttered, pulling my arm from Otylia's grasp and sliding the Thunderstone dagger from its sheathe. "I'm not letting them die for me too."

She grabbed my arm again. Worry filled her eyes, but she nodded as she laid her hand on mine. "Make them pay."

From the moment I stepped past her and joined Xobas and Narcyz, the world became a blur of blades and blood. Sosna bit at the cultists' ankles ahead of us and slowed their advance as I kept behind the shields, ducking in and out with my dagger when the opportunity opened. The rancid smell of death blanketed the area, making me gag as I struggled for a breath of clean air. But none came. The tide of cultists only continued, and we were losing ground.

My chest heaved with every breath. I stabbed and swept behind Narcyz as he thrust his spear through a cultist. Another followed, but as I jabbed my dagger between the attacker's ribs, Narcyz slipped while yanking his spear free. He fell into me, and we collapsed into a heap in the snow.

Cultists swarmed above us. We'd killed nearly half of them, but despite Xobas's skill and Narcyz's grit, numbers weren't on our side.

Though Xobas tried to hold back the attackers as Narcyz struggled to stand, I couldn't find the strength. My heart was heavy, my body beaten. I reached for the dagger. It was too far, stuck in the reddened snow at the cultists' feet. Only fear remained as I examined the black veins cutting across my skin and peering through my torn sleeves. The void of *żityje* in my souls tore me apart bit by bit. When it was over, I wouldn't join Kuba in Nawia's rolling plains. I would die a demon—nothing.

Otylia's screams pierced my mind as the cultists closed in around me. The closest raised his ax.

I closed my eyes just as the sounds of hooves against snow and a blade slicing through flesh filled the air. Cultists wailed as I opened my eyes. Jaryło rode ahead of us, glowing with Kwiecień and his golden shield in his hands as he skewered the cultists. Beneath him, Zofia's pure white coat remained untainted as she stomped a downed cultist and Sosna tore at another's throat.

Just the sight of the god made the remaining cultists turn and flee, but Zofia's gallop was as swift as the winds' furies. Kwiecień twirled through the air with each slice, and when Jaryło leaped off Zofia, he landed ahead of the final three. Seconds later, there was nothing left but a pool of red.

It's over.

Cultists lay dead as far as I could see, the snow discolored and melting. The winds themselves seemed to dance around us as a warm breeze blew in from the east. The storm retreated, and I allowed a relieved smile to cross my face.

Otylia helped me join the others around my physical body. Though the battle was over, I seethed at the cuts and bruises scattered across her torso. She was strong, but it was hard not to feel guilt for her pain.

I peered down the ridge to where Kuba's body lay. "He's gone…" I mumbled as the tears streamed down my face again.

Narcyz held his arm where blood dripped from a deep wound. "Doesn't matter if he was an idiot. That was braver than anything I've seen."

Otylia held the back of my neck, pressing her forehead to mine as her own tears wetted her cheeks. "We won't forget him. He saved both of our lives and defeated one of Marzanna's szeptuchy. I owe him my life. Here or Nawia, it doesn't matter."

"He shouldn't have died!" I sobbed. "It should've been me..."

Narcyz snapped his glare to Jaryło. "Why do you always show up late? Kuba would be alive if you had fought with us!"

"As would Marek," Xobas added, crossing his arms.

"You lot are the least grateful people I have ever met," Jaryło replied. "There were a hundred more cultists and demons in the plains coming to kill you. I ridded you of them."

I pulled away from Otylia. "I saw neither you nor an army of them. The plan was for you to join me against the płanetnik before we returned to the others. Instead, I used everything I had to defeat him and couldn't help finish the rest."

He grinned. "I believed in you, and you followed through quite extraordinarily. Defeating a whole squad of płanetnikami and pulling lightning into yourself—I haven't seen a demon do that in a long time."

Though his flattery tempted the cravings of my demon soul, I saw through his attempt. Too many chiefs had tried the same thing with Father, yet that never worked out well for them. "Are you planning to answer for your unwillingness to follow the plan? Where were you?"

Holding up his arms, he strode toward me with a sharp glare, "Maybe I just wanted to test the extent of your power. It isn't often that a demon as powerful as you falls for a lost goddess."

I hesitated for too long. He lunged forward, grabbing Otylia and holding Kwiecień's sharp edge to her neck in one fluid motion. "Move and your precious goddess dies," he sneered.

"How—" I stammered as Sosna growled. My hands trembled. My blood boiled. I met Otylia's wide eyes as Xobas, Narcyz, and Ara stood by my side with their weapons ready, but they couldn't help. One flick of Jaryło's wrist and she would be dead.

"Father sent me to retrieve his daughter," he replied. "But all of your valiant help to delay Marzanna's advance was very much appreciated before I did so. I wasn't certain Otylia was really her until I saw her power myself. Quite a sight, her breaking free from Yuliya's grasp."

"What is this?" Xobas asked, looking from him to me.

I swallowed. My mind was racing, and it was impossible to think with that Moonblade to Otylia's throat. "The ritual showed us the truth of both of our births. Otylia is the daughter of Dziewanna and Weles. She's... She's a goddess." Turning my attention back to Jaryło, I continued, "Why would you help the god who kidnapped you as a child? Perun is your father."

He laughed. "Perun claimed to war with Weles in order to rescue me, but he never bothered to actually try. All he cares about is defeating his rival. When I returned to him, he didn't even bother to tell me Marzanna was my twin until it was too late! He was no father to me. I am sure you of all people would understand that."

His words struck my heart, and I struggled to find a reply. Neither of our fathers had truly cared for us. He had been raised apart from his position as son of the chief god, not so different than me. "I understand," I finally pled, "but Dziewanna didn't betray you like Perun. He was a terrible father to her as well. Don't punish her and Otylia for Perun's error."

"You know nothing of Weles, demon child. You will never see Nawia, but it is more glorious than Jawia could ever be because of his grace to cater to the dead of this world. Otylia belongs with her father. Do not steal her chance to have what was denied to you—a real family."

I looked from him to Otylia. Her eyes were sharp. I knew this wasn't what she wanted, and I couldn't let him take her. I couldn't...

I stepped forward, my legs straining to hold me while I reached for the winds. Despite my drained body's pleas for it to stop, I grabbed hold of them and found the dagger in the snow. "She deserves the chance that was denied to you. If she wishes to join Weles in Nawia, then that's her choice, not yours."

I felt the dagger's jagged tip with the winds and lifted it into the air. My breaths were weak and my legs trembled, but I let my anger burn away my exhaustion for only a moment. With everything I had left, I sent the dagger flying toward him, collapsing as the shout left his mouth.

Blood seeped from the hole in his chest where the blade pierced him from back to front—Thunderstone capable of killing a god. His body convulsed as he looked down at the wound and muttered, "You fool! Without me, spring has no hope!"

He stumbled, but a smirk crossed his face. Kwiecień's golden edge slid across Otylia's throat, leaving a thin line of red in its wake.

I cried out as her eyes rolled back. "No!"

Otylia dropped into the snow. Jaryło's devilish glare met one last time before Kwiecień slipped from his fingers and his legs gave way. Ara screamed, and both Xobas and Sosna rushed to her as I tried to stand. I couldn't. My heart lay shattered at my feet and my eyes burned as I wept.

Otylia was gone. The girl I would've given anything to save, anything to spend another moment with, was gone in the blink of an eye. *What have I done?*

My knees stung from the snow by the time Xobas helped me stand, but when we reached her body, I dropped to them again, weak and helpless.

I couldn't manage words. Even thoughts were fleeting as I stared down at her face. Her wild green eyes, still frozen open in shock. Her hair, tangled and meshed with the snow. Her red lips that had been pressed to mine only hours before in the happiest moment of my life. And that crescent scar that had glowed like the moon after she'd ripped herself from Yuliya's grasp.

It didn't matter who her mother or father were. She was my goddess, the girl who'd been by my side no matter whether I was the Half-Chief or a demon.

I loved her.

As the tears streamed from the tip of my chin onto her face, I cursed myself for not admitting it to myself sooner, for ever leaving her side and abandoning her when she'd needed me most. I had thought for so long that Father's admiration was what I'd needed— I'd been wrong.

I held her body in my arms as I whispered in her ear, "I'll find you, Otylka." Pulling Dziewanna's amulet from around her neck, I clutched it in my hand so hard it broke skin. "To the ends of the Three Realms, I'll find you. Neither god nor demon will stop me."

The air vibrated, and Jaryło dissolved into golden dust. "No!" I screamed, clinging to Otylia, but I was helpless.

As she glowed, the dust worked its way across her body, from her feet slowly up to her head. The last I saw of her was the thin scar on her cheek before she faded completely.

54

Wacław

She's gone…

THE WORLD WAS BLACK, the ground blood red. Xobas tried to pull me to my feet as Ara wept next to me. He offered something I assumed was condolences. But I was numb, deaf.

Memories of the battle rolled through my mind—the płanetnikami, Eryk's story of his daughter, Kuba's sacrifice, and Jaryło's blade at Otylia's throat. None of the victories mattered as I knelt there, staring down at the amulet of a bow.

Otylia was gone. Kuba was gone. I'd failed.

My heart felt like it had been ripped from my chest as I struggled to stand, but calling the winds had drained what little life I'd had left. I collapsed next to the dagger. Jaryło's blood coated its blade, and when my hand closed around its hilt, Marzanna's voice rang in my mind.

"Wacław, son of Jacek, tamer of demons, and slayer of gods," she said. *"You are quite the surprise."*

Get out of my head!

"He betrayed you, didn't he?"

How did you know?

"It is his way. Do you see now why he must be killed for good, or do you

insist on continuing your futile crusade? You slaughter your own kind when you could help me lead them."

My body shuddered as the entire group watched. We'd found ourselves trapped in the middle of a war we didn't understand. Both Marzanna and Jaryło were selfish and untrustworthy, and as I looked from Xobas to Ara, Narcyz, and Sosna, I knew we could no longer pick a side. We needed to create our own. *I will never help you.*

Her laugh echoed through my brain. *"Then you and everyone you've ever loved will perish like your arrogant father upon your return home. Your victory here is meaningless. My power only grows with each passing day, and soon, all of Jawia will be mine."*

Her voice disappeared as quickly as it had come. Xobas tried to help me up, but I pulled away. Like the last time I had overused my power, I sensed death dragging on my body, calling me to its depths as what little *żityje* I had left faded from my human soul.

Narcyz stepped back as I struggled to look up at them. "Your eyes..." he stammered.

"What?" I asked.

"They're... bleeding."

My hand trembled as I swiped under my eyes, and I gasped at the black blood that coated my fingers. "It's my *żityje*. My demonic soul stole too much from my human one."

"Zurgowie priestesses speak of this," Ara said with a sniffle. Her own eyes were streaked with red, but her tears stopped as she examined me. "They claim that sorcerers who dance with spirits will eventually lose themselves and bleed dark blood from their eyes."

"Last time this happened, I would've died if Otylia hadn't given me her life force. I can feel it again..." I coughed as the black blood continued down my face. "I couldn't save her, and now my own power is killing me."

After losing both Otylia and Kuba, death almost sounded like a warm embrace. Why should I live when they couldn't? But unlike them, I would never see Nawia. My soul would disappear, consumed by Oblivion, and no one would remember the demonic Half-Chief of Dwie Rzeki.

Wacław

"How do we complete the ritual?" Ara asked, kneeling by my side. She wiped the tears from her eyes as determination replaced sorrow. "We *need* you if we're going to get her back."

My mind slipped every second. I tried to fight it, to keep going for Otylia, but it was like swimming upstream in the great Krowik River. Sooner or later, I would be swept away. "Only a szeptucha can conduct it," I mumbled as Sosna approached.

I smiled knowing the ball of orange fur would mourn me, that some bit of Otylia would be with Ara as she searched for the girl I'd fallen for. Her soft nose nudged my hand in the snow, and I stroked her head with the little strength I had left. "Never give up on her."

A hum surrounded me as Sosna yipped and ran to my bag, pushing it open with her nose just enough for the golden egg to be visible.

"That's it!" Ara exclaimed. She scrambled to the egg and brought it to me as the noise pounded my ears. "Dariusz said the gods owe you a gift."

The golden egg's power bled into my hands, and Ara gasped as a light seemed to radiate from it. Through my tired eyes, I watched as the light traveled from it into my frostbitten hand and forced back the blackened veins. Warmth met me, flowing up my arm and through my whole body. Death's grip faded. Soon, I could feel my battered body once again.

When it finished, the egg dissolved to dust, just as Otylia had. I took a shaky breath and examined my arms, now glowing a soft gold—clear of the demonic veins. Sosna nuzzled my hand as Dziewanna's voice flowed from her, "Wacław Lubiewicz, son of Lubena, master of wind and storm, I gift you this last breath of my *żityje* to find my daughter and bring her to me. Only you can free her from Weles, and only she can free me from Marzanna."

Her voiced faded, and Sosna's tail wagged as she hopped around me in excitement. I patted her head weakly and forced myself to stand.

"Why does everything have to keep getting weirder?" Narcyz asked, taking a step away from me.

449

I ignored him and looked to Ara. She'd lost her best friend too, and we embraced each other in a flood of tears.

My mind spun with every thought. We still had a few days' worth of travel left to reach the clans and prevent a war, but I didn't know how to move forward from here. Otylia was gone just hours after our first kiss. Though it felt selfish to think such things after seeing her and Kuba die, my heart didn't care. It just wanted her back. I just wanted both of them back.

"We'll bring her home," Ara said. She shook in my arms and her tears soaked my shoulders, but she needed to cry as much as I did. Though the two of us had never been close, I was glad there was someone else who could share my pain.

"And then we'll make Jaryło pay," I replied.

It was a long time before I finally worked up the strength to step back from Ara. I looked down at my body. With the black veins gone, I still dreaded the return to it. All the bruises were sure to feel much worse, and it was impossible to know what a second time overusing my powers had done to my human soul. But to return was to remain human. If only for now.

All the pain from the battle hit me at once within my physical body. Fire raced through my blood and seared my skin. My throat seized when I breathed, and when I tried to sit up, a stabbing pain shot through my chest. I collapsed back into the snow. The chill seeped through my skull, grounding me to reality—a reality I only wished to leave.

Xobas and Narcyz each took one of my arms before I could ask for help. They lifted me up, and I gritted my teeth as my body ached. "Why does this feel even worse than dying without *żityje*?"

Ara looked to the patch of red where Otylia had lain. "If Dziewanna gave you the last of her *żityje*, then it really is up to us to save Otylia..."

"So it's true?" Xobas asked. "She's a goddess."

"When were you planning to tell us?" Narcyz added.

I groaned and took a deep breath to try to clear my emotions. It didn't work. "Dziewanna didn't want Weles to raise her child, so she hid in Dwie Rzeki. Otylia was that child. We only found out at the Lake of Remembrance, and Otylia wished for it to be kept a secret, so I kept it."

"Letting her push you around already?" Narcyz quipped. "Is she the woman or are you?"

My scowl drove him back. Something twinged in my heart, but I didn't have the energy to yell again. I sighed and gazed over the forest. "Whether she and I are together is not important right now. Weles has her, and I don't care what it takes—I will find her."

Narcyz paced, rubbing his hands along his pant legs as he did. "How you plan to do that?"

"And didn't he say demons can never see the underworld?" Ara added. "I'll do whatever I can to find her, but that's a serious problem."

I clenched and unclenched my fists. "He did..." Jaryło had said demons can't ever go to Nawia, but could my human soul?

Before I could ponder further, though, a glint in the snow caught my eye. I pushed my way past Narcyz to the spot.

"What are you doing now?" he asked.

The smallest of smiles crossed my face as I tapped the brim of my płanetnik hat and bent over to pick up the sword.

When he saw the golden blade, he stepped back. "Whoa..."

Kwiecień shone in my hand—the Moonstone sword of the next moon. It was far lighter than I had expected one of Jaryło's Moonblade to be, but I could sense the power swelling within it, like a *żityje* of its own.

My own weakness forced me to my knees with it in my hands. Xobas rushed toward me, but I held up a hand and dropped to a seated position against the sole tree at the ridge's peak, exhausted. "Jaryło dropped it before he died... Guess we have some good luck for once."

"Why's that?" Ara asked.

"Because as long as he doesn't have it, he can't return during the Kwiecień moon. I don't know how long it takes a god to come back from Nawia, but considering the new moon is in two days, perhaps he'll be trapped there long enough for me to find a way to Otylia."

Xobas rested a hand on my arm. "If Weles truly is her father, then he wouldn't harm her. Besides, that girl is tougher than any of us. She can handle herself. We will figure out a way to bring her back *after* we reach the clans."

"How are you okay with this?" Narcyz asked. "She lied to us, just like Wacław. How do we know she's even a goddess?"

I shook my head. "Dziewanna said it takes time for a young deity to develop their own powers. You can choose whether you want to believe me or not."

Xobas eyed the wounds on my face and arms. "What happened up there?"

"Too much to say now. I defeated the płanetnik and his minions with the winds' help, but when Jaryło appeared and ordered me to kill him, I hesitated. The demon, Eryk, told me the story of his death, how he was forced to hang himself to protect his daughter." I studied my fingers, picturing the sparks that had danced among them. "I gave him my mark, like Marzanna had done to me. In return for me helping him find and save his daughter, he will fight for us against Marzanna."

Narcyz jaw dropped. "You... You can control other demons? That's—"

"Advantageous," Ara replied. "Otylia would've approved."

"I hope," I muttered, not proud of the brand I'd made on the płanetnik's face. Having his power under my command only made me crave more, and after seeing the black veins that had been scattered across my skin, the last thing I wanted was to use my power again.

Narcyz grabbed his hair and groaned. "None of this is normal!"

"I agree that this is cause for concern," Xobas said. "Are you certain this demon can be trusted?"

"All I can say is I saw a man fearing for his daughter's life," I said. "If I can earn his trust, then he could be a powerful ally—something we're lacking right now."

Ara nodded. "When you're as desperate as we are, you take whatever you can get."

Narcyz stormed toward her. "You saw those things. We can't fight alongside them!"

"I saw powerful, broken creatures," Ara replied, crouching to pat the mourning Sosna on her head. "They were people once. If Wacław believes we could turn any of them to our side, then I say we trust him."

Narcyz scowled. "Fine! Not that my opinion matters anyway, but we need to cremate Kuba! Half-Chief might've forgotten his friend, but I haven't. He can't become one of *them*." His eyes widened when he realized he was pointing directly at me instead of the dead. He swallowed and looked toward the sun, his voice hushed. "Kuba died to protect a witch and a demon. We can't let his soul be lost."

"Then it will be done," Xobas said. "Start the fire with Ara. I will prepare the body."

I leaned up to ask how I could help, but before I could, his gaze landed on me. Its weight was enough to warn me not to speak. *How does he do that?*

Narcyz grumbled about Otylia and demons as Xobas led him away. Ara was still watching me with concern. "Are you going to be all right?" she asked.

"All wounds heal in time," I said.

"You know what I meant."

I bit my cheek, too drained to cry anymore. "I want to find her more than anything, but I know we can't until we get to the clans. She would hate me if I fell apart and gave up on this. I just... I just don't know how to keep going after seeing that, after losing her and Kuba."

"Kuba saved all of us. We'll pay him the respect here and in the village that he deserves. Then we'll find Otylia. I promise you're not the only one who wants revenge."

I managed a smile. "Thank you."

She cocked her head to the side. "Why?"

"Because when I failed her, everything fell on you, and you were there for her when I wasn't strong enough."

Sorrow filled her eyes. "I told Otylia I'd follow her anywhere. I never thought that'd mean Nawia, but here we are."

"You're a good friend, and I'm thankful to have you as a part of this. I'm sorry if I never said that before."

"You just stopped eternal winter. Even if it's temporary, I owe you. Everybody does, so no thanks is needed."

I sighed. "Tell that to Mikołaj."

"I will when we get back. He'll know who saved the tribe from the demons and the clans—even if one of them is my own." She flicked the tears from her eyes. "Get some rest. I'm going to help get the fire started."

When she left, I shut my eyes, laid my head back against the tree, and wished for my exhaustion to take me away. *Just a few more days. Finish it for Mom, for Kuba, for Nevenka, for Otylia.* My hand slipped to the amulet of Mokosz around my neck, now joined by Dziewanna's, and as I rested my eyes, I prayed they would give me the will to continue.

55

Wacław

How can they be gone?

KUBA'S CREMATION WAS A QUICK AFFAIR. Though I could've sat next to the fire for hours, mourning the friend who had given his life for mine, Xobas pulled me to my feet and forced me to march into the plains. And march we did.

Dadźbóg's light seemed to hover forever as Ara helped me limp through the meadow. My heart ached with the memory of my kiss with Otylia among those grasses, the waning crescent moon hanging in the sky. I would've given anything to spend another few seconds in that moment. Instead, I was beaten from the inside out, lacking the time to properly grieve. I knew there was no choice, but it still hurt deeply.

There was something wrong about leaving the Mangled Woods to continue to the clans. Part of our hearts, our souls, would always be left in that forest, and when we reached the end of the grasses, I looked back at it one last time. Tears filled my eyes as I saw the speckles of red corn poppies marking what had happened there.

No one spoke for the rest of the day except for Xobas determining the right direction and Ara identifying deer and other animal tracks in order to find potential food sources. There was too much to discuss, to remember, so we addressed none of it. Even my mind was drowned in the river of emotion.

When the moon replaced the sun in the sky, we made camp near what Xobas believed to be the edge of the woods. I hoped he was right as I watched the clouds. A sliver of light was all that lay between us and the demise of the Krowikie tribe—a war we would never win—yet for some reason, it was comforting to know my tribe was in the same situation as me.

"You think the clans will agree to the deal?" Narcyz asked as we sat around the fire, the melting snow turning the ground to a puddle of mud.

I remembered the offer I had proposed—all the southern hills in exchange for their assistance in the war with the Solgawi. Though I disagreed with the war in the west, this was my chance to stop more slaughter. It all seemed so petty now, but Father had approved my plan. It needed to work.

"Jacek was never a father to me," I said, "but if he knew how to do anything, it was to strike a deal for the good of the tribe. I hope it is enough. If it's not, then it will be up to us to find another solution."

"The idea of seeing my clan again grows more frightening the closer we get," Ara replied. "The Zurgowie have lost too much if we've been forced this far west. They won't accept me as more than an outsider anymore. Any friends I had..."

"That is why warriors don't have friends," Xobas said, throwing a log into the fire, his eyes reflecting the flames. "We have brothers."

"And sisters..." she muttered.

He chuckled. "Yes, and sisters. It matters not who has left the clan for a time or not. Friends fade. Family does not, and in war, we give everything to protect our family. When peace is an option, there's no need for such sacrifice." His finger traced his scarred forearm as he studied the stars. "That is better."

I thought of my own scars crisscrossing up my arms and torso. His words made me think that maybe they weren't supposed to be memories of my wounds but memories of what was lost in the clashes I'd survived. "We'll find a way," I said. "For Otylia, Kuba, the tribe, and whatever gods that aren't trying to kill us, we'll find a way. We may have stopped winter's return for now, but until we rescue Dziewanna, life won't return to the wilds—not fully."

Xobas glanced at his cloak. "If we are to make peace in the coming days, we'll all need rest. Facing our enemies will not be easy. Wacław, do you have enough strength in your soul-form to keep watch while you sleep?"

I winced but nodded. Even if I wanted to truly rest, I didn't have the choice.

The rest of the group wrapped themselves in their cloaks, except Narcyz. His fingers dragged in the melted snow as he sat against a tree like me. Though the air lacked some of its chill with Eryk no longer serving Marzanna, the Marzec moon had yet to finish its cycle. The snow was gone, but the world had barely warmed. The trees were still nearly barren. I doubted the crops would fare much better. *We need Dziewanna.*

For a few minutes, I just stared into the fire and thought of Otylia and Kuba with longing and pain in my heart. It soon became too much, and I forced my broken body to its feet before I shuffled over to Narcyz. "Mind if I sit?"

His lip curled, but he voiced no objection, so I did, leaning my back against the tree.

The darkness of the woods seemed infinite during a black moon. On a night like this, though, even the slice of moonlight cast shadows everywhere. It allowed for a different kind of fear. Instead of worrying what lay within the black, I could see it all. Each branch swaying in the winds or animal scurrying across the muck was enough to send a jolt down my spine. After the demons we'd seen in both night and day, I almost preferred blindness.

I lost track of how long we sat there, but I sensed Narcyz growing tenser as time went on. Eventually, his head snapped to me. "What do you want, Half-Chief?"

What do I want? I wasn't sure what had brought me to that tree, but I talked anyway, "I'm sorry."

"For what?"

"For doubting you."

"You never cared. Why would you?"

"Because you and I both went into this journey with something to prove, both to ourselves and everyone else," I said, finally turning my head to meet his gaze. "I know we don't get along—and probably never will—but few warriors can say they fought an army of Marzanna's cultists and lived to tell the tale. You protected my body. I would be dead if it wasn't for you."

A small smile crept across his face as he stared at the ground, his fists clenched over his knees. "Thanks... I... I guess I'm sorry too. You know, for Otylia and Kuba."

"I'm shocked to hear you say her name."

"If she's a goddess, then she might get Perun to throw lightning at me or something."

I smirked. "Fear is quite the motivator."

"It worked on you until you started calling down your *own* lightning."

"Luckily for you, I can only do that when I sleep."

A devious grin crossed his face. "Then maybe not everything is ruined."

We both chuckled and stared at the fire, watching it crackle as a wolf howled in the distance, the call echoing through the night. After a moment, Narcyz responded with his own howl. I shook my head. "You're going to wake everyone up."

His eyes were ablaze as he grabbed hold of his cloak and lay down. With the pelts of wolf fur around him, the howls seemed more appropriate. "The warriors always told stories of their warbands howling to the wolves," he said. "They called them our wild brothers."

I rubbed the wolf bite on my arm, wincing as the memory of it latching on flashed in my mind. "Brothers or not, they truly are wild."

He huffed. "Night, Half-Chief."

"Night," I replied, limping over to my own cloak and wrapping it around me. With a deep breath, I watched the flames dance before fatigue took over and I slid into my soul-form.

The dirt beneath my boots was more exciting than it should've been. For too long we'd slowly hiked through nothing but endless layers of snow. Now that the płanetnik's false winter had faded, we could make the real progress we needed, even if every step sent a stabbing pain through my chest.

The Kwiecień moon approached with each passing day. On this final morning, I'd woken with hope in my heart. We would soon be free of the Mangled Woods and could see life outside of that cursed forest again. When all I had felt since the battle had been sorrow, that was enough.

Xobas sighed as he swung his pack over his shoulder. "My people migrated every year, often more than once. Our lands faded where we left and expanded where we went with sword and arrow. We held no permanent home, so we could never lose it. But leaving the Anshayman Steppe was one of the hardest things I ever did."

"Mother wept for moons after we fled our clan's wars," Ara replied. "I remember more than one of those wars being with your own riders."

"Which is why it's concerning our clans would ally. This Frost-marked Horde must be a powerful force."

I stared into the early morning light as we continued our trek east. "Otylia said they defeated an entire clan's army with almost no losses of their own. If it's true, then all I know is I have no desire to meet them."

"We may not have a choice," Xobas said. "But we do have an opportunity to make an agreement with our clans. They will be powerful allies on the battlefield and off—*if* they agree.

"How do we know they won't kill us on sight?" Narcyz asked.

Ara smirked. "We'll send you first as an offering, just in case."

Xobas gave her a side-eye. "We will have to trust our knowledge of their tongue and culture is enough. Keep your weapons sheathed, no matter what happens."

I touched Kwiecień's hilt at my back. *My two weapons now are the sword of a god and a dagger capable of killing one.* My heart sunk, though. My shield and spear had been destroyed when they had dropped from the clouds. Normally, I wouldn't have cared, but Kuba and I had painted those shields together. It felt as if I'd lost the last piece of him.

It was nearly midday by the time the landscape shifted from warped trees to the open steppe. The divide seemed hardly natural, with a straight line forming the barrier between the two. *More work of the witch?*

I figured I would never know, but it was hard not to be curious as I surveyed the rolling hills of brown and gold. The hard dirt only gave way to the occasional dead bush. These steppe plants had never had a chance to survive the cold. Xobas had spoken many times of the steppe's dry heat, and I doubted anything living within it had been prepared for weeks of unnatural winter.

"As long as they haven't moved since their meeting with the Asti-wie, it's not far now," Xobas said, taking a breath of the steppe air.

"Great," Narcyz quipped as he rolled his eyes. "We're betting on nomads staying still."

Dadźbóg taunted us as we walked over the hills. One moment it seemed he hadn't moved for hours, the next he was sprinting toward the horizon. I tried not to watch his path, but the clans' promise to attack at the start of the Kwiecień moon rung in my mind. We had to find them today or we'd be too late.

The sky darkened as we approached the peak of yet another hill. My hope dragged with my steps, and the others had slowed their pace as well. We'd come so far and lost too much to fail now, but the futility of our search had finally reached me. In the end, it all would have been for nothing. Otylia. Kuba. Marek. Kajetan... All of them had given their lives for us to keep going, for us to save the tribe. How could all of it end without us finding the clans?

But when we crested the hill, the sight in the next valley took my breath away. I dropped to my knees with tears in my eyes and a smile on my face.

"What is it?" Ara asked, rushing to my side.

I couldn't find the words, so I just pointed, and she gasped as she followed my finger. Before us was a camp lit by over a thousand torches. Wood-framed canvas tents covered the entire valley along with more horses than I had ever seen in my life. Banners of both Zurgowie green and Simukie tan fluttered in the winds at the entrance of the camp. From it, two riders galloped toward us, the moon illuminating their dark faces as they moved beyond the torchlight.

Xobas stepped in front of us. He puffed up his chest and raised his chin as the riders approached, slowing to a trot. When they stopped, he held two fingers to the end of his nose before extending his arm toward them. "In lands new and old, we ride," he said in the clans' shared tongue.

One of the riders dismounted, his long ponytail flapping behind him as he patted his horse's neck. With an inquisitive glance, he turned toward us. A tan cape bearing the Simukie emblem of a rearing horse draped from his right shoulder and brushed across the steppe grasses as he approached Xobas and repeated the gesture.

"It seems you have found clans both new and old, commander," the rider said, still in their tongue. "Come. Let us give you new clothes and fresh food. We have awaited your return for a long time, and we have much to discuss."

The second rider looked down on us from her bay horse. Her brow was furrowed and her voice sharper than her counterpart. "The marzban fails to express the severity of the situation." She glanced at me. "Never in our history has the Anshayman Steppe been conquered by a single clan, but this Horde has taken it in mere moons. There is no time to waste if your clans and ours are to survive."

With that, the rider turned her horse and galloped into the valley. The marzban shook his head before waving toward the camp. "Let this new moon grant us all a future free of its darkness."

He and Xobas descended the slope as the others followed. For a

461

moment, though, I could only stand and watch the camp's flames against the stars on the horizon. Tomorrow offered a new day, a new hope, but it would also bring yet another threat, one I would have to face without Otylia.

Narcyz was already halfway down the hill when he glanced over his shoulder. "C'mon, Half-Chief."

"I'm coming," I said to myself more than him. My hand drifted to the Bowmark necklace at my chest as I stared up at the dark, absent moon. "I'm coming, Otylia. Whether it be this moon or the next, I promise I'll find you."

END OF BOOK 1

A Word From The Author

Thank you for joining me on the journey of my first epic fantasy novel. Through rewrites and edits, *A Dagger in the Winds* has been a labor of love from the beginning.

If you have enjoyed reading this story as much as I have writing it, please take the time to post an honest review on whatever retailer you purchased this book from. Every review helps new readers discover the series.

To receive your free copy of *The Rider in the Night*, the prequel novella to The Frostmarked Chronicles, and exclusive first looks at the rest of the series, join my newsletter at www.Brendan-Noble.com.

- Brendan

About the Author

Brendan Noble is a Polish and German-American author currently writing fantasy books based on Slavic mythology. He is fascinated with history, economics, and politics in both reality and fiction.

Brendan is a recent graduate in Economics from Hillsdale College in Michigan. In 2019, he moved from his hometown of Canton, Michigan to Rockford, Illinois when he married his wife, Andrea. Brendan began his writing career in November of 2018 with a challenge from his wife to complete NaNoWriMo (National Novel Writing Month) and has been an author ever since.

Outside of writing, Brendan is a data analyst and soccer referee. His top interests include German, Polish, and American soccer/football, Formula 1, analyzing political elections across the world, playing extremely nerdy strategy video games, exploring with his wife, and reading.